FLASH[MAN] [I]N THE GR[EAT] GAME

George Mac[Donald Fra]ser OBE was a bestselling historical novelist, jour[nalist and s]creenwriter. Having worked on newspapers in Bri[tain and C]anada he is perhaps most famous for his series of [Flashma]n novels and his anti-hero Harry Flashman. In [addition t]o his novels he also wrote numerous screenplays, [including] The Three Musketeers and the James Bond film [. . . G]eorge MacDonald Fraser died in January 200[8 at the age] of 82.

FLASHMAN IN THE GREAT GAME

From *The Flashman Papers,*
1856–58

Edited and Arranged by

George MacDonald Fraser

HARPER

Harper
An imprint of HarperCollins*Publishers*
1 London Bridge Street
London SE1 9GF

www.harpercollins.co.uk

This paperback edition 2015
1

First published in Great Britain by
Barrie & Jenkins 1975

A catalogue record for this book is available from the British Library

ISBN: 978 0 00 721719 9

Typeset in Janson by Palimpsest Book Production Ltd, Falkirk, Stirlingshire
Printed and bound in Great Britain by Clays Ltd, St Ives plc

MIX
Paper from
responsible sources
FSC
www.fsc.org   **FSC C007454**

The following piece was found in the author's study in 2013 by the Estate of George MacDonald Fraser.

How Did I Get the Idea of *Flashman*?

'How did you get the idea of *Flashman*?' and 'When are we going to get his U.S. Civil War memoirs?' are questions which I have ducked more often than I can count. To the second, my invariable response is 'Oh, one of these days'. Followed, when the inquirer is an impatient American, by the gentle reminder that to an old British soldier like Flashman the unpleasantness between the States is not quite the most important event of the nineteenth century, but rather a sideshow compared to the Mutiny or Crimea. Before they can get indignant I add hastily that his Civil War itinerary is already mapped out; this is the only way of preventing them from telling me what it ought to be.

To the question, how did I get the idea, I simply reply that I don't know. Who ever knows? Anthony Hope conceived *The Prisoner of Zenda* on a walk from Westminster to the Temple, but I doubt if he could have said, after the calendar month it took him to write the book, what triggered the idea.

In my case, Flashman came thundering out of the mists of forty years living and dreaming, and while I can list the ingredients that went to his making, heaven only knows how and when they combined.

One thing is sure: the Flashman Papers would never have been written if my fellow clansman Hugh Fraser, Lord Allander, had confirmed me as editor of the *Glasgow Herald* in 1966. But he didn't, the canny little bandit, and I won't say he was wrong. I wouldn't have lasted in the job, for I'd been trained in a journalistic school where editors were gods, and in three months as acting chief my attitude to management, front office, and directors had been that of a seigneur to his serfs – I had even put Fraser's entry to the House of Lords on an inside page, assuring him that it was not for the *Herald*, his own paper, to flaunt his elevation, and that a two-column picture of him was quite big enough. How cavalier can you get?

And doubtless I had other editorial shortcomings. In any event, faced with twenty years as deputy editor (which means doing all the work without getting to the big dinners), I promised my wife I would 'write us out of it'. In a few weeks of thrashing the typewriter at the kitchen table in the small hours, *Flashman* was half-finished, and likely to stay that way, for I fell down a waterfall, broke my arm, and lost interest – until my wife asked to read what I had written. Her reaction galvanised me into finishing it, one draft, no revisions, and for the next two years it rebounded from publisher after publisher, British and American.

I can't blame them: the purported memoir of an unregenerate blackguard, bully, and coward resurrected from a Victorian school story is a pretty eccentric subject. By 1968 I was ready to call it a day, but thanks to my wife's insistence and George Greenfield's matchless knowledge of the publishing scene, it found a home at last with Herbert Jenkins, the manuscript looking, to quote Christopher MacLehose, as though it had been round the world twice. It dam' nearly had.

They published it as it stood, with (to me) bewildering results. It wasn't a bestseller in the blockbuster sense, but the reviewers were enthusiastic, foreign rights (starting with Finland) were sold, and when it appeared in the U.S.A. one-third of forty-odd critics accepted it as a genuine historical memoir, to the undisguised glee of the *New York Times*, which wickedly assembled their reviews. 'The most important discovery since the Boswell Papers' is the one that haunts me still, for if I was human enough to feel my lower ribs parting under the strain, I was appalled, sort of.

You see, while I had written a straightforward introduction describing the 'discovery' of the 'Papers' in a saleroom in Ashby-de-la-Zouche (*that* ought to have warned them), and larded it with editorial 'foot-notes', there had been no intent to deceive; for one thing, while I'd done my best to write, first-person, in Victorian style, I'd never imagined that it would fool anybody. Nor did Herbert Jenkins. And fifty British critics had recognised it as a conceit. (The only one who was half-doubtful was my old chief sub on the *Herald*; called on to review it for another paper, he demanded of the *Herald*'s literary editor: 'This book o' Geordie's isnae true, is it?' and on being assured that it wasn't, exclaimed: 'The conniving bastard!', which I still regard as a high compliment.)

With the exception of one left-wing journal which hailed it as a scathing attack on British imperialism, the press and public took *Flashman*, quite rightly, at face value, as an adventure story dressed up as the memoirs of an unrepentant old cad who, despite his cowardice, depravity and deceit, had managed to emerge from fearful ordeals and perils an acclaimed hero, his only redeeming qualities being his humour and shameless honesty as a memorialist. I was gratified, if slightly puzzled to learn that the great American publisher, Alfred Knopf, had said of the book: 'I haven't heard this voice in fifty years', and that the Commissioner of Metropolitan Police was recommending it to his subordinates. My interest increased as I wrote more Flashman books, and noted the reactions.

I was, several critics agreed, a satirist. Taking revenge on the nineteenth century on behalf of the twentieth, said one. Waging war on Victorian hypocrisy, said another. Plainly under the influence of Conrad, said yet another. A full-page review in a German paper took me flat aback when my eye fell on the word 'Proust' in the middle of it. I don't read German, so for all I know the review may have been maintaining that Proust was a better stand-off half than I was, or used more semi-colons. But there it was, and it makes you think. And a few years ago a highly respected religious journal said that the Flashman Papers deserved recognition as the work of a sensitive moralist, and spoke of service not only to literature and history, but to the study of ethics.

My instant reaction to this was to paraphrase Poins: 'God send me no worse fortune, but I never said so!' while feeling delighted that someone else had said it, and then reflecting solemnly that this was a far cry from long nights with cold tea and cigarettes, scheming to get Flashman into the passionate embrace of the Empress of China, or out of the toils of a demented dwarf on the edge of a snake-pit. But now, beyond remarking that the anti-imperial left-winger was sadly off the mark, that the Victorians were mere amateurs in hypocrisy compared to our own brainwashed, sanctimonious, self-censoring and terrified generation, and that I hadn't read a word of Conrad by 1966 (and my interest in him since has been confined to *Under Western Eyes*, in the hope that I might persuade Dick Lester to film it as only he could), I have no comments to offer on opinions of my work. I know what I'm doing – at least, I think I do – and the aim is to entertain (myself, for a start) while being true to history, to let Flashman comment on human and inhuman nature, and devil take the romantics and the politically correct revisionists both. But my job is writing, not explaining what I've written, and I'm well content and grateful to have others find in Flashy whatever they will (I've even had letters psychoanalysing the brute), and return to the question with which I began this article.

A life-long love affair with British imperial adventure, fed on tupenny bloods, the Wolf of Kabul and Lionheart Logan (where are they now?), the *Barrack-Room Ballads*, films like *Lives of a Bengal Lancer* and *The Four Feathers*, and the stout-hearted stories for boys which my father won as school prizes in the 1890s; the discovery, through Scott and Sabatini and Macaulay, that history is one tremendous adventure story; soldiering in Burma, and seeing the twilight of the Raj in all its splendour; a newspaper-trained lust for finding the truth behind the received opinion; being a Highlander from a family that would rather spin yarns than eat . . . I suppose Flashman was born out of all these things, and from reading *Tom Brown's Schooldays* as a child – and having a wayward cast of mind.

Thanks to that contrary streak (I always half-hoped that Rathbone would kill Flynn, confounding convention and turning the story upside down – Basil gets Olivia, Claude Rains triumphs, wow!), I recognised Flashman on sight as the star of Hughes' book. Fag-roasting rotter and poltroon he might be, he was nevertheless plainly box-office, for he had the looks, swagger and style ('big and strong', 'a bluff, offhand manner', and 'considerable powers of being pleasant', according to this creator) which never fail to cast a glamour on villainy. I suspect Hughes knew it, too, and got rid of him before he could take over the book – which loses all its spirit and zest once Flashy has made his disgraced and drunken exit.

[He was, by the way, a real person; this I learned only recently. A letter exists from one of Hughes' Rugby contemporaries which is definite on the point, but tactfully does not identify him. I have sometimes speculated about one boy who was at Rugby in Hughes' day, and who later became a distinguished soldier and something of a ruffian, but since I haven't a shred of evidence to back up the speculation, I keep it to myself.]

What became of him after Rugby seemed to me an obvious question, which probably first occurred to me when I was about nine, and then waited thirty years for an answer. The Army, inevitably, and since Hughes had given me a starting-point by expelling him in the late 1830s, when Lord Cardigan was in full haw-haw, and the Afghan War was impending. . . just so. I began with no idea of where the story might take me, but with Victorian history to point the way, and that has been my method ever since: choose an incident or campaign, dig into every contemporary source available, letters, diaries, histories, reports, eye-witness, trivia (and fictions, which like the early *Punch* are mines of detail), find the milestones for Flashy to follow, more or less, get impatient to be writing, and turn him loose with the research incomplete, digging for it as I go and changing course as history dictates or fancy suggests.

In short, letting history do the work, with an eye open for the unexpected nuggets and coincidences that emerge in the mining process – for example, that the Cabinet were plastered when they took their final resolve on the Crimea, that Pinkerton the detective had been a trade union agitator in the very place where Flashman was stationed in the first book, that Kipling's *The Man Who Would Be King* had a factual basis, or that Bismarck and Lola Montez were in London in the same week (of 1842, if memory serves, which it often doesn't: whenever Flashman has been a subject on *Mastermind* I have invariably scored less than the contestants).

Visiting the scenes helps; I'd not have missed Little Big Horn, the Borneo jungle rivers, Bent's Fort, or the scruffy, wonderful Gold Road to Samarkand, for anything. Seeking out is half the fun, which is one reason why I decline all offers of help with research (from America, mostly). But the main reason is that I'm a soloist, giving no hints beforehand, even to publishers, and permitting no editorial interference afterwards. It may be tripe, but it's *my* tripe – and I do strongly urge authors to resist encroachments on their brain-children, and trust their own judgment rather than that of some zealous meddler with a diploma in creative punctuation who is just dying to get into the act.

One of the great rewards of writing about my old ruffian has been getting and answering letters, and marvelling at the kindness of readers who take the trouble to let me know they have enjoyed his adventures, or that he has cheered them up, or turned them to history. Sitting on the stairs at 4 a.m. talking to a group of students who have phoned from the

American Midwest is as gratifying as learning from a university lecturer that he is using Flashman as a teaching aid. Even those who want to write the books for you, or complain that he's a racist (of course he is; why should he be different from the rest of humanity?), or insist that he isn't a coward at all, but just modest, and they're in love with him, are compensated for by the stalwarts who've named pubs after him (in Monte Carlo, and somewhere in South Africa, I'm told), or have formed societies in his honour. They're out there, believe me, the Gandamack Delopers of Oklahoma, and Rowbotham's Mosstroopers, and the Royal Society of Upper Canada, with appropriate T-shirts.

I have discovered that when you create – or in my case, adopt and develop – a fictional character, and take him through a series of books, an odd thing happens. He assumes, in a strange way, a life of his own. I don't mean that he takes you over; far from it, he tends to hive off on his own. At any rate, you find that you're not just writing about him: you are becoming responsible for him. You're not just his chronicler: you are also his manager, trainer, and public relations man. It's your own fault – my own fault – for pretending that he's real, for presenting his adventures as though they were his memoirs, putting him in historical situations, giving him footnotes and appendices, and inviting the reader to accept him as a historical character. The result is that about half the letters I get treat him as though he were a person in his own right – of course, people who write to me know that he's nothing of the sort – well, most of them realise it: I occasionally get indignant letters from people complaining that they can't find him in the Army List or the D.N.B., but nearly all of them know he's fiction, and when they pretend that he isn't, they're just playing the game. I started it, so I can't complain.

When Hughes axed Flashman from *Tom Brown's Schooldays*, brutally and suddenly (on page 170, if I remember rightly), it seemed a pretty callous act to abandon him with all his sins upon him, just at the stage of adolescence when a young fellow needs all the help and understanding he can get. So I adopted him, not from any charitable motives, but because I realised that there was good stuff in the lad, and that with proper care and guidance something could be made out of him.

And I have to say that with all his faults (what am I saying, *because* of his faults) young Flashy has justified the faith I showed in him. Over the years he and I have gone through several campaigns and assorted adventures, and I can say unhesitatingly that coward, scoundrel, toady, lecher and dissembler though he may be, he is a good man to go into the jungle with.

George MacDonald Fraser

For the Mad White Woman of Papar River

EXPLANATORY NOTE

One of the most encouraging things about editing the first four volumes of the Flashman Papers has been the generous response from readers and students of history in many parts of the world. Since the discovery of Flashman's remarkable manuscript in a Leicestershire saleroom in 1965, when it was realised that it was the hitherto-unsuspected autobiographical memoir of the notorious bully of *Tom Brown's Schooldays*, letters have reached the editor from such diverse places as Ascension Island, a G.I. rest camp in Vietnam, university faculties and campuses in Britain and America, a modern caravanserai on the Khyber Pass road, a police-station cell in southern Australia, and many others.

What has been especially gratifying has been not only the interest in Flashman himself, but the close historical know-ledge which correspondents have shown of the periods and incidents with which his memoirs have dealt so far – the first Afghan War, the solution of the Schleswig-Holstein Question (involving as it did Count Bismarck and Lola Montez), the Afro-American slave trade, and the Crimean War. Many have contributed interesting observations, and one or two have detected curious discrepancies in Flashman's recollections which, regrettably, escaped his editor. A lady in Athens and a gentleman in Flint, Michigan, have pointed out that Flashman apparently saw the Duchess of Wellington at a London theatre some years after her death, and a letter on Foreign Office notepaper has remarked on his careless reference to a 'British Ambassador' in Washington in 1848, when in fact Her Majesty's representative in the American capital held a less exalted diplomatic title. Such lapses are understandable, if not excusable, in a hard-living octogenarian.

Equally interesting have been such communications as those from a gentleman in New Orleans who claims to be Flashman's illegitimate great-grandson (as the result of a liaison in a military hospital at Richmond, Va., during the U.S. Civil War), and from a British serving officer who asserts that his grandfather lent fifty dollars and a horse to Flashman during the same campaign; neither, apparently, was returned.

It is possible that these and other matters of interest will be resolved when the later papers are edited. The present volume deals with Flashman's adventures in the Indian Mutiny, where he witnessed many of the dramatic moments of that terrible struggle, and encountered numerous Victorian celebrities – monarchs, statesmen, and generals among them. As in previous volumes, his narrative tallies closely with accepted historical fact, as well as furnishing much new information, and there has been little for his editor to do except correct his spelling, deplore his conduct, and provide the usual notes and appendices.

G.M.F.

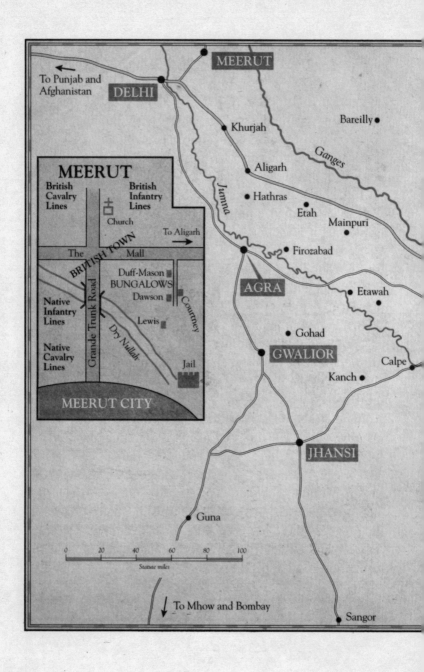

To Punjab and
Afghanistan

DELHI

MEERUT

Khurjah

Bareilly

Ganges

Aligarh

Jumna

Hathras

Etah

Mainpuri

Firozabad

AGRA

Etawah

Gohad

GWALIOR

Calpe

Kanch

JHANSI

Guna

Sangor

To Mhow and Bombay

MEERUT

British
Cavalry
Lines

British
Infantry
Lines

Church

BRITISH TOWN

The Mall

To Aligarh

Duff-Mason
BUNGALOWS

Dawson

Courtney

Native
Infantry
Lines

Grande Trunk Road

Dry Nullah

Lewis

Native
Cavalry
Lines

Jail

MEERUT CITY

| 0 | 20 | 40 | 60 | 80 | 100 |

Statute miles

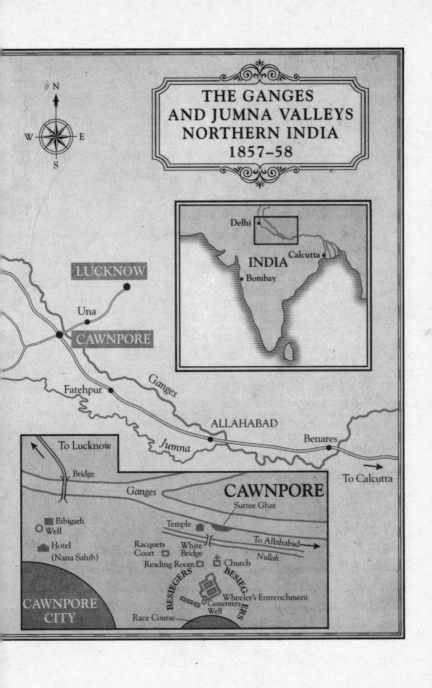

THE GANGES AND JUMNA VALLEYS NORTHERN INDIA 1857–58

N
W — E
S

Delhi

INDIA

Calcutta

Bombay

LUCKNOW

Una

CAWNPORE

Fatehpur

Ganges

ALLAHABAD

Jumna

Benares

To Lucknow

Bridge

Ganges

CAWNPORE

Suttee Ghat

To Allahabad →

To Calcutta →

Bibigarh
Well

Temple

Racquets
Court

White
Bridge

Nullah

Hotel
(Nana Sahib)

Reading Room

Church

BESIEGERS

BESIEGERS

Wheeler's Entrenchment

CAWNPORE
CITY

Cementery
Well

Race Course

They don't often invite me to Balmoral nowadays, which is a blessing; those damned tartan carpets always put me off my food, to say nothing of the endless pictures of German royalty and that unspeakable statue of the Prince Consort standing knock-kneed in a kilt. King Teddy's company is something I'd sooner avoid than not, anyway, for he's no better than an upper-class hooligan. Of course, he's been pretty leery of me for forty-odd years (ever since I misguided his youthful footsteps into an actress's bed, in fact, and brought Papa Albert's divine wrath down on his fat head) and when he finally wheezed his way on to the throne I gather he thought of dropping me altogether – said something about my being Falstaff to his Prince Hal. Falstaff, mark you – from a man with piggy eyes and a belly like a Conestoga wagon cover. Vile taste in cigars he has, too.

In the old Queen's time, of course, I was at Balmoral a great deal. She always fancied me, from when she was a chit of a girl and pinned the Afghan medal on my manly breast, and after I had ridden herd on that same precious Teddy through the Tranby Croft affair and saved him from the worst consequences of his own folly, she couldn't do enough for me. Each September after that, regular as clockwork, there would come a command for 'dear General Flashman' to take the train north to Kailyard Castle, and there would be my own room, with a bowl of late roses on the window-sill, and a bottle of brandy on the side-table with a discreet napkin over it – they knew my style. So I put up with it; she was all right, little Vicky, as long as you gave her your arm to lean on, and let her prattle on endlessly, and the rations were adequate. But even then, I never cottoned to the place. Not only, as I've said, was it furnished in a taste that would have offended the sensibilities of a nigger costermonger, it had the most awful Highland gloom about it – all drizzle and mist and draughts under the door and holy melancholy: even the billiard-room had a print on the wall of a dreadful ancient Scotch couple glowering devoutly. Praying, I don't doubt, for me to be snookered.

But I think what really turns me against Balmoral in my old age is its memories. It was there that the Great Mutiny began for me, and on my rare excursions north nowadays there's a point on the line where the rhythm of the wheels changes, and in my imagination they begin to sing: 'Mera-*Jhansi*-denge-nay, mera-*Jhansi*-denge-nay', over and over, and in a moment the years have dropped away, and I'm remembering how I first came to Balmoral half a century ago; aye, and what it led to – the stifling heat of the parade ground at Meerut with the fettering-hammers clanging; the bite of the muzzle of the nine-pounder jammed into my body and my own blood steaming on the sun-scorched iron; old Wheeler bawling hoarsely as the black cavalry sabres come thundering across the maidan towards our flimsy rampart

2

('No surrender! One last volley, damn 'em, and aim at the horses!'); the burning bungalows, a skeleton hand in the dust, Colin Campbell scratching his grizzled head, the crimson stain spreading in the filthy water below Suttee Ghat, a huge glittering pile of silver and gold and jewels and ivory bigger than anything you've ever seen – and two great brown liquid eyes shadowed with kohl, a single pearl resting on the satin skin above them, open red lips trembling . . . and, blast him, here's the station-master, beaming and knuckling his hat and starting me out of the only delightful part of that waking nightmare, with his cry of 'Welcome back tae Deeside, Sir Harry! Here we are again, then!'

And as he hands me down to the platform, you may be sure the local folk are all on hand, bringing their brats to stare and giggle at the big old buffer in his tweed cape and monstrous white whiskers ('There he is! The V.C. man, Sir Harry Flashman – aye, auld Flashy, him that charged wi' the Light Brigade and killed a' the niggers at Kau-bool – Goad, but isnae he the auld yin? – hip, hooray!'). So I acknowledge the cheers with a wave, bluff and hearty, as I step into the dog-cart, stepping briskly to escape the inevitable bemedalled veteran who comes shuffling after me, hoping I'll slip him sixpence for a dram when he assures me that we once stood together in the Highlanders' line at Balaclava. Lying old bastard, he was probably skulking in bed.

Not that I'd blame him if he was, mark you; given the chance I'd have skulked in mine – and not just at Balaclava, neither, but at every battle and skirmish I've sweated and scampered through during fifty inglorious years of unwilling soldiering. (Leastways, I know they were inglorious, but the country don't, thank heaven, which is why they've rewarded me with general rank and the knighthood and a double row

3

of medals on my left tit. Which shows you what cowardice and roguery can do, given a stalwart appearance, long legs, and a thumping slice of luck. Aye, well whip up, driver, we mustn't keep royalty waiting.)

But to return to the point, which is the Mutiny, and that terrible, incredible journey that began at Balmoral – well, it was as ghastly a road as any living man travelled in my time. I've seen a deal of war, and agree with Sherman that it's hell, but the Mutiny was the Seventh Circle under the Pit. Of course, it had its compensations: for one, I came through it, pretty whole, which is more than Havelock and Harry East and Johnny Nicholson did, enterprising lads that they were. (What's the use of a campaign if you don't survive it?) I did, and it brought me my greatest honour (totally undeserved, I needn't tell you), and a tidy enough slab of loot which bought and maintains my present place in Leicestershire – I reckon the plunder's better employed keeping me and my tenants in drink, than it was decorating a nigger temple for the edification of a gang of blood-sucking priests. And along the Mutiny road I met and loved that gorgeous, wicked witch Lakshmibai – there were others, too, naturally, but she was the prime piece.

One other thing about the Mutiny, before I get down to cases – I reckon it must be about the only one of my campaigns that I was pitched into through no fault of mine. On other occasions, I'll own, I've been to blame; for a man with a white liver a yard wide I've had a most unhappy knack of landing myself neck-deep in the slaughter through my various follies – to wit, talking too much *(that* got me into the Afghan débâcle of '41); playing the fool in pool-rooms (the Crimea); believing everything Abraham Lincoln told me (American Civil War); inviting a half-breed Hunkpapa whore to a regimental ball (the Sioux Rising of '76), and so on; the list's as long as my arm. But my involvement in the Mutiny was all Palmerston's doing (what disaster of the 'fifties wasn't?).

It came out of as clear and untroubled a sky as you could wish, a few months after my return from the Crimea, where, as you may know, I'd won fresh laurels through my terrified inability to avoid the most gruelling actions. I had stood petrified in the Thin Red Streak, charged with the Heavies and Lights, been taken prisoner by the Russians, and after a most deplorable series of adventures (in which I was employed as chief stud to a nobleman's daughter, was pursued by hordes of wolves and Cossacks, and finally was caught up in a private war between Asian bandits and a Ruski army bound for India – it's all in my memoirs somewhere) had emerged breathless and lousy at Peshawar.*

There, as if I hadn't had trouble enough, I was restoring my powers by squandering them on one of those stately, hungry Afghan Amazons, and she must have been a long sight better at coupling than cooking, for something on her menu gave me the cholera. I was on the broad of my back for months, and it took a slow, restful voyage home before I was my own man again, in prime fettle for the reunion with my loving Elspeth and to enjoy the role of a returned hero about town. And, I may add, a *retired* hero; oxen and wainropes weren't going to drag Flashy back to the Front again. (I've made the same resolve a score of times, and by God I've meant it, but you can't fight fate, especially when he's called Palmerston.)

However, there I was in the summer of '56, safely content on half pay as a staff colonel, with not so much as a sniff of

---

* See *Flashman at the Charge*.

war in sight, except the Persian farce, and that didn't matter. I was comfortably settled with Elspeth and little Havvy (the first fruit of our union, a guzzling lout of seven) in a fine house off Berkeley Square which Elspeth's inheritance maintained in lavish style, dropping by occasionally at Horse Guards, leading the social life, clubbing and turfing, whoring here and there as an occasional change from my lawful brainless beauty, and being lionised by all London – well, I'd stood at Armageddon and battled for the Lord (ostensibly) hadn't I, and enough had leaked out about my subsequent secret exploits in Central Asia (though government was damned cagey about them, on account of our delicate peace negotiations with Russia) to suggest that Flashy had surpassed all his former heroics. So with the country in a patriotic fever about its returning braves, I was ace-high in popular esteem – there was even talk that I'd get one of the new Victoria Crosses (for what that was worth) but it's my belief that Airey and Cardigan scotched it between them. Jealous bastards.

I suspect that Airey, who'd been chief of staff to Raglan in Crimea, hadn't forgotten my minor dereliction of duty at the Alma, when the Queen's randy little cousin Willy got his fool head blown off while under my care. And Cardigan loathed me, not least because I'd once emerged drunk, in the nick of time, from a wardrobe to prevent him cocking his lustful leg over my loving Elspeth. (She was no better than I was, you know.) And since coming home, I hadn't given him cause to love me any better.

You see, there was a deal of fine malicious tittle-tattle going about that summer, over Cardigan's part in the Light Brigade fiasco – not so much about his responsibility for the disaster, which was debatable, if you ask me, but for his personal behaviour at the guns. He'd been at the head of the

6

charge, right enough, with me alongside on a bolting horse, farting my fearful soul out, but after we'd reached the battery he'd barely paused to exchange a cut or two with the Ruski gunners before heading for home and safety again. Shocking bad form in a commander, says I, who was trying to hide under a gun limber at the time – not that I think for a moment that he was funking it; he hadn't the brains to be frightened, our Lord Haw-Haw. But he *had* retreated without undue delay, and since he was never short of enemies eager to believe the worst, the gossips were having a field day now. There were angry letters in the press, and even a law-suit,[1] and since I'd been in the thick of the action, it was natural that I should be asked about it.

In fact, it was George Paget, who'd commanded the 4th Lights in the charge, who put the thing to me point-blank in the card-room at White's (can't imagine what I was doing there; must have been somebody's guest) in front of a number of people, civilians mostly, but I know Spottswood was there, and old Scarlett of the Heavies, I think.

'You were neck and neck with Cardigan,' says Paget, 'and in the battery before anyone else. Now, God knows he's not my soul-mate, but all this talk's getting a shade raw. Did you see him in the battery or not?'

Well, I had, but I wasn't saying so – far be it from me to clear his lordship's reputation when there was a chance of damaging it. So I said offhand:

'Don't ask me, George; I was too busy hunting for your cigars,' which caused a guffaw.

'No gammon, Flash,' says he, looking grim, and asked again, in his tactful way: 'Did Cardigan cut out, or not?'

There were one or two shocked murmurs, and I shuffled a pack, frowning, before I answered. There are more ways

7

than one of damning a man's credit, and I wanted to give Cardigan of my best. So I looked uncomfortable, and then growled, slapped the pack down as I rose, looked Paget in the eye, and said:

'It's all by and done with now, ain't it? Let's drop it, George, shall we?' And I went out then and there, leaving behind the impression that bluff, gallant Flashy didn't want to talk about it – which convinced them all that Cardigan had shirked, better than if I'd said so straight out, or called him a coward to his face. I had a chance to do that, too, a bare two hours later, when the man himself came raging up to me with a couple of his toadies in tow, just as Spottswood and I were coming out of the Guards Club. The hall was full of fellows, goggling at the sensation.

'Fwashman! You there, sir!' he croaked – they were absolutely the first words between us since the Charge, nearly two years before. He was breathing frantically, like a man who has been running, his beaky face all mottled and his grey whiskers quaking with fury. 'Fwashman – this is intolewable! My honour is impugned – scandalous lies, sir! And they tell me that you don't deny them! Well, sir? Well? Haw-haw?'

I tilted back my tile with a forefinger and looked him up and down, from his bald head and pop eyes to his stamping foot. He looked on the edge of apoplexy; a delightful sight.

'What lies are these, my lord?' says I, very steady.

'You know vewy well!' he cried. 'Bawacwava, sir – the storming of the battewy! Word George Paget has asked you, in pubwic, whether you saw me at the guns – and you have the effwontewy to tell him you don't know! Damnation, sir! And one of my own officers, too—'

'A former member of your regiment, my lord – I admit the fact.'

'Blast your impudence!' he roared, frothing at me. 'Will you give me the lie? Will you say I was not at the guns?'

I settled my hat and pulled on my gloves while he mouthed.

'My lord,' says I, speaking deliberately clear, 'I saw you in the advance. In the battery itself – I was otherwise engaged, and had no leisure nor inclination to look about me to see who was where. For that matter, I did not see Lord George himself until he pulled me to my feet. I assumed –' and I bore on the word ever so slightly '– that you were on hand, at the head of your command. But I do not *know*, and frankly I do not care. Good day to you, my lord.' And with a little nod I turned to the door.

His voice pursued me, cracking with rage.

'Colonel Fwashman!' he cried. 'You are a viper!'

I turned at that, making myself go red in the face in righteous wrath, but I knew what I was about; he was getting no blow or challenge from me – he shot too damned straight for that.

'Indeed, my lord,' says I. 'Yet I don't wriggle and turn.' And I left him gargling, well pleased with myself. But, as I say, it probably cost me the V.C. at the time; for all the rumours, he was still a power at Horse Guards, and well insinuated at Court, too.

However, our little exchange did nothing to diminish my popularity at large; a few nights later I got a tremendous cheer at the Guards Dinner at Surrey Gardens, with chaps standing on the table shouting 'Huzza for Flash Harry!' and singing 'Garryowen' and tumbling down drunk – how they did it on a third of a bottle of bubbly beat me.[2] Cardigan wasn't there, sensible fellow; they'd have hooted him out of the kingdom. As it was, *Punch* carried a nasty little dig about his absence, and wondered that he hadn't sent along his spurs,

9

since he'd made such good use of them in retiring from the battery.

Of course, Lord Haw-Haw wasn't the only general to come under the public lash that summer; the rest of 'em, like Lucan and Airey, got it too for the way they'd botched the campaign. So while we gallant underlings enjoyed roses and laurels all the way, our idiot commanders were gainfully employed exchanging recriminations, writing furious letters to the papers saying 'twasn't their fault, but some other fellow's, and there had even been a commission set up to investigate their misconduct of the war.

Unfortunately, government picked the wrong men to do the investigating – MacNeill and Tulloch – for they turned out to be honest, and reported that indeed our high command hadn't been fit to dig latrines, or words to that effect. Well, *that* plainly wouldn't do, so another commission had to be hurriedly formed to investigate afresh, and this time get the right answer, and no nonsense about it. Well, they did, and exonerated everybody, hip-hip-hurrah and Rule, Britannia. Which was what you'd have expected any half-competent government to stage-manage in the first place, but Palmerston was in the saddle by then, and he wasn't really good at politics, you know.

To crown it all, in the middle of the scandal the Queen herself had words about it with Hardinge, the Commander-in-Chief, at the Aldershot Review, and poor old Hardinge fell down paralysed and never smiled again. It's true; I was there myself, getting soaked through, and Hardinge went down like a shanghaied sailor, with all his faculties gone, not that he had many to start with. Some said it was a judgement on the Army and government corruption, so there.

All of which mattered rather less to me than the width of

Elspeth's crinolines, but if I've digressed it is merely to show you how things were in England then, and also because I can never resist the temptation to blackguard Cardigan as he deserves. Meanwhile, I was going happily about my business, helping my dear wife spend her cash – which she did like a clipper-hand in port, I'm bound to say – and you would have said we were a blissful young couple, turning a blind eye to each other's infidelities and galloping in harness when we felt like it, which was frequent, for if anything she got more beddable with the passing years.

And then came the invitation to Balmoral, which reduced Elspeth to a state of nervous exultation close to hysterics, and took me clean aback. I'd have imagined that if the Royal family ever thought of me at all, it was as the chap who'd been remiss enough to lose one of the Queen's cousins – but mind you, she had so many of 'em she probably didn't notice, or if she did, hadn't heard that I was to blame for it. No, I've puzzled over it sometimes, and can only conclude that the reason we were bidden to Balmoral that September was that Russia was still very much the topic of the day, what with the new Tsar's coronation and the recent peace, and I was one of the most senior men to have been a prisoner in Russia's hands.

I didn't have leisure to speculate at the time, though, for Elspeth's frenzy at the thought of being 'in attendance', as she chose to call it, claimed everyone's attention within a mile of Berkeley Square. Being a Scotch tradesman's daughter, my darling was one degree more snobbish than a penniless Spanish duke, and in the days before we went north her condescension to her middle-class friends would have turned your stomach. Between gloating, and babbling about how she and the Queen would discuss dressmaking while Albert

11

and I boozed in the gunroom (she had a marvellous notion of court life, you see), she went into declines at the thought that she would come out in spots, or have her drawers fall down when being presented. You must have endured the sort of thing yourself.

'Oh, Harry, Jane Speedicut will be *green*! You and I – guests of Her Majesty! It will be the finest thing – and I have my new French dresses – the ivory, the beige silk, the lilac satin, and the lovely, lovely green which old Admiral Lawson *so* admired – if you think it is not a *leetle* low for the Queen? And my *barrege* for Sunday – will there be members of the nobility staying also? – will there be ladies whose husbands are of lower rank than you? Ellen Parkin – *Lady* Parkin, indeed! – was *consumed* with spite when I told her – oh, and I must have another maid who can manage my hair, for Sarah is too *maladroit* for words, although she is very passable with dresses – what shall I wear to picnics? – for we shall be bound to walk in the lovely Highland countryside – oh, Harry, what do you suppose the Queen reads? – and shall I call the Prince "highness" or "sir"?'

I was glad, I can tell you, when we finally reached Abergeldie, where we had rooms in the castle where guests were put up – for Balmoral was very new then, and Albert was still busy having the finishing touches put to it. Elspeth by this time was too nervous even to talk, but her first glimpse of our royal hosts reduced her awe a trifle, I think. We took a stroll the first afternoon, in the direction of Balmoral, and on the road encountered what seemed to be a family of tinkers led by a small washerwoman and an usher who had evidently pinched his headmaster's clothes. Fortunately, I recognised them as Victoria and Albert out with their brood, and knew enough simply to raise my hat as we passed, for they loathed to be treated as royalty when they were playing at being commoners. Elspeth didn't even suspect who it was until we were past, and when I told her she swooned by the roadside. I revived her by threatening to carry her into the bushes and molest her, and on the way back she observed that really Her Majesty had looked *quite* royal, but in a *common* sort of way.

By the time we were presented at Balmoral, though, the next day, she was high up the scale again, and the fact that we shared the waiting-room beforehand with some lord or other and his beak-nosed lady, who looked at us as though we were riff-raff, reduced my poor little scatterbrain to quaking terror. I'd met the royals before, of course, and tried to reassure her, whispering that she looked a stunner (which was true) and not to be put out by Lord and Lady Puffbuttock, who were now ignoring us with that icy incivility which is the stamp of our lower-class aristocracy. (I know; I'm one myself nowadays.)

It was quite handy that our companions kept their noses in the air, though, for it gave me the chance to loop a ribbon from the lady's enormous crinoline on to an occasional table without her knowing, and when the doors to the royal drawing-room were opened she set off and brought the whole thing crashing down, crockery and all, in full view of the little court circle. I kept Elspeth in an iron grip, and steered her round the wreckage, and so Colonel and Mrs Flashman made their bows while the doors were hurriedly closed behind us, and the muffled sounds of the Puffbuttocks being extricated by flunkeys was music to my ears, even if it did make the Queen look more pop-eyed than usual. The moral is: don't put on airs with Flashy, and if you do, keep your crinolines out of harm's way.

And, as it turned out, to Elspeth's lifelong delight and my immense satisfaction, she and the Queen got on like port and nuts from the first. Elspeth, you see, was one of those females who are so beautiful that even other women can't help liking 'em, and in her idiot way she was a lively and engaging soul. The fact that she was Scotch helped, too, for the Queen was in one of her Jacobite moods just then, and by the grace of God someone had read *Waverley* to Elspeth when she was a child, and taught her to recite 'The Lady of the Lake'.

I had been dreading meeting Albert again, in case he mentioned his whoremongering Nephew Willy, now deceased, but all he did was say:

'Ah, Colonel Flash-mann – haff you read Tocqueville's *L'Ancien Régime?*'

I said I hadn't, yet, but I'd be at the railway library first thing in the morning, and he looked doleful and went on:

'It warns us that bureaucratic central government, far from curing the ills of revolution, can actually arouse them.'

I said I'd often thought that, now that he mentioned it, and he nodded and said: 'Italy is very unsatisfactory,' which brought our conversation to a close. Fortunately old Ellenborough, who'd been chief in India at the time of my Kabul heroics, was among those present, and he buttonholed me, which was a profound relief. And then the Queen addressed me, in that high sing-song of hers:

'Your *dear* wife, Colonel Flashman, tells me that you are *quite* recovered from the rigours of your *Russian* adventures, which you shall tell us of *presently*. They seem to be a quite *extraordinary* people; Lord Granville writes from Petersburg that Lady Wodehouse's Russian maid was found *eating* the contents of one of her ladyship's dressing-table pots – it was

14

castor oil pomatum for the *hair*! What a *remarkable* extravagance, was it not?'

That was my cue, of course, to regale them with a few domestic anecdotes of Russia, and its primitive ways, which went down well, with the Queen nodding approval and saying: 'How barbarous! How strange!' while Elspeth glowed to see her hero holding the floor. Albert joined in in his rib-tickling way to observe that no European state offered such fertile soil for the seeds of socialism as Russia did, and that he feared that the new Tsar had little intellect or character.

'So Lord Granville says,' was the Queen's prim rejoinder, 'but I do not *think* it is quite his place to make such observations on a *royal* personage. Do you not agree, Mrs Flashman?'

Old Ellenborough, who was a cheery, boozy buffer, said to me that he hoped I had tried to civilise the Russians a little by teaching them cricket, and Albert, who had no more humour than the parish trough, looked stuffy and says:

'I am sure Colonel Flash-mann would do no such thing. I cannot unner-stend this passion for cricket; it seems to me a great waste of time. What is the proff-it to a younk boy in crouching motionless in a field for hours on end? Em I nott right, Colonel?'

'Well, sir,' says I, 'I've looked out in the deep field myself long enough to sympathise with you; it's a great fag, to be sure. But perhaps, when the boy's a man, his life may depend on crouching motionless, behind a Khyber rock or a Burmese bush – so a bit of practice may not come amiss, when he's young.'

Which was sauce, if you like, but I could never resist the temptation, in grovelling to Albert, to put a pinch of pepper down his shirt. It was in my character of bluff, no-nonsense Harry, too, and a nice reminder of the daring deeds I'd done.

15

Ellenborough said 'Hear, hear', and even Albert looked only half-sulky, and said all diss-cipline was admirable, but there must be better ways of instilling it; the Prince of Wales, he said, should nott play cricket, but some more constructiff game.

After that we had tea, very informal, and Elspeth distinguished herself by actually prevailing on Albert to eat a cucumber sandwich; she'll have him in the bushes in a minute, thinks I, and on that happy note our first visit concluded, with Elspeth going home on a cloud to Abergeldie.

But if it was socially useful, it wasn't much of a holiday, although Elspeth revelled in it. She went for walks with the Queen, twice (calling themselves Mrs Fitzjames and Mrs Marmion, if you please), and even made Albert laugh when charades were played in the evening, by impersonating Helen of Troy with a Scotch accent. I couldn't even get a grin out of him; we went shooting with the other gentlemen, and it was purgatory having to stalk at his pace. He was keen as mustard, though, and slaughtered stags like a Ghazi on hashish – you'll hardly credit it, but his notion of sport was that a huge long trench should be dug so that we could sneak up on the deer unobserved; he'd have done it, too, but the local ghillies showed so much disgust at the idea that he dropped it. He couldn't understand their objections, though; to him all that mattered was killing the beasts.

For the rest, he prosed interminably and played German music on the piano, with me applauding like hell. Things weren't made easier by the fact that he and Victoria weren't getting on too well just then; she had just discovered (and confided to Elspeth) that she was in foal for the ninth time, and she took her temper out on dear Albert – the trouble was, he was so bloody patient with her, which can drive a

16

woman to fury faster than anything I know. And he was always *right*, which was worse. So they weren't dealing at all well, and he spent most of the daylight hours tramping up Glen Bollocks, or whatever they call it, roaring 'Ze gunn!' and butchering every animal in view.

The only thing that seemed to cheer up the Queen was that she was marrying off her oldest daughter, Princess Vicky – the best of the whole family, in my view, a really pretty, green-eyed little mischief. She was to wed Frederick William of Prussia, who was due at Balmoral in a few weeks, and the Queen was full of it, Elspeth told me.

However, enough of the court gossip; it will give you some notion of the trivial way in which I was being forced to pass my time – toadying Albert, and telling the Queen how many acute accents there were on 'déterminés'. The trouble with this kind of thing is that it dulls your wits, and your proper instinct for self-preservation, so that if a blow falls you're caught clean offside, as I was on the night of September 22, 1856: I recollect the date absolutely because it was the day after Florence Nightingale came to the castle.[3]

I'd never met her, but as the leading Crimean on the premises I was summoned to join in the tête-à-tête she had with the Queen in the afternoon. It was a frost, if you like; pious platitudes from the two of 'em, with Flashy passing the muffins and joining in when called on to agree that what our wars needed was more sanitation and texts on the wall of every dressing-station. There was one near-facer for me, and that was when Miss Nightingale (a cool piece, that) asked me calm as you like what regimental officers could do to prevent their men from contracting certain indelicate social infections from – hem-hem – female camp-followers of a certain sort; I near as dammit put my teacup in the Queen's

17

lap, but recovered to say that I'd never heard of any such thing, not in the Light Cavalry, anyway – French troops another matter, of course. Would you believe it, I actually made her blush, but I doubt if the Queen even knew what we were talking about. For the rest, I thought La Nightingale a waste of good womanhood; handsome face, well set up and titted out, but with that cold don't-lay-a-lecherous-limb-on-me-my-lad look in her eye – the kind, in short, that can be all right if you're prepared to spend time and trouble making 'em cry 'Roger!', but I seldom have the patience. Anywhere else I might have taken a squeeze at her, just by way of research, but a queen's drawing-room cramps your style. (Perhaps it's a pity I didn't; being locked up for indecent assault on a national heroine couldn't have been worse than the ordeal that was to begin a few hours later.)

Elspeth and I spent the following evening at a birthday party at one of the big houses in the neighbourhood; it was a cheery affair, and we didn't leave till close on midnight to drive back to Abergeldie. It was a close, thundery night, with big rain-drops starting to fall, but we didn't mind; I had taken enough drink on board to be monstrously horny, and if the drive had been longer and Elspeth's crinoline less of a hindrance I'd have had at her on the carriage-seat. She got out at the lodge giggling and squeaking, and I chased her through the front door – and there was the messenger of doom, waiting in the hall. A tall chap, almost a swell, but with a jaw too long and an eye too sharp; very respectable, with a hard hat under his arm and a billy in his hip-pocket, I'll wager. I know a genteel strong man from a government office when I see one.

He asked could he speak to me, so I took my arm from Elspeth's waist, patted her towards the stairs with a whispered promise that I'd be up directly to sound the charge, and told him to state his business. He did that smart enough.

'I am from the Treasury, Colonel Flashman,' says he. 'My name is Hutton. Lord Palmerston wishes to speak with you.'

It took me flat aback, slightly foxed that I was. My first thought was that he must want me to go back to London, but then he said: 'His lordship is at Balmoral, sir. If you will be good enough to come with me – I have a coach.'

'But, but . . . you said Lord Palmerston? The Prime . . . what the deuce? Palmerston wants *me*?'

'At once, sir, if you please. The matter is urgent.'

Well, I couldn't make anything of it. I never doubted it was genuine – as I've said, the man in front of me had authority written all over him. But it's a fair start when you come rolling innocently home and are told that the first statesman of Europe is round the corner and wants you at the double – and now the fellow was positively ushering me towards the door.

'Hold on,' says I. 'Give me a moment to change my shoes' – what I wanted was a moment to put my head in the wash-bowl and think, and despite his insistence I snapped at him to wait, and hurried upstairs.

What the devil was Pam doing here – and what could he want with me? I'd only met him once, for a moment, before I went to the Crimea; I'd leered at him ingratiatingly at parties, too, but never spoken. And now he wanted me urgently – me, a mere colonel on half pay. I'd nothing on my conscience, either – leastways, not to interest him. I couldn't see it, but there was nothing but to obey, so I went to my dressing-room, fretting, donned my hat and topcoat against the worsening weather, and remembered that Elspeth, poor child, must even now be waiting for her cross-buttocking lesson. Well, it was hard lines on her, but duty called, so I just popped my head round her door to call a chaste farewell – and there she was, dammit, reclining languorously on the coverlet like one of those randy classical goddesses, wearing nothing but the big ostrich-plume fan I'd brought her from Egypt, and her sniggering maid turning the lamp down low. Elspeth clothed could stop a monk in his tracks; naked and pouting expectantly over a handful of red feathers, she'd have made the Grand Inquisitor burn his books. I hesitated between love and duty for a full second, and then 'The hell with Palmerston, let him wait!' cries I, and was plunging for the bed before the abigail was fairly out of the room. Never miss the chance, as the Duke used to say.

'Lord Palmerston? Oooo-ah! Harry – what *do* you mean?'

'Ne'er mind!' cries I, taking hold and bouncing away.

'But Harry – such impatience, my love! And, dearest – you're wearing your hat!'

'The next one's going to be a boy, dammit!' And for a few glorious stolen moments I forgot Palmerston and minions in the hall, and marvelled at the way that superb idiot woman of mine could keep up a stream of questions while performing like a harem houri – we were locked in an astonishing embrace on her dressing-table stool, I recall, when there was a knock on the door, and the maid's giggling voice piped through to say the gentleman downstairs was getting impatient, and would I be long.

'Tell him I'm just packing my baggage,' says I. 'I'll be down directly,' and presently, keeping my mouth on hers to stem her babble of questions, I carried my darling tenderly back to the bed. Always leave things as you would wish to find them.

'I cannot stay longer, my love,' I told her. 'The Prime

20

Minister is waiting.' And with bewildered entreaties pursuing me I skipped out, trousers in hand, made a hasty toilet on the landing, panted briefly against the wall, and then stepped briskly down. It's a great satisfaction, looking back, that I kept the government waiting in such a good cause, and I set it down here as a deserved tribute to the woman who was the only real love of my life and as the last pleasant memory I was to have for a long time ahead.

It's true enough, too, as Ko Dali's daughter taught me, that there's nothing like a good rattle for perking up an edgy chap like me. It had shaken me for a moment, and it still looked rum, that Palmerston should want to see me, but as we bowled through the driving rain to Balmoral I was telling myself that there was probably nothing in it after all; considering the good odour I stood in just then, hob-nobbing with royalty and being admired for my Russian heroics, it was far more likely to be fair news than foul. And it wasn't like being bidden to the presence of one of your true ogres, like the old Duke or Bismarck or Dr Wrath-of-God Arnold (I've knocked tremulously on some fearsome doors in my time, I can tell you).

No, Pam might be an impatient old tyrant when it came to bullying foreigners and sending warships to deal with the dagoes, but everyone knew he was a decent, kindly old sport at bottom, who put folk at their ease and told a good story. Why, it was notorious that the reason he wouldn't live at Downing Street, but on Piccadilly, was that he liked to ogle the good-lookers from his window, and wave to the cads and crossing-sweepers, who loved him because he talked plain English, and would stump up a handsome subscription for an old beaten prize-pug like Tom Sayers. That was Pam – and if anyone ever tells you that he was a politically

21

unprincipled old scoundrel, who carried things with a high and reckless hand, I can only say that it didn't seem to work a whit worse than the policies of more high-minded statesmen. The only difference I ever saw between them and Pam was that he did his dirty work bare-faced (when he wasn't being deeper than damnation) and grinned about it.

So I was feeling pretty easy as we covered the three miles to Balmoral – and even pleasantly excited – which shows you how damned soft and optimistic I must have grown; I should have known that it's never safe to get within range of princes or prime ministers. When we got to the castle I followed Hutton smartly through a side door, up some back-stairs, and along to heavy double doors where a burly civilian was standing guard; I gave my whiskers a martial twitch as he opened the door, and stepped briskly in.

You know how it can be when you enter a strange room – everything can look as safe and merry as ninepence, and yet there's something in the air that touches you like an electric shock. It was here now, a sort of bristling excitement that put my nerves on edge in an instant. And yet there was nothing out of the ordinary to see – just a big, cheerful panelled room with a huge fire roaring under the mantel, a great table littered with papers, and two sober chaps bustling about it under the direction of a slim young fellow – Barrington, Palmerston's secretary. And over by the fire were three other men – Ellenborough, with his great flushed face and his belly stuck out; a slim, keen-looking old file whom I recognised as Wood, of the Admiralty; and with his back to the blaze and his coat-tails up, the man himself, peering at Ellenborough with his bright, short-sighted eyes and looking as though his dyed hair and whiskers had just been rubbed with a towel – old Squire Pam as ever was. As I came in, his brisk, sharp voice was ringing out (he never gave a damn who heard him):

'. . . so if he's to be Prince Consort, it don't make a ha'porth of difference, you see. Not to the country – or me. However, as long as Her Majesty *thinks* it does – that's what matters, what? Haven't you found that telegraph of Quilter's yet, Barrington? – well, look in the Persian packet, then.'

And then he caught sight of me, and frowned, sticking out his long lip. 'Ha, that's the man!' cries he. 'Come in, sir, come in!'

What with the drink I'd taken, and my sudden nervousness, I tripped over the mat – which was an omen, if you like – and came as near as a toucher to oversetting a chair.

'By George,' says Pam, 'is he drunk? All these young fellows are, nowadays. Here, Barrington, see him to a chair, before he breaks a window. There, at the table.' Barrington pulled out a chair for me, and the three at the fireplace seemed to be staring ominously at me while I apologised and took it, especially Pam in the middle, with those bright steady eyes taking in every inch of me as he nursed his port glass and stuck a thumb into his fob – for all the world like the marshal of a Kansas trail-town surveying the street. (Which is what he was, of course, on a rather grand scale.)

He was very old at this time, with the gout and his false teeth forever slipping out, but he was evidently full of ginger tonight, and not in one of his easygoing moods. He didn't beat about, either.

'Young Flashman,' growls he. 'Very good. Staff colonel, on half pay at present, what? Well, from this moment you're back on the full list, an' what you hear in this room tonight is to go no further, understand? Not to anyone – not even in this castle. You follow?'

23

I followed, sure enough – what he meant was that the Queen wasn't to know: it was notorious that he never told her anything. But that was nothing; it was his tone, and the solemn urgency of his warning, that put the hairs up on my neck.

'Very good,' says he again. 'Now then, before I talk to you, Lord Ellenborough has somethin' to show you – want your opinion of it. All right, Barrington, I'll take that Persian stuff now, while Colonel Flashman looks at the damned buns.'

I thought I'd misheard him, as he limped past me and took his seat at the table-head, pawing impatiently among his papers. But sure enough, Barrington passed over to me a little lead biscuit-box, and Ellenborough, seating himself beside me, indicated that I should open it. I pushed back the lid, mystified, and there, in a rice-paper wrapping, were three or four greyish, stale-looking little scones, no bigger than captain's biscuits.

'There,' says Pam, not looking up from his papers. 'Don't eat 'em. Tell his lordship what you make of those.'

I knew, right off; that faint eastern smell was unmistakable, but I touched one of them to make sure.

'They're chapattis, my lord,' says I, astonished. 'Indian chapattis.'

Ellenborough nodded. 'Ordinary cakes of native food. You attach no signal significance to them, though?'

'Why . . . no, sir.'

Wood took a seat opposite me. 'And you can conjecture no situation, colonel,' says he, in his dry, quiet voice, 'in which the sight of such cakes might occasion you . . . alarm?'

Obviously Ministers of the Crown don't ask damnfool questions for nothing, but I could only stare at him. Pam, apparently deep in his papers at the table-head, wheezing and sucking his teeth and muttering to Barrington, paused to grunt: 'Serve the dam' things at dinner an' they'd alarm me,' and Ellenborough tapped the biscuit box.

'These chapattis came last week from India, by fast steam sloop. Sent by our political agent at a place called Jhansi. Know it? It's down below the Jumna, in Maharatta country. For weeks now, scores of such cakes have been turning up among the sepoys of our native Indian garrison at Jhansi – not as food, though. It seems the sepoys pass them from hand to hand as tokens—'

'Have you ever heard of such a thing?' Wood interrupted.

I hadn't, so I just shook my head and looked attentive, wondering what the devil this was all about, while Ellenborough went on:

'Our political knows where they come from, all right. The native village constables – you know, the *chowkidars* – bake them in batches of ten, and send one apiece to ten different sepoys – and each sepoy is bound to make ten *more*, and pass *them* on, to his comrades, and so on, ad infinitum. It's not new, of course; ritual cake-passing is very old in India. But there are three remarkable things about it: firstly, it happens only rarely; second, even the natives themselves don't know *why* it happens, only that the cakes must be baked and passed; and third –' he tapped the box again '– they believe that the appearance of the cakes foreshadows terrible catastrophe.'

He paused, and I tried to look impressed. For there was nothing out of the way in all this – straight from *Alice in Wonderland*, if you like, but when you know India and the amazing tricks the niggers can get up to (usually in the name of religion) you cease to be surprised. It seemed an interesting superstition – but what was more interesting was that two

Ministers of the Government, and a former Governor-General of India, were discussing it behind closed doors – and had decided to let Flashy into the secret.

'But there's something more,' Ellenborough went on, 'which is why Skene, our political man at Jhansi, is treating the matter as one of urgency. Cakes like these have circulated among native *troops*, quite apart from civilians, on only three occasions in the past fifty years – at Vellore in '06, at Buxar, and at Barrackpore. You don't recall the names? Well, at each place, when the cakes appeared, the same reaction followed among the sepoys.' He put on his House of Lords face and said impressively, 'Mutiny.'

Looking back, I suppose I ought to have thrilled with horror at the mention of the dread word – but in fact all that occurred to me was the facetious thought that perhaps they ought to have varied the sepoys' rations. I didn't think much of the political man Skene's judgement, either; I'd been a political myself, and it's part of the job to scream at your own shadow, but if he – or Ellenborough, who knew India outside in – was smelling a sepoy revolt in a few mouldy biscuits – well, it was ludicrous. I knew John Sepoy (we all did, didn't we?) for the most loyal ass who ever put on uniform – and so he should have been, the way the Company treated him. However, it wasn't for me to venture an opinion in such august company, particularly with the Prime Minister listening: he'd pushed his papers aside and risen, and was pouring himself some more port.

'Well, now,' says he briskly, taking a hearty swig and rolling it round his teeth, 'you've admired his lordship's cakes, what? Damned unappetisin' they look, too. All right, Barrington, your assistants can go – our special leaves at four, does it? Very well.' He waited till the junior secretaries had gone, muttered something about ungodly hours and the Queen's perversity in choosing a country retreat at the North Pole, and paced stiffly over to the fire, where he set his back to the mantel and glowered at me from beneath his gorse-bush brows, which was enough to set my dinner circulating in the old accustomed style.

'Tokens of revolution in an Indian garrison,' says he. 'Very good. Been readin' that report of yours again, Flashman – the one you made to Dalhousie last year, in which you described the discovery you made while you were a prisoner in Russia – about their scheme for invadin' India, while we were busy in Crimea. Course, we say nothin' about *that* these days – peace signed with Russia, all good fellowship an' be damned, et cetera – don't have to tell you. But somethin' in your report came to mind when this cake business began.' He pushed out his big lip at me. 'You wrote that the Russian march across the Indus was to be accompanied by a native risin' in India, fomented by Tsarist agents. Our politicals have been chasin' that fox ever since – pickin' up some interestin' scents, of which these infernal buns are the latest. Now, then,' he settled himself, eyes half-shut, but watching me, 'tell me precisely what you heard in Russia, touchin' on an Indian rebellion. Every word of it.'

So I told him, exactly as I remembered it – how Scud East and I had lain quaking in our nightshirts in the gallery at Starotorsk, and overheard about 'Item Seven', which was the Russian plan for an invasion of India. They'd have done it, too, but Yakub Beg's riders scuppered their army up on the Syr Daria, with Flashy running about roaring with a bellyful of *bhang*, performing unconscious prodigies of valour. I'd set it all out in my report to Dalhousie, leaving out the discreditable bits (you can find *those* in my earlier memoirs, along

27

with the licentious details). It was a report of nicely judged modesty, that official one, calculated to convince Dalhousie that I was the nearest thing to Hereward the Wake he was ever likely to meet – and why not? I'd suffered for my credit.

But the information about an Indian rebellion had been slight. All we'd discovered was that when the Russian army reached the Khyber, their agents in India would rouse the natives – and particularly John Company's sepoys – to rise against the British. I didn't doubt it was true, at the time; it seemed an obvious ploy. But that was more than a year ago, and Russia was no threat to India any longer, I supposed.

They heard me out, in a silence that lasted a full minute after I'd finished, and then Wood says quietly:

'It fits, my lord.'

'Too dam' well,' says Pam, and came hobbling back to his chair again. 'It's all pat. You see, Flashman, Russia may be spent as an armed power, for the present – but that don't mean she'll leave us at peace in India, what? This scheme for a rebellion – by George, if I were a Russian political, invasion or no invasion, I fancy I could achieve somethin' in India, given the right agents. Couldn't I just, though!' He growled in his throat, heaving restlessly and cursing his gouty foot. 'Did you know, there's an Indian superstition that the British Raj will come to an end exactly a hundred years after the Battle of Plassey?' He picked up one of the chapattis and peered at it. 'Dam' thing isn't even sugared. Well, the hundredth anniversary of Plassey falls next June the twenty-third. Interestin'. Now then, tell me – what d'you know about a Russian nobleman called Count Nicholas Ignatieff?'

He shot it at me so abruptly that I must have started a good six inches. There's a choice collection of ruffians whose names you can mention if you want to ruin my digestion for an hour or two – Charity Spring and Bismarck, Rudi Starnberg and Wesley Hardin, for example – but I'd put N. P. Ignatieff up with the leaders any time. He was the brute who'd nearly put paid to me in Russia – a gotch-eyed, freezing ghoul of a man who'd dragged me half way to China in chains, and threatened me with exposure in a cage and knouting to death, and like pleasantries. I hadn't cared above half for the conversation thus far, with its bloody mutiny cakes and the sinister way they kept drag-ging in my report to Dalhousie – but at the introduction of Ignatieff's name my bowels began to play the Hallelujah Chorus in earnest. It took me all my time to keep a straight face and tell Pam what I knew – that Ignatieff had been one of the late Tsar's closest advisers, and that he was a political agent of immense skill and utter ruthlessness; I ended with a reminiscence of the last time I'd seen him, under that hideous row of gallows at Fort Raim. Ellenborough exclaimed in disgust, Wood shuddered deli-cately, and Pam sipped his port.

'Interestin' life you've led,' says he. 'Thought I remem-bered his name from your report – he was one of the prime movers behind the Russian plan for invasion an' Indian rebel-lion, as I recall. Capable chap, what?'

'My lord,' says I, 'he's the devil, and that's a fact.'

'Just so,' says Pam. 'An' the devil will find mischief.' He nodded to Ellenborough. 'Tell him, my lord. Pay close heed to this, Flashman.'

Ellenborough cleared his throat and fixed his boozy spaniel eyes on me. 'Count Ignatieff,' says he, 'has made two clan-destine visits to India in the past year. Our politicals first had word of him last autumn at Ghuznee; he came over the Khyber disguised as an Afridi horse-coper, to Peshawar.

29

There we lost him – as you might expect, one disguised man among so many natives—'

'But my lord, that can't be!' I couldn't help interrupting. 'You can't lose Ignatieff, if you know what to look for. However he's disguised, there's one thing he can't hide – his eyes! One of em's half-brown, half-blue!'

'He can if he puts a patch over it,' says Ellenborough. 'India's full of one-eyed men. In any event, we picked up his trail again – and on both occasions it led to the same place – Jhansi. He spent two months there, all told, usually out of sight, and our people were never able to lay a hand on him. What he was doing, they couldn't discover – except that it was mischief. Now, we see what the mischief was –' and he pointed to the chapattis. 'Brewing insurrection, beyond a doubt. And having done his infernal work – back over the hills to Afghanistan. This summer he was in St Petersburg – but from what our politicals did learn, he's expected back in Jhansi again. We don't know when.'

No doubt it was the subject under discussion, but there didn't seem to be an ounce of heat coming from the blazing fire behind me; the room felt suddenly cold, and I was aware of the rain slashing at the panes and the wind moaning in the dark outside. I was looking at Ellenborough, but in his face I could see Ignatieff's hideous parti-coloured eye, and hear that soft icy voice hissing past the long cigarette between his teeth.

'Plain enough, what?' says Pam. 'The mine's laid, in Jhansi – an' if it explodes . . . God knows what might follow. India looks tranquil enough – but how many other Jhansis, how many other Ignatieffs, are there?' He shrugged. 'We don't know, but we can be certain there's no more sensitive spot than this one. The Russians have picked Jhansi with care

– we only annexed it four years ago, on the old Raja's death, an' we've still barely more than a foothold there. Thug country, it used to be, an' still pretty wild, for all it's one of the richest thrones in India. Worst of all, it's ruled by a woman – the Rani, the Raja's widow. She was old when she married him, I gather, an' there was no legitimate heir, so we took it under our wing – an' she didn't like it. She rules under our tutelage these days – but she remains as implacable an enemy as we have in India. Fertile soil for Master Ignatieff to sow his plots.'

He paused, and then looked straight at me. 'Aye – the mine's laid in Jhansi. But precisely when an' where they'll try to fire it, an' whether it'll go off or not . . . this we must know – an' prevent at all costs.'

The way he said it went through me like an icicle. I'd been sure all along that I wasn't being lectured for fun, but now, looking at their heavy faces, I knew that unless my poltroon instinct was sadly at fault, some truly hellish proposal was about to emerge. I waited quaking for the axe to fall, while Pam stirred his false teeth with his tongue – which was a damned unnerving sight, I may tell you – and then delivered sentence.

'Last week, the Board of Control decided to send an extraordinary agent to Jhansi. His task will be to discover what the Russians have been doing there, how serious is the unrest in the sepoy garrison, and to deal with this hostile beldam of a Rani by persuadin' her, if possible, that loyalty to the British Raj is in her best interest.' He struck his finger on the table. 'An' if an' when this man Ignatieff returns to Jhansi again – to deal with *him*, too. Not a task for an ordinary political, you'll agree.'

No, but I was realising, with mounting horror, who they

31

did think it was a task for. But I could only sit, with my spine dissolving and my face set in an expression of attentive idiocy, while he went inexorably on.

'The Board of Control chose you without hesitation, Flashman. I approved the choice myself. You don't know it, but I've been watchin' you since my time as Foreign Secretary. You've been a political – an' a deuced successful one. I daresay you think that the work you did in Middle Asia last year has gone unrecognised, but that's not so.' He rumbled at me impressively, wagging his great fat head. 'You've the highest name as an active officer, you've proved your resource – you know India – fluent in languages – includin' Russian, which could be of the first importance, what? You know this man Ignatieff, by sight, an' you've bested him before. You see, I know all about you, Flashman,' you old fool, I wanted to shout, you don't know anything of the bloody sort; you ain't fit to be Prime Minister, if that's what you think, 'and I know of no one else so fitted to this work. How old are you? Thirty-four – young enough to go a long way yet – for your country and yourself.' And the old buffoon tried to look sternly inspiring, with his teeth gurgling.

It was appalling. God knows I've had my crosses to bear, but this beat all. As so often in the past, I was the victim of my own glorious and entirely unearned reputation – Flashy, the hero of Jallalabad, the last man out of the Kabul retreat and the first man into the Balaclava battery, the beau sabreur of the Light Cavalry, Queen's Medal, Thanks of Parliament, darling of the mob, with a liver as yellow as yesterday's custard, if they'd only known it. And there was nothing, with Pam's eye on me, and Ellenborough and Wood looking solemnly on, that I could do about it. Oh, if I'd followed my best instincts, I could have fled wailing from the room, or fallen blubbering at some convenient foot – but of course I didn't. With sick fear mounting in my throat, I knew that I'd have to go, and that was that – back to India, with its heat and filth and flies and dangers and poxy niggers, to undertake the damnedest mission since Bismarck put me on the throne of Strackenz.

But this was infinitely worse – Bismarck's crew had been as choice a collection of villains as ever jumped bail or slit a throat, but they were civilised by comparison with Ignatieff. The thought of *dealing* with that devil, as Pam so nicely put it, was enough to send me into a decline. And if that wasn't enough, I was to sneak about some savage Indian kingdom (Thug country, for a bonus), spying on some withered old bitch of an Indian princess and trying to wheedle her to British interest against her will – and she probably the kind of hag whose idea of fun would be to chain malefactors to a rogue elephant's foot. (Most Indian rulers are mad, you know, and capable of anything.) But there wasn't the slightest chance to wriggle; all I could do was put on my muscular Christian expression, look Palmerston fearlessly in the eye, like Dick Champion when the headmaster gives him the job of teaching the fags not to swear, and say I'd do my best.

'Well enough,' says he. 'I know you will. Who knows – perhaps the signs are false, what? Tokens of mutiny, in a place where Russia's been stirrin' the pot, an' the local ruler's chafin' under our authority – it's happened before, an' it may amount to nothin' in the end. But if the signs are true, make no mistake –' and he gave me his steady stare '– it's the gravest peril our country has faced since Bonaparte. It's no light commission we're placin' in your hands, sir – but they're the safest hands in England, I believe.'

So help me God, it's absolutely what he said; it makes you

wonder how these fellows ever get elected. I believe I made some manly sounds, and as usual my sick terror must have been manifesting itself by making me red in the face, which in a fellow of my size is often mistaken for noble resolution. It must have satisfied Pam, anyway, for suddenly he was smiling at me, and sitting back in his chair.

'Now you know why you're sittin' here talkin' to the Prime Minister, what? Been sittin' on eggshells, haven't you? Ne'er mind – I'm glad to have had the opportunity of instructin' you myself – of course, you'll be more fully informed, before you sail, of all the intelligence you'll need – his lordship here, an' Mangles at the Board in London, will be talkin' to you. When d'you take leave of Her Majesty? Another week? Come, that's too long. When does the India sloop sail, Barrington? Monday – you'd best be off to Town on Friday, then. Leave pretty little Mrs Flashman to take care of royalty, what? Stunnin' gal, that – never see her from my window on Piccadilly but it sets me in humour – must make her acquaintance when you come home. Bring her along to Number 96 some evenin' – dinner, an' so forth, what?'

He sat there, beaming like Pickwick. It turned my stomach at the time, and small wonder, considering the stew he was launching me into – and yet, when I think back on Pam nowadays, that's how I see him, painted whiskers, sloppy false teeth and all, grinning like a happy urchin. You never saw such young peepers in a tired old face. I can say it now, from the safety of my declining years: in spite of the hellish pickle he landed me in, I'd swap any politician I ever met for old Pam – damn him.[4]

However, now that he'd put the doom on me, he couldn't get rid of me fast enough; before I'd been properly shooed out of the room he was snapping at Barrington to find some

34

American telegraph or other, and chivvying at Wood that they must soon be off to catch their special train at Aberdeen. It must have been about three in the morning, but he was still full of bounce, and the last I saw of him he was dictating a letter even as they helped him into his coat and muffler, with people bustling around him, and he was breaking off to peer again at the chapattis on the table and ask Ellenborough did the Hindoos eat 'em with meat, or any kind of relish.

'Blasted buns,' says he. 'Might do with jam, d'you think, what? No . . . better not . . . crumble an' get under my confounded teeth, probably . . .' He glanced up and caught sight of me bowing my farewell from the doorway. 'Good night to you, Flashman,' he sings out, 'an' good huntin'. You look out sharp for yourself, mind.'

So that was how I got my marching orders – in a snap of the fingers almost. Two hours earlier I'd been rogering happily away, with not a care in the world, and now I was bound for India on the most dangerous lunatic mission I'd ever heard of – by God, I cursed the day I'd written that report to Dalhousie, glorifying myself into the soup. And fine soup it promised to be – rumours of mutiny, mad old Indian princesses, Thugs, and Ignatieff and his jackals lurking in the undergrowth.

You can imagine I didn't get much rest in what was left of the night. Elspeth was fast asleep, looking glorious with the candlelight on her blonde hair tumbled over the pillow, and her rosebud lips half open, snoring like the town band. I was too fretful to rouse her in her favourite way, so I just shook her awake, and I must say she bore the news of our impending parting with remarkable composure. At least, she wept inconsolably for five minutes at the thought of being bereft while her Hector (that's me) was Braving the Dangers of India, fondled my whiskers and said she and little Havvy would be quite *desolate*, whimpered sadly while she teased me, in an absent-minded way, into mounting her, and then remembered she had left her best silk gloves behind at the evening's party and that she had a spot on her left shoulder which no amount of cream would send away. It's nice to know you're going to be missed.

I had three days still left at Balmoral, and the first of them was spent closeted with Ellenborough and a sharp little creature from the Board of Control, who lectured me in maddening detail about my mission to Jhansi, and conditions in India – I won't weary you with it here, for you'll learn about Jhansi and its attendant horrors and delights in due course. Sufficient to say it did nothing but deepen my misgivings – and then, on the Wednesday morning, something happened which drove everything else clean out of my mind It was such a shock, such an unbelievable coincidence in view of what had gone before (or so it seemed at the time) that I can still think back to it with disbelief – aye, and start sweating at the thought.

I'd had a thoroughly drunken night at Abergeldie, to take my mind off the future, and when I woke cloth-headed and surly on the Wednesday morning, Elspeth suggested that instead of breakfast I'd be better going for a canter. I damned her advice and sent for a horse, left her weeping sulkily into her boiled egg, and ten minutes later was galloping the fumes away along the Balmoral road. I reached the castle, and trotted up as far as the carriage entrance; beyond it, on the far side of the gravel sweep, one of the big castle coaches that brought quality visitors from Aberdeen station was drawn up, and flunkeys were handing down the arrivals and bowing them towards the steps leading to the side door.

Some more poor fools of consequence about to savour the royal hospitality, thinks I, and was just about to turn my horse away when I happened to glance again at the group of gentlemen in travelling capes who were mounting the steps. One of them turned to say something to the flunkeys – and I nearly fell from the saddle, and only saved myself by clutching the mane with both hands. I believe I nearly fainted – for it was something infinitely worse than a ghost; it was real, even if it was utterly impossible. The man on the steps, spruce in the rig of an English country gentleman, and now turning away into the castle, was the man I'd last seen beside the line of carrion gallows at Fort Raim – the man Palmerston was sending me to India to defeat and kill: Count Nicholas Pavlovitch Ignatieff.

'You're sure?' croaked Ellenborough. 'No, no, Flashman – it can't be! Count Ignatieff – whom we were discussing two nights since – here? Impossible!'

'My lord,' says I, 'I've good cause to know him better than most, and I tell you he's in the castle now, gotch-eye and all. Cool as damn-your-eyes, in a tweed cape and deer-stalker hat, so help me! He was there, at the door, not ten minutes ago!'

He plumped down on a chair, mopping at the shaving-soap on his cheeks – I'd practically had to manhandle his valet to be admitted, and I'd left a trail of startled minions on the back-stairs in my haste to get to his room. I was still panting from exertion, to say nothing of shock.

'I want an explanation of this, my lord,' says I, 'for I'll not believe it's chance.'

'What d'ye mean?' says he, goggling.

'Two nights ago we talked of precious little else but this Russian monster – how he'd been spying the length and breadth of India, in the very place to which I'm being sent.

38

And now he turns up – the very man? Is that coincidence?' I was in such a taking I didn't stand on ceremony. 'How comes he in the country, even? Will you tell me Lord Palmerston didn't know?'

'My God, Flashman!' His big mottled face looked shocked. 'What d'you mean by that?'

'I mean, my lord,' says I, trying to hold myself in, 'that there's precious little that happens anywhere, let alone in England, that Lord Palmerston doesn't know about – is it possible that he's unaware that the most dangerous agent in Russia – and one of their leading nobles, to boot – is promenading about as large as life? And never a word the other night, when—'

'Wait! Wait!' cries he, wattling. 'That's a monstrous suggestion! Contain yourself, sir! Are you positive it's Ignatieff?'

I was ready to burst, but I didn't. 'I'm positive.'

'Stay here,' says he, and bustled out, and for ten minutes I chewed my nails until he came back, shutting the door behind him carefully. He had got his normal beetroot colour back, but he looked damned rattled.

'It's true,' says he. 'Count Ignatieff is here with Lord Aberdeen's party – as a guest of the Queen. It seems – you know we have Granville in Petersburg just now, for the new Tsar's coronation? Well, a party of Russian noblemen – the first since the war – have just arrived in Leith yesterday, bringing messages of good will, or God knows what, from the new monarch to the Queen. Someone had written to Aberdeen – I don't know it all yet – and he brought them with him on his way north – with this fellow among 'em. It's extraordinary! The damnedest chance!'

'Chance, my lord?' says I. 'I'll need some convincing of that!'

'Good God, what else? I'll allow it's long odds, but I'm certain if Lord Palmerston had had the least inkling . . .' He trailed off, and you could see the sudden doubt of his own precious Prime Minister written on his jowly face. 'Oh, but the notion's preposterous . . . what purpose could it serve not to tell us? No – he would certainly have told me – and you, I'm sure.'

Well, I wasn't sure – from what I'd heard of Pam's sense of humour I'd have put nothing past him. And yet it would have been folly, surely, with me on the point of setting off for India, ostensibly to undo Ignatieff's work, to have let him come face to face with me. And then, the wildest thought – was it possible Ignatieff *knew* about my mission?

'Never!' trumpets Ellenborough. 'No, that couldn't be! The decision to send you out was taken a bare two weeks since – it would be to credit the Russian intelligence system with super-human powers – and if he did, what could he accomplish here? – dammit, in the Queen's own home! This isn't Middle Asia – it's a civilised country—'

'My lord, that's not a civilised man,' says I. 'But what's to be done? I can't meet him!'

'Let me think,' says he, and strode about, heaving his stomach around. Then he stopped, heavy with decision.

'I think you must,' says he. 'If he has seen you – or finds out that you were here and left before your time . . . wait, though, it might be put down to tact on your part . . . still, no!' He snapped his fingers at me. 'No, you must stay. Better to behave as though there was nothing untoward – leave no room to excite suspicion – after all, former enemies meet in time of peace, don't they? And we'll watch him – by George, we will! Perhaps we'll learn something ourselves! Hah-ha!'

And this was the port-sodden clown who had once

governed India. I'd never heard such an idiot suggestion – but could I shift him? I pleaded, in the name of common sense, that I should leave at once, but he wouldn't have it – I do believe that at the back of his mind was the suspicion that Pam *had* known Ignatieff was coming, and Ellenborough was scared to tinker with the Chief's machinations, whatever they were.

'You'll stay,' he commanded, 'and that's flat. What the devil – it's just a freak of fate – and if it's not, there's nothing this Russian rascal can do. I tell you what, though – I'm not going to miss his first sight of you, what? The man he threatened with torture and worse – disgusting brute! Aye, and the man who bested him in the end. Ha-ha!' And he clapped me on the shoulder. 'Aye – hope nothing happens to embarrass the Queen, though. You'll mind out for that, Flashman, won't you – it wouldn't do – any unpleasantness, hey?'

I minded out, all right. Strangely enough, by the time I came back to the castle with Elspeth that afternoon, my qualms about coming face to face again with that Russian wolf had somewhat subsided; I'd reminded myself that we weren't meeting on his ground any more, but on mine, and that the kind of power he'd once had over me was a thing quite past. Still, I won't pretend I was feeling at ease, and I'd drummed it into Elspeth's head that not a hint must be let slip about my ensuing departure for India, or Pam's visit. She took it in wide-eyed and assured me she would not *dream* of saying a word, but I realised with exasperation that you couldn't trust any warning to take root in that beautiful empty head: as we approached the drawing-room doors she was prattling away about what wedding present she should suggest to the Queen for Mary Seymour, and I, preoccupied, said offhand, why not a lusty young coachman, and immediately regretted it – you couldn't be sure she wouldn't pass it on – and then the doors opened, we were announced, and the heads in the room were all turning towards us.

There was the Queen, in the middle of the sofa, with a lady and gentleman behind; Albert, propping up the mantel-piece, and lecturing to old Aberdeen, who appeared to be asleep on his feet, half a dozen assorted courtiers – and Ellenborough staring across the room. As we made our bows, and the Queen says: 'Ah Mrs Flashman, you are come *just* in time to help with the service of tea,' I was following Ellenborough's glance, and there was Ignatieff, with another Russian-looking grandee and a couple of our own gentry. He was staring at me, and by God, he never so much as blinked or twitched a muscle; I made my little bow towards Albert, and as I turned to face Ignatieff again I felt, God knows why, a sudden rush of to-hell-with-it take hold of me.

'My – dear – Count!' says I, astonished, and everyone stopped talking; the Queen looked pop-eyed, and even Albert left off prosing to the noble corpse beside him.

'Surely it's Count Ignatieff?' cries I, and then broke off in apology. 'Your pardon, ma'am,' says I to Vicky. 'I was quite startled – I had no notion Count Ignatieff was here! Forgive me,' but of course by this time she was all curiosity, and I had to explain that Count Ignatieff was an old comrade-in-arms, so to speak, what? And beam in his direction, while she smiled uncertainly, but not displeased, and Ellenborough played up well, and told Albert that he'd heard me speak of being Ignatieff's prisoner during the late war, but had had no idea this was the same gentleman, and Albert looked disconcerted, and said that was most remarkable.

'Indeed, highness, I had that honour,' says Ignatieff, clicking his heels, and the sound of that chilly voice made my spine tingle. But there was nothing he could do but take the hand I stretched out to him.

'This is splendid, old fellow!' says I, gripping him as though he were my long-lost brother. 'Wherever have you been keeping yourself?' One or two of them smiled, to see bluff Flash Harry so delighted at meeting an old enemy – just what they'd have expected, of course. And when the Queen had been made quite au fait with the situation, she said it was *exactly* like Fitzjames and Roderick Dhu.

So after that it was quite jolly, and Albert made a group with Ignatieff and Ellenborough and me, and questioned me about our acquaintance, and I made light of my captivity and escape, and said what a charming jailer Ignatieff had been, and the brute just stood impassive, with his tawny head bowed over his cup, and looking me over with that amazing half-blue, half-brown eye. He was still the same handsome, broken-nosed young iceberg I remembered – if I'd closed my eyes I could have heard the lash whistling and cracking in Arabat courtyard, with the Cossacks' grip on my arms.

Albert, of course, was much struck by the coincidence of our meeting again, and preached a short sermon about the brotherhood of men-at-arms, to which Ignatieff smiled politely and I cried 'Hear, hear!' It was difficult to guess, but I judged my Muscovite monster wasn't enjoying this too much; he must have been wondering why I pretended to be so glad to see him. But I was all affability; I even presented him to Elspeth, and he bowed and kissed her hand; she was very demure and cool, so I knew she fancied him, the little trollop.

The truth is, my natural insolence was just asserting itself, as it always does when I feel it's safe; when a moment came when Ignatieff and I were left alone together, I thought I'd stick a pin in him, just for sport, so I asked, quietly:

'Brought your knout with you, Count?'

He looked at me a moment before replying. 'It is in Russia,' says he. 'Waiting. So, I have no doubt, is Count Pencherjevsky's daughter.'

'Oh, yes,' says I. 'Little Valla. Is she well, d'you know?'

'I have no idea. But if she is, it is no fault of yours.' He glanced away, towards Elspeth and the others. 'Is it?'

'She never complained to me,' says I, grinning at him. 'On that tack – if *I'm* well, it's no fault of yours, either.'

'That is true,' says he, and the eye was like a sword-point. 'However, may I suggest that the less we say about our previous acquaintance, the better? I gather from your . . . charade, a little while ago – designed, no doubt, to impress your Queen – that you are understandably reluctant that the truth of your behaviour there should be made public.'

'Oh, come now,' says I. ''Twasn't a patch on yours, old boy. What would the Court of Balmoral think if they knew that the charming Russian nobleman with the funny eye was a murderous animal who flogs innocent men to death and tortures prisoners of war? Thought about that?'

'If you think you were tortured, Colonel Flashman,' says he, poker-faced, 'then I congratulate you on your ignorance.' He put down his cup. 'I find this conversation tedious. If you will excuse me,' and he turned away.

'Oh, sorry if you're bored,' says I. 'I was forgetting – you probably haven't cut a throat or burned a peasant in a week.'

It was downright stupid of me, no doubt – two hours earlier I'd been quaking at the thought of meeting him again, and here I was sassing him to my heart's content. But I can never resist a jibe and a gloat when the enemy's hands are tied, as Thomas Hughes would tell you. Ignatieff didn't seem nearly as fearsome here, among the teacups, with chaps toadying the royals, and cress sandwiches being handed round, and Ellenborough flirting ponderously with Elspeth while the Queen complained to old Aberdeen that it was the *press* which had killed Lord Hardinge, in her Uncle Leopold's *opinion*. No, not fearsome at all – without his chains and gallows and dungeons and power of life and death, and never so much as a Cossack thug to bless himself with. I should have remembered that men like Nicholas Ignatieff are dangerous anywhere – usually when you least expect it.

And I was far from expecting anything the next day, the last full one I was to spend at Balmoral. It was a miserable, freezing morning, I remember, with flurries of sleet among the rain, and low clouds rolling down off Lochnagar; the kind of day when you put your nose out once and then settle down to punch and billiards with the boys, and build the fire up high. But not Prince Albert; there were roe deer reported in great numbers at Balloch Buie, and nothing would do but we must be drummed out, cursing, for a stalk.

I'd have slid back to Abergeldie if I could, but he nailed me in the hall with Ellenborough. 'Why, Colonel Flash-mann, where are your gaiters? Haff you nott called for your loader yet? Come, gentlemen, in this weather we haff only a few hours – let us be off!'

And he strutted about in his ridiculous Alpine hat and tartan cloak, while the loaders were called and the brakes made ready, and the ghillies loafed about grinning on the terrace with the guns and pouches – they knew I loathed it, and that Ellenborough couldn't carry his guts more than ten yards without a rest, and the brutes enjoyed our discomfiture. There were four or five other guns in the party, and presently we drove off into the rain, huddling under the tarpaulin covers as we jolted away from the castle on the unmade road.

The country round Balmoral is primitive at the best of times; on a dank autumn day it's like an illustration from Bunyan's *Holy War*, especially near our destination, which was an eerie, dreary forest of firs among the mountains, with great patches of bog, and gullies full of broken rocks, and heather waist-deep on the valley sides. The road petered out there, and we clambered out of the brakes and stood in the pouring wet while Albert, full of energy and blood-lust, planned the campaign. We were to spread out singly, with our loaders, and drive ahead up to the high ground, because the mist was hanging fairly thick by this time, and if we kept together we might miss the stags altogether.

We were just about to start on our squelching climb, when another brake came rolling up the road, and who should pile out but the Russian visitors, with one of the local bigwigs, all dressed for the hill. Albert of course was delighted.

'Come, gentlemen,' cries he, 'this is capital! What? There are no bearss in our Scottish mountains, but we can show you fine sport among the deer. General Menshikof, will you accompany me? Count Ignatieff – ah, where iss Flash-mann?' I was having a quick swig from Ellenborough's flask, and as the Prince turned towards me, and I saw Ignatieff at his elbow, very trim in tweeds and top boots, with a fur cap on his head and a heavy piece under his arm, I suddenly felt as though I'd been kicked in the stomach. In that second I had a vision of those lonely, gully-crossed crags above us, with their great reaches of forest in which you could get lost for days, and mist blotting out sight and sound of all companions – and myself, alone, with Ignatieff down-wind of me, armed, and with that split eye of his raking the trees and heather for a sight of me. It hadn't even occurred to me that he might be in the shooting party,

46

but here he came, strolling across, and behind him a great burly unmistakable *moujik*, in smock and boots, carrying his pouches.

Ellenborough stiffened and shot a glance at me. For myself, I was wondering frantically if I could plead indisposition at the last minute. I opened my mouth to say something, and then Albert was summoning Ellenborough to take the left flank, and Ignatieff was standing watching me coolly, with the rain beating down between us.

'I have my own loader,' says he, indicating the *moujik*. 'He is used to heavy game – bears, as his royal highness says, and wolves. However, he has experience of lesser animals, and vermin, even.'

'I . . . I . . .' It had all happened so quickly that I couldn't think of what to say, or do. Albert was despatching the others to their various starting-points; the first of them were already moving off into the mist. As I stood, dithering, Ignatieff stepped closer, glanced at my own ghillie, who was a few yards away, and said quietly in French:

'I did not know you were going to India, Colonel. My congratulations on your . . . appointment? A regimental command, perhaps?'

'Eh? What d'you mean?' I started in astonishment.

'Surely nothing less,' says he, 'for such a distinguished campaigner as yourself.'

'I don't know what you're talking about,' I croaked.

'Have I been misinformed? Or have I misunderstood your charming wife? When I had the happiness to pay my respects to her this morning, I understood her to say – but there, I may have been mistaken. When one encounters a lady of such exceptional beauty, I fear one tends to look rather than to listen.' He smiled – something I'd never seen him do

47

before: it reminded me of a frozen river breaking up. 'But I think his royal highness is calling you, Colonel.'

'Flash-mann!' I tore myself away from the hypnotic stare of that split eye; there was Albert waving at me impatiently. 'Will you take the lead on the right flank? Come, sir, we are losing time – it will be dark before we can come up to the beasts!'

If I'd had any sense I'd have bolted, or gone into a swoon, or claimed a sprained ankle – but I didn't have time to think. The royal nincompoop was gesticulating at me to be off, my loader was already ploughing into the trees just ahead, one or two of the others had turned to look, and Ignatieff was smiling coldly at my evident confusion. I hesitated, and then started after the loader; as I entered the trees, I took one quick glance back; Ignatieff was standing beside the brake, lighting a cigarette, waiting for Albert to set him on his way. I gulped, and plunged into the trees.

The ghillie was waiting for me under the branches; he was one of your grinning, freckled, red-haired Highlanders, called MacLehose, or something equally unpronounceable. I'd had him before, and he was a damned good shikari – they all are, of course. Well, I was going to stick to him like glue this trip, I told myself, and the farther we got away from our Russian sportsmen in quick time, the better. As I strode through the fir wood, ducking to avoid the whippy branches, I heard Albert's voice faintly behind us, and pressed on even harder.

At the far side of the wood I paused, staring up at the hillside ahead of us. What the devil was I getting in such a stew for? – my heart racing like a trip-hammer, and the sweat running down me, in spite of the chill. This wasn't Russia; it was a civilised shooting-party in Scotland. Ignatieff wouldn't dare to try any devilment here – it had just been the surprise of his sudden appearance at the last minute that had unmanned me . . . wouldn't he, though? By God, he'd try anything, that one – and he knew about my going to India, thanks to that blathering idiot I'd married in an evil hour. Shooters had been hit before, up on the crags, in bad light . . . it could be made to look like an accident . . . mistaken for a stag . . . heavy mist . . . tragic error . . . never forgive himself . . .

'Come on!' I yammered, and stumbled over the rocks for a gully that opened to our left – there was another one straight ahead, but I wasn't having that. The ghillie protested that if we went left we might run into the nearest shooters; that was all right with me, and I ignored him and clambered over the rubble at the gully foot, plunging up to the knee in a boggy patch and almost dropping my gun. I stole a glance back, but there was no sign of anyone emerging from the wood; I sprang into the gully and scrambled upwards.

It was a gruelling climb, through the huge heather-bushes that flanked the stream, and then it was bracken, six feet high, with a beaten rabbit-path that I went up at a run. At the top the gully opened out into another great mass of firs, and not until we were well underneath them did I pause, heaving like a bellows, and the ghillie padded up beside me, not even breathing hard, and grinning surprise on his face.

'Crackey good gracious,' says he, 'you're eager to be at the peasties the day. What's the great running, whatever?'

'Is this piece loaded?' says I, and held it out.

'What for would it be?' says the clown. 'We'll no' be near a deer for half an hour yet. There's no occasion.'

'Load the dam' thing,' says I.

'And have you plowing your pluidy head off, the haste you're in? She'll look well then, right enuff.'

'Damn you, do as you're told!' says I, so he shrugged and spat and looked his disgust as he put in the charge.

'Mind, there's two great pullets in there now,' says he as he handed it back. 'If you've as much sense as a whaup's neb you'll keep the caps in your pooch until we sight the deer.' They've no respect, those people.

I snatched it from him and made off through the wood, and for ten minutes we pushed on, always upwards, through another long gully, and along a rocky ledge over a deep stream, where the mist hung in swirls among the rowan trees, and the foam drifted slowly by on the brown pools. It was as dark as dusk, although it was still early afternoon; there was no sound of another living soul, and nothing moving on the low cliffs above us.

By this time I was asking myself again if I hadn't been over-anxious – and at the same time wondering if it wouldn't be safest to lie up here till dark, and buy the ghillie's silence with a sovereign, or keep moving to our left to reach the other guns. And then he gave a sudden exclamation and stopped, frowning, and putting a hand on his belly. He gave a little barking cough, and his ruddy face was pale as he turned to me.

'Oh!' says he. 'What's this? All of a sudden, my pudden's is pad.'

'What is it?' says I, impatiently, and he sat down on a rock, holding himself and making strained noises.

'I – I don't know. It's my belly – there's some mischief in herself – owf!'

'Are you ill?'

'Oh, goad – I don't know.' His face was green. 'What do these foreign puggers tak' to drink? It's – it must be the spirits yon great hairy fella gave me before we cam' up – oh, mither, isn't it hellish? Oh, stop you, till I vomit!'

But he couldn't, try as he would, but leaned against the rock, in obvious pain, rubbing at himself and groaning. And I watched him, in horror, for there was no doubt what had happened – Ignatieff's man had drugged or poisoned him, so that I'd be alone on the hill. The sheer ruthlessness of it, the hellish calculation, had me trembling to my boots – they would come on me alone, and – but wait, whatever he'd been given, it couldn't be fatal: two corpses on one shoot would be too much to explain away, and one of them poisoned, at that. No, it must just be a drug, to render him helpless, and of course I would turn back down the hill to get help, and they'd be there . . .

'Stay where you are – I'll get help,' says I, and lit out along the ledge, but not in the direction we'd come; it was up and over the hills for Flashy, and my groaning ghillie could be taken care of when time served. I scudded round the corner of rock at the ledge's end, and through a forest of bracken, out into a clear space, and then into another fir wood, where I paused to get my bearings. If I bore off left – but which way *was* left? We'd taken so many turnings, among the confounded bogs and gullies, I couldn't be sure, and there was no sun to help. Suppose I went the wrong way, and ran into them? God knows, in this maze of hills and heather it would be easy enough. Should I go back to the stricken ghillie, and wait with him? I'd be safer, in his company – but they might be up with him by now, lurking on the gully-side, waiting. I stood clutching my gun, sweating.

It was silent as death under the fir-trees, close as a tomb, and dim. I could see out one side, where there was bracken – that would be the place to lie up, so I stole forward on tiptoe, making no noise on the carpet of mould and needles. Near the wood's edge I waited, listening: no sound, except my own breathing. I turned to enter the bracken – and stood frozen, biting back a yelp of fear. Behind me, on the far side of the wood, a twig had snapped.

For an instant I was paralysed, and then I was across the open space of turf and burrowing into the bracken for dear life. I went a few yards, and then writhed round to look back; through the stems and fronds I could see the trees I'd just left, gloomy and silent. But I was deep in cover; if I lay still, not to shake the bracken above me, no one could hope to spot me unless he trod on me. I burrowed down in the sodden grass, panting, and waited, with my ears straining.

For five minutes nothing happened; there was only the dripping of the fronds, and my own heart thumping. What made the suspense so hellish was the sheer unfairness of my predicament – I'd been in more tight corners before than I care to count, but always in some godless, savage part of the world like Afghanistan or Madagascar or Russia or St Louis – it was damnable that I should be lurking in fear of my life in England – or Scotland, even. I hadn't been in this kind of terror on British soil since I'd been a miserable fag at Rugby, carrying Bully Dawson's game bag for him, and we'd had to hide from keepers at Brownsover. They'd caught me, too, and I'd only got off by peaching on Dawson and his pals, and showing the keepers where . . . and suddenly, where there had been nothing a moment ago, a shadow moved in the gloom beneath the trees, stopped, and took on form in the half-light. Ignatieff was standing just inside the edge of the fir wood.

I stopped breathing, while he turned his head this way and that, searching the thickets; he had his gun cocked, and by God he wasn't looking for stags. Then he snapped his fingers, and the *moujik* came padding out of the dimness of the wood;

he was heeled and ready as well, his eyes glaring above his furze of beard. Ignatieff nodded to the left, and the great brute went prowling off that way, his piece presented in front of him; Ignatieff waited a few seconds and then took the way to the right. They both disappeared, noiselessly, and I was left fumbling feverishly for my caps. I slipped them under the hammers with trembling fingers, wondering whether to stay where I was or try to wriggle farther back into the undergrowth. They would be on either side of me shortly, and if they turned into the bracken they might easily . . . and with the thought came a steady rustling to my left, deep in the green; it stopped, and then started again, and it sounded closer. No doubt of it, someone was moving stealthily and steadily towards my hiding place.

It takes a good deal to stir me out of petrified fear, but that did it. I rolled on my side, trying to sweep my gun round to cover the sound; it caught in the bracken, and I hauled frantically at it to get it clear. God, what a din I must be making – and then the damned lock must have caught on a stem, for one barrel went off like a thunderclap, and I was on my feet with a yell, tearing downhill through the bracken. I fairly flung myself through the high fronds, there was the crack of a shot behind me, and a ball buzzed overhead like a hornet. I went bounding through, came out in a clearing with firs on either side, sprang over a bank of ferns – and plunged straight down into a peat cutting. I landed belly first in the stinking ooze, but I was up and struggling over the far side in an instant, for I could hear crashing in the bracken above me, and knew that if I lost an instant he'd get a second shot. I was plastered with muck like a tar-and-feather merchant, but I still had my gun, and then I must have trod on a loose stone, for I pitched headlong, and went rolling and bumping down the slope, hit a rock, and finished up winded and battered in a burn, trying frantically to scramble up, and slithering on the slimy gravel underfoot.

There was a thumping of boots on the bank, I started round, and there was the *moujik*, not ten yards away. I didn't even have time to look for my gun; I was sprawling half out of the burn, and the bastard had his piece at his shoulder, the muzzle looking me straight in the face. I yelled and grabbed for a stone, there was the crash of a gunshot – and the *moujik* dropped his piece, shrieking, and clutched at his arm as he toppled backwards among the rocks.

'Careful, colonel,' says a voice behind me. 'He's only winged.' And there, standing not five yards off, with a smoking revolver in his hand, was a tall fellow in tweeds; he just gave me a nod, and then jumped lightly over the rocks and stood over the *moujik*, who was groaning and clutching his bleeding arm.

'Murderous swine, ain't you?' says the newcomer conversationally, and kicked him in the face. 'It's the only punishment he'll get, I'm afraid,' he added, over his shoulder. 'No diplomatic scandals, you see.' And as he turned towards me, I saw to my amazement who it was – Hutton, the tall chap with the long jaw who'd taken me to Palmerston only a few nights before. He put his pistol back in his arm-pit and came over to me.

'No bones broken? Bless me, but you're a sight.' He pulled me to my feet. 'I'll say this, colonel – you're the fastest man over rough country I ever hope to follow. I lost you in five minutes, but I kept track of our friends, all right. Nice pair, ain't they, though? I wish to God it had been the other one I pulled trigger on – oh, we won't see him again, never fret. Not until everyone's down the hill, and he'll turn up cool as you like, never having been near you all day, what?'

'But – but . . . you mean, you expected this?'

'No-o – not exactly, anyway. But I've been pretty much on hand since the Russian brotherhood arrived, you know. We don't believe in taking chances, eh? Not with customers like Master Ignatieff – enterprising chap, that. So when I heard he'd decided to join the shoot today, I thought I'd look along – just as well I did, I think,' says this astonishing fellow. 'Now, if you've got your wind back, I suggest we make our way down. Never mind our little wounded bird yonder – if he don't bleed to death he'll find his way back to his master. Pity he shot himself by accident, ain't it? That'll be their story, I daresay – and we won't contradict it – here, what are you about, sir?'

I was lunging for my fallen gun, full of murderous rage now that the danger was past. 'I'm going to blow that bloody peasant's head off!' I roared, fumbling with the lock. 'I'll teach—'

'Hold on!' cries he, catching my arm, and he was positively grinning. 'Capital idea, I agree – but we mustn't, you see. One bullet in him can be explained away by his own clumsiness – but not two, eh? We mustn't have any scandal, colonel – not involving Her Majesty's guests. Come along now – let's be moving down, so that Count Ignatieff, who I've no doubt is watching us this minute, can come to his stricken servant's assistance. After you, sir.'

He was right, of course; the irony of it was that although Ignatieff and his brute had tried to murder me, we daren't say so, for diplomacy's sake. God knows what international complications there might have been. This didn't sink in with me at once – but his reminder that Ignatieff was still prowling

55

about was enough to lend me wings down the hill. Not that even he'd have tried another shot, with Hutton about, but I wasn't taking chances.

I'll say this for the secret service – which is what Hutton was, of course – they're damned efficient. He had a gig waiting on the road, one of his assistants was despatched to the help of my ghillie, and within a half-hour I was back in Balmoral through the servants' entrance, being cleaned up and instructed by Hutton to put it about that I'd abandoned the shoot with a strained muscle.

'I'll inform my chiefs in London that Colonel Flashman had a fortunate escape from an unexpected danger, arising from a chance encounter with an old Russian friend,' says he, 'and that he is now fit and well to proceed on the important task ahead of him. And that, in the meantime, I'm keeping an eye on him. No, sir, I'm sorry – I can't answer any of your questions, and I wouldn't if I could.'

Which left me in a fine state of consternation and bewilderment, wondering what to make of it all. My immediate thought was that Palmerston had somehow arranged the whole thing, in the hope that I'd kill Ignatieff, but even in my excited condition that didn't make sense. A likelier explanation was that Ignatieff, coming innocently to Balmoral and finding me on the premises, had decided to take advantage of the chance to murder me, in revenge for the way I'd sold him the previous year. That, knowing the man and his ice-cold recklessness, was perfectly sound reasoning – but there was also the horrid possibility that he had found out about the job Palmerston had given me (God alone knew how – but he'd at least discovered from the idiot Elspeth that I was going to India) and had been out to dispose of me in the way of business.

'A preposterous notion,' was Ellenborough's answer when I voiced my fears to him that night. 'He could *not* know – why, the Board decision was highly secret, and imparted only to the Prime Minister's most intimate circle. No, this is merely another example of the naked savagery of the Russian bear!' He was full of port, and wattling furiously. 'And virtually in Her Majesty's presence, too! Damnable! But, of course, we can say nothing, Flashman. It only remains,' says he, booming sternly, 'for you to mete out conclusive justice to this villain, if you chance to encounter him in India. In the meantime, I'll see that the Lord Chamberlain excludes him from any diplomatic invitations which may be extended to St Petersburg in future. By gad, I will!'

I ventured the cautious suggestion that it might be better, after what had happened, to send someone else to Jhansi – just in case Ignatieff had tumbled to me – but Ellenborough wasn't even listening. He was just full of indignation at Ignatieff's murderous impudence – not on my account, you'll note, but because it might have led to a scandal involving the Queen. (Admittedly, you can't have it getting about that her guests have been trying to slaughter each other; the poor woman probably had enough trouble getting people to visit, with Albert about the place.)

So, of course, we kept mum, and as Hutton had foreseen, it was put about and accepted that Ignatieff's loader had had an accident with a gun, and everyone wagged their heads in sympathy, and the Queen sent the poor unfortunate fellow some shortbread and a tot of whisky. Ignatieff even had the crust to thank her after dinner, and I could feel Ellenborough at my elbow fairly bubbling with suppressed outrage. And to cap it all, the brute had the effrontery to challenge me to a game of billiards – and beat me hollow, too, in the presence of Albert and half a dozen others: I had to be certain there was a good crowd on hand, for God knows what he'd have tried if we'd gone to the pool-room alone. I'll say it for Nicholas Ignatieff – he was a bear-cat for nerve. He'd have been ready to brain me and claim afterwards that it was a mis-cue.

So now – having heard the prelude to my Indian Mutiny adventure, you will understand why I don't care much for Balmoral. And if what happened there that September was trivial by comparison with what followed – well, I couldn't foresee that. Indeed, as I soothed my bruised nerves with brandy fomentations that night, I reflected that there were worse places than India; there was Aberdeenshire, with Ignatieff loose in the bracken, hoping to hang my head on his gunroom wall. I hadn't been able to avoid him here, but if we met again on the coral strand, it wasn't going to be my fault.

I've never been stag-shooting from that day to this, either. Ellenborough was right: the company's too damned mixed.

I remember young Fred Roberts (who's a Field-Marshal now, which shows you what pull these Addiscombe wallahs have got) once saying that everyone hated India for a month and then loved it forever. I wouldn't altogether agree, but I'll allow that it had its attractions in the old days; you lived like a lord without having to work, waited on hand and foot, made money if you set your mind to it, and hardly exerted yourself at all except to hunt the beasts, thrash the men, and bull the women. You had to look sharp to avoid active service, of course, of which there was a lot about; I never fell very lucky that way. But even so, it wasn't a half-bad station, most of the time.

Personally, I put that down to the fact that in my young days India was a middle-class place for the British, where society people didn't serve if they could help it. (Cardigan, for example, took one look and fled.) It's different now, of course; since it became a safe place many of our best and most highly connected people have let the light of their countenances shine on India, with the results you might expect – prices have gone up, service has gone down, and the women have got clap. So they tell me.

Mind you, I could see things were changing even in '56, when I landed at Bombay. My first voyage to India, sixteen years before, had lasted four months on a creaking East Indiaman; this time, in natty little government steam sloops, it had taken just about half that time, even with a vile journey by camel across the Suez isthmus in between. And even from Bombay you could get the smell of civilisation; they'd started the telegraph, and were pushing ahead with the first railways, there were more white faces and businesses to be seen, and people weren't talking, as they'd used to, of India as though it were a wild jungle with John Company strongholds here and there. In my early days, a journey from Calcutta to Peshawar had seemed half round the world, but no longer. It was as though the Company was at last seeing India as one vast country – and realising that now the wars with the Sikhs and Maharattas and Afghans were things of the past, it was an empire that had to be ruled and run, quite apart from fighting and showing a nice profit in Leadenhall Street.

It was far busier than I remembered it, and somehow the civilians seemed more to the fore nowadays than the military. Once the gossip on the verandahs had all been about war in the north, or the Thugs, or the bandit chiefs of the Ghats who'd have to be looked up some day; now it was as often as not about new mills or factories, and even schools, and how there would be a railroad clear over to Madras in the next five years, and you'd be able to journey from Mrs Blackwell's in Bombay to the Auckland in Calcutta without once putting on your boots.

'All sounds very peaceful and prosperous,' says I, over a peg and a whore at Mother Sousa's – like a good little political,

60

you see, I was conducting my first researches in the best gossip-mart I could find (fine mixed clientele, Mother Sousa's, with nothing blacker than quarter-caste and exhibition dances that would have made a Paris gendarme blench – well, if it's scuttle-butt you want, you don't go to a cathedral, do you?). The chap who'd bought me the peg laughed and said:

'Prosperous? I should just think so – my firm's divvy is up forty per cent, and we'll have new factories at Lahore and Allahabad working before Easter. Building churches – and when the universities come there'll be contracts to last out my service, I can tell you.'

'Universities?' says I. 'Not for the niggers, surely?'

'The native peoples,' says he primly – and the little snirp hadn't been out long enough to get his nose peeled – 'will soon be advanced beyond those of any country on earth. Heathen countries, that is. Lie still, you black bitch, can't you see I'm fagged out? Yes, Lord Canning is very strong on education, I believe, and spreading the gospel, too. Well, that's bricks and mortar, ain't it? – that's where to put your money, my boy.'

'Dear me,' says I, 'at this rate I'll be out of a job, I can see.'

'Military, are you? Well, don't fret, old fellow; you can always apply to be sent to the frontiers.'

'Quiet as that, is it? Even round Jhansi?'

'Wherever's that, my dear chap?'

He was just a pipsqueak, of course, and knew nothing; the little yellow piece I was exercising hadn't heard of Jhansi either, and when I asked her at a venture what chapattis were good for except eating, she didn't bat an eye, but giggled and said I was a verree fonnee maan, and must buy her meringues, not chapattis, yaas? You may think I was wasting my time,

61

sniffing about in Bombay, but it's my experience that if there's anything untoward in a country – even one as big as India – you can sometimes get a scent in the most unexpected places, just from the way the natives look and answer. But it was the same whoever I talked to, merchant or military, whore or missionary; no ripples at all. After a couple of days, when I'd got the old Urdu *bat* rolling familiarly off my palate again, I even browned up and put on a *puggaree** and coat and *pyjamys*, and loafed about the Bund bazaar, letting on I was a Mekran coast trader, and listening to the clack. I came out rotten with fleas, stinking of nautch-oil and cheap perfume and cooking *ghee*, with my ears full of beggars' whines and hawkers' jabbering and the clang of the booths – but that was all. Still, it helped to get India back under my hide again, and that's important, if you intend to do anything as a political.

Hullo, says you, what's this? – not Flashy taking his duty seriously for once, surely. Well, I was, and for a good reason. I didn't take Pam's forebodings seriously, but I knew I was bound to go to Jhansi and make some sort of showing in the task he'd given me – the thing was to do it quickly. If I could have a couple of official chats with this Rani woman, look into the business of the sepoys' cakes, and conclude that Skene, the Jhansi political, was a nervous old woman, I could fire off a report to Calcutta and withdraw gracefully. What I must not do was linger – because if there *was* any bottom to Pam's anxieties, Jhansi might be full of Ignatieff and his jackals before long, and I wanted to be well away before that happened.

So I didn't linger in Bombay. On the third day I took the road north-east towards Jhansi, travelling in good style by

---

* Turban.

bullock-hackery, which is just a great wooden room on wheels, in which you have your bed and eat your meals, and your groom and cook and bearer squat on the roof. They've gone out now, of course, with the railway, but they were a nice leisurely way of travelling, and I stopped off at messes along the road, and kept my ears open. None of the talk chimed with what I'd heard at Balmoral, and the general feeling was that the country had never been so quiet. Which was heartening, even if it was what you'd expect, down-country.

I purposely kept clear of any politicals, because I wanted to form my own judgements without getting any uncomfortable news that I didn't want to hear. However, up towards Mhow, who should I run into but Johnny Nicholson, whom I hadn't seen since Afghanistan, fifteen years before, trotting along on a Persian pony and dressed like a Baluchi robber with a beard down to his belly, and a couple of Sikh lancers in tow. We fell on each other like old chums – he didn't know me well, you see, but mostly by my fearsome reputation; he was one of your play-up-and-fear-God paladins, full of zeal and athirst for glory, was John, and said his prayers and didn't drink and thought women were either nuns or mothers. He was very big by now, I discovered, and just coming down for leave before he took up as resident at Peshawar.

By rights I shouldn't have mentioned my mission to anyone, but this was too good a chance to miss. There wasn't a downier bird in all India than Nicholson, or one who knew the country better, and you could have trusted him with anything, money even. So I told him I was bound for Jhansi, and why – the chapattis, the Rani, and the Russians. He listened, fingering his beard and squinting into the distance, while we squatted by the road drinking coffee.

'Jhansi, eh?' says he. 'Pindari robber country – Thugs, too. Trust you to pick the toughest nut south of the Khyber. Maharatta chieftains – wouldn't turn my back on any of 'em, and if you tell me there have been Russian agitators at work, I'm not surprised. Any number of ugly-looking copers and traders have been sliding south with the caravans up our way this year past, but not many guns, you see – that's what we keep our accounts by. But I don't like this news about chapattis passing among the sepoys.'

'You don't think it amounts to anything, surely?' I found all his cheerful references to Thugs and Pindaris damned disconcerting; he was making Jhansi sound as bad as Afghanistan.

'I don't know,' says he, very thoughtful. 'But I do know that this whole country's getting warm. Don't ask me how I know – Irish instinct if you like. Oh, I know it looks fine from Bombay or Calcutta, but sometimes I look around and ask myself what we're sitting on, out here. Look at it – we're holding a northern frontier against the toughest villains on earth: Pathans, Sikhs, Baluchis, and Afghanistan thrown in, with Russia sitting on the touchline waiting their chance. In addition, down-country, we're nominal masters of a collection of native states, half of them wild as Barbary, ruled by princes who'd cut our throats for three-pence. Why? Because we've tried to civilise 'em – we've clipped the tyrants' wings, abolished abominations like *suttee* and *thugee*, cancelled their worst laws and instituted fair ones. We've reformed 'em until they're sick – and started the telegraph, the railroad, schools, hospitals, all the rest of it.'

This sounded to me like a man riding his pet hobby; I couldn't see why any of this should do anything but please the people.

'The people don't count! They never do. It's the rulers that matter, the rajas and the nabobs – like this rani of yours in Jhansi. They've squeezed this country for centuries, and Dalhousie put a stop to it. Of course it's for the benefit of the poor folk, but they don't know that – they believe what their princes tell 'em. And what they tell 'em is that the British Sirkar is their enemy, because it stops them burning their widows, and murdering each other in the name of Kali, and will abolish their religion and force Christianity on them if it can.'

'Oh, come, John,' says I, 'they've been saying that for years.'

'Well, there's something in it.' He looked troubled, in a stuffy religious way. 'I'm a Christian, I hope, or try to be, and I pray I shall see the day when the Gospel is the daily bread of every poor benighted soul on this continent, and His praise is sung in a thousand churches. But I could wish our people went more carefully about it. These are a devout people, Flashman, and their beliefs, misguided though they are, must not be taken lightly. What do they think, when they hear Christianity taught in the schools – in the jails, even – and when colonels preach to their regiments?[5] Let the prince, or the agitator, whisper in their ears "See how the British will trample on thy holy things, which they respect not. See how they will make Christians of you." They will believe him. And they are such simple folk, and their eyes are closed. D'you know,' he went on, 'there's a sect in Kashmir that even worships *me*?'

'Good for you,' says I. 'D'ye take up a collection?'

'I try to reason with them – but it does no good. I tell you, India won't be converted in a day, or in years. It must come slowly, if surely. But our missionaries – good, worthy men – press on apace, and cannot see the harm they may do.' He sighed. 'Yet can one find it in one's heart to blame them, old fellow, when one considers the blessings that God's grace would bring to this darkened continent? It is very hard.' And he looked stern and nobly anguished; Arnold would have loved him. Then he frowned and growled, and suddenly burst out:

'It wouldn't be so bad, if we weren't so confounded soft! If we would only carry things with a high hand – the reforms, and the missionary work, even. Either let well alone, or do the thing properly. But we don't, you see; we take half-measures, and are too gentle by a mile. If we are going to pull down their false gods, and reform their old and corrupt states and amend their laws, and *make* 'em worthy men and women – then let us do it with strength! Dalhousie was strong, but I don't know about Canning. I know if I were he, I'd bring these oily, smirking, treacherous princes under my heel—' his eyes flashed as he ground his boot in the dust. 'I'd give 'em government, firm and fair. I'd be less soft with the sepoys, too – and with some of our own people. That's half the trouble – you haven't been back long enough, but depend upon it, we send some poor specimens out to the army nowadays, and to the Company offices. "Broken-down tapsters and serving men's sons", eh? Well, you'll see 'em – ignorant, slothful fellows of poor class, and we put 'em to officer high-caste Hindoos of ten years' service. They don't know their men, and treat 'em like children or animals, and think of nothing but drinking and hunting, and – and . . .' he reddened to the roots of his enormous beard and looked aside. 'Some of them consort with . . . with the worst type of native women.' He cleared his throat and patted my arm. 'There, I'm sorry, old fellow; I know it's distasteful to talk of such things, but it's true, alas.'

I shook my head and said it was heart-breaking.

'Now you see why your news concerns me so? These omens at Jhansi – they may be the spark to the tinder, and I've shown you, I hope, that the tinder exists in India, because of our own blindness and softness. If we were stronger, and dealt firmly with the princes, and accompanied our enlightenment of the people with proper discipline – why, the spark would be stamped out easily enough. As it is—' he shook his head again. 'I don't like it. Thank God they had the wit to send someone like you to Jhansi – I only wish I could come with you, to share whatever perils may lie ahead. It's a strange, wild place, from all I've heard,' says this confounded croaker with pious satisfaction, as he shook my hand. 'Come, old fellow, shall we pray together – for your safety and guidance in whatever dangers you may find yourself?'

And he plumped down there and then on his knees, with me alongside, and gave God his marching orders in no uncertain fashion, telling him to keep a sharp eye on his servant. I don't know what it was about me, but holy fellows like Nicholson were forever addressing heaven on my behalf – even those who didn't know me well seemed to sense that there was a lot of hard graft to be done if Flashy was ever to smell salvation. I can see him yet – his great dark head and long nose against the sunset, his beard quivering with exhortation, and even the freckles on the back of his clasped hands. Poor wild John – he should have canvassed the Lord on his own behalf, perhaps, for while I'm still here after half a century, he was stiff inside the year, shot in the midriff by a pandy sniper in the attack on Delhi, and left to die by inches at the roadside. That's what his duty earned for him;

if he'd taken proper precautions he'd have made viceroy. And Delhi would have fallen just the same.[6]

Whatever his prayers accomplished for my solid flesh, his talk about Jhansi had done nothing for my spirits. 'A strange wild place,' he'd said, and talked of the Pindari bandits and Thugs and Maharatta scoundrels – well, I knew it had been hell's punch-bowl in the old days, but I'd thought since we'd annexed it that it must be quieter now. Mangles, at the Board of Control in London, had described it as 'tranquil beneath the Company's benevolent rule', but he was a pompous ass with a talent for talking complete bosh about subjects on which he was an authority.

As I pushed on into Bandelkand it began to look as though he was wrong and Nicholson was right – it was broken, hilly country, with jungle on the slopes and in the valleys, never a white face to be seen, and the black ones getting uglier by the mile. The roads were so atrocious, and the hackery jolted and rolled so sickeningly, that I was forced to take to my Pegu pony; there was devil a sign of civilisation, but only walled villages and every so often a sinister Maharatta fort squatting on a hilltop to remind you who really held the power in this land. 'The toughest nut south of the Khyber' – I was ready to believe it, as I surveyed those unfriendly jungly hills, seeing nothing cheerier than a distant tiger skulking among the waitabit thorn. And this was the country that we were 'ruling' – with one battalion of suspect sepoy infantry and a handful of British civilians to collect the taxes.

My first sight of Jhansi city wasn't uplifting either. We rounded a bend on the hill road, and there it was under a dull evening sky – a massive fort, embattled and towered, on a great steep rock, and the walled city clustered at its foot. It was far bigger than I'd imagined; the walls must have been four miles round at least, and the air over the city was thick with the smoke of a thousand cooking fires. On this side of the city lay the orderly white lines of the British camp and cantonment – God, it looked tiny and feeble, beneath that looming vastness of Jhansi fort. My mind went back to Kabul, and how our camp had seemed dwarfed by the Bala Hissar – and even at Kabul, with an army of ten thousand, only a handful of us had escaped. I told myself that here it was different – that less than a hundred miles ahead of me there were our great garrisons along the Grand Trunk, and that however forbidding Jhansi might look, it was a British state nowadays, and under the Sirkar's protection. Only there wasn't much sign of that protection – just our pathetic little village like a flea on the lion's lip, and somewhere in that great citadel, where our troops never went, that brooding old bitch of a Rani scheming against us, with her thousands of savage subjects waiting for her word. Thus my imagination – as if it hadn't been full enough already, what with Ignatieff and Thugs and wild Pindaris and dissident sepoys and Nicholson's forebodings.

My first task was to look up Skene, the political whose reports had started the whole business, so I headed down to the cantonment, which was a neat little compound of perhaps forty bungalows, with decent gardens, and the usual groups already meeting on the verandahs for sundown pegs and cordials; there were a few carriages waiting with their grooms and drivers to take people out for dinner, and one or two officers riding home, but I drove straight through, and got a *chowkidar*'s direction to the little Star Fort, where Skene had his office – he'd still be there, the *chowkidar* said, which argued a very conscientious political indeed.

Frankly, I hoped to find him scared or stupid; he wasn't either. He was one of these fair, intent young fellows who fall over themselves to help, and will work all the hours God sends. He hopped from one leg to another when I presented myself, and seemed fairly overwhelmed to meet the great Flashy, but the steady grey eye told you at once that here was a boy who didn't take alarm at trifles. He had clerks and bearers running in all directions to take my gear to quarters, saw to it that I was given a bath, and then bore me off for dinner at his own bungalow, where he lost no time in getting down to business.

'No one knows why you're here, sir, except me,' says he. 'I believe Carshore, the Collector, suspects, but he's a sound man, and will say nothing. Of course, Erskine, the Commissioner at Saugor, knows all about it, but no one else.' He hesitated. 'I'm not quite clear myself, sir, why they sent you out, and not someone from Calcutta.'

'Well, they wanted an assassin, you see,' says I, easily, just for bounce. 'It so happens I'm acquainted with the Russian gentleman who's been active in these parts – and dealing with him ain't a job for an ordinary political, what?' It was true, after all; Pam himself had said it. 'Also, it seems Calcutta and yourself and Commissioner Erskine – with all respect – haven't been too successful with this titled lady up in the city palace. Then there are these cakes; all told, it seemed better to Lord Palmerston to send me.'

'Lord Palmerston?' says he, his eyes wide open. 'I didn't know it had gone that far.'

I assured him he'd been the cause of the Prime Minister's losing a night's sleep, and he whistled and reached for the decanter.

'That's neither here nor there, anyway,' says I. 'You cost *me* a night's sleep, too, for that matter. The first thing is: have any of these Russian fellows been back this way?'

To my surprise, he looked confused. 'Truth is, sir – I never knew they'd been near. That came to me from Calcutta – our frontier people traced them down this way, three times, I believe, and I was kept informed. But if they hadn't told me, I'd never have known.'

That rattled me, if you like. 'You mean, if they *do* come back – or if they're loose in your bailiwick now – you won't know of it until Calcutta sees fit to tell you?'

'Oh, our frontier politicals will send me word as soon as any suspected person crosses over,' says he. 'And I have my own native agents on the look-out now – some pretty sharp men, sir.'

'They know especially to look out for a one-eyed man?'

'Yes, sir – he has a curious deformity which he hides with a patch, you know – one of his eyes is half-blue, half-brown.'

'You don't say,' says I. By George, I hadn't realised our political arrangements were as ramshackle as this. 'That, Captain Skene, is the man I'm here to kill – so if any of your . . . sharp men have the chance to save me the trouble, they may do it with my blessing.'

'Oh, of course, sir. Oh, they will, you know. Some of them,' says he, impressively, 'are Pindari bandits – or used to be, that is. But we'll know in good time, sir, before any of these Ruski fellows get within distance.'

I wished I could share his confidence. 'Calcutta has no notion what the Russian spies were up to down here?' I asked him, but he shook his head.

'Nothing definite at all – only that they'd been here. We were sure it must be connected with the chapattis going round, but those have dried up lately. None have passed since October, and the sepoys of the 12th N.I. – that's the regiment here, you know – seem perfectly quiet. Their colonel swears they're loyal – has done from the first, and was quite offended that I reported the cakes to Calcutta. Perhaps he's right; I've had some of my men scouting the sepoy lines, and they haven't heard so much as a murmur. And Calcutta was to inform me if cakes passed at any other place, but none have, apparently.'

Come, thinks I, this is decidedly better; Pam's been up a gum-tree for nothing. All I had to do was make a show of brief activity here, and then loaf over to Calcutta after a few weeks and report nothing doing. Give 'em a piece of my mind, too, for causing me so much inconvenience.

'Well, Skene,' says I, 'this is how I see it. There's nothing to be done about what the Prime Minister calls "those blasted buns" – unless they make a reappearance, what? As to the Russians – well, *when* we get word of them, I'll probably drop out of sight, d'you see?' I would, too – to some convenient haven which the Lord would provide, and emerge when the coast was clear. But I doubted it would even come to that. 'Yes, you won't see me – but I'll be about, never fear, and if our one-eyed friend, or any of his creatures, shows face . . . well . . .'

He looked suitably impressed, with a hint of that awe which my fearsome reputation inspires. 'I understand, sir. You'll wish to . . . er, work in your own way, of course.' He blinked at me, and then exclaimed reverently: 'By Jove, I don't envy those Ruski fellows above half – if you don't mind my saying so, sir.'

'Skene, old chap,' says I, and winked at him. 'Neither do I.' And believe me, he was my slave for life, from that moment.

'There's the other thing,' I went on. 'The Rani. I have to try to talk some sense into her. Now, I daresay there isn't much I can do, since I gather she's shown you and Erskine that she's not disposed to be friendly, but I'm bound to try, you see. So I'll be obliged to you if you'll arrange an audience for me the day after tomorrow – I'd like to rest and perhaps look around the city first. For the present, you can tell me your own opinion of her.'

He frowned, and filled my glass. 'You'll think it's odd, sir, I daresay, but in all the time I've been here, I've never even seen her. I've met her, frequently, at the palace, but she speaks from behind a purdah, you know – and as often as not her chamberlain does the talking for her. She's a stickler for form, and since government granted her diplomatic immunity after her husband died – as a sop, really, when we assumed suzerainty – well, it makes it difficult to deal with her satisfactorily. She was friendly enough with Erskine at one time – but I've had no change out of her at all. She's damned bitter, you see – when her husband died, old Raja Gangadar, he left no children of his own – well, he was an odd bird, really,' and Skene blushed furiously and avoided my eye. 'Used to go about in female dress most of the time, and wore bangles and . . . and perfume, you see—'

'No wonder she was bitter,' says I.

'No, no, what I mean is, since he left no legitimate heir, but only a boy whom he'd adopted, Dalhousie wouldn't recognise the infant. The new succession law, you know. So the state was annexed – and the Rani was furious, and petitioned the Queen, and sent agents to London, but it was no go. The adopted son, Damodar, was dispossessed, and the Rani, who'd hoped to be regent, was deprived of her power – officially. Between ourselves, we let her rule pretty well as she pleases – well, we can't do otherwise, can we? We've one battalion of sepoys, and thirty British civilians to run the state administration – but she's the law, where her people are concerned, absolute as Caesar.'

'Doesn't that satisfy her, then?'

'Not a bit of it. She detests the fact that officially she only holds power by the Sirkar's leave, you see. And she's still wild about the late Raja's will – you'd think that with a quarter of a million in her treasury she'd be content, but there was some jewellery or other that Calcutta confiscated, and she's never forgiven us.'

'Interesting lady,' says I. 'Dangerous, d'you think?'

He frowned. 'Politically, yes. Given the chance, she'd pay *our* score off, double quick – that's why the chapatti business upset me. She's got no army, as such – but with every man in Jhansi a born fighter, and robber, she don't need one, do she? And they'll jump if she whistles, for they worship the ground she treads on. She's proud as Lucifer's sister, and devilish hard, not to say cruel, in her own courts, but she's uncommon kind to the poor folk, and highly thought of for her piety – spends five hours a day meditating, although she was a wild piece, they say, when she was a girl. They brought her up like a Maharatta prince at the old Peshwa's court – taught her to ride and shoot and fence with the best of them. They say she still has the fiend's own temper,' he added, grinning, 'but she's always been civil enough to me – at a distance. But make no mistake, she's dangerous; if you can sweeten her, sir, we'll all sleep a deal easier at nights.'

There was that, of course. However withered an old trot she might be, she'd be an odd female if she was altogether impervious to Flashy's manly bearing and cavalry whiskers – which was probably what Pam had in mind in the first place. Cunning old devil. Still, as I turned in that night I wasn't absolutely looking forward to poodle-faking her in two days' time, and as I glanced from my bungalow window and saw Jhansi citadel beetling in the starlight, I thought, we'll take a nice little escort of lancers with us when we go to take tea with the lady, so we will.

But that was denied me. I had intended to pass the next day looking about the city, perhaps having a discreet word with Carshore the Collector and the colonel of the sepoys, but as the *syce** was bringing round my pony to the dak-bungalow, up comes Skene in a flurry. When he'd sent word to the palace that Colonel Flashman, a distinguished soldier of the Sirkar, was seeking an audience for the following day, he'd been told that distinguished visitors were expected to present themselves immediately as a token of proper respect to her highness, and Colonel Flashman could shift his distinguished rump up to the palace forthwith.

'I . . . I thought in the circumstances of your visit,' says Skene, apologetically, 'that you might think it best to comply.'

'You did, did you?' says I. 'Does every Briton in Jhansi leap to attention when this beldam snaps her fingers, then?'

'Shall we say, we find it convenient to humour her highness,' says he – he was more of a political than he looked, this lad, so I blustered a bit, to be in character, and then said he might find me an escort of lancers to convoy me in.

'I'm sorry, sir,' says he. 'We haven't any lancers – and if we had, we've agreed not to send troop formations inside the city walls. Also, since I was excluded from the, er . . . invitation, I fear you must go alone.'

'What?' says I. 'Damnation, who governs here – the Sirkar or this harridan?' I didn't fancy above half risking my hide unguarded in that unhealthy-looking fortress, but I had to

---

* Groom.

cover it with dignity. 'You've made a rod for your own backs by being too soft with this . . . this woman. She's not Queen Bess, you know!'

'She thinks she is,' says he cheerfully, so in the end of course I had to lump it. But I changed into my lancer fig first, sabre, revolver and all – for I could guess why she was ensuring that I visited her alone: up-country, on the frontier, they judge a man on his own looks, but down here they go on the amount and richness of your retinue. One mounted officer wasn't going to impress the natives with the Sirkar's power – well, then, he'd look his best, and be damned to her. So I figged up, and when I regarded myself in Skene's cracked mirror – blue tunic and breeches, gold belt and epaulettes, white gauntlets and helmet, well-bristled whiskers, and Flashy's stalwart fourteen stone inside it all, it wasn't half bad. I took a couple of packages from my trunk, stowed them in my saddlebag, waved to Skene, and trotted off to meet royalty, with only the *syce* to show me the way.

Jhansi city lies about a couple of miles from the cantonment, and I had plenty of time to take in the scenery. The road, which was well-lined with temples and smaller buildings, was crowded into the city, with bullock-carts churning up the dust, camels, palankeens, and hordes of travellers both mounted and on foot. Most of them were country folk, on their way to the bazaars, but every now and then would come an elephant with red and gold fringed howdah swaying along, carrying some minor nabob or rich lady, or a portly merchant on his mule with a string of porters behind, and once the *syce* pointed out a group who he said were members of the Rani's own bodyguard – a dozen stalwart Khyberie Pathans, of all things, trotting along very military in double file, with mail coats and red silk scarves wound round their spiked helmets.

The Rani might not have a army, but she wasn't short of force, with those fellows about: there was a hundred years' Company service among them if there was a day.

And her city defences were a sight to see – massive walls twenty feet high, and beyond them a warren of streets stretching for near a mile to the castle rock, with its series of curtain walls and round towers – it would be the deuce of a place to storm, after you'd fought through the city itself; there were guns in the embrasures, and mail-clad spearmen on the walls, all looking like business.

We had to force our horses through a crowded inferno of heat and smells and noise and jostling niggers to get to the palace, which stood apart from the fort near a small lake, with a shady park about it; it was a fine, four-square building, its outer walls beautifully decorated with huge paintings of battles and hunting scenes. I presented myself to another Pathan, very splendid in steel back-and-breast and long-tail *puggaree*, who commanded the gate guard, and sat sweating in the scorching sun while he sent off a messenger for the chamberlain. And as I chafed impatiently, the Pathan walked slowly round me, eyeing me up and down, and presently stopped, stuck his thumbs in his belt, and spat carefully on my shadow.

Now, close by the gate there happened to be a number of booths and side-shows set up – the usual things, lemonade-sellers, a fakir with a plant growing through his palm, sundry beggars, and a kind of punch-and-judy show, which was being watched by a group of ladies in a palankeen. As a matter of fact, they'd already taken my eye, for they were obviously Maharatta females of quality, and four finer little trotters you never saw. There was a very slim, languid-looking beauty in a gold sari reclining in the palankeen, another plump piece in scarlet trousers and jacket beside her, and a third, very black, but fine-boned as a Swede, with a pearl headdress that must have cost my year's pay, sitting in a kind of camp-chair alongside – even the ladies' maid standing beside the palankeen was a looker, with great almond eyes and a figure inside her plain white sari like a Hindoo temple goddess. I was in the act of touching my hat to them when the Pathan started expectorating. At this the maid giggled, the ladies looked, and the Pathan sniffed contemptuously and spat again.

Well, as a rule anyone can insult me and see how much it pays him, especially if he's large and ugly and carrying a *tulwar*.* But for the credit of the Sirkar, and my own face in front of the women, I had to do something, so I looked the Pathan up and down, glanced away, and said quietly in Pushtu:

'You would spit more carefully if you were still in the Guides, *hubshi*.'†

He opened his eyes at that, and swore. 'Who calls me *hubshi*? Who says I was in the Guides? And what is it to thee, *feringhee*‡ pig?'

'You wear the old coat under your breastplate,' says I. 'But belike you stole it from a dead Guide. For no man who had a right to that uniform would spit on Bloody Lance's shadow.'

That set him back on his heels. 'Bloody Lance?' says he. 'Thou?' He came closer and stared up at me. 'Art thou that same Iflass-man who slew the four Gilzais?'

'At Mogala,' says I mildly. It had caused a great stir at the time, in the Gilzai country, and won me considerable fame (and my extravagant nickname) along the Kabul road – in fact, old Mohammed Iqbal had killed the four horsemen,

---

* A sword.

† Literally, 'woolly-haired' – a negro.

‡ Christian, a white man.

while I lit out for the undergrowth, but nobody living knew that.* And obviously the legend endured, for the Pathan gaped and swore again, and then came hastily to attention and threw me a *barra salaam*† that would have passed at Horse Guards.

'Sher Khan, *havildar*‡ lately of Ismeet Sahib's company of the Guides,[7] as your honour says,' croaks he. 'Now, shame on me and mine that I put dishonour on Bloody Lance, and knew him not! Think not ill of me, *husoor*,§ for—'

'Let the ill think ill,' says I easily. 'The spittle of a *durwan*¶ will not drown a soldier.' I was watching out of the corner of my eye to see how the ladies were taking this, and noted with satisfaction that they were giggling at the Pathan's discomfiture. 'Boast to your children, O *Ghazi***-that-was-a-Guide-and-is-now-a-Rani's-porter, that you spat on Bloody Lance Iflass-man's shadow – and lived.' And I walked my horse past him into the courtyard, well pleased; it would be all round Jhansi inside the hour.

It was a trifling enough incident, and I forgot it with my first glance at the interior of the Rani's palace. Outside it had been all dust and heat and din, but here was the finest garden courtyard you ever saw – a cool, pleasant enclosure where little antelopes and peacocks strutted on the lawns, parrots and monkeys chattered softly in the surrounding trees, and a dazzling white fountain played; there were shaded archways

---

* See *Flashman*.
† Great Salute.
‡ Sergeant.
§ Sir, Lord.
¶ Door-keeper.
** Hero.

79

in the carved walls, where well-dressed folk whom I took to be her courtiers sat and talked, waited on by bearers. One of the richest thrones in India, Pam had said, and I could believe it – there were enough silks and jewellery on view there to stuff an army with loot, the statuary was of the finest, in marble and coloured stones that I took to be jade, and even the pigeons that pecked at the spotless pavements had silver rings on their claws. Until you've seen it, of course, you can't imagine the luxury in which these Indian princes keep themselves – and there are folk at home who'll tell you that John Company were the robbers!

I was kept waiting there a good hour before a major-domo came, salaaming, to lead me through the inner gate and up a narrow winding stair to the durbar room on the first storey; here again all was richness – splendid silk curtains on the walls, great chandeliers of purple crystal hanging from the carved and gilded ceiling, magnificent carpets on the floor (with good old Axminster there among the Persian, I noticed) and every kind of priceless ornament, gold and ivory, ebony and silverwork, scattered about. It would have been in damned bad taste if it hadn't all been so bloody expensive, and the dozen or so men and women who lounged about on the couches and cushions were dressed to match; the ones down in the courtyard must have been their poor relations. Handsome as Hebe the women were, too – I was just running my eye over one alabaster beauty in tight scarlet trousers who was reclining on a shawl, playing with a parakeet, when a gong boomed somewhere, everyone stood up, and a fat little chap in a huge turban waddled in and announced that the durbar had begun. At which music began to play, and they all turned and bowed to the wall, which I suddenly realised wasn't a wall at all, but a colossal ivory screen, fine as lace, that cut the room in two. Through it you could just make out movement in the space beyond, like shadows behind thick gauze; this was the Rani's purdah screen, to keep out prying heathen eyes like mine.

I seemed to be first man in, for the chamberlain led me to a little gilt stool a few feet from the screen, and there I sat while he stood at one end of the screen and cried out my name, rank, decorations, and (it's a fact) my London clubs; there was a murmur of voices beyond, and then he asked me what I wanted, or words to that effect. I replied, in Urdu, that I brought greetings from Queen Victoria, and a gift for the Rani from Her Majesty, if she would graciously accept it. (It was a perfectly hellish photograph of Victoria and Albert looking in apparent stupefaction at a book which the Prince of Wales was holding in an attitude of sullen defiance; all in a silver frame, too, and wrapped up in muslin.) I handed it over, the chamberlain passed it through, listened attentively, and then asked me who the fat child in the picture was. I told him, he relayed the glad news, and then announced that her highness was pleased to accept her sister-ruler's gift – the effect was spoiled a trifle by a clatter from behind the screen which suggested the picture had fallen on the floor (or been thrown), but I just stroked my whiskers while the courtiers tittered behind me. It's hell in the diplomatic, you know.

There was a further exchange of civilities, through the chamberlain, and then I asked for a private audience with the Rani; he replied that she never gave them. I explained that what I had to say was of mutual but private interest to Jhansi and the British government; he looked behind the screen for instructions, and then said hopefully:

'Does that mean you have proposals for the restoration of her highness's throne, the recognition of her adopted son, and the restitution of her property – all of which have been stolen from her by the Sirkar?'

Well, it didn't, of course. 'What I have to say is for her highness alone,' says I, solemnly, and he stuck his head round the screen and conferred, before popping back.

'There are such proposals?' says he, and I said I could not talk in open durbar, at which there were sounds of rapid female muttering from behind the screen. The chamberlain asked what I could have to say that could not be said by Captain Skene, and I said politely that I could tell that to the Rani, and no other. He conferred again, and I tried to picture the other side of the screen, with the Rani, sharp-faced and thin in her silk shawl, muttering her instructions to him, and puzzled to myself what the odd persistent noise was that I could hear above the soft pipes of the hidden orchestra – a gentle, rhythmic swishing from beyond the screen, as though a huge fan were being used. And yet the room was cool and airy enough not to need one.

The chamberlain popped out again, looking stern, and said that her highness could see no reason for prolonging the interview; if I had nothing new from the Sirkar to impart to her, I was permitted to withdraw. So I got to my feet, clicked my heels, saluted the screen, picked up the second package which I had brought, thanked him and his mistress for their courtesy, and did a smart about-turn. But I hadn't gone a yard before he stopped me.

'The packet you carry,' says he. 'What is that?'

I'd been counting on this; I told him it was my own.

'But it is wrapped as the gift to her highness was wrapped,' says he. 'Surely it also is a present.'

'Yes,' says I, slowly. 'It was.' He stared, was summoned behind the screen, and came out looking anxious.

'Then you may leave it behind,' says he.

I hesitated, weighing the packet in my hand, and shook my head. 'No, sir,' says I. 'It was my own personal present, to her highness – but in my country we deliver such gifts face to face, as honouring both giver and receiver. By your leave,' and I bowed again to the screen and walked away.

'Wait, wait!' cries he, so I did; the rhythmic sound from behind the screen had stopped now, and the female voice was talking quietly again. The chamberlain came out, red-faced, and to my astonishment he bustled everyone else from the room, shooing the silken ladies and gentlemen like geese. Then he turned to me, bowed, indicated the screen, and effaced himself through one of the archways, leaving me alone with my present in my hand. I listened a moment; the swishing sound had started again.

I paused to give my whiskers a twirl, stepped up to the end of the screen, and rapped on it with my knuckles. No reply. So I said: 'Your highness?', but there was nothing except that damned swishing. Well, here goes, I thought; this is what you came to India for, and you must be civil and adoring, for old Pam's sake. I stepped round the screen, and halted as though I'd walked into a wall.

It wasn't the gorgeously carved golden throne, or the splendour of the furniture which outshone even what I'd left, or the unexpected sensation of walking on the shimmering Chinese quilt on the floor. Nor was it the bewildering effect of the mirrored ceiling and walls, with their brilliantly coloured panels. The astonishing thing was that from the ceiling there hung, by silk ropes, a great cushioned swing, and sitting in it, wafting gently to and fro, was a girl – the only soul in the room. And such a girl – my first impression was of great, dark, almond eyes in a skin the colour of milky coffee, with a long straight nose above a firm red mouth and chin, and hair as black as night that hung in a jewelled tail down her back. She was dressed in a white silk bodice and sari which showed off the dusky satin of her bare arms and midriff, and on her head was a little white jewelled cap from which a single pearl swung on her forehead above the caste-mark.

I stood and gaped while she swung to and fro at least three times, and then she put a foot on the carpet and let the swing drag to a halt. She considered me, one smooth dusky arm up on the swing rope – and then I recognised her: she was the ladies' maid who had been standing by the palankeen at the palace gate. The Rani's maid? – then the lady of the palankeen must be . . .

'Your mistress?' says I. 'Where is she?'

'Mistress? I have no mistress,' says she, tilting up her chin and looking down her nose at me. 'I am Lakshmibai, Maharani of Jhansi.'

For a moment I didn't believe it: I had become so used to picturing her over the past three months as a dried-up old shrew with skinny limbs that I just stood and gaped.[8] And yet, as I looked at her, there couldn't be any doubt: the richness of her clothes shouted royalty at you, and the carriage of her head, with its imperious dark eyes, told you as nothing else could that here was a woman who'd never asked permission in her life. There was strength in every line of her, too, for all her femininity – by George, I couldn't remember when I'd seen bouncers like those, thrusting like pumpkins against the muslin of her blouse, which was open to the jewelled clasp at her breast bone – if it hadn't been for a couple of discreetly embroidered flowers on either side, there would have been nothing at all concealed. I could only stand speechless before such queenly beauty, wondering what it would be like to tear the muslin aside, thrust your whiskers in between 'em, and go brrrrr!

'You have a gift to present,' says she, speaking in a quick, soft voice which had me recollecting myself and clicking my heels as I presented my packet. She took it, weighed it in her hand, still half-reclining in her swing, and asked sharply: 'Why do you stare at me so?'

'Forgive me, highness,' says I. 'I did not expect to find a queen who looked so . . .' I'd been about to say 'young and lovely', but changed it hurriedly for a less personal compliment. 'So like a queen.'

'Like that queen?' says she, and indicated the picture of Vicky and Albert, which was lying on a cushion.

'Each of your majesties,' says I, with mountainous diplomacy, 'looks like a queen in her own way.'

She considered me gravely, and then held the packet out to me. 'You may open it.'

I pulled off the wrapping, opened the little box, and took out the gift. You may smile, but it was a bottle of perfume – you see, Flashy ain't as green as he looks; it may be coals to Newcastle to take perfume to India, but in my experience, which isn't inconsiderable, there's not a woman breathing who isn't touched by a gift of scent, and it don't matter what age she is, either. And it was just the gift a blunt, honest soldier would choose, in his simplicity – furthermore, it was from Paris, and had cost the dirty old goat who presented it to Elspeth a cool five sovs. (She'd never miss it.) I handed it over with a little bow, and she touched the stopper daintily on her wrist.

'French,' says she. 'And very costly. Are you a rich man, colonel?'

That took me aback; I muttered something about not calling on a queen every day of my life.

'And why have you called?' says she, very cool. 'What is there that you have to say that can be said only face to face?' I hesitated, and she suddenly stood up in one lithe movement

86

– by Jove, they jumped like blancmanges in a gale. 'Come and tell me,' she went on, and swept off out on to the terrace at that end of the room, with a graceful swaying stride that stirred the seat of her sari in a most disturbing way. She jingled as she walked – like all rich Indian females, she seemed to affect as much jewellery as she could carry, with bangles at wrist and ankle, a diamond collar beneath her chin, and even a tiny pearl cluster at one nostril. I followed, admiring the lines of the tall, full figure, and wondering for the umpteenth time what I *should* say to her, now that the moment had come.

Pam and Mangles, you see, had given me no proper directions at all: I was supposed to wheedle her into being a loyal little British subject, but I'd no power to make concessions to any of her grievances. And it wasn't going to be easy; an unexpected stunner she might be, and therefore all the easier for me to talk to, but there was a directness about her that was daunting. This was a queen, and intelligent and experienced (she even knew French perfume when she smelled it); she wasn't going to be impressed by polite political chat. So what must I say? The devil with it, thinks I, there's nothing to lose by being as blunt as she is herself.

So when she'd settled herself on a daybed, and I'd forced myself to ignore that silky midriff and the shapely brown ankle peeping out of her sari, I set my helmet on the ground and stood up four-square.

'Your highness,' says I, 'I can't talk like Mr Erskine, or Captain Skene even. I'm a soldier, not a diplomat, so I won't mince words.' And thereafter I minced them for all I was worth, telling her of the distress there was in London about the coolness that existed between Jhansi on the one hand and the Company and Sirkar on the other; how this state of

87

affairs had endured for four years to the disadvantage of all parties; how it was disturbing the Queen, who felt a sisterly concern for the ruler of Jhansi not only as a monarch, but as a woman, and so on – I rehearsed Jhansi's grievances, the willingness of the Sirkar to repair them so far as was possible, threw in the information that I came direct from Lord Palmerston, and finished on a fine flourish with an appeal to her to open her heart to Flashy, plenipotentiary extraordinary, so that we could all be friends and live happy ever after. It was the greatest gammon, but I gave it my best, with noble compassion in my eye and a touch of ardour in the curl shaken down over my brow. She heard me out, not a muscle moving in that lovely face, and then asked:

'You have the power to make redress, then? To alter what has been done?'

I said I had the power to report direct to Pam, and she said that so, in effect, had Skene. Her agents in London had spoken direct to the Board of Control, without avail.

'Well,' says I, 'this is a little different, highness, don't you see? His lordship felt that if I heard from you at first-hand, so to speak, and we talked—'

'There is nothing to talk about,' says she. 'What can I say that has not been said – that the Sirkar does not know? What can you—'

'I can ask, maharaj', what actions by the Sirkar, short of removing from Jhansi and recognising your adopted son, would satisfy your grievances – or go some way to satisfying them.'

She came up on one elbow at that, frowning at me with those magnificent eyes. For what I was hinting at – without the least authority, mind you – was concessions, and devil a smell of those she'd had in four years.

'Why,' says she, thoughtfully. 'They know well enough. They have been told my grievances, my just demands, for four years now. And yet they have denied me. How can repetition serve?'

'A disappointed client may find a new advocate,' says I, with my most disarming smile, and she gave me a long stare, and then got up and walked over to the balustrade, looking out across the city. 'If your highness would speak your mind to me, openly—'

'Wait,' says she, and stood for a moment, frowning, before she turned back to me. She couldn't think what to make of this, she was suspicious, and didn't dare to hope, and yet she was wondering. God, she was a black beauty, sure enough – if I'd been the Sirkar, she could have had Jhansi and a pound of tea with it, just for half an hour on the daybed.

'If Lord Palmerston,' says she at last – and old Pam himself would have been tempted to restore her throne just to hear the pretty way she said 'Lud Pammer-stan' – 'wishes me to restate the wrongs that have been done me, it can only be because he has discovered some interest to serve by redressing them – or promising redress. I do not know what that interest is, and you will not tell me. It is no charitable desire to set right injustices done to my Jhansi—' and she lifted her head proudly. 'That is certain. But if he wishes my friendship, for whatever purpose of his own, he may give an earnest of his good will by restoring the revenues which should have come to me since my husband's death, but which the Sirkar has confiscated.' She stopped there, chin up, challenging, so I said:

'And after that, highness? What else?'

'Will he concede as much? Will the Company?'

'I can't say,' says I. 'But if a strong case can be made – when I report to Lord Palmerston . . .'

'And you will put the case, yourself?'

'That is my mission, maharaj'.'

'And such other . . . cases . . . as I may advance?' She looked the question, and there was just a hint of a smile on her mouth. 'So. And I must first put them to you – and no doubt you will suggest to me how they may best be phrased . . . or modified. You will advise, and . . . persuade?'

'Well,' says I, 'I'll help your highness as I can . . .'

To my astonishment she laughed, with a flash of white teeth, her head back, and shaking most delightfully.

'Oh, the subtlety of the British!' cries she. 'Such delicacy, like an elephant in a swamp! Lord Palmerston wishes, for his own mysterious reasons of policy, to placate the Rani of Jhansi. So he invites her to repeat the petition which has been repeatedly denied for years. But does he send a lawyer, or an advocate, or even an official of the Company? No – just a simple soldier, who will discuss the petition with her, and how it may best be presented to his lordship. Could not a lawyer have advised her better?' She folded her hands and came slowly forward, sauntering round me. 'But how many lawyers are tall and broad-shouldered and . . . aye, quite handsome – and persuasive as Flashman *bahadur*?* Not a doubt but *he* is best fitted to convince a silly female that a modest claim is most likely to succeed – and she will abate her demands for *him*, poor foolish girl, and be less inclined to insist on fine points, and stand upon her rights. Is this not so?'

'Highness, you misunderstand entirely . . . I assure you—'

'Do I?' says she, scornfully, but laughing still. 'I am not sixteen, colonel; I am an old lady of twenty-nine. And I may

---

* Title of honour, champion.

not know Lord Palmerston's purpose, but I understand his methods. Well, well. It may not have occurred to his lordship that even a poor Indian lady may be persuasive in her turn.' And she eyed me with some amusement, confident in her own beauty, the damned minx, and the effect it was having on me. 'He paid me a poor compliment, do you not think?'

What could I do but grin back at her? 'Do his lordship justice, highness,' says I. 'He'd never seen you. How many have, since you are *purdah-nishin*?'*

'Enough to have told him what I am like, I should have hoped. How did he instruct you – humour her, whatever she is, fair or foul, young and silly or old and ugly? Charm her, so that she keeps her demands cheap? Captivate her, as only a hero can.' She stirred an eyebrow. 'Who could resist the champion who killed the four Gilzais – where was it?'

'At Mogala, in Afghanistan – as your highness heard at the gate. Was it to test me that you had the Pathan spit on my shadow?'

'His insolence needed no instruction,' says she. 'He is now being flogged for it.' She turned away from me and sauntered back into the durbar room. 'You may have the tongue which insulted you torn out, if you wish,' she added over her shoulder.

That brought me up sharp, I can tell you. We'd been rallying away famously, and I'd all but forgotten who and what she was – an Indian prince, with all the capricious cruelty of her kind under that lovely hide. Unless she was just mocking me with the reminder – whether or no, I would play my character.

'Not necessary, highness,' says I. 'I had forgotten him.'

---

* Literally, 'one who sits behind a curtain'.

She nodded, and struck a little silver gong with her wrist-bangle. 'It is time for my noon meal, and this afternoon I hold my court. You may return tomorrow, and we shall discuss the representations you are to make to the subtle Lord Palmerston.' She smiled slightly in dismissal. 'And I thank you for your gift, colonel.'

Her maids were coming in, and the little fat chamberlain, so I made my bow.

'Maharaj',' says I. 'Your most humble obedient.'

She inclined her head regally, and turned away, but as I backed out round the screen I noticed that she had picked up my perfume-bottle from the table, and was inviting her maids to have a sniff at it.

I came away from that audience thinking no small diplomatic beer of myself. At least I seemed to have got further with her than any other representative of the Sirkar had ever done, even if I'd had to lie truth out of Jhansi to do it. God knew I'd not the slightest right to promise redress of any of her grievances against the Raj, and if I trotted back a list of them to London the Board would turn 'em down flat again, no question. But she didn't know that, and if I could jolly her along for a week for two, hinting at this or that possible concession, she might grow more friendly disposed – which was what Pam wanted, after all. Her hopes would revive, and while they were sure to be dashed in the end, I'd be back snug in England by then.

That was the official aspect, of course; the important thing was the delightful surprise that the old beldam of Jhansi was as prime a goer as ever wriggled a hip, and just ripe for my kind of diplomacy. She was a cocky bitch, with a fine sense of her queenly consequence, but I wasn't fooled by her airs, or the set-down she'd tried to give me by warning me not to try to come round her with whiskery blandishments. That was pure flirtation, to put me on my mettle – I know these beauties, you see, and it don't matter whether they're queens or commoners, when they start to play the cool, mocking grand dame it's a sure sign that they're wondering what kind of a mount you'll make. I'd seen the glint in this one's eye when she walked round me, and thought quietly to myself, we'll have you gasping for more, my girl, before this fortnight's out.

You may think me a presumptuous ambassador on short notice, especially since the object of my carnal ambitions was royal, clever, dangerously powerful, and a high-caste Hindoo lady of reputed purity to boot. But that means nothing when a woman fancies a buck like me; besides, I knew about these high-born Indian wenches – randy as ferrets, the lot of them, and with all the opportunity to gratify it, too. A woman with a shape and face like Lakshmibai's hadn't let it go to waste in four years' widowhood (after being married to some prancing old quean, too), not with the stallions of her palace guard available at the crook of her little finger. Well, I'd make a rare change of bedding for her – and if her lusty inclinations needed any prompting, she might find it in the thought that being amiable to ambassador Flashy was the likeliest way of getting what she wanted for herself and her state. Dulce et decorum est pro patria rogeri, she could say to herself – and I cantered back to the cantonments full of cheery thoughts, imagining what that voluptuous tawny body would look like when I peeled the sari off it, and speculating on the novel uses to which the pair of us could put that swing of hers, in the interests of diplomatic relations.

In the meantime, I had Pam's other business to attend to, so I spent the afternoon in the Native Infantry lines, looking at the Company sepoys to gauge for myself what their temper was. I did it idly enough, for they seemed a properly smart and docile lot, and yet it was a momentous visit. For it led to an encounter that was to save my life, and set me on one of the queerest and most terrifying adventures of my career, and perhaps shaped the destiny of British India, too.

I had just finished chatting to a group of the *jawans*,* and telling 'em that in my view they'd never be called on to serve overseas, in spite of the new act,[9] when the officer with me – fellow called Turnbull – asked me if I'd like to look at the irregular horse troop who had their stables close by. Being a cavalryman, I said yes, and a fine mixed bunch they were, too, Punjabis and frontiersmen mostly, big, strapping ruffians with oiled whiskers and their shirts inside their breeches, laughing and joking as they worked on their leather, and as different from the smooth-faced infantry as Cheyennes are from hottentots. I was having a good crack with them, for these were the kind of scoundrels with whom I'd ridden (albeit reluctantly) in my Afghan days, when their *rissaldar*† came up – and at the sight of me he stopped dead in the stable door, gaping as though he couldn't believe his eyes. He was a huge, bearded *Ghazi* of a fellow, Afghan for certain by the devil's face of him – I'd have said Gilzai or Dourani – with a skull-cap on the back of his head, and the old yellow coat of Skinner's riders over his shoulders.[10]

'Jehannum!' says he, and stared again, and then stuck his hands on his hips and roared with laughter.

'Salaam, *rissaldar*,' says I, 'what do you want with me?'

'A sight of thy left wrist, Bloody Lance,' says he, grinning

---

* Soldiers.

† native officer commanding a cavalry troop.

like a death's head. 'Is there not a scar, there, to match this?—' and he pulled up his sleeve, while I stared in disbelief at the little puckered mark, for the man who bore it should have been dead, fifteen years ago – and he'd been a mere slip of a Gilzai boy when it had been made, with his bleeding fore-arm against mine, and his mad father, Sher Afzul, doing the honours and howling to heaven that his son's life was pledged eternally to the service of the White Queen.

'Ilderim?' says I, flabbergasted. 'Ilderim Khan, of Mogala?' And then he flung his arms round me, roaring, and danced me about while the *sowars** grinned and nudged each other.

'Flashman!' He pounded my back. 'How many years since ye took me for the Sirkar? Stand still, old friend, and let me see thee! Bismillah, thou hast grown high and heavy in the service – such a *barra sahib*,† and a colonel, too! Now praise God for the sight of thee!'

And then he was showing me off to his fellows, telling them how we'd met in the old Kabul days, when his father had held the passes south, and how I'd killed the four Gilzais (strange, the same lying legend coming up twice in a day), and he'd been pledged to me as a hostage, and we'd lost sight of each other in the Great Retreat. It's all there, in my earlier memoirs, and pretty gruesome, too, even if it was the basis of my glorious career.‡

So now it was Speech Day with a vengeance, while we relived old memories and slapped each other on the shoulder for half an hour or so. And then he asked me what I was doing here, and I answered vaguely that I was on a mission

* Troopers.
† Great lord, important man.
‡ See *Flashman*.

to the Rani, but soon to go home again; and at this he looked at me shrewdly, but said nothing more until I was leaving.

'It will be *palitikal*, beyond doubt,' says he. 'Do not tell me. Listen, instead, to a friend's word. If ye speak with the Rani, be wary of her; she is a Hindoo woman, and knows too much for a woman's good.'

'What d'you know about her?' says I.

'Little enough,' says he, 'except that she is like the silver krait, in that she is beautiful and cunning and loves to bite the sahibs. The Company have made a *cutch-rani** of her, Flashman, but she still has fangs. This,' he added bitterly, 'comes of soft government in Calcutta, by *ducks* and *mulls*†who have been too long in the heat. So beware of her, and go with God, old friend. And remember, while thou art in Jhansi, Ilderim is thy shadow – or if not me, then these *loose-wallahs* and *jangli-admis*‡ of mine. They have their uses—' And he jerked a thumb towards his troopers.

That, coming from an Afghan *upper roger*§ who was also a friend, was the best kind of insurance policy you could wish – not that I now had any fears, fool that I was, about my stay in Jhansi. As to what he'd said of the Rani – well, I knew it already, and Afghans' views on women are invariably sour

---

* 'Cutch' in this sense means inferior, as opposed to 'pukka', meaning first-rate. E.g. *pukka road*, a macadam surface, *cutch road*, a mere track. Thus *cutch-rani*, a nominal queen, without power.

† *Ducks and mulls* – Bombay Anglo-Indians and Madras Anglo-Indians. Slang expressions current among the British in India, but probably seldom used by Indians themselves.

‡ Thieves and jungle-men.

§ A young chief – Sansk., 'yuva rajah'. For this and other curiosities of Anglo-Indian slang, see *Hobson-Jobson*, by H. Yule (1886).

– beastly brutes. Anyway, I didn't doubt my ability to handle Lakshmibai, in every sense of the word.

Still, I found his simile coming to mind next day, when I attended her durbar again, and watched her sitting enthroned to hear petitions, dressed in a cloth-of-silver sari that fitted her like a skin, with a silver-embroidered shawl framing that fine dark face; when she moved it was for all the world like a great gleaming snake stirring. She was very grave and queenly, and her courtiers and suppliants fairly grovelled, and scuttled about if she raised her pinky; when the last petitioner had been heard, and a gong had boomed to end the durbar, she sat with her chin in the air while the mob bowed itself out backwards, leaving only me and her two chief councillors standing there – and then she slipped out of her throne with a little cry of relief, hissed at one of her pet monkeys and chased it out on to the terrace, clapping her hands in mock anger, and then returned, perfectly composed, to lounge on her swing.

'Now we can talk,' says she, 'and while my *vakeel** reads out the matter of my "petition", you may refresh yourself, colonel—' and she indicated a little table with flasks and cups on it. 'Ah, and see,' she added, flicking a flimsy little hand-kerchief from her sari, 'I am wearing French perfume today – do you care for it? My lady Vashki thinks I am no better than an infidel.'

It was my perfume, right enough; I bowed acknowledge-ment while she smiled and settled herself, and the *vakeel* began to drone out her petition in formal Persian.

It's worth repeating, perhaps, for it was a fair sample of the objections that many Indian princes had to British rule

---

* Legal representative (possibly used here ironically).

– the demand for restoration of her husband's revenues, compensation for the slaughter of sacred cows, reappointment of court hangers-on dismissed by the Sirkar, restitution of confiscated temple funds, recognition of her authority as regent, and the like. All a waste of time, had she but known it, but splendid stuff for me to talk to her about over the next week or two while I pursued the really important work of charming her into a recumbent position.

I had no doubt she was willing enough for me to make the running there – she was wearing my scent, and letting me know it, and she was as pleasant as pie in her cool way at that meeting – nodding graciously as I talked to her wise men about the petition, smiling if I ventured a joke, inviting them to admire my reasoning (which they fell over themselves to do, absolutely), even asking my advice occasionally, and always considering me languidly with those dark slanting eyes as I talked. All of which might have seemed suspiciously amiable after her frankness at our first encounter – but since then she'd had time to weigh the political advantages of being pleasant to me, and was setting out to make me enjoy my work.

But I knew politics wasn't the half of it – I know when a woman's got that little flutter in her midriff about me, and in our ensuing meetings I could watch her enjoying using her beauty on me – and she could do that with a touch that Montez might have envied. I'll admit it now, I found her enchanting; she had the advantage of being a queen, of course, which makes a beauty all the more tantalising – well, even I, on short acquaintance, could hardly have taken her belly in one hand, her bum in the other, and fondled her flat on her back with passionate murmurs, as one would do in ordinary circumstances. No, with royalty you have to wait a little. Not that I wasn't tempted, in those early talks, when she had dismissed her councillors, and we were alone, and just once or twice, from the warm gleam in her eye as she swayed on her swing or lay on her daybed, I wondered if perhaps . . . but I decided to make haste slowly, and play the bowling as it came down.

It came mighty fast, too, sometimes, for if she was generally content just to politick flirtatiously, I soon discovered that she could be dead serious when Jhansi and her own ambitions were concerned; let the talk turn that way, and you saw the passion of her feeling.

'Five years ago, how many beggars were on the streets?' she rounded on me once. 'One for every ten today. And who has accomplished this? Who but the Sirkar, by assuming the affairs of the state, so that one white sahib comes to do the work that employed a dozen of our people, who must be turned out to starve. Who guards the state? Why, the Company soldiers – so Jhansi's army must be disbanded, and they, too, can shift or steal or go hungry!'

'Well now, highness,' says I, 'it's hard to blame the Sirkar for being efficient, and as for your unemployed soldiers, they'll be more than welcome in the Company service—'

'In a foreign army? And will there be room in its ranks, too, for the Indian craftsmen whom the Sirkar's efficiency has put out of work? For the traders whose commerce has decayed under the benevolent rule of the Raj?'

'You must give us a little time, maharaj',' says I, humouring her. 'And it ain't all bad, you know. Banditry has ceased; the poor folk are safe from dacoits and Thugs – why, your own throne is secure against greedy neighbours like Kathe Khan and the Dewan of Orcha—'

'*My* throne is safe?' says she, stopping the swing on which she had been swaying, and lifting her brows at me. 'Oh, very safe – for the Sirkar to enjoy its revenues, and usurp my place, and disinherit my son – ha! As to Kathe Khan and that jackal of Orcha, whom the Company in their wisdom allow to live – if I ruled this state, and had my soldiers, Kathe Khan and his fellow-viper would come against me once –' she picked up a fruit from the tray at her elbow, considered it, and nibbled daintily '– and crawl home again – without their hands and feet.'

'No doubt, ma'am,' says I. 'But the fact is that when Jhansi ruled itself, it couldn't deal with these foes. Nor were the Thugs put down—'

'Oh, aye – we hear much of them, and how the Company suppressed their wickedness. And why – because they slew travellers, or was it because they served a Hindoo god and so offended the Christian Company?' She eyed me contemptuously. 'Belike had the Thugs been Jesus-worshippers, they would have been roaming yet – especially if they had chosen Hindoo victims.'

You can't argue with gross prejudice, so I just looked amiable and said:

'And doubtless had *suttee*, that fine old Hindoo custom whereby widows were tortured to death, been a Christian practice, we would have encouraged it? But in our ignorance and spite, we forbade it – along with the law which condemned those widows who had escaped burning to a life of slavery and degradation with their heads shaved and heaven knows what else. Come, maharaj' – can we do nothing right?' And without thinking I added: 'I'd have thought your highness, as a widow, would have cause to thank the Sirkar for that at least.'

As soon as the words were out, I saw I'd put my foot in

it. The swing stopped abruptly, and she sat upright, with a face like a mask, staring at me.

'I?' says she. 'I? Thank the Sirkar?' And she suddenly flung her fruit across the room and stood upright, blazing at me. 'You dare to suggest that?'

Well, I could grovel, or face it out – but I don't hold with grovelling to pretty women, not unless the danger's desperate or I'm short of cash. So I started to hum and haw placatingly, while she snapped in a voice like ice:

'I owe the Company nothing! If the Company had never been, do you think I would have submitted to *suttee*, or allowed myself to be made a menial? Do you take me for a fool?'

'By God, no, ma'am,' says I hastily. 'Anything but, and if I've offended, I beg your pardon. I simply thought that the law was binding on all, ah . . . ladies, you see, and . . .'

'The Maharani makes the law,' says she, all Good Queen Bess damning the dagoes, and I hurriedly cried thank heaven for that, at which she looked down her nose at me.

'That is not the view of your Company or your country. Why should you be different? Why should you care?'

That was my cue, of course; I hesitated a second, and then looked at her, very frank and manly. 'Because I've seen your highness,' says I quietly. 'And . . . well . . . I do care, a great deal, you see.' I stopped there, giving her my steadiest smile, with a touch of ardent admiration thrown in, and after a long moment her stare softened, and she even smiled as she sat down again and said:

'Shall we return to the confiscated temple funds?'

Altogether it was a rum game in those first few days – rum for her, because she was a fair natural tyrant, yet whenever a disagreement in our discussions arose, she would allow it to smooth over, with that warm mysterious smile, and rum for me, because here I was day after day closeted with this choice piece of rump, and not so much as touching her, let alone squeezing and grappling. But I had to bide my time, and since she took such obvious and natural pleasure in my company, I contained my horniness for the moment, in the interests of diplomacy.

In the meantime, I occasionally paid attention to the other side of Pam's business, talking with Skene, and Carshore the Collector, and reassuring myself that all continued to go well among the sepoys. There wasn't a hint of agitation now, my earlier fears about Ignatieff and his scoundrels were beginning to seem like a distant nightmare, and now that I was so well established in the Rani's good graces, the last cloud over my mission appeared to have been dispelled. Laughable, you may think, when you recollect that this was 1856 drawing to a close – you will ask how I, and the others, could have been so blind to the fact that we were living on the very edge of hell, but if you'd been there, what would you have seen? A peaceful native state, ruled by a charming young woman whose grievances were petty enough, and who gave most of her time to seducing the affections of a dashing British colonel; a contented native soldiery; and a tranquil, happy, British cantonment.

I was about it a great deal, and all our people were so placid and at ease – I remember a dinner at Carshore's bungalow, with his family, and Skene and his pretty little wife so nervous and pleased in her new pink gown, and jolly old Dr McEgan with his fund of Irish stories, and the garrison men with their red jackets, slung on the backs of their chairs, matching their smiling red faces, and their gossipy wives, and myself raising a laugh by coaxing one of the Wilton girls to eat a 'country captain'* with the promise that it would make her hair curl when she grew older.

It was all so comfy and easy, it might have been a dinner-party at home, except for the black faces and gleaming eyes of the bearers standing silent against the chick-screens, and the big moths fluttering round the lamps; afterwards there was a silly card game, and Truth or Consequences, and local scandal, and talk of leave and game-shooting with our cheroots and port on the verandah. Trivial enough memories, when you think what happened to all of them – I can still feel the younger Wilton chit pulling at my arm and crying:

'Oh, Colonel Flashman, Papa says if I ask you ever so nicely you will sing us "The Galloping Major" – will you please, oh, please do!' And see those shining eyes, and the ringlets, as she tugged me to where her sister was sitting at the piano.

We couldn't see ahead, then, and life was pleasant – especially for me, with my diplomatic duties to attend to, and they became more enjoyable by the hour; I'll say that for Rani Lakshmibai, she knew how to make business a pleasure. Much of the time we didn't talk in the palace at all; she was, as Skene had told me, a fine horsewoman, and loved nothing better than to put on her jodhpurs and turban, with two little silver pistols in her sash, and gallop on the maidan, or go hawking along a wooded river not far from the city. There was a charming little pavilion there, of about a dozen rooms on two storeys, hidden among the trees, and once or twice I was taken on picnics with a few of her courtiers and attendants. At other times we would talk in the palace garden, among the scores of pet beasts and birds which she kept, and

---

* A type of curry.

once she had me into one of her hen-parties in the durbar room, at which she entertained all the leading ladies of Jhansi to tea and cakes, and I found myself called on to discourse on European fashions to about fifty giggling Indian females in saris and bangles and kohl-dark eyes – excellent fun, too, although the questions they asked about crinolines and panniers would have made a sailor blush.

But her great delight was to be out of doors, riding or playing with her adopted son Damodar, a grave-faced imp of eight, or inspecting her guards at field exercise; she even watched their wrestling matches in the courtyard, and a race-meeting in which some of our garrison officers took part – I was intrigued to see that on this occasion she wore a purdah veil and an enveloping robe, for about the palace she went bare-faced – and pretty bare-bodied, too. And if she could be as formal as a stockbroker with a new-bought peerage, she had a delightful way with the ordinary folk – she was never so gay and happy as when she held a party for children from the city in her garden, letting them run among the birds and monkeys, and at one of her almsgivings I saw her quite concerned as her treasurer scattered coins among the mob of hideous and stinking beggars clamouring at her gate. Not at all like a Rani, sometimes – she was a queer mixture of schoolgirl and sophisticated woman, all scatter one moment, all languor and dignity the next. Damned unpredictable – oh, and captivating; there were times when even I found myself regarding her with an interest that wasn't more than four-fifths lustful – and that ain't like me. It was directly after that alms-giving, when we rode out to her pavilion among the trees, and I had just remarked that what was needed for India was a Poor Law and a few parish workuses, that she suddenly turned in her saddle, and burst out:

'Can you not see that that is not our way – that none of our ways are your ways? You talk of your reforms, and the benefits of British law and the Sirkar's rule – and never think that what seems ideal to you may not suit others; that we have our own customs, which you think strange and foolish, and perhaps they are – but they are ours – our own! You come, in your strength, and your certainty, with your cold eyes and pale faces, like . . . like machines marching out of your northern ice, and you will have everything in order, tramping in step like your soldiers, whether those you conquer and civilise – as you call it – whether they will or no. Do you not see that it is better to leave people be – to let them alone?'

She wasn't a bit angry, or I'd have agreed straight off, but she was as intense as I'd known her, and the great dark eyes were almost appealing, which was most unusual. I said that all I'd meant was that instead of thousands going sick and ragged and hungry about her city, it might be better to have some system of relief; come cheaper on her, too, if they had the beggars picking yarn or mending roads for their dole.

'You talk of a system!' says she, striking her riding crop on the saddle. 'We do not care for systems. Oh, we admire and respect those which you show us – but we do not want them; we would not choose them for ourselves. You remember we spoke of how twelve Indian babus* did the work of one white clerk—'

'Well, that's waste, ma'am,' says I respectfully. 'There's no point—'

'Wasteful or not, does it matter – if people are happy?' says she, impatiently. 'Where lies the virtue of your boasted

* Clerks.

105

progress, your telegraphs, your railway trains, when we are content with our sandals and our ox-carts?'

I could have pointed out that the price of *her* sandals would have kept a hundred Jhansi coolie families all their lives, and that she'd never been within ten yards of an ox-cart, but I was tactful.

'We can't help it, maharaj',' says I. 'We have to do the best we can, don't you know, as we see it. And it ain't just telegraphs and trains – though you'll find those useful enough, in time – why, I'm told there are to be universities, and hospitals—'

'To teach philosophies that we do not want, and sciences that we do not need. And a law that is foreign to us, which our people cannot understand.'

'Well, that doesn't leave 'em far behind the average Englishman,' says I. 'But it's fair law – and with respect that's more than you can say for most of your Indian courts. Look now – when there was a brawl in the street outside your palace two days since, what happened? Your guards didn't catch the culprits – so they laid hands on the first poor soul they met, haled him into your *divan*,* guilty or not – and you have him hanging by his thumbs and sun-drying at the scene of the crime for two solid days. Fellow near died of it – and he'd done nothing! I ask you, ma'am, is that justice?'

'He was a *badmash*,† and well known,' says she, wide-eyed. 'Would you have let him go?'

'For that offence, yes – since he was innocent of it. We punish only the guilty.'

'And if you cannot find them? Is there to be no example

---

* Court.
† Scoundrel.

made? There will be no more brawls outside the palace, I think.' And seeing my look, she went on: 'I know it is not your way, and it seems unfair and even barbarous to you. But we understand it – should that not be enough? You find it strange – like our religions, and our forbidden things, and our customs. But can your Sirkar not see that they are as precious to us as yours are to you? Why is it not enough to your Company to drive its profit? Why this greed to order people's lives?'

'It isn't greed, highness,' says I. 'But you can't drive trade on a battlefield, now can you? There has to be peace and order, surely, and you can't have 'em without . . . well, a strong hand, and a law that's fair for all – or for most people, anyway.' I knew she wouldn't take kindly if I said the law was as much for her as for her subjects. 'And when we make mistakes, well, we try to put 'em right, you see – which is what I'm here for, to see that justice – our justice, if you like – is done to you—'

'Do you think that is all that matters?' says she. We had stopped in the pavilion garden, and the horses were cropping while her attendants waited out of earshot. She was looking at me, frowning, and her eyes were very bright. 'Do you think it is the revenues, and the jewels – even my son's rights; do you think that is all I care for? These are the things that can be redressed – but what of the things that cannot? What of this life, this land, this country that you will change – as you change everything you touch? Today, it is still bright – but you will make it grey; today, it is still free – oh, and no doubt wrong and savage by your lights – and you will make it tame, and orderly, and bleak, and the people will forget what they once were. That is what you will do – and that is why I resist as best I can. As you, and Lord Palmerston

107

would. Tell him,' says she, and by George, her voice was shaking, but the pretty mouth was set and hard, 'when you go home, that whatever happens, I will not give up my Jhansi. *Mera Jhansi denge nay.* I will not give up my Jhansi!'

I was astonished; I'd never been in doubt that under the delectable feminine surface there was a tigress of sorts, but I hadn't thought it was such a passionately sentimental animal. D'you know, for a moment I was almost moved, she seemed such a damned spunky little woman; I felt like saying 'There, there', or stroking her hand, or squeezing her tits, or something – and then she had taken a breath, and sat upright in the saddle, as though recovering herself, and she looked so damned royal and so damned lovely that I couldn't help myself.

'Maharaj' – you don't need me to say it. Go to London yourself, and tell Lord Palmerston – and I swear he'll not only give you Jhansi but Bombay and Hackney Wick as well.' And I meant it; she'd have been a sensation – had 'em eating out of her dusky little palm. 'See the Queen herself – why don't you?'

She stared thoughtfully ahead for a moment, and then murmured under her breath: 'The Queen . . . God save the Queen – what strange people you British are.'

'Don't you worry about the British,' says I, 'they'll sing "God save the Queen", all right – and they'll be thinking of the Queen of Jhansi.'

'Now that is disloyal, colonel,' says she, and the languid smile was back in her eyes, as she turned her horse and trotted off with me following.

Now, you may be thinking to yourself, what's come over old Flash? He ain't going soft on this female, surely? Well, you know, I think the truth is that I was a bit soft on all my girls – Lola and Cassie and Valla and Ko Dali's daughter and Susie the Bawd and Takes-Away-Clouds-Woman and the rest of 'em. Don't mistake me; it was always the meat that mattered, but I had a fair affection for them at the same time – every now and then, weather permitting. You can't help it; feeling randy is a damned romantic business, and it's my belief that Galahad was a bigger beast in bed than ever Lancelot was. That's by the way, but worth remembering if you are to understand about me and Lakshmibai – and I've told you a good deal about her on purpose, because she was such a mysterious, contrary female that I can't hope to explain her (any more than historians can) but must just leave you to judge for yourselves from what I've written – and from what was to follow.

For on the morning after that talk at the pavilion – two weeks to the day since I'd arrived in Jhansi – things began to happen in earnest. To me, at any rate.

I sensed there was something up as soon as I presented myself in the durbar room; she was perfectly pleasant, vivacious even, as she told me about some new hunting-cheetah she'd been given, but her *vakeel* and chief minister weren't meeting her eye, and her foot was tap-tapping under the edge of her gold sari; ah, thinks I, someone's been getting the sharp side of missy's tongue. She didn't have much mind to business, either, and once or twice I caught her eyeing me almost warily, when she would smile quickly – with anyone else I would have said it was nervousness. Finally she cut the discussion off abruptly, saying enough for today, and we would watch the guardsmen fencing in the courtyard.

Even there, I noticed her finger tapping on the balcony as we looked down at the Pathans sabring away – damned active, dangerous lads they looked, too – but in a little while she began to take notice, talking about the swordplay and applauding the hits, and then she glanced sidelong at me, and says:

'Do you fence as well as you ride, colonel?'

I said, pretty fair, and she gave me her lazy smile and says:

'Then we shall try a bout,' and blow me if she didn't order a couple of foils up to the durbar room, and go off to change into her jodhpurs and blouse. I waited, wondering – of course, Skene had said she'd been brought up with boys, and could handle arms with the best of them, but it seemed deuced odd – and then she was back, ordering her attendants away, tying up her hair in a silk scarf, and ordering me on guard very business-like. They'll never believe this at home, thinks I, but I obeyed, indulgently enough, and she touched me three times in the first minute. So I settled down, in earnest, and in the next minute she hit me only once, laughing, and told me to try harder.

That nettled me, I confess; I wasn't having this, royalty or not, so I went to work – I'm a strong swordsman, but not too academic – and I pushed her for all I was worth. She was better-muscled than she looked, though, and fast as a cat, and I had to labour to make her break ground, gasping with laughter, until her back was against one of the glass walls. She took to the point, holding me off, and then un-accountably her guard seemed to falter, I jumped in with the old heavy cavalry trick, punching my hilt against the forte of her blade, her foil spun out of her hand – and for a moment we were breast to breast, with me panting within inches of that dusky face and open, laughing mouth – the great dark eyes were wide and waiting – and then my foil was clattering on the floor and I had her in my arms, crushing my lips on hers and tasting the sweetness of her tongue, with that soft

110

body pressed against me, revelling in the feel and fragrance of her. I felt her hands slip up my back to my head, holding my face against hers for a long delicious moment, and then she drew her lips away, sighing, opened her eyes, and said:

'How well do you shoot, colonel?'

And then she had slipped from my arms and was walking quickly towards the door to her private room, with me grunting endearments in pursuit, but as I came after her she just raised a hand, without turning or breaking stride, and said firmly:

'The durbar is finished . . . for the moment.' The door closed behind her, and I was left with the fallen foils, panting like a bull before business, but thinking, my boy, we're home – the damned little teaser. I hesitated, wondering whether to invade her boudoir, when the little chamberlain came pottering in, eyeing the foils in astonishment, so I took my leave and presently was riding back to the cantonment, full of buck and anticipation – I'd known she'd call 'Play!' in the end, and now there was nothing to do but enjoy the game.

That was why she'd been jumpy earlier, of course, wondering how best to bring me to the boil, the cunning minx. 'How well do you shoot?' forsooth – she'd find out soon enough, when we finished the durbar – tomorrow, no doubt. So by way of celebration I drank a sight more bubbly than was good for me at dinner, and even took a magnum back to my bungalow for luck. It was as well I did, for about ten Ilderim dropped by for a prose – as he'd taken to doing – and there's nobody thirstier than a dry Gilzai – if you think all Muslims abstain, I can tell you of one who didn't. So we popped the cork, and gassed about the old days, and smoked, and I was enjoying myself with carnal thoughts about my Lucky Lakshmibai and thinking about turning in, when there

111

came a scraping on the chick at the back of the bungalow, and the *khitmagar** appeared to tell me that there was a *bibi*[†] who insisted on seeing me.

Ilderim grinned and wagged his ugly head, and I cursed, thinking here was some bazaar houri plying her trade where it was least wanted, but I staggered out, and sure enough at the foot of the steps was a veiled woman in a sari, but with a burly-looking escort standing farther back at the gate. She didn't look like a slut, somehow, and when I asked what she wanted she came quickly up the steps, salaamed, and held out a little leather pouch. I took it, wondering; inside there was a handkerchief, and even through the champagne fumes there was no mistaking – it was heavy with my perfume.

'From my mistress,' says the woman, as I goggled at it.

'By God,' says I, and sniffed it again. 'Who the blazes—'

'Name no names,' says she, and it was a well-spoken voice, for a Hindoo. 'My mistress sends it, and bids you come to the river pavilion in an hour.' And with that she salaamed again, and slipped down the steps. I called after her, and took an unsteady step, but she didn't stop, and she and her escort vanished in the dark.

Well, I'm damned, thinks I, surprise giving way to delight – she couldn't wait, by heaven . . . and of course the river pavilion at night was just the place . . . far better than the palace, where all sorts of folk were prying. Nice and secluded, very discreet – just the place for a rowdy little Rani to entertain. '*Syce*!' I shouted, and strode back inside, a trifle unsteadily, damning the champagne, but chortling as I

---

* Bearer, waiter.

† Lady.

examined my chin in the glass, decided it would do, and roared for a clean shirt.

'Now where away?' says Ilderim, who was squatting on the rug. 'Not after some trollop from the bazaar, at this time?'

'No, brother,' says I. 'Something much better than a trollop. If you could see this one you'd forswear small boys and melons for good.' By Jove, I was feeling prime; I dandied myself up in no time, rinsed my face to clear some of the booze away, and was out champing on the verandah as the *syce* brought my pony round.

'You're mad,' growls Ilderim. 'Do you go alone – where to?'

'I'm not sharing her, if that's what you mean. I'll take the *syce*.' For I wasn't too sure of the way at night, and it was pitch black. I must have been drunker than I felt, for it took me three shots to mount, and then, with a wave to Ilderim, who was glowering doubtfully from the verandah, I trotted off, with the *syce* scrambling up behind.

Now, I'll admit I was woozy, and say at the same time that I'd have gone if I'd been cold sober. I don't know when I've been pawing the ground quite so hard for a woman – probably the two weeks' spooning had worked me up, and I couldn't cover the two miles to the pavilion fast enough. Fortunately the *syce* was a handy lad, for he not only guided us but held me from tumbling out of the saddle; I don't remember much of the journey except that it lasted for ages, and then we were among trees, with the hooves padding on grass, the *syce* was shaking my arm, and there ahead was the pavilion, half-hidden by the foliage.

I didn't want the *syce* spying, so I slid down and told him to wait, and then I pushed on. In spite of the night air, the booze seemed to have increased its grip, but I navigated well

113

enough, leaning on a trunk every now and then. I surveyed the pavilion; there were dim lights on the ground floor, and in one room upstairs, and by George, there was even the sound of music on the slight breeze. I beamed into the dark – what these Indians don't know about the refinements of romping isn't worth knowing. An orchestra underneath, privacy and soft lights upstairs, and no doubt refreshments to boot – I rubbed my face and hurried forward through the garden to the outside staircase leading to the upper rooms, staggering quietly so as not to disturb the hidden musicians, who were fluting sweetly away behind the screens.

I mounted the staircase, holding on tight, and reached the little landing. There was a small passage, and a slatted door at the end, with light filtering through it. I paused, to struggle out of my loose trousers – at least I wasn't so tight that I'd been fool enough to come out in boots – took a great lusty breath, padded unsteadily forward, and felt the door give at my touch. The air was heavy with perfume as I stepped in, stumbled into a muslin curtain, swore softly as I disentangled myself, took hold of a wooden pillar for support, and gazed round into the half-gloom.

There were dim pink lamps burning, on the floor against the walls, giving just enough light to show the broad couch, shrouded in mosquito net, against the far wall. And there she was, silhouetted against the glow, sitting back among the cushions, one leg stretched out, the other with knee raised; there was a soft tinkle of bangles, and I leaned against my pillar and croaked:

'Lakshmibai? Lucky? – it's me, darling . . . *chabeli** . . . I'm here!'

* Sweetheart.

114

She turned her head, and then in one movement raised the net and slipped out, standing motionless by the couch, like a bronze statue. She was wearing bangles, all right, and a little gold girdle round her hips, and some kind of metal headdress from which a flimsy veil descended from just beneath her eyes to her chin – not another stitch. I let out an astonishing noise, and was trying to steady myself for a plunge, but she checked me with a lifted hand, slid one foot forward, crooked her arms like a nautch-dancer, and came gliding slowly towards me, swaying that splendid golden nakedness in time to the throbbing of the music beneath our feet.

I could only gape; whether it was the drink or admiration or what, I don't know, but I seemed paralysed in every limb but one. She came writhing up to me, bangles tinkling and dark eyes gleaming enormously in the soft light; I couldn't see her face for the veil, but I wasn't trying to; she retreated, turning and swaying her rump, and then approached again, reaching forward to brush me teasingly with her fingertips; I grabbed, gasping, but she slid away, faster now as the tempo of the music increased, and then back again, hissing at me through the veil, lifting those splendid breasts in her hands, and this time I had the wit to seize a tit and a buttock, fairly hooting with lust as she writhed against me and lifted the veil just enough to bring her mouth up to mine. Her right foot was slipping up the outside of my left leg, past the knee, up to the hip, and round so that her heel was in the small of my back – God knows how they do it, double joints or something – and then she was thrusting up and down like a demented monkey on a stick, raking me with her nails and giving little shrieks into my mouth, until the torchlight procession which was marching through my loins suddenly

115

exploded, she went limp in my arms, and I thought, oh Lord, now lettest thou thy servant depart in peace, as I slid gently to the floor in ecstatic exhaustion with that delightful burden clinging and quivering on top of me.

The instructors who taught dancing to young Indian royalty in those days must have been uncommon sturdy; she had just about done for me, but somehow I must have managed to crawl to the couch, for the next I knew I was there with my face cradled against those wonderful perfumed boobies – I tried feebly to go brrr! but she turned my head and lifted a cup to my lips. As if I hadn't enough on board already, but I drank greedily and sank back, gasping, and was just deciding I might live, after all, when she set about me again, lips and hands questing over my body, fondling and plaguing, writhing her hips across my groaning carcase until she was astride my thighs with her back to me, and the torchlight procession staggered into marching order once more, eventually erupting yet again with shattering effect. After which she left me in peace for a good half-hour, as near as I could judge in my intoxicated state – one thing I'm certain of, that if I'd been sober and in my right mind she could never have teased me into action a third time, as she did, by doing incredible things which I still only half-believe as I recall them. But I remember those great eyes, over the veil, and the pearl on her brow, and her perfume, and the tawny velvet skin in the half-light . . .

I came awake in an icy sweat, my limbs shivering, trying to remember where I was. There was a cold wind from somewhere out in the dark, and I turned my aching head; the pink lamps were burning, casting their shadows, but she was no longer there. Someone was, though, surely, over by the door; there was a dark figure, but it wasn't naked, for I

116

could see a white loin-cloth, and instead of the gold head-dress, there was a tight white turban. A man? And he was holding something – a stick? No, it had a strange curved head on it – and there was another man, just behind him, and even as I watched they were gliding stealthily into the room, and I saw that the second one had a cloth in his right hand.

For perhaps ten seconds I lay motionless, gazing – and then it rushed in on me that this wasn't a dream, that they were moving towards the couch, and that this was horrible, inexplicable danger. The net was gone from the couch, and I could see them clearly, the white eyes in the black faces – I braced for an instant and then hurled myself off the couch away from them, slipped, recovered, and rushed at the shutters in the screen-wall. There was a snarl from behind me, something swished in the air and thudded, and I had a glimpse of a small pick-axe quivering in the shutter as I flung myself headlong at the screen, yelling in terror. Thank God I'm fourteen stone – it came down with a splintering crash, and I was sprawling on the little verandah, thrashing my way out of the splintered tangle and heaving myself on to the verandah rail.

From the tail of my eye I saw a dark shape springing for me over the couch; there was a tree spreading its thick foliage within five feet of the verandah, and I dived straight into it, crashing and scraping through the branches, clutching vainly and taking a tremendous thump across the hips as I struck a limb. For a second I seemed suspended, and then I shot down and landed flat on my back with a shock that sickened me. I rolled over, trying to heave myself up, as two black figures dropped from the tree almost on top of me; I blundered into one of them, smashed a fist into its face, and then

117

something flicked in front of my eyes, and I only just got a hand up in time to catch the garotte as it jerked back on to my throat.

I shrieked, hauling at it; my wrist was clamped under my chin by the strangler's scarf, but my right arm was free, and as I staggered back into him I scrabbled behind me, was fortunate enough to grab a handful of essentials, and wrenched for all I was worth. He screamed in agony, the scarf slackened, and he went down, but before I could flee for the safety of the wood the other one was on my back, and he made no mistake; the scarf whipped round my windpipe, his knee was into my spine, and I was flailing helplessly with his breath hissing in my ear. Five seconds, it flashed across my mind, is all it takes for an expert garotter to kill a man – oh, Jesus, my sight was going, my head was coming off, with a horrible pain tearing in my throat, I was dying even as I fell, floating down to the turf – and then I was on my back, gasping down huge gulps of air, and the faces that were swimming in front of my eyes, glaring horribly, were merging into one – Ilderim Khan was gripping my shoulders and urging:

'Flashman! Be still! There – now lie a moment, and breathe! Inshallah! The strangler's touch is no light thing.' His strong fingers were massaging my throat as he grinned down at me. 'See what comes of lusting after loose women? A moment more, and we would have been sounding retreat over thee – so give thanks that I have a suspicious mind, and followed with my *badmashes* to see what kind of *cunchunee** it was who bade thee to her bed so mysteriously. How is it, old friend – can you stand?'

'What happened?' I mumbled, trying to rise.

---

* Dancing girl.

'Ask why, rather. Has she a jealous husband, perhaps? We saw the lights, and heard music, but presently all was still, and many came out, to a palankeen in which ladies travel, and so away. But no sign of thee, till we heard thee burst out, with these hounds of hell behind thee.' And following his nod, I saw there were two of his ruffians squatting in the shadows over two dark shapes lying on the grass – one was ominously still, but the other was gasping and wheezing, and from the way he clutched himself I imagine he was the assassin whose courting-tackle I'd tried to rearrange. One of Ilderim's *sowars* was ostentatiously cleaning his Khyber knife with a handful of leaves, and presently a third came padding out of the dark.

'The sahib's *syce* is dead yonder,' says he. 'Bitten with a tooth from Kali's mouth!'*

'What?' says Ilderim, starting up. 'Now, in God's name—' and he went quickly to the body of the dead strangler, snatching a lantern from one of his men, and peering into the dead face. I heard him exclaim, and then he beckoned me. 'Look there,' says he, and pulled down the dead man's eyelid with his finger; even in the flickering light I could see the crude tattoo on the skin.

'Thug!'[11] says Ilderim through his teeth. 'Now, Flashman, what does this mean?'

I was trying to take hold of my senses, with my head splitting and my neck feeling as though it had been through the mangle. It was a nightmare – one moment I'd been in a drunken frenzy of fornication with Lakshmibai, with a houseful of musicians beating time – and the next I was being murdered by professional stranglers – and Thugs at that. But I was too

* Stabbed with a Thug pick-axe.

119

shocked to think, so Ilderim grunted and turned to the groaning prisoner.

'This one shall tell us,' says he, and seized him by the throat. 'Look now – thou art dead already. But it can be swift, or I can trim off the appurtenances and extremities from thy foul carcase and make thee eat them. That, for a beginning. So choose – who sent thee, and why?'

The Thug snarled, and spat at him, so Ilderim says: 'Take him to the tree yonder,' and while they did he hauled out his knife, stropped it on his sole, says 'Bide here, *husoor*,' and then strode grimly after them.

I couldn't have moved, if I'd wanted to. It was a nightmare, unbelievable, but in those few minutes, while dreadful grunts and an occasional choked-off scream came out of the dark, I strove to make some sense of it. Lakshmibai had plainly left me asleep – or drunk, or drugged, or both – in the pavilion, and shortly after the Thugs had arrived. But why – why should she seek my death? It made no sense – no, by God, because if she *had* just been luring me out for assassination, she'd have had me ambushed on the way – she'd certainly not have pleasured me like a crazy spinster first. And there was no earthly reason why she should want me killed – what had I done to merit that? She'd been so friendly and straight and kind – I could have sworn she'd been falling in love with me for two weeks past. Oh, I've known crafty women, sluts who'd tickle your buttons with one hand and reach for a knife with the other – but not her. I couldn't swallow that; I wouldn't.

I could even understand her slipping out and leaving me – it had been a clandestine gallop, after all; she had a reputation to consider. What better way of concluding it than by vanishing swiftly back to the palace, leaving her partner to find his own way home – I reflected moodily that she'd probably done the same thing, countless times, in that very pavilion, whenever she felt like it. She was no novice, that was certain – no wonder her late husband had lost interest and curled up and died: the poor devil must have been worn to a shadow.

But who then had set Thugs on me? Or were they just stray, indiscriminate killers – as Thugs usually were, slaying anyone who happened in their way, for fun and religion? Had they just spotted me, out at night, and decided to chalk up another score for Kali – and then Ilderim came striding out of the dark, whipping his knife into the turf, and squatting down beside me.

'Stubborn,' says he, rubbing his beard, 'but not too stubborn. Flashman – it is ill news.' He stared at me with grave eyes. 'There is a fellowship – hunting thee. They have been out this week past – the brotherhood of deceivers, whom everyone thought dead or disbanded these years past – with orders to seek out and slay the Colonel Flashman sahib at Jhansi. That one yonder is a chief among them – six nights since he was at Firozabad, where his lodge met to hear a strange fakir who offered them gold, and –' he tapped my knee '– an end to the Raj in due time, and a rebirth of their order of *thugee*. They were to prepare against the day – and as grace before meat they were to sacrifice thee to Kali. I knew all along,' says he with a grim satisfaction, 'that this was *palitikal*, and ye walked a perilous road. Well, thou art warned in time – but it must be a fast horse to the coast, and ship across the *kala pani*,* for if these folk are riding thy tail, then this land is death to thee; there will not be a safe nook from the Deccan to the Khyber Gate.'

---

* Black water, i.e., the ocean.

121

I sat limp and trembling, taking this horror in; I was afraid to ask the question, but I had to know.

'This fakir,' I croaked. 'Who is he?'

'No one knows – except that he is from the north, a one-eyed man with a fair skin from beyond the passes. There are those who think he is a sahib, but not of thy people. He has money, and followers in secret, and he preaches against the *sahib-log** in whispers . . .'

Ignatieff – I almost threw up. So it had happened, as Pam had thought it might: the bastard was back, and had tracked me down – and devil a doubt he knew all about my mission, too, somehow – and he and his agents were spreading their poison everywhere, and seeking to revive the devilish *thugee* cult against us, with me at the top of the menu – and Ilderim was right, there wasn't a hope unless I could get out of India – but I couldn't! This was what I was meant to be here for – why Pam in his purblind folly had sent me out: to tackle Ignatieff at his own game and dispose of him. I couldn't run squealing to Bombay or Calcutta bawling 'Gangway – and a first-class ticket home, quick!' This was the moment I was meant to earn my corn – against bloody dacoits and Ruski agents? I gulped and sweated – and then another thought struck me.

Was Lakshmibai part of this? God knew she'd no cause to love the Sirkar – was she another of the spiders in this devilish web, playing Delilah for the Russians? – but no, no, even to my disordered mind one thing remained clear: she'd never have walloped the mattress with me like that if she'd been false. No, this was Ignatieff, impure and anything but simple, and I had to think as I'd never thought before, with

* Lord-people, i.e., the British.

Ilderim's eye on me while I took my head in my hands and wondered, Christ, how can I slide out this time. And then inspiration dawned, slowly – I couldn't leave India, or be seen to be running away, but I'd told Skene that if the crisis came I might well vanish from sight, locally, to go after Ignatieff in my own way – well, now I would vanish, right enough; that shouldn't be difficult. I schemed it fast, as I can when I'm truly up against it, and turned to Ilderim.

'Look, brother,' says I. 'This is a great *palitikal* affair, as you guessed. I cannot tell thee, and I cannot leave India—'

'Then thou art dead,' says he, cheerfully. 'Kali's hand will be on thee, through these messengers—' and he pointed at the dead Thug.

'Hold on,' says I, sweating. 'They're looking for Colonel Flashman – but if Colonel Flashman becomes, say – a Khyekeen pony-pedlar, or an Abizai who has done his time in the Guides or lancers, how will they find him then? I've done it before, remember? Dammit, I speak Pushtu as well as you do, and Urdu even better – wasn't I an agent with Sekundar Sahib? All I need is a safe place for a season, to lie up and sniff the wind before –' and I started lying recklessly, for effect '– before I steal out again, having made my plans, to break this one-eyed fakir and his rabble of stranglers and *loose-wallahs*. D'you see?'

'Inshallah!' cries he, grinning all over his evil face. 'It is the great game! To lie low in disguise, and watch and listen and wait, and conspire with the other *palitikal* sahibs of the Sirkar, until the time is ripe – and then go against these evil subverters in a secret *razzia*!* And when that time comes – I

---

* An attack on unbelievers.

may share the sport, and *hallal** these Hindoo and foreign swine, with my lads? – thou wouldst not forget thy old friend then?' He grabbed my hand, the bloodthirsty devil. 'Thou'd send me word, surely, when the knives are out – thy brother Ilderim?'

You'll wait a long time for it, my lad, thinks I; give me a good disguise and a pony and you'll not see me again – not until everything has safely blown over, and some other idiot has disposed of Ignatieff and his bravos. That's when I'd emerge, with a good yarn to spin to Calcutta (and Pam) about how I'd gone after him secretly, and dammit, I'd missed the blighter, bad luck. That would serve, and sound sufficiently mysterious and convincing – but for the moment my urgent need was a disguise and a hiding place at a safe distance. Some jungly or desert spot might be best; I'd lived rough that way before, and as I'd told Ilderim, I could pass as a frontiersman or Afghan with any of 'em.

'When there are Ruski throats to be cut, you'll be the first to know,' I assured him, and he embraced me, chuckling, and swearing I was the best of brothers.

The matter of disguise reminded me that I was still stark naked, and shivering; I told him I wanted a kit exactly like that of his *sowars*, and he swore I'd have it, and a pony, too.

'And you may tell Skene sahib from me,' says I, 'that the time has come – and he can start feeling sorry for the Ruskis – he'll understand.' For I wasn't going back to the cantonment; I wanted to ride out tonight, wherever I was going. 'Tell him of the one-eyed fakir, that the Thugs are abroad again, and the axles are getting hot. You may say I've had a

---

* Ritual throat-cutting.

124

brush with the enemy already – but you needn't tell him what else I was doing tonight.' I winked at him. 'Understand? Oh, aye – and if he has inquiries after me from the Rani of Jhansi, he may say I have been called away, and present my apologies.'

'The Rani?' says he, and his eye strayed towards the pavilion. 'Aye.' He coughed and grinned. 'That was some rich lady's palankeen I saw tonight, and many servants. Perchance, was it—'

"A Gilzai and a grandmother for scandal',' I quoted. 'Mind your own dam' business. And now, be a good lad, and get me that outfit and pony.'

He summoned one of his rascals, and asked if the tortured Thug was dead yet.

'Nay, but he has no more to tell,' says the other. 'For he said nothing when I—' You wouldn't wish to know what he said next. 'Shall I pass him some of his own tobacco?'[12] he added.

'Aye,' says Ilderim. 'And tell Rafik Tamwar I want all his clothes, and his knife, and his horse. Go thou.'

For answer the *sowar* nodded, took out his Khyber knife, and stepped back under the trees to where his companions were guarding the prisoner, or what was left of him. I heard him address the brute – even at that time and place it was an extraordinary enough exchange to fix itself in my mind; one of the most astonishing things I ever heard, even in India.

'It is over, deceiver,' says he. 'Here is the knife – in the throat or the heart? Choose.'

The Thug's reply was hoarse with agony. 'In the heart, then – quickly!'

'You're sure? As you wish.'

125

'No – wait!' gasps the Thug. 'Put the point . . . behind . . . my ear – so. Thrust hard – thus I will bleed less, and go undisfigured. Now!'

There was a pause, and then the *sowar*'s voice says: 'He was right – he bleeds hardly at all. Trust a deceiver to know.'

A few moments later and Rafik Tamwar appeared, grumbling, in a rag of loin-cloth, with his clothes over his arm, and leading a neat little pony. I told Ilderim that Skene sahib must see his kit replaced, and he could have my own Pegu pony, at which the good Tamwar grinned through his beard, and said he would willingly make such an exchange every day. I slipped into his shirt and cavalry breeches, drew on the soft boots, donned his hairy *poshteen*,* stuck the Khyber cleaver in my sash, and was winding the *puggaree* round my head and wishing I had a revolver as well, when Ilderim says thoughtfully:

'Where wilt thou go, Flashman – have ye an eyrie to wait in where no enemy can find thee?'

I confessed I hadn't, and asked if he had any suggestions, at which he frowned thoughtfully, and then smiled, and then roared with laughter, and rolled on his back, and then stood up, peering and grinning at me.

'Some juice for thy skin,' says he. 'Aye, and when thy beard has grown, thou'lt be a rare Peshawar ruffler – so ye swagger enough, and curl thy hair round thy finger, and spit from the back of thy throat—'

'I know all about that,' says I, impatiently. 'Where d'you suggest I do all these things?'

'In the last place any ill-willer would ever look for a British colonel sahib,' says he, chortling. 'Look now – wouldst thou

---

* Sheepskin coat.

126

live easy for a spell, and eat full, and grow fat, what time thou art preparing to play the game against these enemies of the Raj? Aye, and get well paid for it – 24 rupees a month, and *batta** also?' He slapped his hands together at my astonishment. 'Why not – join the Sirkar's army! What a recruit for the native cavalry – why, given a month they'll make thee a *daffadar*!'† He stuck his tongue in his cheek. 'Maybe a *rissaldar* in time – who knows?'

'Are you mad?' says I. 'Me – enlist as a *sowar*? And how the devil d'you expect me to get away with that?'

'What hinders? Thou hast passed in Kabul bazaar before today, and along the Kandahar road. Stain thy face, as I said, and grow thy beard, and thou'lt be the properest Sirkar's bargain in India! Does it not meet thy need – and will it not place thee close to affairs – within reach of thine own folk, and ready to move at a finger-snap?'

It was ridiculous – and yet the more I thought of it, the more obvious it was. How long did I want to hide – a month? Two or three perhaps? I would have to live, and for the life of me I couldn't think of a more discreet and comfortable hiding place than the ranks of a native cavalry regiment – I had all the qualifications and experience . . . if I was careful. But I'd have to be that, whatever I did. I stood considering while Ilderim urged me, full of enthusiasm.

'See now – there is my mother's cousin, Gulam Beg, who was *malik*‡ in one of my father's villages, and is now

---

* Field allowance.

† Cavalry commander of ten.

‡ Headman.

woordy-major* in the 3rd Cavalry at Meerut garrison. If thou goest to him, and say Ilderim sent thee, will he not be glad of such a fine sturdy trooper – ye may touch the hilt, and eat the salt, and belike he'll forget the *assami*† for my sake. Let me see, now,' says this mad rascal, chuckling as he warmed to his work, 'thou art a Yusufzai Pathan of the Peshawar Valley – no, no, better still, we'll have thee a Hasanzai of the Black Mountain – they are a strange folk, touched, and given to wild fits, so much may be excused thee. Oh, it is rare! Thou art – Makarram Khan, late of the Peshawar police, and so familiar with the ways of the sahibs; thou hast skirmished along the line, too. Never fear, there *was* a Makarram Khan,[13] until I shot him on my last furlough; he will give thee a *shabash*‡ from hell, for he was a stout rider in his time. Careless, though – or he'd have watched the rocks as he rode. Well, Makarram –' says he, grinning like a wolf in the gloom '– wilt thou carry a lance for the Sirkar?'

I'd been determining even as he talked; I was in the greatest fix, and there was no other choice. If I'd known what it would lead to, I'd have damned Ilderim's notion to his teeth, but it seemed inspired at the time.

'Bind thy *puggaree* round thy jaw at night, lest thou babble in English in thy sleep,' says he at parting. 'Be sullen, and speak little – and be a good soldier, blood-brother, for the credit of Ilderim Khan.' He laughed and slapped my saddle as we shook hands in the dark under the trees. 'When thou

---

* Native adjutant of Indian irregular cavalry. (Since the 3rd were not irregulars, Flashman seems to have misused the term here.)
† In this sense, a deposit paid by a recruit on enlistment.
‡ Hurrah, bravo.

comest this way again, go to Bull Temple, beyond the Jokan Bagh – I will have a man waiting for an hour at sunrise and sunset. Salaam, *sowar*!' cries he, and saluted, and I dug my heels into my pony and cantered off in the dawn, still like a man in a wild dream.

You might think it impossible for a white man to pass himself off as a native soldier in John Company's army, and indeed I doubt if anyone else has ever done it. But when you've been called on to play as many parts as I have, it's a bagatelle. Why, I've been a Danish prince, a Texas slave-dealer, an Arab sheik, a Cheyenne Dog Soldier, and a Yankee navy lieutenant in my time, among other things, and none of 'em was as hard to sustain as my lifetime's impersonation of a British officer and gentleman. The truth is we all live under false pretences much of the time; you just have to put on a bold front and brazen it through.

I'll admit my gift of languages has been my greatest asset, and I suppose I'm a pretty fair actor; anyway, I'd carried off the role of an Asian-Afghan nigger often enough, and before I was more than a day's ride on the way to Meerut I was thoroughly back in the part, singing Kabuli bazaar songs through my nose, sneering sideways at anyone I passed, and answering greetings with a grunt or a snarl. I had to keep my chin and mouth covered for the first three days, until my beard had sprouted to a disreputable stubble; apart from that, I needed no disguise, for I was dark and dirty-looking enough to start with. By the time I struck the Grand Trunk my own mother wouldn't have recognised the big, hairy Border ruffian jogging along so raffishly with his boots out of his stirrups, and his love-lock curling out under his *puggaree*; on the seventh day, when I cursed and shoved my pony through the crowded streets of Meerut city, spurning the rabble aside as a good Hasanzai should, I was even *thinking* in Pushtu, and if you'd offered me a seven-course dinner at the Café Royal I'd have turned it down for mutton-and-rice stew with boiled dates to follow.

My only anxiety was Ilderim's cousin, Gulam Beg, whom I had to seek out in the native cavalry lines beyond the city; he would be sure to run a sharp eye over a new recruit, and if he spotted anything queer about me I'd have a hard job keeping up the imposture. Indeed, at the last minute my nerve slackened a little, and I rode about for a couple of hours before I plucked up the courage to go and see him – I rode on past the native infantry lines, and over the Nullah Bridge up to the Mall in the British town; it was while I was sitting my pony, brooding under the trees, that a dog-cart with two English children and their mother went by, and one of the brats squealed with excitement and said I looked just like Ali Baba and the Forty Thieves. That cheered me up, for some reason – anyway, I had to have a place to eat and sleep while I shirked my duty, so I finally presented myself at the headquarters of the 3rd Native Light Cavalry, and demanded to see the *woordy-major*.

I needn't have worried. Gulam Beg was a stout, white-whiskered old cove with silver-rimmed spectacles on the end of his nose, and when I announced that Ilderim Khan of

Mogala was my sponsor he was all over me. Hasanzai, was I, and late of the *polis*? That was good – I had the look of an able man, yes – doubtless the Colonel Sahib would look favourably on such a fine upstanding recruit. I had seen no military service, though? – hm . . . he looked at me quizzically, and I tried to slouch a bit more.

'Not in the Guides, perhaps?' says he, with his head on one side. 'Or the *cutch*-cavalry? No? Then doubtless it is by chance that you stand the regulation three paces from my table, and clench your hand with the thumb forward – and that the pony I see out yonder is girthed and bridled like one of ours.' He chuckled playfully. 'A man's past in his own affair, Makarram Khan – what should it profit us to pry and discover that a new "recruit" had once quit the Sirkar's service over some small matter of feud or blood-letting, eh? You come from Ilderim – it is enough. Be ready to see the Colonel Sahib at noon.'

He'd spotted me for an old soldier, you see, which was all to the good; having detected me in a small deception, it never occurred to him to look for a large one. And he must have passed on his conclusion to the Colonel, for when I made my *salaam* to that worthy officer on the orderly-room verandah, he looked me up and down and says to the *woordy-major* in English:

'Shouldn't wonder if you weren't right, Gulam Beg – he's heard 'Boots and Saddles' before, that's plain. Probably got bored with garrison work and slipped off one night with half a dozen rifles on his back. And now, having cut the wrong throat or lifted the wrong herd, he's come well south to avoid retribution.' He sat back, fingering the big white moustache which covered most of his crimson face. 'Ugly-looking devil, ain't he though? Hasanzai of the Black

132

Mountain, eh? – yes, that's what I'd have thought. Very good . . .' He frowned at me and then said, very carefully:

'*Company cavalry apka mangta?*' which abomination of bad Urdu I took to mean: did I want to join the Company cavalry? So I showed my teeth and says: '*Han*, sahib,' and thought I might as well act out my part by betraying some more military knowledge – I ducked my head and leaned over and offered him the hilt of my sheathed Khyber knife, at which he burst out laughing and touched it,[14] saying that Gulam Beg was undoubtedly right, and I wasn't half knowledgeable for a chap who pretended never to have been in the Army before. He gave instructions for me to be sworn in, and I took the oath on the sabre-blade, ate a pinch of salt, and was informed that I was now a skirmisher of the 3rd Native Light Cavalry, that my *daffadar* was Kudrat Ali, that I would be paid one rupee per day, with a quarter-anna dyeing allowance, and that since I had brought my own horse I would be excused the customary recruit deposit. Also that if I was half as much a soldier as the Colonel suspected, and kept my hands off other people's throats and property, I might expect promotion in due course.

Thereafter I was issued with a new *puggaree*, half-boots and *pyjamy* breeches, a new and very smart silver-grey uniform coat, a regulation sabre, a belt and bandolier, and a tangle of saddlery which was old and stiff enough to have been used at Waterloo (and probably had), and informed by a betel-chewing *havildar* that if I didn't have it reduced to gleaming suppleness by next morning, I had best look out. Finally, he took me to the armoury, and I was shown (mark this well) a new rifled Enfield musket, serial number 4413 – some things a soldier never forgets – which I was informed was mine henceforth, and more precious than my own mangy carcase.

Without thinking, I picked it up and tested the action, as I'd done a score of times at Woolwich – and the Goanese store-wallah gaped.

'Who taught you that?' says he. 'And who bade you handle it, *jangli* pig? It is for you to see – you touch it only when it is issued on parade.' And he snatched it back from me. I thought another touch of character would do no harm, so I waited till he had waddled away to replace it in the rack, and then whipped out my Khyber knife and let it fly, intending to plant it in the wall a foot or so away from him. My aim was off though – the knife imbedded itself in the wall all right, but it nicked his arm in passing, and he squealed and rolled on the floor, clutching at his blood-smeared sleeve.

'Bring the knife back,' I snarled, baring my fangs at him, and when he had scrambled up, grey-faced and terrified, and returned it, I touched the point on his chest and says: 'Call Makarram Khan a pig just once more, *ulla kabaja*,* and I will carry thine eyes and genitals on this point as kebabs.' Then I made him lick the blood off the blade, spat in his face, and respectfully asked the *havildar* what I should do next. He, being a Mussulman, was all for me, and said, grinning, that I should make a fair recruit; he told my *daffadar*, Kudrat Ali, about the incident, and presently the word went round the big, airy barrack-room that Makarram Khan was a genuine saddle-and-lance man, from up yonder, who would strike first and inquire after – doubtless a Border lifter, and a feud-carrier, but a man who knew how to treat Hindoo insolence, and therefore to be properly respected.

So there I was – Colonel Harry Paget Flashman, late of the 11th Hussars, 17th Lancers and the Staff, former aide

---

* Son of an owl.

to the Commander-in-Chief, and now acting-*sowar* and rear file in the skirmishing squadron, 3rd Cavalry, Bengal Army, and if you think it was a mad-brained train of circumstance that had taken me there – well, so did I. But once I had got over the unreality of it all, and stopped imagining that everyone was going to see through my disguise, I settled in comfortably enough.

It was an eerie feeling, though, at first, to squat on my *charpai** against the wall, with my *puggaree* off, combing my hair or oiling my light harness, and look round that room at the brown, half-naked figures, laughing and chattering – of all the things that soldiers talk about, women, and officers, and barrack gossip, and women, and rations, and women – but in a foreign tongue which, although I spoke it perfectly and even with a genuine frontier accent, was still not my own. While I'd been by myself, as I say, I'd even been thinking in Pushtu, but here I had to hold on tight and remember what I was meant to be – for one thing, I wasn't used to being addressed in familiar terms by native soldiers, much less ordered about by an officious *naik*† who'd normally have leaped to attention if I'd so much as looked in his direction. When the man who bunked next to me, Pir Ali, a jolly rascal of a Baluch, tapped my shoulder in suggesting that we might visit the bazaar that first evening, I absolutely stared at him and just managed to bite back that 'Damn your impudence' that sprang to my tongue.

It wasn't easy, for a while; quite apart from remembering obeisances at the prescribed times, and making a show at

---

* Cot.
† Corporal.

cooking my own dinner at the *choola*,* there were a thousand tiny details to beware of – I must remember not to cross my legs when sitting, or blow my nose like a European, or say 'Mmh?' if someone said something I couldn't catch, or use the wrong hand, or clear my throat in the discreet British fashion, or do any of the things that would have looked damned odd in an Afghan frontiersman.[15]

Of course I made mistakes – once or twice I was just plain ignorant of things that I ought to have known, like how to chew a *majoon*† when Pir Ali offered me one (you have to spit into your hand from time to time, or you'll end up poisoned), or how to cut a sheep-tail for curry, or even how to sharpen my knife in the approved fashion. When I blundered, and anyone noticed, I found the best way was to stare them down and growl sullenly.

But more often than not my danger lay in betraying knowledge which Makarram Khan simply wouldn't have had. For example, when Kudrat Ali was giving us sword exercise I found myself once falling into the 'rest' position of a German schlager-fencer (not that anyone in India was likely to recognise that), and again, daydreaming about fagging days at Rugby while cleaning my boots one evening, I found myself humming 'Widdicombe Fair' – fortunately under my breath. My worst blunder, though, was when I was walking near a spot where the British officers were playing cricket, and the ball came skipping towards me – without so much as thinking I snapped it up, and was looking to throw down the wicket when I remembered, and threw it back as clumsily as I could. Once or two of them stared, though, and I heard someone

---

* Cooking-place, camp oven of clay.
† Green sweetmeat containing *bhang*.

say that big nigger was a deuced smart field. That rattled me, and I trod even more carefully than before.

My best plan, I soon discovered, was to do and say as little as possible, and act the surly, reserved hillman who walked by himself, and whom it was safest not to disturb. The fact that I was by way of being a protégé of the *woordy-major*'s, and a Hasanzai (and therefore supposedly eccentric), led to my being treated with a certain deference; my imposing size and formidable looks did the rest, and I was left pretty much alone. Once or twice I walked out with Pir Ali, to lounge in the Old Market and ogle the bints, or dally with them in the boutique doorways, but he found my grunts a poor return for his own cheery prattle, and abandoned me to my own devices.

It wasn't, as you can guess, the liveliest life for me at first – but I only had to think of the alternative to resign myself to it for the present. It was easy enough soldiering, and I quickly won golden opinions from my *naik* and *jemadar*** for the speed and intelligence with which I appeared to learn my duties. At first it was a novelty, drilling, working, eating, and sleeping with thirty Indian troopers – rather like being on the other side of the bars of a monkey zoo – but when you're closed into a world whose four corners are the barrack-room, the *choola*, the stables, and the maidan, it can become maddening to have to endure the society of an inferior and foreign race with whom you've no more in common than if they were Russian *moujiks* or Irish bog-trotters. What makes it ten times worse is the outcast feeling that comes of knowing that within a mile or two your own kind are enjoying all the home comforts, damn 'em – drinking *barra* pegs, smoking

---

* Under-officer.

decent cigars, flirting and ramming with white women, and eating ices for dessert. (I was no longer so enamoured of mutton *pilau* in *ghee*,* you gather.) Within a fortnight I'd have given anything to join an English conversation again, instead of listening to Pir Ali giggling about how he'd bullocked the headman's wife on his last leave, or the endless details of Sita Gopal's uncle's law-suit, or Ram Mangal's reviling of the *havildar*, or Gobinda Dal's whining about how he and his brothers, being soldiers, had lost much of the petty local influence they'd formerly enjoyed in their Oudh village, now that the Sirkar had taken over.

When it got too bad I would loaf up to the Mall, and gape at the mem-sahibs with their big hats and parasols, driving by, and watch the officers cantering past, flicking their crops as I clumped my big boots and saluted, or squat near the church to listen to them singing 'Greenland's Icy Mountains' of a Sunday evening. Dammit, I missed my own folk then – far worse than if they'd been a hundred miles away. I missed Lakshmibai, too – odd, ain't it, but I think what riled me most was the knowledge that if she'd seen me as I now was – well, she wouldn't even have noticed me. However, it had to be stuck out – I just had to think of Ignatieff – so I would trudge back to barracks and lie glowering while the *sowars* chattered. It had this value – I learned more about Indian soldiers in three weeks than I'd have done in a lifetime's ordinary service.

You'll think I'm being clever afterwards, but I soon realised that all wasn't as well with them as I'd have thought at first sight. They were Northern Muslims, mostly, with a sprinkling of high-caste Oudh Hindoos – the practice of separating

---

* Native butter, cooking-fat.

the races in different companies or troops hadn't come in then. Good soldiers, too; the 3rd had distinguished itself in the last Sikh War, and a few had frontier service. But they weren't happy – smart as you'd wish on parade, but in the evening they would sit about and croak like hell – as first I thought it was just the usual military sore-headedness, but it wasn't.

At first all I heard was vague allusions, which I didn't inquire about for fear of betraying a suspicious ignorance – they talked a deal about one of the padres in the garrison, Reynolds sahib, and how Colonel Carmik-al-Ismeet (that was the 3rd's commander, Carmichael-Smith) ought to keep him off the post, and there was a fairly general repeated croak about polluted flour, and the Enlistment Act, but I didn't pay much heed until one night, I remember, an Oudh *sowar* came back from the bazaar in a tremendous taking. I don't even remember his name, but what had happened was that he'd been taking part in a wrestling match with some local worthy, and before he'd got his shirt back on afterwards, some British troopers from the Dragoon Guards who were there at the time had playfully snapped the sacred cord which he wore over his shoulder next the skin – as his kind of Hindoos did.

'*Banchuts*!* Scum!' He was actually weeping with rage. 'It is defiled – I am unclean!' And for all that his mates tried to cheer him up, saying he could get a new one, blessed by a holy man, he went on raving – they take these things very seriously, you know, like Jews and Muslims with pork. If it seems foolish to you, you may compare it with how you'd feel if a nigger pissed in the font at your own church.

* A highly offensive term.

'I shall go to the Colonel sahib!' says he finally, and one of the Hindoos, Gobinda Dal, sneered:

'Why should he care – the man who will defile our *atta**
will not rebuke an English soldier for this!'

'What's all this about the *atta*?' says I to Pir Ali, and he shrugged.

'The Hindoos say that the sahibs are grinding cow bones into the sepoys' flour to break their caste. For me, they can break any Hindoo's stupid caste and welcome.'

'Why should they do that?' says I, and Sita Gopal, who overheard, spat and says:

'Where have you lived, Hasanzai? The Sirkar will break every man's caste – aye, and what passes for caste even among you Muslims: there are pig bones in the *atta*, too, in case you didn't know it. *Naik* Shere Afzul in the second troop told me; did he not see them ground at the sahibs' factory at Cawnpore?'

'Wind from a monkey's backside,' says I. 'What would it profit the sahibs to pollute your food – since when do they hate their soldiers?'

To my astonishment about half a dozen of them scoffed aloud at this – 'Listen to the Black Mountain *munshi*!'† 'The sahibs love their soldiers – and so the *gora*-cavalry broke Lal's string for him tonight!' 'Have you never heard of the Dum-Dum sweeper, Makarram Khan?' and so on. Ram Mangal, who was the noisiest croaker of them all, spat out:

'It is of a piece with the padre sahib's talk, and the new regulation that will send men across the *kala pani* – they will break our caste to make us Christians! Do they not know

---

* Flour.
† Teacher.

this even where you come from, hillman? Why, it is the talk of the army!'

I growled that I didn't put any faith in latrine-gossip – especially if the latrine was a Hindoo one, and at this one of the older men, Sardul something-or-other, shook his head and says gravely:

'It was no latrine-rumour, Makarram Khan, that came out of Dum-Dum arsenal.' And for the first time I heard the astonishing tale that was, I discovered, accepted as gospel by every sepoy in the Bengal army – of the sweeper at Dum-Dum who'd asked a caste sepoy for a drink from his dish, and on being refused, had told the sepoy that he needn't be so dam' particular because the sahibs were going to do away with caste by defiling every soldier in the army by greasing their cartridges with cow and pig fat.

'This thing is known,' says old Sardul, positively, and he was the kind of old soldier that men listen to, thirty years' service, Aliwal medal, and clean conduct sheet, damn your eyes. 'Is not the new Enfield musket in the armoury? Are not the new greased cartridges being prepared? How can any man keep his religion?'

'They say that at Benares the *jawans* have been permitted to grease their own loads,' says Pir Ali,[16] but they hooted him down.

'They say!' cries Ram Mangal. 'It is like the tale they put about that all the grease was mutton-fat – if that were so, where is the need for anyone to make his own grease? It is a lie – just as the Enlistment Act is a lie, when they said it was a provision only, and no one would be asked to do foreign service. Ask the 19th at Behrampore – where their officers told them they must serve in Burma if they refused the cartridge when it was issued! Aye, but they will refuse – then

141

we'll see!' He waved his hands in passion. 'The polluted *atta* is another link in the chain – like the preaching of that owl Reynolds sahib with his Jesus-talk, which Carmik-al-Ismeet permits to our offence. He *wants* to put us to shame!'

'It is true enough,' says old Sardul, sadly. 'Yet I would not believe it if such a sahib as my old Colonel MacGregor – did he not take a bullet meant for me at Kandahar? – were to look in my eye and say it was false. The pity is that Carmik-al-Ismeet is not such a sahib – there are none such nowadays,' says he with morbid satisfaction, 'and the Army is but a poor ruin of what it was. You do not know today what officers were – if you had seen Sale sahib or Larrinsh* sahib or Cotton sahib, you would have seen men!' (Since he'd served in Afghanistan I'd hoped he would mention Iflass-man sahib, but he didn't, the croaking old bastard.) 'They would have died before they would have put dishonour on their sepoys; their children, they used to call us, and we would have followed them to hell! But now,' he wagged his head again, 'these are *cutch*-sahibs, not *pakka*-sahibs – and the English common soldiers are no better. Why, in my young day, an English trooper would call me brother, give me his hand, offer me his water-bottle (not realising that I could not take it, you understand). And now – these common men spit on us, call us monkeys and *hubshis* – and break Lal's string!'

Most of their talk was just patent rubbish, of course, and I'd no doubt it was the work of agitators, spreading disaffection with their nonsense about greased cartridges and polluted food. I almost said so, but decided it would be unwise to draw attention to myself – and anyway it wasn't such a burning

---

* 'Lawrence' – any one of the famous Lawrence brothers who served on the frontier, and later in the Mutiny.

topic of conversation most of the time that one could take it seriously. I knew they put tremendous store by their religion – the Hindoos especially – and I supposed that whenever an incident like Lal's string stirred them up, all the old grievances came out, and were soon forgotten. But I'll confess that what Sardul had said about the British officers and troops reminded me of John Nicholson's misgivings. I had hardly seen a British officer on parade since my enlistment; they seemed content to leave their troops to the *jemadars* and n.c.o.s – Addiscombe[17] tripe, of course – and there was no question the British rankers in the Meerut garrison were a poorer type than, say, the 44th whom I'd known in the old Afghan days, or Campbell's Highlanders.

I got first-hand evidence of this a day or two later, when I accidentally jostled a Dragoon in the bazaar, and the brute turned straight round and lashed out with his boot.

'Aht the way, yer black bastard!' says he. 'Think yer can shove a sahib arahnd – *banchut*!' And he would have taken a swipe at me with his fist, too, but I just put my hand on my knife-hilt and glared at him – it wouldn't have been prudent to do more. 'Christ!' says he, and took to his heels until he got to the end of the street, where he snatched up a stone and flung it at me – it smashed a plate on a booth nearby – and then made off. I'll remember you, my lad, thinks I, and the day'll come when I'll have you triced up and flogged to ribbons. (And I did, as good luck had it.) I've never been so wild – that the scum of a Whitechapel gutter should take his boot to *me*! I'll be honest and say that if I'd seen him do it to a native two months earlier I wouldn't have minded a bit – and still wouldn't, much: it's a nigger's lot to be kicked. But it ain't mine, and I can't tell you how I felt afterwards – filthy, in a way, because I hadn't been able to pay the swine back. That's by the way; the point is that old Sardul was right. There wasn't the respect for *jawans* among the British that there had been in my young day; we probably lashed and kicked niggers just as much (I know I did), but there was a higher regard for the sepoys at least, on the whole.

I doubt if any commander in the old days would have done what Carmichael-Smith did in the way of preaching-parades, either. I hadn't believed it in the barrack gossip, but sure enough, the next Sunday this coffin-faced Anglican *fakir*, the Rev. Reynolds, had a muster on the maidan, and we had to listen to him expounding the Parable of the Prodigal Son, if you please. He did it through a brazen-lunged *rissaldar* who interpreted for him, and you never heard the like. Reynolds lined it out in English, from the Bible, and the *rissaldar* stood there with his staff under his arm, at attention, with his whiskers bristling, bawling his own translation:

'There was a *zamindar*,* with two sons. He was a mad *zamindar*, for while he yet lived he gave to the younger his portion of the inheritance. Doubtless he raised it from a moneylender. And the younger spent it all whoring in the bazaar, and drinking *sherab*.† And when his money was gone he returned home, and his father ran to meet him, for he was pleased – God alone knows why. And in his foolishness, the father slew his only cow – he was evidently not a Hindoo – and they feasted on it. And the older son, who had been dutiful and stayed at home, was jealous, I cannot tell for what reason, unless the cow was to have been part of his inheritance. But his father, who did not like him, rebuked the older son. This story was told by Jesus the Jew, and if you believe

---

* Farmer.
† Strong drink.

it you will not go to Paradise, but instead will sit on the right-hand side of the English Lord God Sahib who lives in Calcutta. And there you will play musical instruments, by order of the Sirkar. Parade – dismiss!'

I don't know when I've been more embarrassed on behalf of my church and country. I'm as religious as the next man – which is to say I'll keep in with the local parson for form's sake and read the lessons on feast-days because my tenants expect it, but I've never been fool enough to confuse religion with belief in God. That's where so many clergymen, like the unspeakable Reynolds, go wrong – and it makes 'em arrogant, and totally blind to the harm they may be doing. This idiot was so drunk with testaments that he couldn't conceive how ill-mannered and offensive he was making himself look; I suppose he thought of high-caste Hindoos as being like wilful children or drunken costermongers – perverse and misguided, but ripe for salvation if he just pointed 'em the way. He stood there, with his unctuous fat face and piggy eyes, blessing us soapily, while the Muslims, being worldly in their worship, tried not to laugh, and the Hindoos fairly seethed. I'd have found it amusing enough, I daresay, if I hadn't been irritated by the thought that these irresponsible Christian zealots were only making things harder for the Army and Company, who had important work to do. It was all so foolish and unnecessary – the heathen creeds, for all their nonsensical mumbo-jumbo, were as good as any for keeping the rabble in order, and what else is religion for?

In any event, this misguided attempt to cure Hindoo souls took place, not just at Meerut but elsewhere, according to the religious intoxication of the local commanders, and in my opinion was the most important cause of the mischief that followed.[18] I didn't appreciate this at the time – and couldn't have done anything if I had. Besides, I had more important matters to engage my attention.

A few days after that parade, there was a gymkhana on the maidan, and I rode for the skirmishers in the *nezabazi*.* Apart from languages and fornication, horsemanship is my only accomplishment, and I'd been well-grounded in tent-pegging by the late Muhammed Iqbal, so it was no surprise that I took the greatest number of pegs, and would have got even more if I'd had a pony that I knew, and my lance hadn't snapped in a touch peg on the last round. It was enough to take the cup, though, and old Bloody Bill Hewitt, the garrison commander, slipped the handle over my broken lance-point in front of the marquee where all the top numbers of Meerut society were sitting applauding politely, the ladies in their crinolines and the men behind their chairs.

'*Shabash, sowar*,' says Bloody Bill. 'Where did you learn to manage a lance?'

'Peshawar Valley, *hussor*,' says I.

'Company cavalry?' says he, and I said no, Peshawar police.

'Didn't know they was lancers,' says he, and Carmichael-Smith, who was on hand, laughed and said to Hewitt in English:

'No more they are, sir. It's a rather delicate matter, I suspect – this bird here pretends he's never served the Sirkar before, but he's got Guide written all over him. Shouldn't wonder if he wasn't *rissaldar* – *havildar* at least. But we don't ask embarrassing questions, what? He's a dam' good recruit, anyway.'

'Ah,' says Hewitt, grinning; he was a fat, kindly old buffer. ''Nough said, then.' And I was in the act of saluting when a little puff of wind sprang up, scattering the papers which

---

* Tent-pegging with a lance.

146

were on the table behind him, and blowing them under the pony's hooves. Like a good little toady, I slipped out of the saddle and gathered them up, and without thinking set them on the table and put the ink-pot on top of them, to hold them steady – a simple, ordinary thing, but I heard an exclamation, and looked up to see Duff Mason, one of the infantry colonels, staring at me in surprise. I just salaamed and saluted and was back in my saddle in a second, while they called up the next man for his prize, but as I wheeled my pony away I saw that Mason was looking after me with a puzzled smile on his face, and saying something to the officer next to him.

Hollo, thinks I, has he spotted something? But I couldn't think I'd done anything to give myself away – until next morning, when the *rissaldar* called me out of the ranks, and told me to report to Mason's office in the British lines forthwith. I went with my heart in my mouth, wondering what the hell I was going to do if he had seen through my disguise, only to find it was the last thing my guilty conscience might have suspected.

'Makarram Khan, isn't it?' says Mason, when I stood to attention on his verandah and went through the ritual of hilt-touching. He was a tall, brisk, wiry fellow with a sharp eye which he cast over me. 'Hasanzai, Peshawar policeman – but only a few weeks' Army service?' He spoke good Urdu, which suggested he was smarter than most, and my innards quaked.

'Well, now, Makarram,' says he, pleasantly. 'I don't believe you. Nor does your own Colonel. You're an old soldier – you ride like one, you stand like one, and what's more you've held command. Don't interrupt – no one's trying to trap you, or find out how many throats you've cut in the Khyber country in your time: that's nothing to me. You're here now, as an ordinary *sowar* – but a sowar who gathers up papers as though he's as used to handling 'em as I am. Unusual, in a Pathan – even one who's seen service, don't you agree?'

'In the police, husoor,' says I woodenly, 'are many *kitabs**
and papers.'

'To be sure there are,' says he, and then added, ever so easily, in English, 'What's that on your right hand?'

I didn't look, but I couldn't help my hand jerking, and he chuckled and leaned back in his chair, pleased with himself.

'I guessed you understood English when the commander and your Colonel were talking in front of you yesterday,' says he. 'You couldn't keep it out of your eyes. Well, never mind; it's all to the good. But see here, Makarram Khan – whatever you've done, whatever you've been, where's the sense in burying yourself in the ranks of a native cavalry *pultan*?† You've got education and experience; why not use 'em? How long will it take you to make *subedar*,‡ or *havildar* even, in your present situation? Twenty years, thirty – with down-country cavalry? I'll tell you what – you can do better than that.'

Well, it was a relief to know my disguise was safe enough, but the last thing I wanted was to be singled out in any way. However, I listened respectfully, and he went on:

'I had a Pathan orderly, Ayub Jan; first-class man, with me ten years, and now he's gone back home, to inherit. I need someone else – well, you're younger than he was, and a sight smarter, or I'm no judge. And he wasn't a common orderly

---

* Books.
† Regiment.
‡ Native officer.

148

– never did a menial task, or anything of that order; wouldn't have asked him to, for he was Yusufzai – and a gentleman, as I believe you are, d'you see?' He looked at me very steady, smiling. 'So what I want is a man of affairs who is also a man of his hands – someone I can trust as a soldier, messenger, steward, aide, guide, shield-on-shoulder—' He shrugged. 'When I saw you yesterday, I thought "That's the kind of man." Well – what d'ye say?'

I had to think quickly about this. If I could have looked at myself in the mirror, I suppose I was just the sort of ruffian I'd have picked myself, in Duff Mason's shoes. Pathans make the best orderly-bodyguards-comrades there are, as I'd discovered with Muhammad Iqbal and Ilderim. And it would be a pleasant change from barracks – but it was risky. It would draw attention to me; on the other hand my character was established by now, and any lapses into Englishness might be explained from the past which Mason and Carmichael-Smith had wished upon me. I hesitated, and he said quietly:

'If you're thinking that coming out of the ranks may expose you to greater danger of – being recognised by the police, say, or some inconvenient acquaintance from the past . . . have no fear of that. At need, there'll always be a fast horse and a *dustuck** to see you back to the Black Mountain again.'

It was ironic – he thought I went in fear of discovery as a deserter or Border raider, when my only anxiety was that I'd be unmasked as a British officer. Bit of a lark, really – and on that thought I said very good, I'd accept his offer.

'Thank you, Makarram Khan,' says he, and nodded to a table that was set behind his chair, against the chick: there was a drawn sabre lying on it, and I knew what was expected

---

* Permit.

of me. I went past him, and put my hand on the blade – it had been so arranged that with my body in between, he couldn't see from where he sat whether I was touching the steel or not. The old dodge, thinks I, but I said aloud:

'On the haft and hilt, I am thy man and soldier.'

'Good,' says he, and as I turned he held out his hand. I took it, and just for devilment I said:

'Have no fear, *husoor* – you will smell the onion on your fingers.' I knew, you see, that in anticipation of the oath, he would have rubbed onion on the blade, so that he could tell afterwards if I'd truly touched it while I swore. A Pathan who intended to break his oath wouldn't have put his hand on the steel, and consequently wouldn't have got the onion-smell on his fingers.

'By Jove!' says he, and quickly sniffed his hand. Then he laughed, and said I was a Pathan for wiliness, all right, and we would get along famously.

Which I'm bound to say we did – mind you, our association wasn't a long one, but while it lasted I thoroughly enjoyed myself, playing major-domo in his household, for that's what it amounted to, as I soon discovered. His bungalow was a pretty big establishment, you see, just off the east end of the Mall, near the British infantry lines, with about thirty servants, and since there was no proper mem-sahib, and his *khansamah** was almost senile, there was no order about the place at all. Rather than have me spend my time dogging him about his office, where there wasn't much for me to do except stand looking grim and impressive, Duff Mason decided I should make a beginning by putting his house and its staff into *pukka* order (as I gathered Ayub Jan had done

* Butler.

in his time) and I set about it. Flashy, Jack-of-all-trades, you see: in the space of a few months I'd already been a gentleman of leisure, staff officer, secret political agent, ambassador, and sepoy, so why not a nigger butler for a change?

You may think it odd – and looking back it seems damned queer to me, too – but the job was just nuts to me. I was leading such an unreal existence, anyway, and had become so devilish bored in the sepoy barracks, that I suppose I was ready enough for anything that occupied my time without too much effort. Duff Mason's employ was just the ticket: it gave me the run of a splendid establishment, the best of meat and drink, a snug little bunk of my own, and nothing to do but bully menials, which I did with a hearty relish that terrified the brutes and made the place run like clockwork. All round, I couldn't have picked a softer billet for my enforced sojourn in Meerut if I'd tried. (Between ourselves, I've a notion that had I been born in a lower station in life I'd have made a damned fine butler for some club or Town house, yes-me-lording the Quality, ordering flunkeys about, putting upstarts in their place, and pinching the port and cigars with the best of them.)

I've said there were no proper mem-sahibs in the house, by which I mean that there was no colonel's lady to supervise it – hence the need for me. But in fact there were two white women there, both useless in management – Miss Blanche, a thin, twitchy little spinster who was Duff Mason's sister, and Mrs Leslie, a vague relative who was either a grass widow or a real one, and reminded me rather of a sailor's whore – she was a plumpish, pale-skinned woman with red frizzy hair and a roving eye for the garrison officers, with whom she went riding and flirting when she wasn't lolling on the verandah eating sweets. (I didn't do more than run a brisk eye over either of 'em when Duff Mason brought me to the house, by the way – we nigger underlings know our place, and I'd already spotted a nice fat black little kitchen-maid with a saucy lip and a rolling stern.)

However, if neither of the resident ladies was any help in setting me about my duties, there was another who was – Mrs Captain MacDowall, who lived farther down the Mall, and who bustled in on my first afternoon on the pretext of taking tea with Miss Blanche, but in fact to see that Duff Mason's new orderly started off on the right foot. She was a raw-boned old Scotch trot, not unlike my mother-in-law; the kind who loves nothing better than to interfere in other folk's affairs, and put their lives in order for them. She ran me to earth just as I was stowing my kit; I salaamed respectfully, and she fixed me with a glittering eye and demanded if I spoke English.

'Now then, Makarram Khan, this is what you'll do,' says she. 'This house is a positive disgrace; you'll make it what it should be – the best in the garrison after General Hewitt's, mind that. Ye can begin by thrashing every servant in the place – and if you're wise you'll do it regularly. My father,' says she, 'believed in flogging servants every second day, after breakfast. So now. Have you the slightest – the slightest notion – of how such an establishment as this should be run? I don't suppose ye have.'

I said, submissively, that I had been in a sahib's house before.

'Aye, well,' says she, 'attend to me. Your first charge is the kitchen – without a well-ordered kitchen, there's no living in a place. Now – I dined here two nights since, *and I was disgusted*. So I have lists here prepared—' she whipped some papers from her bag. 'Ye can't read, I suppose? No, well, I'll tell you what's here, and you'll see to it that the cook – who is none too bad, considering – prepares her menus accordingly. I shouldn't need to be doing this –' she went on, with a withering glance towards the verandah, where Miss Blanche and Mrs Leslie were sitting (reading *The Corsair* aloud, I recall) '– but if I don't, who will, I'd like to know? Hmf! Poor Colonel Mason!' She glared at me. 'That's none of your concern – you understand?' She adjusted her spectacles. 'Breakfast . . . aye. Chops-steaks-quail-fried-fish-baked-minced-chicken-provided-the-bird's-no-more-than-a-day-old. *No* servants in the breakfast room – it can all be placed on the buffet. Can ye make tea – I mean tea that's fit to drink?'

Bemused by these assaults, I said I could.

'Aye,' says she, doubtfully. 'A mistress should always make the tea herself, but here . . .' She sniffed. 'Well then, always two teapots, with no more than three spoonfuls to each, and a pinch of carbonate of soda in the milk. See that the cook makes coffee, very strong, first thing in the morning, and adds *boiling* water during the course of the day. *Boiling*, I said – and *fresh* hot milk, or cold whipped cream. Now, then—' and she consulted another list.

'Luncheon – also on the buffet. Mutton-broth-almond-soup-mulligatawny-white-soup-cold-clear-soup-milk-pudding-stewed-fruit. *No heavy cooked dishes*—' this with a glare over her spectacles. 'They're unhealthy. Afternoon tea – brown bread and butter, scones, Devonshire cream, and cakes. Have ye any apostle spoons?'

'Mem-sahib,' says I, putting my hands together and ducking my head. 'I am only a poor soldier, I do not know what—'

'I'll have two dozen sent round. Dinner – saddle-of-mutton-boiled-fowls-roast-beef . . . ach!' says she, 'I'll tell the cook myself. But you –' she wagged a finger like a marlin-spike '– will mind what I've said, and see that my instructions are followed and that the food is cleanly and promptly served. And see that the salt is changed every day, and that no one in the kitchen wears woollen clothes. And if one of them cuts a finger – straight round with them to my bungalow. Every inch of this house will be dusted twice a day, before callers come between noon and two, and before dinner. Is that clear?'

'*Han* mem-sahib, *han* mem-sahib,' says I, nodding vigorously, heaven help me. She regarded me grimly, and said she would be in from time to time to see that all was going as it should, because Colonel Mason *must* be properly served, and if *she* didn't attend to it, and see that I kept the staff *hard* at their duties, well . . . This with further sniffy looks towards the verandah, after which she went to bully the cook, leaving me to reflect that there was more in an orderly's duties than met the eye.[19]

I tell you this, because although it may seem not to have much to do with my story, it strikes me it has a place; if you're to understand India, and the Mutiny, and the people who were caught up in it, and how they fared, then women like Mrs Captain MacDowall matter as much as Outram or Lakshmibai or old Wheeler or Tantia Tope. Terrible women, in their way – the memsahibs. But it would have been a different country without 'em – and I'm not sure the Raj would have survived the year '57, if they hadn't been there, interfering.

At all events, under her occasional guidance and blistering rebukes, I drove Mason's menials until the place was running like a home-bound tea clipper. You'll think it trivial, perhaps, but I got no end of satisfaction in this supervising

– there was nothing else to occupy me, you see, and as Arnold used to say, what thy hand findeth to do . . . I welted the backsides off the sweepers, terrorised the *mateys,** had the bearers parading twice a day with their dusters, feather brooms, and polish bottles, and stalked grimly about the place pleased as punch to see the table-tops and silver polished till they gleamed, the floors bone-clean, and the *chota hazri*† and *darwazaband*‡ trays carried in on the dot. Strange, looking back, to remember the pride I felt when Duff Mason gave a dinner for the garrison's best, and I stood by the buffet in my best grey coat and new red sash and *puggaree*, with my beard oiled, looking dignified and watching like a hawk as the *khansamah* and his crew scuttled round the candle-lit table with the courses. As the ladies withdrew Mrs Captain MacDowall caught my eye, and gave just a little nod – probably as big a compliment, in its way, as I ever received.

So a few more weeks went by, and I was slipping into this nice easy life, as is my habit whenever things are quiet. I reckoned I'd give it another month or so, and then slide out one fine night for Jhansi, where I'd surprise Skene by turning up *à la* Pathan and pitch him the tale about how I'd been pursuing Ignatieff in secret and getting nowhere. I'd see Ilderim, too, and find if the Thugs were still out for me; if it seemed safe I'd shave, become Flashy again, and make tracks for Calcutta, protesting that I'd done all that could be done. Might even pay my respects to Lakshmibai on the

---

* Waiters.

† Lit. 'little breakfast' – early morning tea.

‡ '*Darwazaband*', not at home. Presumably the salver used for calling-cards.

way . . . however, in the meantime I'd carry on as I was, eating Duff Mason's rations, seeing that his bearer laid out his kit, harrying his servants, and tupping his kitchen-maid – she was a poor substitute for my Rani, and once or twice, when it seemed to me that Mrs Leslie's eye lingered warmly on my upstanding Pathan figure or my swarthy bearded countenance, I toyed with the idea of having a clutch at her. Better not, though – too many prying eyes in a bungalow household, which is what made life hard for grass widows and unattached white females in Indian garrisons – they couldn't do more than flirt in safety.

Every now and then I had to go back to barracks. Carmichael-Smith had been willing enough to detach me to Duff Mason, but I still had to muster on important parades, when all sepoys on the regimental strength were called in. It was on one of these that I heard the rumour flying that the 19th N.I. had rioted at Behrampore over the greased cartridge, as sepoy Ram Mangal had predicted.

'They have been disbanded by special court,' says he to me out of the corner of his mouth as we clattered back to the armoury to hand in our rifles; he was full of excitement. 'The sahibs have sent the *jawans* home, because the Sirkar fears to keep such spirited fellows under arms! So much for the courage of your British colonels – they begin to fear. Aye, presently they will have real cause to be fearful!'

'It will need to be better cause than a pack of whining monkeys like the 19th,' says Pir Ali. 'Who minds if a few Hindoos get cow-grease on their fingers?'

'Have you seen this, then?' Mangal whipped a paper from under his jacket and thrust it at him. 'Here are your own people – you Mussulmen who so faithfully lick the sahibs' backsides – even they are beginning to find their manhood!

156

Read here of the great *jihad** that your *mullahs*† are preaching against the infidels – not just in India, either, but Arabia and Turkestan. Read it – and learn that an Afghan army is preparing to seize India, with Ruski guns and artillerymen – what does it say? "Thousands of Ghazis, strong as elephants".' He laughed jeeringly. 'They may come to help – but who knows, perhaps they will be behind the fair? The goddess Kali may have destroyed the British already – as the wise men foretold.'

It was just another scurrilous pamphlet, no doubt, but the sight of that grinning black ape gloating over his sedition riled me; I snatched the paper and rubbed it deliberately on the seat of my trousers. Pir Ali and some of the sepoys grinned, but the rest looked pretty glum, and old Sardul shook his head.

'If the 19th have been false to their salt, it is an ill thing,' says he, and Mangal broke in excitedly to say hadn't the sahibs broken faith first, by trying to defile the sepoys' caste?

'First Behrampore – then where?' cries he. 'Which *pultan* will be next? It is coming, brothers – it is coming!' And he nodded smugly, and went off chattering with his cronies.[20]

I didn't value this, at the time, but it crossed my mind again a couple of nights later, when Duff Mason had Archdale Wilson, the *binky-nabob*,‡ and Hewitt and Carmichael-Smith and a few others on his verandah, and I heard Jack Waterfield, a senior man in the 3rd Native Cavalry, talking about Behrampore, and wondering if it was wise to press ahead with the issue of the new cartridge.

---

* Holy war.
† Preachers.
‡ Artillery commander.

'Of course it is,' snaps Carmichael-Smith. 'Especially now, when it's been refused at Behrampore. Give way on this – and where will it end? It's a piece of damned nonsense – some crawling little agitator fills the sepoys' heads with rubbish about beef-grease and pig-fat, when it's been made perfectly plain by the authorities that the new cartridge contains nothing that could possibly offend Muslim or Hindoo. But it serves as an excuse for the troublemakers – and there are always some.'

'Fortunately not in our regiment,' says another – Plowden, who commanded my own company. By God, thinks I, that's all you know, and then Carmichael-Smith was growling on that he'd like to see one of his sepoys refuse the issue, by God he would.

'No chance of that, sir,' says another major of the 3rd, Richardson. 'Our fellows are too good soldiers, and no fools. Can't think what happened with the 19th – too many senior officers left regimental service for the staff, I shouldn't wonder. New men haven't got the proper grip.'

'But suppose our chaps did refuse?' says one young fellow in the circle. 'Mightn't it—'

'That is damned croaking!' says Carmichael-Smith angrily. 'You don't know sepoys, Gough, and that's plain. I do, and I won't countenance the suggestion that my soldiers would have their heads turned by this . . . this seditious bosh. What the devil – they know their duty! But if they get the notion that any of us have doubts, or might show weakness – well, that's the worst thing imaginable. I'll be obliged if you'll keep your half-baked observations to yourself!'

That shut up Gough, sharp enough, and Duff Mason tried to get the pepper out of the air by saying he was sure

Carmichael-Smith was right, and if Gough had misgivings, why not settle them then and there.

'Your colonel won't mind, I'm sure, if I put it to one of his own *sowars* – don't fret, Smith, he's a safe man.' And he beckoned me from where I stood in the shadows by the serving-table from which the bearers kept the glasses topped up.

'Now, Makarram Khan,' says he. 'You know about this cartridge nonsense. Well – you're a Muslim . . . will you take it?'

I stood respectfully by his chair, glancing round the circle of faces – Carmichael-Smith red and glistening, Waterfield thin and shrewd, young Gough flustered, old Hewitt grinning and belching quietly.

'If it will drive a ball three hundred yards, and straight, *husoor*,' says I, 'I shall take it.'

They roared, of course, and Hewitt said there was a real Pathan answer, what?

'And your comrades?' asks Archdale Wilson.

'If they are told, truly, by the colonel sahib, that the cartridge is clean, why should they refuse?' says I, and they murmured agreement. Well, thinks I, that's a plain enough hint, and Carmichael-Smith can put Master Mangal's croaking into the shade.

He might have done, too, but the very next day the barracks was agog with a new rumour – and we heard for the first time a name that was to sweep across India and the world.

'Pandy?' says I to Pir Ali. 'Who may he be?'

'A sepoy of the 34th, at Barrackpore,' says he. 'He shot at his captain sahib on the parade ground – they say he was drunk with *sharab* or *bhang*, and called on the sepoys to rise against their officers.[21] What do I know? Perhaps it is true, perhaps it is rumour – Ram Mangal is busy enough convincing those silly Hindoo sheep that it really happened.'

So he was, with an admiring crowd round him in the middle of the barrack-room, applauding as he harangued them.

'It is a lie that the sepoy Pandy was drunk!' cries he. 'A lie put about by the sahibs to dishonour a hero who will defend his caste to the death! He would not take the cartridge – and when they would have arrested him, he called to his brothers to beware, because the British are bringing fresh battalions of English soldiers to steal away our religion and make slaves of us. And the captain sahib at Barrackpore shot Pandy with his own hands, wounding him, and they keep him alive for torture, even now!'

He was working himself into a terrible froth over this – what surprised me was that no one – not even the Muslims – contradicted him, and *Naik* Kudrat Ali, who was a good soldier, was standing by chewing his lip, but doing nothing. Eventually, when Mangal had raved himself hoarse, I thought I'd take a hand, so I asked him why he didn't go to the Colonel himself, and find out the truth, whatever it was, and ask for reassurance about the cartridge.

'Hear him!' cries he scornfully. 'Ask a sahib for the truth? Hah! Only the *gora-colonel*'s lapdog would suggest it! Maybe I will speak to Carmik-al-Ismeet, though – in my own time!' He looked round at his cronies with a significant, ugly grin. 'Yes, maybe I will . . . we shall see!'

Well, one swallow don't make a summer, or one ill-natured agitator a revolt – no doubt what I'm telling you now about barrack-room discontent among the sepoys looks strong evidence of trouble brewing, but it didn't seem so bad then. Of course there was discontent, and Ram Mangal played on

160

it, and every rumour, for all he was worth – but you could go into any barracks in the world, you know, at any time, and find almost the same thing happening. No one *did* anything, just sullen talk; the parades went on, and the sepoys did their duty, and the British officers seemed content enough – anyway, I was only occasionally in the barracks myself, so I didn't hear much of the grumbling. When the word came through that Sepoy Pandy had been hanged at Barrackpore for mutiny, I thought there might be some kind of stir among our men, but they never let cheep.

In the meantime, I had other things to claim my attention: Mrs Leslie of the red hair and lazy disposition had begun to take a closer interest in me. It started with little errands and tasks that put me in her company, then came her request to Duff Mason that I should ride escort on her and Miss Blanche when they drove out visiting ('it looks so much better to have Makarram Khan attending us than an ordinary *syce*'), and finally I found myself accompanying her when she went riding alone – the excuse was that it was convenient to her to have an attendant who spoke English, and could answer her questions about India, in which she professed a great interest.

I know what interests you, my girl, thinks I, but you'll have to make the first move. I didn't mind; she was a well-fleshed piece in her way. It was amusing, too, to see her plucking up her courage; I was a black servant to her, you see, and she was torn between a natural revulsion and a desire to have the big hairy Pathan set about her. On our rides, she would flirt a very little, in a hoity-toity way, and then think better of it; I maintained my correct and dignified noble animal pose, with just an occasional ardent smile, and a slight squeeze when I helped her dismount. I knew she was getting ready for the plunge when she said one day:

161

'You Pathans are not truly . . . Indian, are you? I mean . . . in some ways you look . . . well, almost . . . white.'

'We are not Indian at all, mem-sahib,' says I. 'We are descended from the people of Ibrahim, Ishak and Yakub, who were led from the Khedive's country by one Moses.'

'You mean – you're Jewish?' says she. 'Oh.' She rode in silence for a while. 'I see. How strange.' She thought some more. 'I . . . I have Jewish acquaintances . . . in England. Most respectable people. And quite white, of course.'

Well, the Pathans believe it, and it made her happy, so I hurried the matter along by suggesting next day that I show her the ruins at Aligaut, about six miles from the city; it's a deserted temple, very overgrown, but what I hadn't told her was that the inside walls were covered with most artistically carved friezes depicting all the Hindoo methods of fornicating – you know the kind of thing: effeminate-looking lads performing incredible couplings with fat-titted females. She took one look and gasped; I stood behind with the horses and waited. I saw her eyes travel round from one impossible carving to the next, while she gulped and went crimson and pale by turns, not knowing whether to scream or giggle, so I stepped up behind her and said quietly that the forty-fifth position was much admired by the discriminating. She was shivering, with her back to me, and then she turned, and I saw that her eyes were wild and her lips trembling, so I gave my swarthy ravisher's growl, swept her up in my arms, and then down on to the mossy floor. She gave a little frightened moan, opened her eyes wide, and whispered:

'You're sure you're Jewish . . . not . . . not Indian?'

'*Han*, mem-sahib,' says I, thrusting away respectfully, and she gave a contented little squeal and grappled me like a wrestler.

We rode to Aligaut quite frequently after that, studying Indian social customs, and if the forty-fifth position eluded us, it wasn't for want of trying. She had a passion for knowledge, did Mrs Leslie, and I can think back affectionately to that cool, dim, musty interior, the plump white body among the ferns, and the thoughtful way she would gnaw her lower lip while she surveyed the friezes before pointing to the lesson for today. Pity for some chap she never re-married. Aye, and more of a pity for her she never got the chance.

For by now April had turned into May, the temperature was sweltering, and there was a hot wind blowing across the Meerut parade ground and barracks that had nothing to do with the weather. You could feel the tension in the air like an electric cloud; the sepoys of the 3rd N.C. went about their drill like sullen automatons, the native officers stopped looking their men in the eye, the British officers were quiet and wary or explosively short-tempered, and there were more men on report than anyone could remember. There were ugly rumours and portents: the 34th N.I. – the executed Sepoy Pandy's regiment – had been disbanded at Barrackpore, a mysterious fakir on an elephant had appeared in Meerut bazaar predicting that the wrath of Kali was about to fall on the British, chapattis were said to be passing in some barrackrooms, the Plassey legend was circulated again. Out of all the grievances and mistrust that folk like Ram Mangal had been voicing, a great, discontented unease grew in those few weeks – and one thing suddenly became known throughout the Meerut garrison: without a word said, the certainty was there. When the new greased cartridge was issued, the 3rd Native Cavalry would refuse it.

Now, you may say, knowing what followed, something should have been done. I, with respect, will ask: what? The thing was, while everyone *knew* that feeling was rising by the hour, no one could foresee for a moment what was about to happen. It was unimaginable. The British officers couldn't conceive that their beloved sepoys would be false to their salt – dammit, neither could the sepoys. If there's one thing I will maintain, it is that not a soul – not even creatures like Ram Mangal – thought that the bitterness could explode in violence. Even if the cartridge was refused – well, the worst that could follow was disbandment, and even that was hard to contemplate. I didn't dream of what lay ahead – not even with all my forewarning over months. And I was there – and no one can take fright faster than I. So when I heard that Carmichael-Smith had ordered a firing-parade, at which the skirmishers (of whom I was one) would demonstrate the new cartridge, I simply thought: well, this will settle it – either they'll accept the new loads, and it'll all blow over, or they won't and Calcutta will have to think again.

Waterfield tried to smooth things beforehand, singling out the older skirmishers and reassuring them that the loads were not offensively greased, but they wouldn't have it – they even pleaded with him not to ask them to take the cartridge. I think he tried to reason with Carmichael-Smith – but the word came out that the firing-parade would take place as ordered.

After Waterfield's failure, this was really throwing down the gauntlet, if you like – I'd not have done it, if I'd been Carmichael-Smith, for one thing I've learned as an officer is never to give an order unless there's a good chance of its being obeyed. And if you'd fallen in with the skirmishers that fine morning, having seen the sullen faces as they put on their belts and bandoliers and drew their Enfields from the armoury, you'd not have wagered a quid to a hundred on their taking the cartridge. But Carmichael-Smith, the ass, was determined, so there we stood, in extended line between the other squadrons of the regiment facing inwards, the native officers at ease before their respective troops, and the *rissaldar* calling us to attention as Carmichael-Smith, looking thunderous, rode up and saluted.

We waited, with our Enfields at our sides, while he rode along the extended rank, looking at us. There wasn't a sound; we stood with the baking sun at our backs; every now and then a little puff of warm wind would drive a tiny dust-devil across the ground; Plowden's horse kept shying as he cursed and tried to steady it. I watched the shadows of the rank swaying with the effort of standing rigid, and the sweat rivers were tickling my chest. *Naik* Kudrat Ali on my right was straight as a lance; on my other side old Sardul's breathing was hoarse enough to be audible. Carmichael-Smith completed his slow inspection, and reined up almost in front of me; his red face under the service cap was as heavy as a statue's. Then he snapped an order, and the *havildar-major* stepped forward, saluted, and marched to Carmichael-Smith's side, where he turned to face us. Jack Waterfield, sitting a little in rear of the colonel, called out the orders from the platoon exercise manual.

'Prepare to load!' says he, adding quietly: 'Rifle-at-full-extent-of-left-arm.' The *havildar-major* shoved out his rifle.

'Load!' cries Jack, adding again: 'Cartridge-is-brought-to-the-left-hand-right-elbow-raised-tear-off-top-of-cartridge-with-fingers-by-dropping-elbow.'

This was the moment; you could feel the rank sway forward ever so little as the *havildar-major*, his bearded face intent, held up the little shiny brown cylinder, tore it across, and poured the powder into his barrel. A hundred and eighty eyes watched him do it; there was just a suspicion of a sigh from the rank as his ramrod drove the charge home; then he came to attention again. Waterfield gave him the 'present' and 'fire', and the single demonstration shot cracked across the great parade ground. On either side, the rest of the regiment waited, watching us.

'Now,' says Carmichael-Smith, and although he didn't raise his voice, it carried easily across the parade. 'Now, you have seen the loading drill. You have seen the *havildar-major*, a soldier of high caste, take the cartridge. He knows the grease with which it is waxed is pure. I assure you again – nothing that could offend Hindoo or Muslim is being offered to you – I would not permit it. Carry on, *havildar-major*.'

What happened was that the *havildar-major* came along the rank, with two *naiks* carrying big bags of cartridges, of which he offered three to each skirmisher. I was looking straight to my front, sweating and wishing the back of my leg would stop itching; I couldn't see what was happening along the rank, but I heard a repeated murmur as the *havildar-major* progressed – '*Nahin, havildar-major sahib; nahin, havildar-major sahib.*' Carmichael-Smith's head was turned to watch; I could see his hand clenched white on his rein.

The *havildar-major* stopped opposite Kudrat Ali, and held out three cartridges. I could feel Kudrat stiffen – he was a big, rangy Punjabi Mussulman, a veteran of Aliwal and the frontier, proud as Lucifer of his stripes and himself, the kind of devoted ass who thinks his colonel is his father and even breaks wind by numbers. I stole a glance at him; his mouth was trembling under his heavy moustache as he muttered:

'*Nahin, havildar-major sahib.*'

Suddenly, Carmichael-Smith broke silence; his temper must have boiled higher with each refusal.

'What the devil do you mean?' His voice cracked hoarsely. 'Don't you recognise an order? D'you know what insubordination means?'

Kudrat started violently, but recovered. He swallowed with a gulp you could have heard in Poona, and then says:

'Colonel sahib – I cannot have a bad name!'

'Bad name, by God!' roars Smith. 'D'you know a worse name than mutineer?' He sat there glowering and Kudrat trembled; then the *havildar-major*'s hand was thrust out to me, his blood-shot brown eyes glaring into mine; I looked at the three little brown cylinders, aware that Waterfield was watching me intently, and old Sardul was breathing like a walrus on my other side.

I took the cartridges – there was a sudden exclamation farther along the rank, but I stuffed two of them into my belt, and held up the third. As I glanced at it, I realised with a start that it wasn't greased – it was waxed. I tore it across with a shaky hand, poured the powder into the barrel, stuffed the cartridge after it, and rammed it down.[22] Then I returned to attention, waiting.

Old Sardul was crying. As the cartridges were held out to him he put up a shaking hand, but not to take them. He made a little, feeble gesture, and then sings out:

'Colonel sahib – it is not just! Never – never have I disobeyed – never have I been false to my salt! Sahib – do not ask this of me – ask anything – my life, even! But not my honour!' He dropped his Enfield, wringing his hands. 'Sahib, I—'

'Fool!' shouts Carmichael-Smith. 'D'you suppose I would ask you to hurt your honour? When did any man know me do such a thing? The cartridges are clean, I tell you! Look at the *havildar-major* – look at Makarram Khan! Are they men of no honour? No – and they're not mutinous dogs, either!'

It wasn't the most tactful thing to say, to that particular sepoy; I thought Sardul would go into a frenzy, the way he wept – but he wouldn't touch the cartridges. So it went, along the line; when the end had been reached only four other men out of ninety had accepted the loads – four and that stalwart pillar of loyalty, Flashy Makarram Khan (he knew his duty, and which side his bread was buttered).

So there it was. Carmichael-Smith could hardly talk for sheer fury, but he cussed us something primitive, promising dire retribution, and then dismissed the parade. They went in silence – some stony-faced, others troubled, a number (like old Sardul) weeping openly, but mostly just sullen. For those of us who had taken the cartridges, by the way, there were no reproaches from the others – proper lot of long-suffering holy little Tom Browns they were.

That, of course, was something that Carmichael-Smith didn't understand. He thought the refusal of the cartridges was pure pig-headedness by the sepoys, egged on by a few malcontents. So it was, but there was a genuine religious feeling behind it, and a distrust of the Sirkar. If he'd had his wits about him, he'd have seen that the thing to do now was to drop the cartridge for the moment, and badger Calcutta to issue a new one that the sepoys could grease themselves (as was done, I believe, in some garrisons). He might even have made an example of one or two of the older disobedients, but no, that wasn't enough for him. He'd been defied by his own men, and by God, he wasn't having that. So the whole eighty-five were court-martialled, and the court, composed entirely of native officers, gave them all ten years' hard labour.

I can't say I had much sympathy with 'em – anyone who's fool enough to invite ten years on the rock-pile for his superstitions deserves all he gets, in my view. But I'm bound to say that once the sentence had been passed, it couldn't have been worse carried out – instead of shipping the eighty-five quietly off to jail the buffoon Hewitt decided to let the world – and other sepoys especially – see what happened to mutineers, and so a great punishment parade was ordered for the following Saturday.

As it happened, I quite welcomed this myself, because I had to attend, and so was spared an excursion to Aligaut with Mrs Leslie – that woman's appetite for experiment was increasing, and I'd had a wearing if pleasurable week of it. But from the official point of view, that parade was a stupid, dangerous farce, and came near to costing us all India.

It was a red morning, oppressive and grim, with a heavy, overcast sky, and a hot wind driving the dust in stinging volleys across the maidan. The air was suffocatingly close, like the moment before thunder. The whole Meerut garrison was there – the Dragoon Guards with their sabres out; the Bengal Artillery, with their British gunners and native assistants in leather breeches standing by their guns; line on line of red-coated native infantry completing the hollow square, and in the middle Hewitt and his staff with Carmichael-Smith and the regimental officers, all mounted. And then the eighty-five were led out in double file, all in full uniform, but for one thing – they were in their bare feet.

I don't know when I've seen a bleaker sight than those two grey ranks standing there hangdog, while someone bawled out the court's findings and sentence, and then a drum began to roll, very slow, and the ceremony began.

Now I've been on more punishment parades than I care

to remember, and quite enjoyed 'em, by and large. There's a fascination about a hanging, or a good flogging, and the first time I saw a man shot from a gun – at Kabul, that was – I couldn't take my eyes off it. I've noticed, too, that the most pious and humanitarian folk always make sure they get a good view, and while they look grim or pitying or shocked they take care to miss none of the best bits. Really, what happened at Meerut was tame enough – and yet it was different from any other drumming-out or execution I remember; usually there's excitement, or fear, or even exultation, but here there was just a doomed depression that you could feel, hanging over the whole vast parade.

While the drum beat slowly, a *havildar* and two *naiks* went along the ranks of the prisoners, tearing the buttons off the uniform coats; they had been half cut off beforehand, to make the tearing easy, and soon in front of the long grey line there were little scattered piles of buttons, gleaming dully in the sultry light; the grey coats hung loose, like sacks, each with a dull black face above it.

Then the fettering began. Groups of armourers, each under a British sergeant, went from man to man, fastening the heavy lengths of irons between their ankles; the fast clanging of the hammers and the drum-beat made the most uncanny noise, clink-clank-boom! clink-clank-clink-boom! and a thin wailing sounded from beyond the ranks of the native infantry.

'Keep those damned people quiet!' shouts someone, and there was barking of orders and the wailing died away into a few thin cries. But then it was taken up by the prisoners themselves; some of them stood, others squatted in their chains, crying; I saw old Sardul, kneeling, smearing dust on his head and hitting his fist on the ground; Kudrat Ali stood stiff at attention, looking straight ahead; my half-section, Pir Ali – who to my astonishment had refused the cartridge in the end – was jabbering angrily to the man next to him; Ram Mangal was actually shaking his fist and yelling something. A great babble of noise swelled up from the line, with the *havildar-major* scampering along the front, yelling '*Chubbarao*! Silence!' while the hammers clanged and the drum rolled – you never heard such an infernal din. Old Sardul seemed to be appealing to Carmichael-Smith, stretching out his hands; Ram Mangal was bawling the odds louder than ever; close beside where I was an English sergeant of the Bombay Artillery knocked out his pipe on the gun-wheel, spat, and says:

'There's one black bastard I'd have spread over the muzzle o' this gun, by Jesus! Scatter his guts far enough, eh, Paddy?'

'Aye,' says his mate, and paced about, scratching his head. ''Tis a bad business, though, Mike, right enough. Dam' niggers! Bad business!'

'Oughter be a bleedin' sight worse,' says Mike. 'Pampered sods – lissen 'em squeal! If they 'ad floggin' in the nigger army, they'd 'ave summat to whine about – touch o' the cat'd 'ave them bitin' each other's arses, never mind cartridges. But all they get's the chokey, an' put in irons. That's what riles me – Englishmen get flogged fast enough, an' these black pigs can stand by grinnin' at it, but somebody pulls their buttons off an' they yelp like bleedin' kids!'[23]

'Ah-h,' says the other. 'Disgustin'. An' pitiful, pitiful.'

I suppose it was, if you're the pitying kind – those pathetic-looking creatures in their shapeless coats, with the irons on their feet, some yelling, some pleading, some indifferent, some silently weeping, but mostly just sunk in shame

– and out in front Hewitt and Carmichael-Smith and the rest sat their horses and watched, unblinking. I'm not soft, but I had an uneasy feeling just then – you're making a mistake, Hewitt, thinks I, you're doing more harm than good. He didn't seem to know it, but he was trampling on their pride (I may not have much myself, but I recognise it in others, and it's a chancy thing to tamper with). And yet he could have seen the danger, in the sullen stare of the watching native infantry; they were feeling the shame, too, as those fetters went on, and the prisoners wept and clamoured, and old Sardul grovelled in the dust for one of his fallen buttons, and clenched it against his chest, with the tears streaming down his face.

He was one, I confess, that I felt a mite sorry for, when the fettering was done, and the band had struck up 'The Rogue's March', and they shuffled off, dragging their irons as they were herded away to the New Jail beyond the Grand Trunk Road. He kept turning and crying out to Carmichael-Smith – it reminded me somehow of how my old guv'nor had wept and pleaded when I saw him off for the last time to the blue-devil factory in the country where he died bawling with delirium tremens. Damned depressing – and as I walked my pony off with the four other loyal skirmishers, and glanced at their smug black faces, I thought, well, you bloody toadies – after all, they were Hindoos; I wasn't.

However, I soon worked off my glums back at Duff Mason's bungalow, by lashing the backside off one of the bearers who'd lost his oil-funnel. And then I had to be on hand for the dinner that was being given for Carmichael-Smith that night (doubtless to celebrate the decimation of his regiment), and Mrs Leslie, dressed up to the nines for the occasion, was murmuring with a meaning look that she intended to have a long ride in the country next day, so I must see picnic prepared, and there were the *mateys* to chase, and the kitchen-staff to swear at, and little Miss Langley, the riding-master's daughter, to chivvy respectfully away – she was a pretty wee thing, seven years old, and a favourite of Miss Blanche's, but she was the damnedest nuisance when she came round the back verandah in the evenings to play, keeping the servants from their work and being given sugar cakes.

With all this, I'd soon forgotten about the punishment parade, until after dinner, when Duff Mason and Carmichael-Smith and Archdale Wilson had taken their pegs and cheroots on to the verandah, and I heard Smith's voice suddenly raised unusually loud. I stopped a *matey* who was taking out a tray to them, and took it myself, so I was just in time to hear Smith saying:

'. . . of all the damned rubbish I ever heard! Who is this *havildar*, then?'

'Imtiaz Ahmed – and he's a good man, sir.' It was young Gough, mighty red in the face, and carrying his crop, for all he was in dinner kit.

'Damned good croaker, you mean!' snaps Smith, angrily. 'And you stand there and tell me that he has given you this cock-and-bull about the cavalry plotting to march on the jail and set the prisoners free? Utter stuff – and you're a fool for listening to—'

'I beg your pardon, sir,' says Gough, 'but I've been to the jail – and it looks ugly. And I've been to barracks; the men are in a bad way, and—'

'Now, now, now,' says Wilson, 'easy there, young fellow. You don't know 'em, perhaps, as well as we do. Of course they're in a bad way – what, they've seen their comrades marched off in irons, and they're upset. They're like that – they'll cry their eyes out, half of 'em . . . All right, Makarram Khan,' says he, spotting me at the buffet, 'you can go.' So that was all I heard, for what it was worth, and since nothing happened that night, it didn't seem to be worth too much.[24]

Next morning Mrs Leslie wanted to make an early start, so I fortified myself against what was sure to be a taxing day with half a dozen raw eggs beaten up in a pint of stout, and we rode out again to Aligaut. She was in the cheeriest spirits, curse her, climbing all over me as soon as we reached the temple, and by the end of the afternoon I was beginning to wonder how much more Hindoo culture I could endure, delightful though it was. I was a sore and weary native orderly by the time we set off back, and dozing pleasantly in my saddle as we passed through the little village which lies about a mile east of the British town – indeed, I could just hear the distant chiming of the church bell for evening service – when Mrs Leslie gave an exclamation and reined in her pony.

'What's that?' says she, and as I came up beside her, she hushed me and sat listening. Sure enough, there was another sound – a distant, indistinct murmur, like the sea on a far shore. I couldn't place it, so we rode quickly forward to where the trees ended, and looked across the plain. Straight ahead in the distance were the bungalows at the end of the Mall, all serene; far to the left, there was the outline of the Jail, and beyond it the huge mass of Meerut city – nothing out of the way there. And then beyond the Jail, I saw it as I peered at the red horizon – where the native cavalry and infantry lines lay, dark clouds of smoke were rising against the orange of the sky, and flickers of flame showed in the dusk. Buildings were burning, and the distant murmur was resolving itself into a thousand voices shouting, louder and ever louder. I sat staring, with a horrid suspicion growing in my mind, half-aware that Mrs Leslie was tugging at my sleeve, demanding to know what was happening. I couldn't tell her, because I didn't know; nobody knew, in that first moment, on a peaceful, warm May evening when the great Indian Mutiny began.

If I'd had my wits about me, or more than an inkling of what was happening, I'd have turned our ponies north and ridden for the safety of the British infantry lines a mile away. But my first thought was: Gough was right, some crazy bastards are rioting and trying to break the prisoners loose – and of course they'll fail, because Hewitt'll have British troops marching down to the scene at once; maybe they're there already, cutting up the niggers. I was right – and wrong, you see, but above all I was curious, once my first qualms had settled. So it wasn't in any spirit of chivalry that I sang out to Mrs Leslie:

'Ride to the bungalow directly, mem-sahib! Hold tight, now!' and cut her mare hard across the rump. She squealed as it leaped forward, and called to me, but I was already wheeling away down towards the distant Jail – I wanted to see the fun, whatever it was, and I had a good horse under me to cut out at the first sign of danger. Her plaintive commands echoed after me, but I was putting my pony to a bank, and clattering off towards the outlying buildings of the native city bazaar, skirting south so that I'd pass the Jail at a distance and see what was happening.

At first there didn't seem to be much; this side of the bazaar was strangely empty, but in the gathering dark I could hear rather than see confused activity going on between the Jail and the Grand Trunk – shouting and the rush of hurrying feet, and sounds of smashing timber. I wheeled into the bazaar, following the confusion of noise ahead; the whole of the sky to my front beyond the bazaar was glowing orange now, whether with fire or sundown you couldn't tell, but the smoke was hanging in a great pall beyond the city – it's a hell of a fine fire, thinks I, and forged on into the bazaar, between booths where dim figures seemed to be trying to get their goods away, or darting about in the shadows, chattering and wailing. I bawled to a fat vendor, who was staring down the street, asking what was up, but he just waddled swiftly into his shop, slamming his shutters – try to get sense out of an excited Indian, if you like. Then I reined up, with a *chico** scampering almost under my hooves, and the mother after it, crouching and shrieking, and before I knew it there was a swarm of folk in the street, all wailing and running in panic; stumbling into my pony, while I cursed and lashed out with my quirt; behind them the sounds of riot were suddenly closer – hoarse yelling and chanting, and the sudden crack of a shot, and then another.

Time to withdraw to a safer distance, thinks I, and wheeled my pony through the press into a side-alley. Someone went down beneath my hooves, they scattered like sheep – and then down the alley ahead of me, running pell-mell for his life, was a man in the unmistakable stable kit of the Dragoon

* Child.

Guards, bare-headed and wild-eyed, and behind him, like hounds in full cry, a screaming mob of niggers.

He saw me ahead, and yelled with despair – of course, what he saw was a great hairy native villain blocking his way. He darted for a doorway, and stumbled, and in an instant they were on him, a clawing, animal mob, tearing at him while he lashed out, yelling obscenities. For an instant he broke free, blood pouring from a wound in his neck, and actually scrambled under my pony; the mob was round us in a trice, dragging him out bodily while I struggled to keep my seat – there was no question of helping him, even if I'd been fool enough to try. They bore him up, everyone shrieking like madmen, and smashed him down on the table of a pop-shop, holding his limbs while others broke the pop-bottles and slashed and stabbed at him with the shards.

It was a nightmare. I could only clutch my reins and stare at that screaming, thrashing figure, half-covered in the pop foam, as those glittering glass knives rose and fell. In seconds he was just a hideous bloody shape, and then someone got a rope round him, and they swung him up to a beam, with his life pouring out of him.[25] In panic I drove my heels into the pony, blundered to the corner, and rode for dear life.

It was the shocking unexpectedness of it that had unmanned me – to see a white man torn to pieces by natives. Perhaps you can't imagine what that meant in India; it was something you could not believe, even when you saw it. For a few moments I must have ridden blind, for the next thing I knew I was reining up on the edge of the Grand Trunk where it comes north out of Meerut city, gazing at a huge rabble pouring up towards the British town; to my amazement half of them were sepoys, some of them just in their jackets, others in full fig down to the cross-belts, brandishing muskets and bayonets, and yelling in unison: '*Mat Karo! Mat Karo!* * *Sipahi Jai!*' and the like – slogans of death and rebellion. There was one rascal on a cart, brandishing ankle-irons above his head, and a heaving mass of sepoys and bazaarwallahs pushing his vehicle along, yelling like drunkards.

Beyond the road the native cavalry barracks were in full flame; even as I watched I saw one roof cave in with an explosion of sparks. Behind me there were buildings burning in the bazaar, and even as I turned to look I saw a gang of ruffians hurling an oil-lamp into a booth, while others were steadily thrashing with clubs at the fallen body of the owner; finally they picked him up and tossed him into the blaze, dancing and yelling as he tried vainly to struggle out; he was a human torch, his mouth opening and closing in unheard screams, and then he fell back in the burning ruin.

I don't know how long I sat there, staring at these incredible things, but I know it was dark, with flames leaping up everywhere, and an acrid reek pervading the air, before I came to my senses enough to realise that the sooner I lit out the better – of course, I was safe enough in that I was to all outward appearance a native, and a big, ugly one at that, but it made no sense to linger; any moment there must be the sound of bugles up the road, heralding a British detachment, and I didn't want to be caught up in the ensuing brawl. So I put my pony's nose north, and trotted along the edge of the road, with that stream of mad humanity surging in the same direction at my elbow.

Even then I hadn't determined what it all meant, but any doubts I might have had were resolved as I came level with the Jail, and there was a huge crowd, clamouring and

---

* 'Kill!'

applauding round a bonfire, and forming up, in their prison *dhotis*,* but with their ankles freed, were some of the prisoners – I recognised Gobinda, and one or two others, and a sepoy whom I didn't know was standing on a cart, haranguing the mob, although you could hardly hear him for the din:

'It is done! . . . Death to the *gora-log*!† . . . sahibs are already running away . . . see the broken chains! . . . On, brothers, kill! kill! To the white town!'

The whole mob screamed as one man, leaping up and down, and then bore the prisoners shoulder-high, streaming out on to the Grand Trunk towards the distant Mall – God, I could see flames up there already, out towards the eastern end. There must be bungalows burning on this side of the Mall, beyond the Nullah.

There was only one way for me to go. Behind was Meerut city and the bazaar, which was being smashed up and looted by the sound of things; to my left lay the burning native barracks; ahead, between me and the British Town, the road was jammed with thousands of crazy fanatics, bent on blood and destruction. I waited till the press thinned a little, and swung right, heading for the Nullah north of the Jail; I would cross the east bridge, and make a long circle north past the Mall to come to the British camp lines.

The first part was easy enough; I crossed the Nullah, and skirted the east end of the British Town, riding carefully in the half-dark, for the moon wasn't up yet. It was quiet here, in the groves of trees; the tumult was far off to my left, but now and then I saw little groups of natives – servant-women, probably, scurrying among the bushes, and one ominous sign

---

* Loin-cloths.

† British.

that some of the killers had come this way – an old *chowkidar*, with his broken staff beside him, lying with his skull beaten in. Were they butchering anyone, then – even their own folk? Of course – any natives suspected of loyalty would be fair game – including the *gora-colonel*'s lapdog, as Ram Mangal had charmingly called me. I pressed on quickly; not far behind me, I could hear chanting voices, and see torchlight among the trees. The sooner I . . .

'Help! Help! In God's name, help us!'

It came from my right; a little bungalow, behind a white gate, and as I stopped, uncertain, another voice cried:

'Shut up, Tommy! God knows who it is . . . see the lights yonder!'

'But Mary's dead!' cries the first voice, and it would have made your hair stand up. 'She's dead, I tell you – they've—'

They were English, anyway, and without thinking I slipped from the saddle, vaulted the gate, and cried: 'It's a friend! Who are you?'

'Oh, thank God!' cries the first voice. 'Quickly – they've killed Mary . . . Mary!'

I glanced back; the torches were still two hundred yards away among the trees. If I could get the occupants of the bungalow moving quickly, they might get away. I strode up the verandah steps, looked through the space where a chick had been torn down, and saw a wrecked room, with an oil-lamp burning feebly, and a white man, his left leg soaked in blood, lying against the wall, a sabre in his hand, staring at me with feverish eyes.

'Are you . . .?' he began, and then yelled. 'Christ – it's a mutineer – 3rd Cavalry! Jim!'

And I hadn't got my mouth open when out of the shadows

someone sprang; I had an instant's vision of a white face, red moustache, staring eyes, and whirling sabre, and then I was locked with him, crashing to the floor, while I yelled:

'You bloody idiot! I'm English, damn you!'

But he seemed to have gone mad; even as I wrestled his sabre from him and sprang away he yelled to his pal, who feebly shoved his sabre towards him; the next thing he was slashing at me, yelling curses, and I was guarding and trying to shout sense at him. I broke ground, fell over something soft, and realised as I struck the ground that it was a white woman, in evening dress – or rather it was her body, for she was lying in a pool of blood. I flung up my sabre to guard another maniac slash, but too late; I felt a fiery pain across my skull, just above the left ear, and the fellow on the floor screams:

'Go it, Jim! Finish him, finish—'

The crash of musketry filled the room; the fellow above me twisted grotesquely, dropping his sabre, and tumbled down across my legs; there were black faces grinning at the window above me through the powder smoke, and then they were in the room, yelling with triumph as they drove their bayonets into the wounded Tommy, hacking at him, smashing the furniture, and finally one of them was helping me up, shouting:

'Just in time, brother! Thank the 11th N.I., *sowar*! Aieee! Three of the pigs! God be praised – have ye been at their goods, then?'

I was dizzy with pain, so he dropped me, and while they ransacked the bungalow, growling like beasts, I crawled out on to the verandah and into the bushes. I lay there, staunching the blood that was running down my cheek; it wasn't a bad wound – no worse than the schlager cut beside it, which de

Gautet had given me years ago. But I didn't come out, even after they'd gone, taking my pony with them; I was too shaken and scared – that idiot Jim had come within an ace of finishing me – my God, it had been Jim Lewis, of course – the veterinary. I'd bowed him out of Mason's bungalow only a couple of nights before. And now, he was dead, and his wife Mary – and I was alive, saved by the mutineers who'd murdered them.

I lay there, still half-dazed, trying to make sense of it. This was mutiny, no doubt of it, and on the grand scale – the 3rd Cavalry were out, of course, and I'd seen 20th N.I. men under arms on the Grand Trunk; the fellows who'd inadvertently saved me were 11th N.I., so that was the whole Indian garrison of Meerut. But where the devil were the two British regiments? – their lines weren't more than a half-mile from where I was lying, beyond the Mall, but although two or three hours must have passed since the rioting started, there wasn't a sign of any activity by the authorities. I lay listening to the crackle of firing, and the distant tumult of voices and wrecking and burning – there were no bugle calls, no sound of volleys, no shouted orders, no heavy gunfire amidst the confusion. Hewitt couldn't just be sitting doing nothing – a terrible thought struck me: they couldn't have been wiped out, surely? No, you can't beat two thousand disciplined soldiers with a mutinous mob – but what the hell was keeping 'em quiet, then?[26]

In the long run I decided I'd have to make a break for it, up to the Mall and across towards the British infantry lines; it would take me past Duff Mason's bungalow, and the MacDowalls', so I could see what was happening there, though no doubt the people would have withdrawn already to the safety of the British camps. Yes, I could see, when I

183

stood up, that some of the bungalows south of the Mall were burning, and there was a hell of a din and shooting coming from the British Town farther west; I would have to keep well clear of that.

I moved cautiously through the trees, and found the little drive that led up to the eastern end of the Mall. There was a bungalow burning like blazes a hundred yards ahead, and half a dozen sepoys standing by its fence, cursing and occasionally firing a shot into it; on the other side of the road, a crowd of servants were huddled under a tree, and as I stole quietly towards them in the shadows I could hear them wailing. That was Surgeon Dawson's bungalow; as I came level with it, I remembered that Dawson had been down with smallpox – he and his wife and children had all been confined to the house – and there was its roof caving in with a thunderous whoosh of sparks. I felt giddy and ill at the thought – and then hurried on, past that hellish scene; the drive ahead was deserted as far as I could see in the light of the rising moon.

Our bungalow wasn't burning, anyway – but just before I reached it my eye was caught by something on the verandah of the Courtneys' place across the way. Something was moving; it was a human figure, trying to crawl. I hesitated fearfully, and then slipped through the gate and up the path; the figure was wheezing horribly; it suddenly rolled over on its back, and I saw it was a native servant, with a bayonet buried in his chest. As I stood appalled his head rolled, and he saw me; he tried to lift a hand, pointing towards the house, and then he flopped back, groaning.

For the life of me I can't think what made me go inside, and I wish I hadn't. Mrs Courtney was dead in her chair, shot and bayoneted, with her head buried in the cushions, and when I looked beyond I vomited on the spot – her three children were there as well. It was a sight to blast your eyes; the place was like a slaughter-house, stinking with blood – I turned and ran, retching, and didn't stop until I found myself stumbling on to Duff Mason's verandah.

The place was still as death – but I had to go in, for I knew that in Duff Mason's bottom desk-drawer there was a Colt and a box of ammunition, and I wanted them both as I wanted my next breath. I glanced through the trees towards the Dawsons' burning home, but there was no sign of approaching mutineers, so I slipped through the chick-door into the hall. And there I fainted dead away – something I haven't done more than twice in my life.

The reason I'll tell you quickly – Mrs Leslie's head was lying on the hall table. Her body, stripped naked – that same plump white body that I'd fondled only a few hours earlier, was lying a few feet beyond, unspeakably gashed. And in the doorway to the dining-room, Mrs Captain MacDowall was huddled grotesquely against the jamb, with a tulwar pinning her to the wall; clenched in one hand was a small vase, with the flowers it had held scattered on the boards – I realised that she must have snatched it up as a weapon.

I don't remember getting Duff Mason's revolver, but I know that later I was standing in the hall, keeping my eyes away from those ghastly things on the floor, loading it with cartridges and weeping and cursing to myself together. Why – why the hell should they do this? – I found myself blubbering it aloud. I've seen death and horror more than most men, but this was worse than anything – it was beyond bestiality. Gobinda? Pir Ali? Old Sardul? Ram Mangal, even? They couldn't have done this – they wouldn't have done it to the wives of their bitterest enemies. But it had been done

185

– if not by them, then by men like them. It was mad, sense-less, incredible – but it was there, and if I tell you of it now, it is not to horrify, but to let you understand what happened in India in '57, and how it was like nothing that any of us had ever seen before. And none of us – not even I – was ever the same again.

You know me, and what a damned coward and scoundrel I am, and not much moved by anything – but I did an odd thing in that house. I couldn't bring myself to touch Mrs Leslie, or even to look again at that ghastly head, with its frizzy red hair and staring eyes – but before I left I went to Mrs Captain MacDowall, and forced the vase from her fingers, and I collected the flowers and put them in it. I was going to set it on the floor beside her, and then I remembered that carping Scotch voice, and her contemptuous sniff – so I set it on a little table instead, with a napkin under it, just so. I took one more look round – at the wreckage of the place that my bearers had made the finest house on the station; the polished wood scarred and broken, the ornaments smashed, the rug matted with blood, the fine chandelier that had been Miss Blanche's pride wantonly shattered in a corner – and I went out of that house with such hate in my heart as I've never felt before or since. There was something I wanted to do – and quickly; I had my chance in the next five minutes, as I slipped up to the corner of the drive, and looked westward along the Mall.

The shots were still crackling in the British Town – were there any of our folk left alive down there, I wondered. How many bungalows, burned or whole, contained the same horrors that I'd found? I wasn't going to look – and I wasn't going a step farther, either. Burning buildings, screaming mobs, death and wreckage – they were all there, ahead of me; as I looked north through the trees I could see torchlight and hear yelling between me and the British lines. Whatever Hewitt and Carmichael-Smith and the rest of them were doing – supposing they were still alive – I'd now decided they could do without me: all I wanted was to get out of Meerut, and away from that hell, as fast as I could, and find peace and safety, and rest the hellish pain in my wounded head. But first I must do what I lusted above all things to do – and here came the chance, in the shape of a trooper, cantering along the Mall, swaying in his saddle, singing drunkenly to himself as he rode. Behind him, against the distant flames, there were a few parties of sepoys straggling on the Mall; eastward the road was quite empty.

I stepped into the Mall as he rode up; he had a bloody *tulwar* in one hand, a foolish animal grin on his filthy black face, and the grey coat of the 3rd Cavalry on his back. Seeing me in the same rig he let out a whoop and reined in unsteadily.

'*Ram-ram,** sowar,*' says I, and forced myself to leer at him. 'Have you slain as many as I have, eh? And whose blood is that?' I pointed at his sword.

'Hee-hee-hee-hee,' giggles he, lurching in the saddle. 'Is it blood? It is? Whose – why, maybe it is Carmik-al-Ismeet's?' He waved the blade, goggling drunkenly. 'Or Hewitt Sahib's? Nay, nay, nay!'

'Whose, then?' says I, genially, and laid a hand on his crupper.

'Ah, now,' says he, studying the blade. 'The Riding-Master Langley Sahib's – eh? That son of a stinking mangy pork-eating dog! Nay, nay, nay!' He leaned precariously from the

---

* Hello.

saddle. 'Not Langley. Hee-hee-hee-hee! He will have no grand-children by his daughter! Hee-hee-hee-hee!'

And I'd chased her growling, off the verandah, just the previous night. I had to hold on to his leather to keep my balance, biting back the bile that came into my mouth. I took another quick glance along the Mall; the nearest sepoys were still some distance off.

'*Shabash*!' says I. 'That was a brave stroke.' And as he leered and chortled I brought my hand up with the Colt in it, aimed carefully just above his groin, and fired.

He reared up, and I clutched the bridle to steady the horse as he went flying from the saddle; a second and I had it managed, then I was up and in his place, and he was threshing on the ground, screaming in agony – with luck he would take days to die. I circled him once, snarling down at him, looked back along the Mall, at those distant black figures like Dante's demons against the burning inferno behind them, and then I was thundering eastward, past the last bungalows, and the sights and sounds of horror were fading behind me.[27]

God knows how far I rode that night – probably no great distance. I don't think I was quite right in the head, partly from the shock of what I'd seen, but much more from the pain of my wound, which began to act up most damnably. It felt as though my left temple was wide open, and white heat was getting into my brain; I could hardly see out of my left eye, and was haunted by the fear that the cut would send me blind. I had enough sense, though, to know which way I wanted to go – south by east at first to skirt Meerut city, and then south by west until I struck the Delhi road at a safe distance. Delhi meant the safety of a great British garrison (or so I thought), and since there were telegraph lines between it and Meerut I felt certain that I'd meet help coming along it. I wasn't to know that the fool Hewitt hadn't even sent a message to tell of the Meerut outbreak.

So that was the course I followed, half-blind with pain, and constantly losing my bearings, even in the bright moonlight, so that I had to stop and cast about among the groves and hamlets. I forged ahead, and when I came on the Delhi road at last, what did I see but two companies of sepoys tramping along under the moon, in fair order, singing and chanting as they went, with their muskets slung and the *havildars* calling the step. For an instant I thought they must be reliefs from Delhi, and then it dawned on me that they were marching in the wrong direction – but I was too done up to care; I just sat my pony by the roadside, and when they spotted me half a dozen of them broke ranks, crying that it was a 3rd Cavalryman, and cheering me until they saw the blood on my face and coat. Then they helped me down, and sponged my head and gave me a drink, and their *havildar* says:

'You're in no case to catch your *pultan* tonight, *bhai*.* They must be half way to Delhi by now,' at which the rest of them cheered and threw up their hats.

'Are they so?' says I, wondering what the devil he meant.

'Aye, first among the loot, as usual,' cries another. 'They have the advantage of us, on their ponies – but we'll be there, too!' And they all cheered and laughed again, black faces with grinning white teeth looking down at me. Even in my bemused state this seemed to mean only one thing.

'Has Delhi fallen, then?' I asked, and the *havildar* says, not yet, but the three regiments there would surely rise, and

---

* Brother.

with the whole of the Meerut garrison marching to help them the sahibs would be overthrown and slaughtered within the day.

'We were only the beginning!' says he, sponging away at my wound. 'Soon Delhi – then Agra, Cawnpore, Jaipur – aye, and Calcutta itself! The Madras army is on the move also, and from one end of the Grand Trunk to the other the sahibs have been driven into their compounds like mice into their holes. The North is rising – there, lie still, man – there will be sahibs enough for your knife-edge, when your wound is healed. Best come with us, if you can travel; see, we hold together in good company, like soldiers – lest the sahibs send out riders who may snap us up piecemeal.'

'No – no,' says I, struggling up. 'I'll ride on to join my *pultan*.' And despite their protests I clambered on to my pony again.

'He thirsts for white blood!' shouts one. '*Shabash, sowar!* But leave enough for the rest of us to drink!'

I shouted something incoherent, about wanting to be first in at the death, and as they halloed encouragement after me I put my pony to a trot, hanging on grimly, and set off down the road. The other company was yelling and singing as I passed – I remember noting that they were wearing flower garlands round their necks. I carried on until I had distanced them, my head splitting at every step and swelling up like a balloon, and then I remember swinging off into the forest, and blundering until I slumped out of the saddle and lay where I fell, utterly exhausted.

When I came to – if you can call it that – I was extremely ill. I've no clear idea of what followed, except that there were long periods of confused dreaming, and moments of vivid clarity, but it's difficult to tell one from the other. I'm sure that at one point I was lying face-down in a tank, gulping down brackish water while a little girl with a goat stood and watched me – I can even remember that the goat had a red thread round its horns. On the other hand, I doubt if Dr Arnold truly did come striding through the trees in an enormous turban, crying: 'Flashman, you have been fornicating with Lakshmibai during first lesson; how often must I tell you there is to be no galloping after morning prayers, sir!' Or that John Charity Spring stood there four-square shouting: 'Amo, amas, amat! Lay into him, doctor! The horny young bastard is always amo-ing! *Hae nugae in seria ducent mala*,* by God!' And then they changed into a wrinkled old native woman and a scrawny nigger with a white moustache; she was holding a *chatti*† to my mouth – it felt hard and cold, but it became suddenly soft and warm, and the *chatti* was Mrs Leslie's lips against mine, and what was running into my mouth wasn't water, but blood, and I screamed silently while all the grinning faces whirled round me, and the whole world was burning while a voice intoned: 'Cartridge is brought to the left hand with right elbow raised' . . . and then the old man and woman were there again, peering anxiously down at me while I slipped into black unconsciousness.

It was in their hut that I finally came to myself, with a half-healed wound on my temple, having lost heaven knows how much blood and weight, verminous and stinking and weak as a kitten – but with my head just clear enough to remember what had happened. Unfortunately, it wasn't to prove quite so clear about thinking ahead.

I've since calculated that I lay ill and delirious in their

---

* These trifles will lead to grave evils.
† Pot, drinking cup.

hovel for nearly three weeks, perhaps longer. They didn't seem to know – apart from being the lowest kind of creatures, they were scared stiff of me, and it wasn't until I'd prevailed on them to fetch someone from a nearby village that I could get any notion of what was happening. They finally drummed up an ancient pensioner, who shied off as soon as he saw me – my cavalry coat and gear, and my filthy appearance must have marked me as a mutineer par excellence – but before he could get out of the door I had soothed him with my revolver, held in a shaky hand, and in no time he was crouching beside my charpoy, babbling like the man from Reuters, while the rest of his village peeped through cracks in the walls, shivering.

Delhi had fallen – he had been there, and there had been a terrible slaughter of sahibs, and all their folk. The King of Delhi had been proclaimed and now ruled all India. It had been the same everywhere – Meerut, Bareilly, Aligarh, Etawah, Mainpuri (all of which were within a hundred miles or so), the splendid sepoys had triumphed all along the line, and soon every peasant in the land would receive a rupee and a new chicken. (Sensation.) The sahibs had tried to fall treacherously on the native soldiers at Agra, Cawnpore and Lucknow, but there was no doubt that these places would succumb also – two regiments of mutineers had passed through his own village last night, with cannon, to assist in the overthrow of Agra – everywhere there were dead sahibs, obviously there would soon be none left in the world. Bombay had risen, Afghan fighters were pouring in from the north, a great Muslim *jihad* had been proclaimed, fort after fort of the hated *gora-log* was going down, with fearful slaughter. Doubtless I had already borne my part? – excellent, I would certainly be rewarded with a nawab's throne and treasure and flocks of amorous women. What less did I deserve? 3rd Cavalry, was I not? Doughty fighters – he had been in the Bombay Sappers, himself, thirty-one years' service, and not so much as a *naik*'s stripes to swell his miserable *pinshun* – aieee, it was time the mean, corrupt and obscene Sirkar was swept away . . .

Some of his news would be exaggerated bosh, of course, but I couldn't judge how much, and I didn't doubt his information about the local mutinies (which proved accurate enough, by the way: half the stations between Meerut and Cawnpore had been overrun by this time). Perhaps I was too ready to swallow his gammon about Afghan invasion and Bombay being in flames – but remember, I'd *seen* the stark, staring impossible happen at Meerut – after that, anything was credible. After all, there was only one British soldier in India for every fifty sepoys, to say nothing of banditti, frontiersmen, dacoits, bazaar ruffians and the like – dear God, if the thing spread there wasn't an earthly damned reason why they shouldn't swallow every British garrison, cantonment and residency from Khyber to Coromandel. And it would spread – I didn't doubt it, as I sat numb and shaking on my *charpai*.

Coward's reasoning, if you like, but I don't know any other kind, thank heaven; at least it prepares you for the worst. And there couldn't be much worse than my present situation, plumb in the eye of the storm – damnation, of all the places to hide in, what malign fate had taken me to Meerut? And how to get away? – my native disguise was sound enough, but I couldn't skulk round India forever as a footloose nigger. I'd have to find a British garrison – a large, safe one . . . Cawnpore? Not by a mile – the whole Ganges valley seemed to be ablaze. North wasn't any good, Delhi was gone and

Agra on the brink . . . South? Gwalior? Jhansi? Indore? I found myself chattering the names aloud, and repeating one over and over – 'Jhansi, Jhansi!'

Now, you must remember I was in my normal state of great pusillanimity, and half-barmy to boot, as a result of shock and the clout I'd taken. Otherwise I'd never have dreamed of Jhansi, two hundred and fifty miles away – but Ilderim was at Jhansi, and if there was one thing certain in this dreadful world, it was that he'd keep his tryst, and would either wait for me at Bull Temple as he'd promised, or leave word. And Jhansi must be safe – dammit, I'd spent weeks with its ruler, in civilised discussion and hectic banging; she was a lovely, wonderful girl, and would have her state well in hand, surely? Yes, Jhansi – it was madness, and I know it now, but in my weak, feverish state it seemed the only course at the time.

So south I went, talking to myself most of the time, and shying away from everyone and everything except the meanest villages, where I put in for provisions; I didn't stand on ceremony, but just lurched in snarling and brandishing my Colt, kicking the cowed inhabitants aside, and lifting whatever I fancied – I've never been more grateful for my English public school upbringing than I was then. Whether I was unlucky or not I don't know, but as I worked my way south past Khurjah and Hathras and Firozabad, over the river and down past Gohad to the Jhansi border, everything I saw confirmed my worst fears. I must have skulked in the brush a dozen times to avoid bands of sepoys – one of 'em a full regiment, blow me, with colours and band tootling away, but plainly mutineers from the din they made and the slovenly way they marched. I know now that there were British-held towns and stations along the way, and even bands of our

194

cavalry scouring the country, but I never ran across them. What I did see was a sickening trail of death – burned-out bungalows, looted villages, bodies all swollen up and half-eaten by vultures and jackals. I remember one little garden, beside a pretty house, and three skeletons among the flowers – picked clean by ants, I daresay. Two were full-grown, and one was a baby. Now and then I would see smoke on the horizon, or over the trees, and crowds of villagers fleeing with their miserable belongings – it was like the end of the world to me, then, and if you'd known India you'd have thought the same – imagine it in Kent or Hampshire, for that's how it seemed to us.

Fortunately, thanks to my curiously light-headed condition, my recollections of that wandering ride are not too clear; it wasn't until the very morning that I came down out of the low hills to Jhansi city, and saw the distant fort-crowned rock above the town, that my mind seemed to give a little snap – I remember sitting my pony, with my brain clearing, understanding what I'd done, and why I was here, breaking out in a sweat at my own temerity, and then realising that I'd perhaps done the wise thing, after all. It all looked peaceful enough, although I was on the wrong side of the city to see the British cantonment; I decided to lie up during the afternoon, and then slip into Bull Temple, which was not far from the Jokan Bagh, a garden of little beehive temples not far outside the town. If Ilderim's messenger wasn't there by sundown, I'd scout the cantonment, and if all was well I'd ride in and report myself to Skene.

The sun was just slipping away and the shadows lengthening when I skirted the woods where Lakshmibai's pavilion lay – who knows, thinks I, perhaps we'll dance another Haymarket hornpipe before long – and came down to Bull

Temple just after dusk. I didn't see a soul as I came, but I was cheered by the sound of a bugle-call in the distance, and I was pressing ahead more boldly up towards the temple ruin when someone clicked his tongue in the shadows, and I reined up sharply.

'Who goes there?' says I, fingering the Colt, and a man lounged out, spreading his hands to show they were empty. He was a Pathan, skull-cap and *pyjamys* and all, and as he came to my horse's head I recognised the *sowar* who'd given me his gear and pony when I'd left Jhansi – Rafik Tamwar.

'Flashman *husoor*,' says he, softly. 'Ilderim said you would come.' And without another word he jerked his thumb towards the temple itself, put his hands to his mouth, and hooted softly like an owl; there was an answering hoot from the ruins, and Tamwar nodded to me to go ahead.

'Ilderim is yonder,' says he, and before I could ask him what the devil it meant, he had dissolved into the shadows and I was staring uneasily across the tangle of weeds and broken masonry that marked the old temple garden; there was a glare of firelight from the doorway in the half-fallen shell of the dome, and a man was standing waiting – even at that distance I knew it was Ilderim Khan, and a moment later I was face to bearded grinning face with him, shaking with very relief as his one sound arm clasped me round the shoulders – the other was bound up in a sling – and he was chuckling in his throat and growling that I must have a pact with Shaitan since I was alive to keep the rendezvous.

'For we have heard of Meerut,' says he, as he drew me in to the fire, and the half-dozen *sowars* crouched round it made space for us. 'And Delhi, Aligarh and the rest—'

'But what the blazes are you doing here?' says I. 'Since

when have irregular cavalry taken to bivouacking in ruins when they have their own quarters?'

He stared at me, stopping in the act of throwing a billet on the fire, and something in that look turned my blood to ice. They were all staring at me; I glanced from one grim bearded face to another, and in a voice suddenly hoarse I asked:

'What does it mean? Your officer – Henry sahib? Has anything—'

Ilderim threw the billet on the fire, and squatted down beside me. 'Henry sahib is dead, brother,' says he quietly. 'And Skene sahib. And the Collector sahib. And all their women, and their children also. They are all dead.'

I can see it now as vividly as I saw it then – the dark hawk-face silhouetted against the temple wall that glowed ruddy in the firelight, and the bright stream of a tear on his cheek. You don't often see a Pathan cry, but Ilderim Khan cried as he told me what had happened at Jhansi.

'When the news came of Meerut, that black Hindoo bitch who calls herself Maharani summoned Skene sahib, and says she needs must enlarge her bodyguard, for the safety of her person and the treasure in her palace. These being unquiet times. She spoke very sweetly, and Skene, being young and foolish, gave her what she wished – aye, he even said that we of the free cavalry might serve her, and Kala Khan (may he rot in hell) took her salt and her money, and two others with him. But most of her new guard were the scum of the bazaar – *badmashes* and *klifti-wallahs** and street-corner ten-to-one assassins and the sweepings of the jail.

'Then, two weeks ago, there was stirring among the sepoys

* Thieves.

198

of the 12th N.I., and chapattis and lotus flowers passed, and some among them burned a bungalow by night. But the colonel sahib spoke with them, and all seemed well, and a day and a night passed. Then Faiz Ali and the false swine Kala Khan, with a great rabble of sepoys and these new heroes of the Rani's guard, fell on the Star Fort, and made themselves masters of the guns and powder, and marched on the cantonment to put it to the fire, but Skene sahib had warning from a true sepoy, and while some dozen sahibs were caught and butchered by these vermin, the rest escaped into the little Town Fort, and the mem-sahibs and little ones with them, and made it good against the mutineers. And for five days they held it – do I not know? For I was there, with Rafik Tamwar and Shadman Khan and Muhammed Din, whom you see here. And I took this –' he touched his wounded arm '– the seventh time they tried to storm the wall.'

'They came like locusts,' growls one of the *sowars* round the fire. 'And like locusts they were driven.'

'Then the food was gone, and the water, and no powder remained for the *bundooks*,'* says Ilderim. 'And Skene sahib – have ye seen a young man grow old in a week, brother? – said we could hold no longer, for the children were like to die. So he sent three men, under a white flag, to the Rani, to beg her help. And she – she told them she had no concern for the English swine.'

'I don't believe it,' says I.

'Listen, brother – and believe, for I was one of the three, and Muhammed Din here another, and we went with Murray sahib to her palace gate. Him only they admitted, and flung

---

* Firearms.

us two in a stinking pit, but they told us what passed after-wards – that she had spurned Murray sahib, and afterwards he was racked to pieces in her dungeon.' He turned to stare at me with blazing eyes. 'I do not know – it is what I was told; only hear what followed, and then – judge thou.'

He stared into the fire, clenching and unclenching his fist, and then went on:

'When no word went back to Skene sahib, and seeing the townsfolk all comforting the mutineers, and jeering at his poor few, he offered to surrender. And Kala Khan agreed, and they opened the fort gates, and trusted to the mercy of the mutineers.'

It was then I saw the tear run down into his beard; he didn't look at me, but just continued gazing at the flames and speaking very softly:

'They took them all – men, and women, and children – to the Jokan Bagh, and told them they must die. And the women wept, and threw themselves on their knees, and begged for the children's lives – mem-sahibs, brother, you understand, such ladies as you know of, grovelled at the boots of the filth of the bazaar. I saw it!' He suddenly shouted. 'And the untouchable scum – these high-caste worms who call them-selves men, and will shudder away if a real man's shadow falls across their *chattis* – these creatures laughed and mocked the mem-sahibs and kicked them aside.

'I saw it – I, and Muhammed Din here, for they brought us out to the Jokan Bagh saying, "See thy mighty sahibs; see thy proud mem-sahibs who looked on us as dirt; see them crawl to us before they die."'

'There is a furnace thrice-heated waiting,' says one of the *sowars*. 'Remember that, *rissaldar* sahib.'

'If they burn forever it will not be hot enough,' says Ilderim.

200

'They killed the sahibs first – the Collector sahib, Andrews sahib – Gordon, Burgess, Taylor, Turnbull – all of them. They held them in a row, and chopped them down with cleavers. Skene sahib they slew last of all; he asked to embrace his wife, but they laughed at him and struck him, and bade him kneel for the knife. "I will die on my feet," says he, "with no regret save that I am polluted by the touch of dishonoured lice like you. Strike, coward – see, my hands are tied." And Bakshish Ali, the jail daroga, cut him down. And through all this they made the women and children watch, crying "See, thy husband's blood! See, baby, it is thy father's head – ask him to kiss thee, baby!" And then they killed the mem-sahibs, in another row, while the townsfolk watched and cheered, and threw marigolds at the executioners. And Skene mem-sahib said to Faiz Ali, "If it pleases you, you may burn me alive, or do what you will, if you will spare the children." But they threw dirt in her face, and swore the children should die.'

One of the *sowars* says: 'There will be a red thread round her wrist, as for a *Ghazi*.'

'And I,' says Ilderim, 'fought like a tiger and foamed and swore as they held me. And I cried out: "*Shabash*, mem-sahib!" and "Heep-heep-heep-hoora", as the sahibs do, to comfort her. And they cut her down.' He was crying openly now, his mouth working. 'And then they took the children – twenty of them – little children, that cried out and called for their dead mothers, and they cut them all in pieces, with axes and butchers' knives. And there they left them all, in the Jokan Bagh, without burial.'[28]

Hearing something, however horrible, can never be as ghastly as seeing it; the mind may take it in, but mercifully the imagination can't. Even while I shuddered and felt sickened, listening, I couldn't conjure up the hideous scene he was describing – all I could think of was McEgan's jolly red face as he told his awful jokes, and little Mrs Skene so anxious in case her dress was wrong for the Collector's dinner, and Andrews talking about Keats's poetry, and Skene saying it wasn't a patch on Burns, and that dainty little Wilton girl singing 'bobbity-bobbity-bob' along with me and laughing till she was breathless. It didn't seem possible they were all dead – cut down like beasts in a slaughter-house. Yet what shocked me most, I think, was to see that great Gilzai warrior, whom you could have roasted alive and got nothing but taunts and curses, sobbing like a child. There was nothing to say; after a moment I asked him how he came to be still alive.

'They put Muhammed and me in the jail, with promises of death by torture, but these others of my troop broke us out at night, and we escaped. Until yesterday we hid in the woods, but then the mutineers departed, God knows whither, and we came here. Shadman and two others have gone for horses; we wait for them – and for thee, brother.' He wiped his face and forced a grin, and gripped me by the shoulder.

'But the Rani, then?'

'God send that fair foulness a lover made of red-hot metal to bed her through eternity,' says he, and spat. 'She is in her citadel yonder, while Kala Khan marshals her guard on the maidan – perchance ye heard his bugles? – and sends out for levies to raise her an army. For why? – hear this and laugh. Some of the mutineers chose Sadasheo Rao of Parola as their leader – he has taken Karera Fort, and calls himself Raja of Jhansi in defiance of her.' He laughed harshly. 'They say she will crucify him with his own bayonets – God send she does. Then she will march against Kathe Khan and the Dewan of

Orcha, to bring them under her pretty heel. Oh, an enterprising lady, this Rani, who knows how to take advantage of a world upside down – and meanwhile they say she sends messages to the British protesting her loyalty to the Sirkar – rot her for a lying, faithless, female pi-dog!'

'Maybe she is,' says I. 'Loyal, I mean. Very well, I don't doubt your story, or what you saw and were told – but, look here, Ilderim. I know something of her – and while I'll allow she's deep, I'll not credit that she would have children slaughtered – it isn't in her. Do you know for a fact that she joined the mutineers, or encouraged them – or could have prevented them?' The fact is, I didn't want to believe she was an enemy, you see.

Ilderim glanced at me witheringly, and bit his nail in scorn.

'Bloody Lance,' says he, 'ye may be the bravest rider in the British Army, and God knows thou art no fool – but with women thou art a witless infant. Thou has coupled this Hindoo slut, hast thou not?'

'Damn your impudence—'

'I thought as much. Tell me, blood-brother, how many women hast thou covered, in thy time?' And he winked at his mates.

'What the devil d'you mean?' I demanded.

'How many? Come, as a favour to thy old friend.'

'Eh? What's it to you, dammit? Oh, well, let's see . . . there's the wife, and . . . er . . . and, ah—'

'Aye – ye have fornicated more times than I have passed water,' says this elegant fellow. 'And just because they let thee have thy way, didst thou trust them therefore? Because they were beautiful or lecherous – wert thou fool enough to think it made them honest? Like enough. This Rani has beglamoured thee – well then, go thou up and knock on her palace gate tonight, and cry "Beloved, let me in." I shall stand under the wall to catch the pieces.'

When he put it that way, of course, it was ridiculous. Whether she was loyal or not – and I could hardly credit that she wasn't – it didn't seem quite the best time to test the matter, with her state running over at the edges with mutineers. Good God, was there nowhere safe in this bloody country? Delhi, Meerut, Jhansi – how many garrisons remained, I asked Ilderim, and told him the stories I'd heard, and the sights I'd seen, on my way south.

'No one knows,' says he grimly. 'But be sure the sepoys have not won, as they would have the world believe. They have made the land between Ganges and Jumna a ruin of fire and blood, and gone undefeated – as yet. They range the country in strength – but already there is word that the British are marching on Delhi, and bands of sahibs who escaped when their garrisons were overthrown are riding abroad in growing numbers. Not only men who have lost their regiments, but civilian sahibs also. The Sirkar still has teeth – and there are garrisons that hold out in strength. Cawnpore for one – a bare four days' ride from here. They say the old General Wheeler sahib is in great force there, and has shattered an army of sepoys and *badmashes*. When Shadman brings our horses, it is there we will ride.'

'Cawnpore?' I almost squeaked the word in consternation, for it was back in the dirty country with a vengeance. Having come out of that once, I'd no wish to venture in again.

'Where else?' says he. 'There is no safer road from Jhansi. Farther south ye dare not go, for there are few sahib places, and no great garrisons. Nor are there to the west. Over the Jumna the country may be hot with mutineers, but it is where thine own folk are – and they are mine, too, and my lads'.'

I looked at the ugly villains round the fire, hard-bitten frontier rough-necks to a man in their dirty old *poshteens* and the big Khyber knives in their belts – by George, I'd be a sight safer going north again in their company than striking out anywhere else on my own. What Ilderim said was probably true, too; Cawnpore and the other river strong-holds would be where our generals would concentrate – I could get back among my own kind, and shed this filthy beard and sepoy kit and feel civilised again. Wouldn't have to spin any nonsense about why I'd disappeared from Jhansi, either, in supposed pursuit of Ignatieff – my God, I'd forgotten him entirely, and the Thugs, and all the rest. My mission to Jhansi – Pam and his cakes and warnings – it was all chaff in the wind now, forgotten in this colossal storm that was sweeping through India. No one was going to fret about where I'd sprung from, or what I'd been doing. I felt my spirits rising by the minute – when I thought of the escape I'd had, leaving Jhansi in the first place, I could say that even my horrible experience at Meerut had been worth while.

That's another thing about being a windy beggar – if you scare easily, you usually cheer up just as fast when the danger is past. Well, not past yet, perhaps – but at least I was with friends again, and by what Ilderim said the Mutiny wasn't by any means such a foregone thing as I'd imagined – why, once our people got their second wind, it would be the bloody rebels who'd be doing the running, no doubt, with Flashy roaring on the pursuit from a safe distance. And I might have been rotting out yonder with the others at Jokan Bagh – I shuddered at the ghastly memory of Ilderim's story – or burned alive with the Dawsons at Meerut. By Jove, things weren't so bad after all.

'Right,' says I. 'Cawnpore let it be.' How was I to know I was almost speaking my own epitaph?

In the meantime, I had one good night's sleep, feeling safe for the first time in weeks with Ilderim's rascals around me, and next day we just lay up in the temple ruins while one *sowar* went to scout for Shadman Khan, who was meant to be out stealing horses for us. It was the rummest fix to be in, for all day we could hear the bugles tootling out on the plain where the Rani's army was mustering for her own private little wars with Jhansi's neighbours; Ilderim reported in the evening that she had assembled several hundred foot soldiers, and a few troops of Maharatta riders, as well as half a dozen guns – not a bad beginning, in a troubled time, but of course with a treasury like Jhansi's she could promise regular pay for her soldiers, as well as the prospect of Orcha's loot when she had dealt with the Dewan.

With the second dawn came Shadman himself, cackling at his own cleverness: he and his pals had laid hands on six horses already, they were snug in a thicket a couple of miles from the town, and he had devised a delightful plan for getting another half-dozen mounts as well.

'The Hindoo bitch needs riders,' says he. 'So I marched into her camp on the maidan this afternoon and offered my services. "I can find six old Company *sowars* who will ride round Jehannum and back for a rupee a day and whatever spoil the campaign promises," says I to the noseless pig who is master of her cavalry, "if ye have six good beasts to put under them." "We have horses and to spare," says he, "bring me your six *sowars* and they shall have five rupees a man down payment, and a carbine and embroidered saddle-cloth apiece." I beat him up to ten rupees each – so tomorrow let six of us join her cavalry, and at nightfall we shall unjoin, and meet thee, *rissaldar*, and all ride off rejoicing. Is it not a brave scheme – and will cost this slut of a Rani sixty rupees as well as her steeds and furniture?'

There's nothing as gleeful as a Pathan when he's doing the dirty; they slapped their knees in approval and five of them went off with him that afternoon. Ilderim and I and the remaining three waited until nightfall, and then set off on foot to the thicket where we were to rendezvous – there were the first six horses and a *sowar* waiting, and round about midnight Shadman and his companions came clattering out of the dark to join us, crowing with laughter. Not only had they lifted the six horses, they had cut the lines of a score more, slit the throat of the cavalry-master as he lay asleep, and set fire to the fodder-store, just to keep the Rani's army happy.

'Well enough,' growls Ilderim, when he had snarled them to silence. 'It will do – till we ride to Jhansi again, some day. There is a debt to pay, at the Jokan Bagh. Is there not, blood-brother?' He gripped my shoulder for a moment as we sat our mounts under the trees, and the others fell in two by two behind us. In the distance, very black against the starlit purple of the night sky, was the outline of the Jhansi fortress with the glow of the city beneath it; Ilderim was staring towards it bright-eyed – I remember that moment so clearly, with the warm gloom and the smell of Indian earth and horse-flesh, the creak of leather and the soft stamping of the beasts. I was thinking of the horror that lay in the Jokan Bagh – and of that lovely girl, in her mirrored palace yonder with its swing and soft carpets and luxurious furniture, and trying to make myself believe that they belonged in the same world.

'It will take more than one dead rebel and a few horses

to settle the score for Skene sahib and the others,' says he. 'Much more. So – to Cawnpore? Walk-march, trot!'

He had said it was a bare four days' ride, but it took us that long to reach the Jumna above Haminpur, for on my advice we steered clear of the roads, and kept to the country-side, where we sighted nothing bigger than villages and poor farms. Even there, though, there was ample sign of the turbu-lence that was sweeping the land; we passed hamlets that were just smoking, blackened ruins, with buzzing carcases, human and animal, lying where they had been shot down, or strung up to branches; and several times we saw parties of mutineers on the march, all heading north-east like ourselves. That was enough to set me wondering if I wasn't going in the wrong direction, but I consoled myself that there was safety in numbers – until the morning of the fourth day, when Ilderim aroused me in a swearing passion with the news that eight of our party had slipped off in the night, leaving only the two of us with Muhammed Din and Rafik Tamwar.

'That faithless thieving, reiving son of a Kabuli whore, Shadman Khan, has put them up to this!' He was livid with rage. 'He and that other dung-beetle Asaf Yakub had the dawn watch – they have stolen off and left us, and taken the food and fodder with them!'

'You mean they've gone to join the mutineers?' I cried.

'Not they! We would never have woken again if that had been their aim. No – they will be off about their trade, which is loot and murder! I should have known! Did I not see Shadman licking his robber's lips when we passed the sacked bungalows yesterday? He and the others see in this broken countryside a chance to fill their pockets, rather than do honest service according to their salt. They will live like the bandits they were before the Sirkar enlisted them in an evil hour, and when they have ravaged and raped their fill they will be off north to the frontier again. They have not even the stomach to be honest mutineers!' And he spat and stamped, raging.

'Never trust an Afridi,' says Tamwar philosophically. 'I knew Shadman was a *badmash* the day he joined. At least they have left us our horses.'

That was little consolation to me as we saddled up; with eleven hardy riders round me I'd felt fairly secure, but now that they were reduced to three – and only one of those really trustworthy – I fairly had the shakes again. However, having come this far there was nothing for it but to push on; we weren't more than a day's ride from Cawnpore by my reckoning, and once we were behind Wheeler's lines we would be safe enough. My chief anxiety was that the closer we got, the more likely we would be to find mutineers in strength, and this was confirmed when, a few hours after sun-up, we heard, very faint in the distance, the dull thump of gunfire. We had stopped to water our beasts at a tank beside the road, which at that point was enclosed by fairly thick forest either side; Ilderim's head came up sharp at the sound.

'Cawnpore!' says he. 'Now what shall that shooting mean? Can Wheeler sahib be under siege? Surely—'

Before I could reply there was a sudden drumming of hooves, and round a bend in the road not two hundred yards ahead came three horsemen, going like hell's delight; I barely had time to identify them as native cavalrymen of some sort, and therefore probably mutineers, when into view came their pursuers – and I let out a yell of delight, for out in the van was an undoubted white officer, with his sabre out and view-hallooing like a good 'un. At his heels came a motley gang of riders, but I hadn't time to examine them – I was crouched down at the roadside with my Colt out, drawing a bead on the foremost fugitive. I let blaze, and his horse gave a gigantic bound and crashed down, thrashing in the dust; his two companions swung off to take to the woods, but one of the mounts stumbled and threw its rider, and only the other won to the safety of the trees, with a group of the pursuers crashing after him.

The others pounced on the two who'd come to grief, while I ran towards them, yelling:

'Hurrah! Bravo, you fellows! It's me, Flashman! Don't shoot!'

I could see now that they were Sikh cavalry, mostly, although there were at least half a dozen white faces among them, staring at me as I came running up; suddenly one of them, with a cry of warning, whips out his revolver and covers me.

'Don't move,' he bawls. 'Drop that pistol – sharp, now!'

'No, no!' cries I. 'You don't understand! I'm a British officer! Colonel Flashman!'

'The devil you are!' He stared from me to Ilderim, who had come up behind me. 'You look like it, don't you? And who the hell is he – the Duke of Cambridge?'

'He's a *rissaldar* of irregular cavalry. And I, old fellow, believe it or not, beneath this fine beard and homely native garb, am Colonel Harry Paget Flashman – of whom I daresay you've heard?' I was positively burbling with relief as I held out my hand to him.

'You look bloody like a pandy* to me,' says he. 'Keep your distance!'

'Well, you don't exactly look straight from Horse Guards

---

* Mutineer (see Note 21).

yourself, you know,' says I, laughing. None of them did; apart from the Sikhs, who were a fairly wild-looking bunch, his white companions were the oddest crowd, in bits and pieces of uniform from half a dozen regiments, with their gear slung any old how. Some had *puggarees*, some helmets, and one fat chap with a white beard had a straw hat and frock coat; they were all dirty and unshaven after weeks in the saddle, and the only thing uniform about them was that they were fairly bristling with weapons – pistols, carbines, swords, knives in their belts, and one or two with pig spears.

'May I ask who I have the honour of addressing?' says I, as they crowded up. 'And if you have a commanding officer, perhaps you might convey my compliments to him.'

That impressed him, although he still looked suspicious.

'Lieutenant Cheeseman, of Rowbotham's Mosstroopers,' says he. 'But if you're one of us, what the dooce are you going about dressed as a nigger for?'

'You say you're Flashman?' says another – he was wearing a pith helmet and spectacles, and what looked like old cricket flannels tucked into his top-boots. 'Well, if you are – an' I must say you don't look a bit like him – you ought to know me. Because Harry Flashman stood godfather to my boy at Lahore in '42 – what's my name, eh?'

I had to close my eyes and think – it had been on my triumphal progress south after the Jalallabad business. An Irish name – yes, by God, it was unforgettable.

'O'Toole!' says I. 'You did me the honour of having your youngster christened Flashman O'Toole – I trust he's well?'

'By God I did!' says he, staring. 'It must be him, Cheeseman! Here, where's Colonel Rowbotham?'

I confess I was curious myself – Rowbotham's Mosstroopers was a new one on me, and if their commander was anything like his followers he must be a remarkable chap. There was a great rumpus going on in the road behind the group who surrounded me, and I saw that one of the fugitives was being dragged up between two of the Sikhs, and thrown forward in the dust before one of the riders, who was leaning down from his saddle looking at the still form of the fellow whose horse I'd shot.

'Why, this one's dead!' he exclaimed, peevishly. 'Of all the confounded bad luck! Hold on to that other scoundrel, there! Here, Cheeseman, what have you got – is it some more of the villains?'

He rode over the dead man, glaring at me, and I don't think I've ever seen an angrier-looking man in my life. Everything about him was raging – his round red face, his tufty brindle eyebrows, his bristling sandy whiskers, even the way he clenched his crop, and when he spoke his harsh, squeaky voice seemed to shake with suppressed wrath. He was short and stout, and sat his pony like a hog on a hurdle; his pith helmet was wrapped in a long *puggaree*, and he wore a most peculiar loose cape, like an American poncho, clasped round with a snake-clasp belt. Altogether a most ridiculous sight, but there was nothing funny about the pale, staring eyes, or the way his mouth worked as he considered me.

'Who's this?' he barked, and when Cheeseman told him, and O'Toole, who had been eyeing me closely, said he believed I was Flashman after all, he growled suspiciously and demanded to know why I was skulking about dressed as a native, and where had I come from. So I told him, briefly, that I was a political, lately from Jhansi, where I and my three followers had escaped the massacre.

'What's that you say?' cries he. 'Massacre – at Jhansi?' And the others crowded their horses round, staring and exclaiming, while I reported what had happened to Skene and the rest – even as I told it, I was uncomfortably aware of something not quite canny in the way they listened: it was a shocking story enough, but there was an excitement about them, in the haggard faces and the bright eyes, as though they had some fever, that I couldn't account for. Usually, when Englishmen listen to a dreadful tale, they do it silently, at most with signs of disgust or disbelief, but this crowd stirred restlessly in their saddles, muttering and exclaiming, and when I'd finished the little chap burst into tears, gritting his teeth and shaking his crop.

'God in Heaven!' cries he. 'Will it never cease? How many innocents – twenty children, you say? And all the women? My God!' He rocked in his saddle, dashing the tears away, while his companions groaned and shook their fists – it was an astonishing sight, those dozen scarecrows who looked as though they'd fought a long campaign in fancy-dress costume, swearing and addressing heaven; it occurred to me that they weren't quite right in the head. Presently the little chap regained his composure, and turned to me.

'Your pardon, colonel,' says he, and if his voice was low it was shaking with emotion. 'This grievous news – this shocking intelligence – it makes me forget myself. Rowbotham, James Kane Rowbotham, at your service; these are my moss-troopers – my column of volunteer horse, sir, banded after the rebellion at Delhi, and myself commissioned by Governor Colvin at Agra.'

'Commissioned . . . by a civilian?' It sounded deuced odd, but then he and his gang looked odd. 'I gather, sir, that you ain't . . . er, Army?'

He flew up at that. 'We are soldiers, sir, as much as you! A month ago I was a doctor, at Delhi . . .' His mouth

213

worked again, and his tongue seemed to be impeding his speech. 'My . . . my wife and son, sir . . . lost in the uprising . . . murdered. These gentlemen . . . volunteers, sir, from Agra and Delhi . . . merchants, lawyers, officials, people of all classes. Now we act as a mobile column, because there are no regular cavalry to be spared from the garrisons; we strive to keep the road open between Agra and Cawnpore, but since the mutineers are now before Cawnpore in force, we scour the country for news of their movements and fall on them when we can. Vermin!' He choked, glaring round, and his eye fell on the prisoner, prone in the dust with a Sikh keeping a foot on his neck. 'Yes!' cries he, 'we may not be soldiers, sir, in your eyes, but we have done some service in putting down this abomination! Oh, yes! You'll see – you'll see for yourself! Cheeseman! How many have we now?'

'Seven, sir, counting this one.' Cheeseman nodded at the prisoner. 'Here comes Fields with the others now.'

What I took to be the rest of Rowbotham's remarkable regiment was approaching down the road at a brisk trot, a dozen Sikhs and two Englishmen in the same kind of outlandish rig as the others. Running or staggering behind, their wrists tied to the Sikhs' stirrup-leathers, were half a dozen niggers in the last stages of exhaustion; three or four of them were plainly native infantrymen, from their coats and breeches.

'Bring them up here!' cries Rowbotham violently, and when they had been untied and ranged in a straggled line in front of him, he pointed to the trees behind them. 'Those will do excellently – get the ropes, Cheeseman! Untie their hands, and put them under the branches.' He was bouncing about in his saddle in excitement, and there were little flecks of spittle among the stubble of his chin. 'You'll see, sir,' says he to me. 'You'll see how we deal with these filthy butchers of women and children! It has been our custom to hang them in groups of thirteen, as an appropriate warning – but this news of Jhansi which you bring – this new horror – makes it necessary . . . makes it necessary . . .' He broke off incoherently, twisting the reins in his hands. 'We must make an immediate example, sir! This cancer of mutiny . . . what? Let these serve as a sacrifice to those dead innocent spirits so cruelly released at Jhansi!'

He wasn't mad, I'd decided; he was just an ordinary little man suddenly at war. I've seen it scores of times. He had reason, too; I, who had been at Meerut and Jhansi, was the last to deny that. His followers were the same; while the Sikhs threw lines over the branches, they sat and stared their hatred at the prisoners; I glanced along and noted the bright eyes, the clenched teeth, the tongues moistening the lips, and thought to myself, you've taken right smartly to nigger-killing, my boys. Well, good luck to you; you'll make the pandies sorry they ever broke ranks before you're done.

They didn't look sorry at the moment, mind, just sullen as the Sikhs knotted the ropes round their necks – except for one of them, a fat scoundrel in a *dhoti* who shrieked and struggled and blubbered and even broke free for a moment and flung himself grovelling before Rowbotham until they dragged him back again. He collapsed in the dust, beating the earth with his hands and feet while the others stood resigned; Cheeseman says:

'Shall we put 'em on horses, sir – makes it quicker?'

'No!' cries Rowbotham. 'How often must I tell you – I do not wish to make it quicker for these . . . these villains! They are being hanged as a punishment, Mr Cheeseman – it is not my design to make it easy for them! Let them suffer – and the longer the better! Will it atone for the atrocities they have wrought? No, not if they were flayed alive! You hear that, you rascals?' He shook his fist at them. 'You know now the price of mutiny and murder – in a moment you shall pay it, and you may thank whatever false God you worship that you obtain a merciful death – you who did not scruple to torture and defile the innocent!' He was raving by now, with both hands in the air, and then he noticed again the dead fellow lying in the road, and roared to the Sikhs to string him up as well, so that they should all hang together as a token of justice. While they were manhandling the corpse he rode along behind the prisoners, examining each knot jealously, and then, so help me, he whipped off his hat and began to pray aloud, beseeching a Merciful God, as he put it, to witness what just retribution they were meting out in His name, and putting in a word for the condemned, although he managed to convey that a few thousand years in hell wouldn't do them any harm.

Then he solemnly told the Sikhs to haul away, and they tailed on the ropes and swung the pandies into the air, the fat one screeching horribly. He wasn't a mutineer, I was certain, but it probably wouldn't have been tactful to mention that just then. The others gasped and thrashed about, clutching at their halters – now I saw why they hadn't tied their hands, for three of them managed to clutch the ropes and haul themselves up, while the others choked and turned blue and presently hung there, twitching and swaying gently in the sunlight. Everyone was craning to watch the struggles of the three who had got their hands on the ropes, pulling themselves up to take the choking strain off their necks; they kicked and screamed now, swinging wildly to and fro; you could see their muscles quivering with the appalling strain.

'Five to one on the Rajput,' says O'Toole, fumbling in his pockets.

'Gammon,' says another. 'He's no stayer; I'll give evens on the little 'un – less weight to support, you see.'

'Neither of 'em's fit to swing alongside that artillery *havildar* we caught near Barthana,' says a third. 'Remember, the one old J.K. found hiding under the old woman's charpoy. I thought he'd hang on forever – how long was it, Cheese?'

'Six and a half minutes,' says Cheeseman. He had his foot cocked up on his saddle and was scribbling in a notebook. 'That's eighty-six, by the way, with today's batch—' he nodded towards the struggling figures. 'Counting the three shot last night, but not the ones we killed in the Mainpuri road ambush. Should knock up our century by tomorrow night, with luck.'

'I say, that's not bad – hollo, O'Toole, there goes your Rajput! Bad luck, old son – five chips, what? Told you my bantam was the form horse, didn't I?'

'Here – he'll be loose in a moment, though! Look!' O'Toole pointed to the small sepoy, who had managed to pull himself well up his rope, getting his elbow in the bight of it, and was tugging at the noose with his other hand. One of the Sikhs sprang up to haul at his ankles, but Rowbotham barked an order and then, drawing his revolver, took careful aim and shot the sepoy through the body. The man jerked convulsively and then fell, his head snapping back as the rope tightened; someone laughed and sang out 'Shame!' while another huzzaed, and then they all had their pistols out, banging away at the hanging figures which twitched and swung under the impact of the bullets.

'Take that, you bastard!' 'There – that's for little Jane! And that – and that!' 'How d'ye like it now, you black pig of a mutineer? I wish you had fifty lives to blow away!' 'Die, damn you – and roast in hell!' 'That's for Johnson – that's for Mrs Fox – that, that, and that for the Prices!' They wheeled their mounts under the corpses, which were running with blood now, blasting at them point-blank.

'Too bloody good for 'em!' cries the white-bearded chap in the straw hat, as he fumbled feverishly to reload. 'The colonel's right – we ought to be flaying 'em alive, after what they've done! Take that, you devil! Or burning the brutes. I say, J.K., why ain't we burnin' 'em?'

They banged away, until Rowbotham called a halt, and their frenzy died down; the smoking pistols were put away, and the column fell in, with the flies buzzing thickly over the eight growing pools of blood beneath the bodies. I wasn't surprised to see the riders suddenly quiet now, their excitement all spent; they sat heavy in their saddles, breathing deeply, while Cheeseman checked their dressing. It's the usual way, with civilians suddenly plunged into war and given the chance to kill; for the first time, after years spent pushing pens and counting pennies, they're suddenly free of all restraint, away from wives and families and responsibility, and able to indulge their animal instincts. They go a little crazy after a while, and if you can convince 'em they're doing the Lord's work, they soon start enjoying it. There's nothing like a spirit of righteous retribution for kindling cruelty in a decent, kindly, God-fearing man – I, who am not one, and have never needed any virtuous excuse for my bestial indulgences, can tell you that. Now, having let off steam, they were sated, and some a little shocked at themselves, just as if they'd been whoring for the first time – which, of course, was something they'd never have dreamed of doing, proper little Christians that they were. If you ask me what I think of what I'd just witnessed – well, personally, I'd have backed O'Toole's Rajput, and lost my money.

However, now that the bloody assizes was over, and Rowbotham and his merry men were ready to take the road again, I was able to get back to the business in hand, which was getting myself safely into Cawnpore. Fortunately they were headed that way themselves, since two weeks spent slaughtering pandies in the countryside had exhausted their forage and ammunition (the way they shot up corpses, I wasn't surprised). But when, as we rode along, I questioned Rowbotham about how the land lay, and what the cannonading to the north signified, I was most disagreeably surprised by his answer; it couldn't have been much worse news.

Cawnpore was under siege, right enough, and had been for two weeks. It seemed that Wheeler, unlike most commanders, had seen the trouble coming; he didn't trust his sepoys a damned inch, and as soon as he heard of the Meerut rising he'd prepared a big new fortification in barracks on the eastern edge of Cawnpore city, with entrenchments and guns, so that if his four native regiments mutinied he could get inside it with every British civilian and loyal rifle in the place. He knew that the city itself, a great straggling place along the Ganges, was indefensible, and that he couldn't have hoped to secure the great numbers of white civilians, women and children and all, unless he packed them into his new stronghold, which was by the racecourse, and had a good level field of fire all round.

So when the pandies did mutiny, there he was, all prepared, and for a fortnight he'd been giving them their bellyful, in spite of the fact that the mutineers had been reinforced by the local native prince, Nana Dondu Pant Sahib, who'd turned traitor at the last minute. Rowbotham hadn't the least doubt that the place would hold; rumours had reached him that help was already on its way, from Lucknow, forty miles to the north, and from Allahabad, which lay farther off, east along the Ganges.

This was all very well, but we were going to have to run the gauntlet to get inside, as I pointed out; wouldn't it be better to skirt the place and make for Lucknow, which by all accounts was still free from mutiny? He wouldn't have that, though; his troops needed supplies badly, and in the uncertain state of the country he must make for the nearest British garrison. Besides, he anticipated no difficulty about getting in; his Sikhs had already scouted the pandy besiegers, and while they were in great strength there was no order about their lines, and plenty of places to slip through. He'd even got a message in to Wheeler, giving him a time and signal for our arrival, so that we could win to the entrenchment without any danger of being mistaken for the enemy.

For a sawbones he was a most complete little bandolero, I'll say that for him, but what he said gave me the blue fits straight off. Plainly, I'd jumped from the Jhansi frying-pan into the Cawnpore fire, but what the devil could I do about it? From what Rowbotham said, there wasn't a safe bolthole between Agra and Allahabad; no one knew how many garrisons were still holding, and those that were couldn't offer any safer refuge than Cawnpore; I daren't try a run for Lucknow with Ilderim (God knew what state it might be in when we got there). A rapid, fearful calculation convinced me that there wasn't a better bet than to stick with this little madman, and pray to God he knew what he was doing. After all, Wheeler was a good man – I'd known him in the Sikh War – and Rowbotham was positive he'd hold out easily and be relieved before long.

'And that will be the end of this wicked, abominable insurrection,' says he, when we made camp that night ten miles closer to Cawnpore, with the distant northern sky lighting to the flashes of gunfire, rumbling away unceasingly. 'We know that our people are already investing Delhi, and must soon break down the rebel defences and pull that unclean creature who calls himself King off his traitor's throne – that will be to root out the mischief at its heart. Then, when Lawrence moves south from Lucknow, and our other forces push up the river, this nest of rebels about Cawnpore will be trapped; destroy them, and the thing is done. Then it will only remain to restore order, and visit a merited punishment upon these scoundrels; they must be taught such a lesson as will never be forgotten – aye, if we have to destroy them by tens of thousands –' he was away again on that fine, rising bray which reminded me of the hangings that afternoon; his troopers, round the camp-fire, growled enthusiastically '– hundreds of thousands, even. Nothing less will serve if this foulness is to be crushed once for all. Mercy will be folly – it will be construed as mere weakness.'

This sermon provoked a happy little discussion on whether, when all the mutineers had been rounded up, they should be blown from guns, or hanged, or shot. Some favoured burning alive, and others flogging to death; the chap in the straw hat was strong for crucifixion, I remember, but another fellow thought that would be blasphemous. They got quite heated about it – and before you throw up your hands in pious horror, remember that many of them had seen their own families butchered in the kind of circumstances I'd witnessed myself at Meerut, and were thirsting to pay the pandies back with interest, which was reasonable enough. Also, they were convinced that if they didn't make a dreadful

221

example, it would lead to more outbreaks, and the slaughter of every white person in India – the fear of that, and the knowledge of the kind of wantonly cruel foe they were up against, hardened them as nothing else could have done.

It was all one to me, I may say; I was too anxious about coming safe into Cawnpore to worry about how they disposed of the mutineers – it seemed a trifle premature to me. They were the rummest lot, though; when they'd tired of devising means of execution they got into a great argument about whether hacking and carrying should be allowed in football, and as I was an old Rugby boy my support was naturally enlisted by the hackers – it must have been the strangest sight, when I come to think of it, me in my garb of hairy Pathan with *poshteen* and *puggaree*, maintaining that if you did away with scrimmaging you'd be ruining the manliest game there was (not that I'd go near a scrimmage if you paid me), and the white-bearded wallah, with the blood splashes still on his coat, denouncing the handling game as a barbarism. Most of the others joined in, on one side or the other, but there were some who sat apart brooding, reading their Bibles, sharpening their weapons, or just muttering to themselves; it wasn't a canny company, and I can get the shivers thinking about them now.

They could soldier, though; how Rowbotham had licked them into shape in less than a month (and where *he'd* got the genius from) beat me altogether, but you never saw anything more workmanlike than the way they disposed their march next day, with flank riders and scouts, a twenty-pound forage bag behind each saddle, all their gear and arms padded with cloth so that they didn't jingle, and even leather night-shoes for the horses slung on their cruppers. Pencherjevsky's Cossacks and Custer's scalp-hunters couldn't have made a braver show than that motley gang of clerks and counter-jumpers that followed Rowbotham to Cawnpore.

We were coming in from the east, and since the pandy army was all concentrated close to Wheeler's stronghold and in the city itself, we got within two or three miles before Rowbotham said we must lie up in a wood and wait for dark. Before then, by the way, we'd pounced on an outlying pandy picket in a grove and killed two of them, taking three more prisoner: they were strung up on the spot. Two more stragglers were caught farther on, and since there wasn't a tree handy Rowbotham and the Sikh *rissaldar* cut their heads off. The Sikh settled his man with one swipe, but Rowbotham took three; he wasn't much with a sabre. (Ninety-three not out, as Cheeseman put it.)

We lay up in the stuffy, sweltering heat of the wood all afternoon, listening to the incessant thunder of the cannonading; one consolation was the regular crash of the artillery salvoes, which indicated that Wheeler's gunners were making good practice, and must still be well stocked with powder and shot. Even after nightfall they still kept cracking away, and one of the Sikhs, who had wormed his way up to within a quarter-mile of the entrenchment, reported that he had heard Wheeler's sentries singing out 'All's well!' regular as clockwork.

About two in the morning Rowbotham called us together and gave his orders. 'There is a clear way to the Allahabad road,' says he, 'but before we reach it we must bear right to come in behind the rebel gun positions, no more than half a mile from the entrenchment. At precisely four o'clock I shall fire a rocket, on which we shall burst out of cover and ride for the entrenchment at our uttermost speed; the sentries, having seen our rocket, will pass us through. The word is

223

"Britannia". Now, remember, for your lives, that our goal lies to the left of the church, so keep that tower always to your right front. Our rush will take us past the racecourse and across the cricket pitch –'

'Oh, I say!' says someone. 'Mind the wicket, though.'

'– and then we must put our horses to the entrenchment bank, which is four feet high. Now, God bless us all, and let us meet again within the lines or in Heaven.'

That's just the kind of pious reminder of mortality I like, I must say; while the rest of 'em were shaking hands in the dark I was carefully instructing Ilderim that at all costs he must stick by my shoulder. I was in my normal state of chattering funk, and my spirits weren't raised as we were filing out of the wood and I heard someone whisper:

'I say, Jinks, what's the time?'

'Ten past three,' says Jinks, 'on the bright summer morning of June the twenty-second – and let's hope to God we see the twenty-third.'

June twenty-third; I knew that date – and suddenly I was back in the big panelled room at Balmoral, and Pam was saying '. . . the Raj will come to an end a hundred years after the battle of Plassey . . . next June twenty-third.' By George, there was an omen for you! And now all round was the gloom, and the soft pad of the walking horses, and the reins sweating in my palms as we advanced interminably, my eyes glued to the faint dark shape of the rider ahead; there was a mutter of voices as we halted, and then we waited in the stifling dark between two rows of ruined houses – five minutes, ten, fifteen, and then a voice called 'Ready, all!' There was the flare of a match, a curse, then a brighter glare, and suddenly a rush of sparks and an orange rocket shot up into the purple night sky, weaving like a comet, and as it burst to a chorus of cries and yells from far ahead Rowbotham shouts 'Advance!' and we dug in our heels and fairly shot forward in a thundering mass.

There was a clear space ahead, and then a grove of trees, and beyond more level ground with dim shapes moving. As we bore down on them I realised that they must be pandies; we were charging the rear of their positions, and it was just light enough to make out the guns parked at intervals. There were shrieks of alarm and a crackle of shots, and then we were past, swerving between the gun-pits; there were horsemen ahead and either side and Ilderim crouched low in the saddle at my elbow. He yelled something and pointed right, and I saw an irregular tumbled outline which must be the church; to its left, directly ahead, little sparks of light were flashing in the distance – the entrenchment defenders were firing to cover us.

Someone sang out: 'Bravo, boys!' and then all hell burst loose behind us; there was a crashing salvo of cannon, the earth ahead rose up in fountains of dust, and shot was whistling over our heads. A horse screamed, and I missed by a whisker a thrashing tangle of man and mount which I passed so close that a lashing limb caught me smack on the knee. Voices were roaring in the dark, I heard Rowbotham's frantic 'Close up! Ride for it!' A dismounted man plunged across my path and was hurled aside by my beast; behind me I heard the shriek of someone mortally hit, and a riderless horse came neighing and stretching frantically against my left side. Another shattering volley burst from the guns in our rear, and that hellish storm swept through us – it was Balaclava all over again, and in the dark, to boot. Suddenly my pony stumbled, and I knew from the way he came up that he was hit; a stinging cloud of earth and gravel struck me across the face, a shot howled overhead, and Ilderim was sweeping past ahead of me.

'Stop!' I bawled. 'My screw's foundered! Stop, blast you – give me a hand!'

I saw his shadowy form check, and his horse rear; he swung round, and as my horse sank under me his arm swept me out of the saddle – by God, he was strong, that one. My feet hit the ground, but I had hold of his bridle, and for a few yards I was literally dragged along, with Ilderim above hauling to get me across the crupper. Someone cannoned into us, and then as I pulled myself by main force across the crupper I felt a sudden shock, and Ilderim pitched over me and out of the saddle.

Even as I righted myself on the horse's back the whole scene was suddenly bathed in glaring light – some swine had fired a flare, and its flickering illumination shone on a scene that looked like a mad artist's hell. Men and horses seemed to be staggering and going down all round me under the hail of fire, throwing grotesque shadows as they fought and struggled. I saw Rowbotham pinned under a fallen horse only a few yards away; Cheeseman, his face a bloody mask, was stretched supine beside him, his limbs asprawl; Ilderim, with his left arm dangling, was half-up on one knee, clutching at my stirrup. A bare hundred yards ahead the entrenchment was in plain view, with the defenders' heads visible, and some ass standing atop of it waving his hat; behind us, the red explosions of the cannon suddenly died, and to my horror I saw, pounding out under the umbrella of light cast by the flare, a straggling line of riders – sepoy cavalry with their sabres out, bearing down at the charge, and not more than a furlong away. Ilderim seized my stirrup and bawled:

'On, on! Ride, brother!'

226

I didn't hesitate. He'd turned back to rescue me, and his noble sacrifice wasn't going to be in vain if I could help it. That was certain death bearing down on us; I jammed in my heels, the horse leaped forward, and Ilderim was almost jerked off his feet. For perhaps five paces he kept up, with the yells and hoof-beats growing behind us, and then he stumbled and went down. I did my damnedest to shake him free, but in that instant the bloody bridle snapped, and I hurled out of the saddle and hit the ground with a smash that jarred every bone in my body. A shocking pain shot through my left ankle – Christ, it was caught in the stirrup, and the horse was tearing ahead, dragging me behind at the end of a tangle of leatherwork which somehow was still attached to its body.

If any of you young fellows ever find yourself in this predicament, where you're dragged over rough, iron-hard ground, with or without a mob of yelling black fiends after you, take a word of advice from me. Keep your head up (screaming helps), and above all try to be dragged on your back – it will cost you a skinned arse, but that's better than having your organs scraped off. Try, too, to arrange for some stout lads to pour rapid fire into your pursuers, and for a handy Gilzai friend to chase after you and slash the stirrup-leather free in the nick of time before your spine falls apart. I was half-conscious and virtually buttockless when Ilderim – God knows, wounded as he was, where he'd got the speed and strength – hauled me up below the entrenchment and pitched me almost bodily over the breastwork. I went over in a shocking tangle, roaring: 'Britannia! Britannia, for Christ's sake! I'm a friend!' and then a chap was catching me and lowering my battered carcase to earth and inquiring:

'Will you have nuts or a cigar, sir?'

Then a musket was being pushed into my hand, and in

shocked confusion I found myself at the rampart, banging away at red-coated figures who came out of the smoke and dust, and I know Ilderim was alongside me, relieving me of my revolver and loosing off shots into the brown. All round there was the crash of volleys, and a great bass voice was yelling. 'Odds, fire! Reload! Evens, fire! Reload!' The pain from my ankle was surging up my leg, into my body, making me sick and dizzy, I was coughing with the reek of powder smoke, there was a bugle sounding, and a confused roar of cheering – and the next thing I remember I was lying in the half-light of dawn, with my back against a sand-bagged wall, staring at a big, shot-torn barrack building, while a tall, bald-headed cove with a pipe was getting my boot off, and applying a damp cloth to my swollen ankle.

There were a couple of chaps with muskets looking on, and Ilderim was having his arm bandaged by a fellow in a kepi and spectacles. There were others, moving about, carrying people towards the barrack, and along the parapet there were haggard-looking fellows, white and sepoy, with their pieces at the ready. A horrid smell seemed to hang over the place, and everything was filthy, with gear and litter all over the dusty ground, and the people seemed to be moving slowly. I was still feeling pretty dazed, but I guessed it must all be a dream anyway, for the chap third along the parapet to my left, with a handkerchief knotted round his head, was undoubtedly young Harry East. There couldn't be two snub noses like that in the world, and since the last time I'd seen him I'd been pinned under a sledge in the snows of southern Russia, and he had been lighting out for safety, it didn't seem reasonable that he should have turned up here.

I'll tell you a strange thing about pain – and Cawnpore. That ankle of mine, which I'd thought was broken, but which in fact was badly sprained, would have kept me flat on my back for days anywhere else, bleating for sympathy; in Cawnpore I was walking on it within a few hours, suffering damnably, but with no choice but to endure it. That was the sort of place it was; if you'd had both legs blown off you were rated fit for only light duties.

Imagine a great trench, with an earth and rubble parapet five feet high, enclosing two big single-storey barracks, one of them a burned-out shell and the other with half its roof gone. All round was flat plain, stretching hundreds of yards to the encircling pandy lines which lay among half-ruined buildings and trees; a mile or less to the north-west was the great straggling mass of Cawnpore city itself, beside the river – but when anyone of my generation speaks of Cawnpore he means those two shattered barracks with the earth wall round them.

That was where Wheeler, with his ramshackle garrison,

had been holding out against an army for two and a half weeks. There were nine hundred people inside it when the siege began, nearly half of them women and children; of the rest four hundred were British soldiers and civilians, and a hundred loyal natives. They had one well, and three cannon; they were living on two handfuls of mealies a day, fighting off a besieging force of more than three thousand mutineers who smashed at them constantly with fifteen cannon, subjected them to incessant musket-fire, and tried to storm the entrenchment. The defenders lost over two hundred dead in the first fortnight, men, women, and children, from gunfire, heat and disease; the hospital barrack had been burned to ashes with the casualties inside, and of the three hundred left fit to fight, more than half were wounded or ill. They worked the guns and manned the wall with muskets and bayonets and whatever they could lay hands on.

This, I discovered to my horror, was the place I'd fled to for safety, the stronghold which Rowbotham had boasted was being held with such splendid ease. It was being held – by starved ghosts half of whom had never fired a musket before, with their women and children dying by inches in the shot-torn, stifling barrack behind them, in the certainty that unless help came quickly that entrenchment would be their common grave. Rowbotham never lived to discover how mistaken he'd been: he and half his troop were lying stark out on the plain – his final miscalculation having been to time our rush to coincide with a pandy assault.

I was the senior officer of those who'd got safely (?) inside, and when they'd discovered who I was and bound up my ankle I was helped into the little curtained corner of the remaining barrack where Wheeler had his office. We stared at each other in disbelief, he because I was still looking like

Abdul the Bulbul, and I because in place of the stalwart, brisk commander I'd known ten years ago there was now a haggard, sunken ancient; with his grimy, grizzled face, his uniform coat torn and filthy, and his breeches held up with string, he looked like a dead gardener.

'Good God, you're never young Harry Flashman!' was his greeting to me. 'Yes, you are though! Where the dooce did you spring from?' I told him – and in the short time I took to tell him about Meerut and Jhansi, no fewer than three round-shot hit the building, shaking the plaster; Wheeler just brushed the debris absently off his table, and then says:

'Well, thank God for twenty more men – though what we'll feed you on I cannot think. Still, what matter a few more mouths? – you see the plight we're in. You've heard nothing of . . . our people advancing from Allahabad, or Lucknow?' I said I hadn't and he looked round at his chief officers, Vibart and Moore, and gave a little gesture of despair.

'I suppose it was not be expected,' says he. 'So . . . we can only do our duty – how much longer? If only it was not for the children, I think we could face it well enough. Still – no croaking, eh?' He gave me a tired grin. 'Don't take it amiss if I say I'm glad to see you, Flashman, and will welcome your presence in our council. In the meantime, the best service you can do is to take a place at the parapet. Moore here will show you – God bless you,' says he, shaking hands, and it was from Moore, a tall, fair-haired captain with his arm in a blood-smeared sling, that I learned of what had been happening in the past two weeks, and how truly desperate our plight was.

It may read stark enough, but the sight of it was terrible. Moore took me round the entrenchment, stooping as he walked and I hobbled, for the small-arms fire from the distant

231

sepoy lines kept whistling overhead, smacking into the barrack wall, and every so often a large shot would plump into the enclosure or smash another lump out of the building. It was terrifying – and yet no one seemed to pay it much attention; the men at the parapet just popped up for an occasional look, and those moving in the enclosure, with their heads hunched down, never even broke step if a bullet whined above them. I kept bobbing nervously, and Moore grinned and said:

'You'll soon get used to it – pandy marksmen don't hit a dam' thing they aim at. It's the random shots that do the damage – damnation!' This as a cloud of dust, thrown up by a round-shot hitting the parapet, enveloped us. 'Stretcher, there! Lively now!' There was a body twitching close by where the shot had struck; at Moore's shout two fellows doubled out from the barrack to attend to it. After a brief look one of them shook his head, and then they picked up the body between them and carried it off towards what looked like a well; they just pitched it in, and Moore says:

'That's our cemetery. I've worked it out that we put someone in there every two hours. Over there – that's the wet well, where we get our water. We won't go too close – the pandy sharpshooters get a clear crack at it from that grove yonder, so we draw our water at night. Jock McKillop worked it for a week, until they got him. Heaven only knows how many we've lost on water-drawing since.'

What seemed so unreal about it, and still does, was the quiet conversational way he talked. There was this garrison, being steadily shot to bits, and starving in the process, and he went on pointing things out, cool as dammit, with the crackle of desultory firing going on around us. I stomached it so long, and then burst out:

232

'But in God's name – it's hopeless! Hasn't Wheeler tried to make terms?'

He laughed straight out at that. 'Terms? Who with? Nana Sahib? Look here, you were at Meerut, weren't you? Did *they* make terms? They want us dead, laddie. They slaughtered everything white up in the city yonder, and God knows how many of their own folk as well. They tortured the native goldsmiths to death to get at their loot; Nana's been blowing loyal Indians from guns as fast as they can trice 'em over the muzzles! No,' he shook his head, 'there'll be no terms.'

'But what the devil – I mean, what . . .?'

'What's going to come of it? Well, I don't need to tell you, of all people – either a relief column wins through from Allahabad in three days at most, or we'll be so starved and short of cartridge that the pandies will storm over that wall. Then . . .' He shrugged. 'But of course, we don't admit that – not in front of the ladies, anyway, however much some of 'em may guess. Just grin and assure 'em that Lawrence will be up with the rations any day, what?'

I won't trouble to describe my emotions as this sank in, along with the knowledge that for once there was nowhere to bolt to – and I couldn't have run anyway, with my game ankle. It was utterly hopeless – and what made it worse, if anything, was that as a senior man I had to pretend, like Wheeler and Moore and Vibart and the rest, that I was ready to do or die with the best. Even I couldn't show otherwise – not with everyone else steady and cheery enough to sicken you. I'll carry to my grave the picture of that blood-sodden ground, with the flies droning everywhere, and the gaunt figures at the parapet; the barrack wall honeycombed with the shots that slapped into it every few seconds; the occasional cry of a man struck; the stretcher parties running – and

233

through it all Moore walking about with his bloody arm, grinning and calling out jokes to everyone; Wheeler, with his hat on his head and the pistol through the cord at his waist, staring grim-faced at the pandy lines and scratching his white moustache while he muttered to the aide scribbling notes at his elbow; a Cockney sergeant arguing with a private about the height of the pillars at Euston Square station, while they cut pieces from a dead horse for the big copper boiler against the barrack wall.

'Stew today,' says Moore to me. 'That's thanks to you fellows coming in. Usually, if we want meat, we have to let a pandy cavalryman charge up close, and then shoot the horse, not the rider.'

'More meat on the 'orse than there is on the pandy, eh, Jasper?' says the sergeant, winking, and the private said it was just as well, since some non-coms of his acquaintance, namin' no names, would as soon be cannibals as not.

These are the trivial things that stick in memory, but none clearer than the inside of that great barrack-room, with the wounded lying in a long, sighing, groaning line down one wall, and a few yards away, behind roughly improvised screens of chick and canvas, four hundred women and children, who had lived in that confined, sweating furnace for two weeks. The first thing that struck you was the stench, of blood and stale sweat and sickness, and then the sound – the children's voices, a baby crying, the older ones calling out, and some even laughing, while the firing cracked away outside; the quiet murmur of the women; the occasional gasp of pain from the wounded; the brisk voices from the curtained corner where Wheeler had his office. Then the gaunt patient faces – the weary-looking women, some in ragged aprons, others in soiled evening dresses, nursing or minding the children or tending the wounded; the loyal sepoys, slumped against the wall, with their muskets between their knees; an English civilian sitting writing, and staring up in thought, and then writing again; beside him an old babu in a *dhoti*, mouthing the words as he read a scrap of newspaper through steel-rimmed spectacles; a haggard-looking young girl stitching a garment for a small boy who was waiting and hitting out angrily at the flies buzzing round his head; two officers in foul suits that had once been white, talking about pig-sticking – I remember one jerking his arm to shoot his linen, and him with nothing over his torso but his jacket; an *ayah**** smiling as she piled toy bricks for a little girl; a stocky, tow-headed corporal scraping his pipe; a woman whispering from the Bible to a pallid Goanese-looking fellow lying on a blanket with a bloody bandage round his head; an old, stern, silver-haired mem-sahib rocking a cradle.

They were all waiting to die, and some of them knew it, but there was no complaint, no cross words that I ever heard. It wasn't real, somehow – the patient, ordinary way they carried on. 'It beats me,' I remember Moore saying, 'when I think how our dear ladies used to slang and back-bite on the verandahs, to see 'em now, as gentle as nuns. Take my word for it, they'll never look at their fellow-women the same way again, if we get out of this.'

'Don't you believe it,' says another, called Delafosse. 'It's just lack of grub that's keeping 'em quiet. A week after it's all over, they'll be cutting Lady Wheeler dead in the street, as usual.'

It's all vague memory, though, with no sense of time to it; I couldn't tell you when it was that I came face to face with

* Native nursemaid.

Harry East, and we spoke, but I know that it was near Wheeler's curtain, where I'd been talking with two officers called Whiting and Thomson, and a rather pretty girl called Bella Blair was sitting not far away reading a poem to some of the children. I must have got over my funks to some extent, for I know I was sufficiently myself to be properly malicious to him.

'Hallo, Flashman,' says he.

'Hallo, young Scud East,' says I, quite cool. 'You got to Raglan, I hear.'

'Yes,' says he, blushing. 'Yes, I did.'

'Good for you,' says I. 'Wish I could have come along – but I was delayed, you recollect.'

This was all Greek to the others, of course, so the young ass had to blurt it out for their benefit – how we'd escaped together in Russia, and he'd left me behind wounded (which, between ourselves, had been the proper thing to do, since there was vital news to carry to Raglan at Sevastopol), and the Cossacks had got me. Of course, he hadn't got the style to make the tale sound creditable to himself, and I saw Whiting cock an eyebrow and sniff. East stuttered over it, and blushed even redder, and finally says:

'I'm so glad you got out, in the end, though, Flashman. I . . . I hated leaving you, old fellow.'

'Yes,' says I. 'The Cossacks were all for it, though.'

'I . . . I hope they didn't – I mean, they didn't use you too badly . . . that they didn't . . .' He was making a truly dreadful hash of it, much to my enjoyment. 'It's been on my conscience, you know . . . having to go off like that.'

Whiting was looking at the ceiling by this. Thomson was frowning, and the delectable Bella had stopped reading to listen.

'Well,' says I, after a moment, 'it's all one now, you know.' I gave a little sigh. 'Don't fret about it, young Scud. If the worst comes to the worst here – I won't leave *you* behind.'

It hit him like a blow; he went chalk-white, and gasped, and then he turned on his heel and hurried off. Whiting said, 'Good God!' and Thomson asked incredulously: 'Did I understand that right? He absolutely cut out and left you – saved his own skin?'

'Um? What's that?' says I, and frowned. 'Oh, now, that's a bit hard. No use both of us being caught and strung up in a dungeon and . . .' I stopped there and bit my lip. 'That would just have meant the Cossacks would have had two of us to . . . play with, wouldn't it? Doubled the chance of one of us cracking and telling 'em what they wanted to know. That's why I wasn't sorry he cleared out . . . I knew I could trust myself, you see . . . But, Lord, what am I rambling about? It's all past.' I smiled bravely at them. 'He's a good chap, young East; we were at school together, you know.'

I limped off then, leaving them to discuss it if they wanted to, and what they said I don't know, but later than evening Thomson sought me out at my place on the parapet, and shook my hand without a word, and then Bella Blair came, biting her lip, and kissed me quickly on the cheek and hurried off. It's truly remarkable, if you choose a few words carefully, how you can enhance your reputation and damage someone else's – and it was the least I could do to pay back that pious bastard East. Between me and his own precious Arnold-nurtured conscience he must have had a happy night of it.

I didn't sleep too well myself. A cupful of horse stew and a handful of flour don't settle you, especially if you're shaking with the horrors of your predicament. I even toyed with the idea of resuming my Pathan dress – which I had exchanged for army shirt and breeches – slipping over the parapet, lame as I was, and trying to escape, but the thought of being caught in the pandy lines was more than I could bear. I just lay there quaking, listening to the distant crack of the rebel snipers, and the occasional crump of a shot landing in the enclosure, tortured by thirst and hunger cramps, and I must have dozed off, for suddenly I was being shaken, and all round me people were hurrying, and a brazen voice was bawling 'Stand to! Stand to! Loading parties, there!' A bugle was blaring, and orders were being shouted along the parapet – the fellow next me was ramming in a charge hurriedly, and when I demanded what was the row he just pointed out over the barricade, and invited me to look for myself.

It was dawn, and across the flat maidan, in front of the pandy gun positions, men were moving – hundreds of them. I could see long lines of horsemen in white tunics, dim through the light morning mist, and in among the squadrons were the scarlet coats and white breeches of native infantry. Even as I looked there was the red winking of fire from the gun positions, and then the crash of the explosions, followed by the whine of shot and a series of crashes from the barracks behind. Clouds of dust billowed down from the wall, to the accompaniment of yells and oaths, and a chorus of wails from the children. A kettledrum was clashing, and here were the loading parties, civilians and followers and even some of the women, and a couple of *bhistis*,* and then Wheeler himself, with Moore at his heels, bawling orders, and behind him on the barrackroof the torn Union Jack was being hauled up to flap limply in the warm dawn air.

'They're coming, rot 'em!' says the man next to me. 'Look

---

* Native water-carriers.

at 'em, yonder – 56th N.I., Madras Fusiliers. An' Bengal Cavalry, too – don't I know it! Those are my own fellows, blast the scoundrels – or were. All right, my bucks, your old riding-master's waiting for you!' He slapped the stock of his rifle. I'll give you more pepper than I ever did at stables!'

The pandy guns were crashing away full tilt now, and the whistle of small arms shot was sounding overhead. I was fumbling with my revolver, pressing in the loads; all down the parapet there was the scraping of ramrods, and Wheeler was shouting:

'Every piece loaded, mind! Loading parties be ready with fresh charges! Three rifles to each man! All right, Delafosse! Moore, call every second man from the south side – smartly, now! Have the fire-parties stand by! Sergeant Grady, I want an orderly with bandages every ten yards on this parapet!'

He could hardly be heard above the din of the enemy firing and the crash of the shots as they plumped home; the space between the parapet and the barracks was swirling with dust thrown up by the shot, and we lay with our heads pressed into the earth below the top of the barrier. Someone came forward at a crouching run and laid two charged muskets on the ground beside me; to my astonishment I saw it was Bella Blair – the fat babu I'd seen reading the previous night was similarly arming the riding-master, and the chap on t'other side of me had as his loader a very frail-looking old civilian in a dust-coat and cricket cap. They lay down behind us; Bella was pale as death, but she smiled at me and pushed the hair out of her eyes; she was wearing a yellow calico dress, I recall, with a band tied round her brows.

'All standing to!' roars Wheeler. He alone was on his feet, gaunt and bare-headed, with his white hair hanging in wisps down his cheeks; he had his revolver in one hand, and his sabre stuck point-first in the ground before him. 'Masters – I want a ration of flour and half a cup of water to each—'

A terrific concerted salvo drowned out the words; the whole entrenchment seemed to shake as the shots ploughed into it and smashed clouds of brick dust from the barracks. Farther down the line someone was screaming, high-pitched, there was a cry for the stretchers, the dust eddied round us and subsided, and then the noise gradually ebbed away, even the screams trailed off into a whimper, and a strange, eerie stillness fell.

'Steady, all!' It was Wheeler, quieter now. 'Riflemen – up to the parapet! Now hold your fire, until I give you the word! Steady, now!'

I peered over the parapet. Across the maidan there was silence, too, suddenly broken by the shrill note of a trumpet. There they were, looking like a rather untidy review – the ranks of red-coated infantry, in open order, just forward of the ruined buildings, and before them, within shot, the horse squadrons, half a dozen of them well spaced out. A musket cracked somewhere down the parapet, and Wheeler shouted:

'Confound it, hold that fire! D'you hear?'

We waited and watched as the squadrons formed, and the riding-master cursed under his breath.

'Sickenin',' says he, 'when you think I taught 'em that. As usual – C Troop can't dress! That's *Havildar* Ram Hyder for you! Look at 'em, like a bloody Paul Jones! Take a line from the right-hand troop, can't you? Rest of 'em look well enough, though, don't they? There now, steady up. That's better, eh?'

The man beyond him said something, and the riding-master laughed. 'If they must charge us I'd like to see 'em do it proper, for my own credit's sake, that's all.'

I tore my eyes away from that distant mass of men, and glanced round. The babu, flat on the ground, was turning his head to polish his spectacles; Bella Blair had her face hidden, but I noticed her fists were clenched. Wheeler had clapped his hat on, and was saying something to Moore; one of the *bhistis* was crawling on hands and knees along the line, holding a chaggle for the fellows to drink from. Suddenly the distant trumpet sounded again, there was a chorus of cries from across the maidan, a volley of orders, and now the cavalry were moving, at a walk, and then at a trot, and there was a bright flicker along their lines as the sabres came out.

Oh, Christ, I thought, this is the finish. There seemed to be hordes of them, advancing steadily through the wisps of mist, the dust coming up in little clouds behind them, and the crackle of the sharpshooters started up again, the bullets whining overhead.

'Steady, all!' roars Wheeler again. 'Wait for the word, remember!'

I had laid by my revolver and had my musket up on the parapet. My mouth was so dry I couldn't swallow – I was remembering those masses of horsemen that had poured down from the Causeway Heights at Balaclava, and how disciplined fire had stopped them in their tracks – but those had been Campbell's Highlanders shooting then, and we had nothing but a straggling line of sick crocks and civilians. They must break over us like a wave, brushing past our feeble volleys –

'Take aim!' yells Wheeler, 'make every shot tell, and wait for my command!'

They were coming at the gallop now, perhaps three hundred yards off, and the sabres steady against the shoulders;

241

they were keeping line damned well, and I heard my riding-master muttering:

'Look at 'em come, though! Ain't that a sight? – and ain't they shaping well! Hold 'em in there, *rissaldar*, mind the dressing—'

The thunder of the beating hooves was like surf; there was a sudden yell, and all the points came down, with the black blobs of faces behind them as the riders crouched forward and the whole line burst into the charge. They came sweeping in towards the entrenchment, I gripped my piece convulsively, and Wheeler yelled 'Fire!'

The volley crashed out in a billow of smoke – but it didn't stop them. Horses and men went down, and then we were seizing our second muskets and blazing away, and then our third – and still they came, into that hell of smoke and flame, yelling like madmen; Bella Blair ws beside me, thrusting a musket into my hand, and hurrying feverishly to reload the others. I fired again, and as the smoke cleared we looked out on to a tangle of fallen beasts and riders, but half of them were still up and tearing in, howling and waving their sabres. I seized my revolver and blasted away; there were three of them surging in towards my position, and I toppled one from the saddle, another went rolling down with his mount shot under him, and the third came hurtling over the entrenchment, with the man on my right slashing at him as he passed.

Behind him pressed the others – white coats, black faces, rearing beasts, putting their horses to the parapet; I was yelling incoherent obscenities, scrabbling up the muskets as fast as they were reloaded, firing into the mass; men were struggling all along the entrenchment, bayonets and swords against sabres, and still the firing crashed out. I heard Bella scream, and then there was a dismounted rider scrambling up the barrier directly before me; I had a vision of glaring eyes in a black face and a sabre upraised to strike, and then he fell back shrieking into the smoke. Behind me Wheeler was roaring, and I was grabbing for another musket, and then they were falling back, thank God, wheeling and riding back into the smoke, and the *bhisti* was at my elbow, thrusting his chaggle at my lips.

'Stand to!' shouts Wheeler, 'they're coming again!'

They were re-forming, a bare hundred yards off; the ground between was littered with dead and dying beasts and men. I had barely time to gulp a mouthful of warm, muddy water and seize my musket before they were howling in at us once more, and this time there were pandy infantrymen racing behind them.

'One more volley!' bawls Wheeler. 'Hold your fire, there! Aim for the horses! No surrender! Ready, present – fire!'

The whole wall blasted fire, and the charge shook and wavered before it came rushing on again; half a dozen of them were rearing and plunging up to the entrenchment, the sabres were swinging about our heads, and I was rolling away to avoid the smashing hooves of a rider coming in almost on top of me. I scrambled to my feet, and there was a red-coated black devil leaping at me from the parapet; I smashed at him with my musket butt and sent him flying, and then another one was at me with his sabre, lunging. I shrieked as it flew past my head, and then we had closed, and I was clawing at his face, bearing him down by sheer weight. His sabre fell, and I plunged for it; another pandy was rushing past me, musket and bayonet extended, but I got my hand on the fallen hilt, slashing blindly; I felt a sickening shock on my head, and fell, a dead weight landed on top of me, and the next thing I knew I was on my hands and knees, with the earth swimming round me, and Wheeler was bawling,

'Cease fire! Cease fire! Stretchers, there!' and the noise of yelling and banging had died away, while the last of the smoke cleared above the ghastly shambles of the parapet.

There seemed to be dead and dying everywhere. There must have been at least a dozen pandies sprawled within ten yards of where I knelt; the ground was sticky with blood. Wheeler himself was down on one knee, supporting the fat babu, who was wailing with a shattered leg; the frail civilian was lying asprawl, his cricket cap gone and his head just a squashed red mess. One of the pandies stirred, and pulled himself up on one knee; Wheeler, his arm still round the babu, whipped up his revolver and fired, and the pandy flopped back in the dust. The stretcher-parties were hurrying up; I looked out over the parapet, across a maidan littered with figures of men that crawled or lay still; there were screaming horses trying to rise, and others that lay dead among the fallen riders. Two hundred yards off there were men running – the other way, thank God; farther down the parapet someone sent up a cheer, and it gradually spread along the entrenchment in a ghastly, croaking yell. My mouth was too dry, and I was too dazed to cheer – but I was alive.

Bella Blair was dead. She was lying on her side, her hands clutched on the stock of a musket whose bayonet was buried in her body. I heard a moan behind me, and there was the riding-master, flopped against the parapet, his shirt soaked in blood, trying to reach for the fallen water-chaggle. I stumbled over to him, and held it up to his lips; he sucked it, groaning, and then let his head fall back.

'Beat 'em, did we?' says he, painfully. I could only nod; I took a gulp at the chaggle myself, and offered him another swig, but he turned his head feebly aside. There was nothing to be done for him; his life was running out of him where he lay.

'Beat 'em,' says he again. 'Dam' good. Thought . . . they was going to ride . . . clean over us there . . . for a moment.' He coughed blood, and his voice trailed away into a whisper. 'They shaped well, though . . . didn't they . . . shape well? My Bengalis . . .' He closed his eyes. 'I thought they shaped . . . uncommon well . . .'

I looked down the entrenchment. About half the defenders were on their feet at the parapet, I reckoned. In between, the sprawled, silent figures, the groaning, writhing wounded waiting for the stretchers, the tangle of gear and fallen weapons, the bloody rags – and now the pandy guns again, pounding anew at the near-dead wreck of the Cawnpore garrison, with its tattered flag still flapping from the mast. Well, thinks I, they can walk in now, any time they like. There's nothing left to stop 'em.

But they didn't. That last great assault of June twenty-third, which had come within an ace of breaking us, had sickened the pandies. The maidan was strewn with their dead, and although they pounded us with gunfire for another two terrible days, they didn't have the stomach for another frontal attack. If only they'd known it, half the men left on our parapet were too done up with fatigue and starvation to lift a musket, the barrack was choked with more than three hundred wounded and dying, the well was down to stinking ooze, and our remaining flour was so much dust. We couldn't have lasted two minutes against a determined assault – yet why should they bother, when hunger and heat and the

245

steady rate of casualties from bombardment were sure to finish us soon anyway?

Three folk went mad, as I remember, in those forty-eight hours; I only wonder now that we all didn't. In the furnace of the barrack the women and children were too reduced by famine even to cry; even the younger officers seemed to be overcome by the lethargy of approaching certain death. For that, Wheeler now admitted, was all that remained.

'I have sent a last message out to Lawrence,' he told us senior men on the second night. 'I have told him that we have nothing left but British spirit, and that cannot last forever. We are like rats in a cage. Our best hope is that the rebels will come in again, and give us a quick end; better that than watch our women and little ones die by inches.'[29]

I can still see the gaunt faces in the flickering candlelight round his table; someone gave a little sob, and another swore softly, and after a moment Vibart asked if there was no hope that Lawrence might yet come to our relief.

Wheeler shook his head. 'He would come if he could, but even if he marched now he could not reach us in under two days. By then . . . well, you know me, gentlemen. I haven't croaked in fifty years' soldiering, and I'm not croaking now, when I say that short of a miracle it is *all up*. We're in God's hands, so let each one of us make his preparations accordingly.'

I was with him there, only my preparations weren't going to be spiritual. I still had my Pathan rig-out stowed away, and I could see that the time was fast approaching when, game ankle or no, Flashy was going to have to take his chance over the wall. It was that or die in this stinking hole, so I left them praying and went to my place on the parapet to think it out; I was in a blue funk at the thought of trying to

246

decamp, but the longer I waited, the harder it might become. I was still wrestling with my fears when someone hove up out of the gloom beside me, and who should it be but East.

'Flashman,' says he, 'may I have a word with you?'

'If you must,' says I. 'I'll be obliged if you'll make it a brief one.'

'Of course, of course,' says he. 'I understand. As Sir Hugh said, it is time for each of us to make his own soul; I won't intrude on your meditations a moment longer than I must, I promise. The trouble is . . . my own conscience. I . . . I need your help, old fellow.'

'Eh?' I stared at him, trying to make out his face in the dark. 'What the deuce—?'

'Please . . . bear with me. I know you're bitter, because you think I abandoned you in Russia . . . left you to die, while I escaped. Oh, I know it was my duty, and all that, to get to Raglan . . . but the truth is –' he broke off and had a gulp to himself '– the truth is, I was *glad* to leave you. There – it's out at last . . . oh, if you knew how it had been tormenting me these two years past! That weight on my soul – that I abandoned you in a spirit of hatred and sinful vengeance. No . . . let me finish! I hated you then . . . because of the way you had treated Valla . . . when you flung her from that sledge, into the snow! I could have killed you for it!'

He was in a rare taking, no error; a Rugby conscience pouring out is a hell of a performance. He wasn't telling me a thing I hadn't guessed at the time – I know these pious bastards better than they know themselves, you see.

'I loved her, you see,' he went on, talking like an old man with a hernia. 'She meant everything to me . . . and you had cast her away so . . . brutally. Please, please, hear me out! I'm confessing, don't you see? And . . . and asking for your forgiveness. It's late in the day, I know – but, well, it looks as though we haven't much longer, don't it? So . . . I wanted to tell you . . . and shake your hand, old school-fellow, and hear from you that my . . . my sin is forgiven me. If you can find it in your heart, that is.' He choked resoundingly. 'I . . . I trust you can.'

I've heard some amazing declarations in my time, but this babbling was extraordinary. It comes of Christian upbringing, of course, and taking cold baths, all of which implants in the impressionable mind the notion that repentance can somehow square the account. At any other time, it would have given me some malicious amusement to listen to him; even in my distracted condition, it was interesting enough for me to ask him:

'D'ye mean that if I *hadn't* given you cause to detest me, you'd have stayed with me, and let Raglan's message go hang?'

'What's that?' says he. 'I . . . I don't know what you mean. I . . . I . . . please, Flashman, you must see my agony of spirit . . . I'm trying to . . . make you understand. Please – tell me, even now, what I can do.'

'Well,' says I, thoughtfully, 'you could go and fart in a bottle and paint it.'

'What?' says he, bewildered. 'What did you say?'

'I'm trying to indicate that you can take yourself off,' says I. 'You're a selfish little swine, East. You admit you've behaved like a scoundrel to me, and if that wasn't enough, you have the cheek to waste my time – when I need it for prayer. So go to hell, will you?'

'My God, Flashman . . . you can't mean it! You can't be so hard. It only needs a word! I own I've wronged you, terribly . . . maybe in more ways than I know. Sometimes . . . I've wondered if perhaps you too loved Valla . . . if you did,

248

and placed duty first . . .' He gulped again, and peered at me. 'Did you . . . love her, Flashman?'

'About four or five times a week,' says I, 'but you needn't be jealous; she wasn't nearly as good a ride as her Aunt Sara. You should have tried a steam-bath with that one.'

He gave a shocked gasp, and I absolutely heard his teeth chatter. Then: 'God, Flashman! Oh . . . oh, you are unspeakable! You are vile! God help you!'

'Unspeakable and vile I may be,' says I, 'but at least I'm no hypocrite, like you: the last thing you want is for God to help me. You don't want my forgiveness, either; you just want to be able to forgive yourself. Well, you run along and do it, Scud, and thank me for making it easy for you. After what you've heard tonight, your conscience needn't trouble you any longer about having left old Flashy to his fate, what?'

He stumbled off at that, and I was able to resume my own debate about whether it was best to slide out or stay. In the end, my nerve failed me, and I curled up in the lee of the parapet for the night. Thank God I did, for on the next morning Wheeler got his miracle.

She was the most unlikely messenger of grace you ever saw – a raddled old *chee-chee** biddy with clanking earrings and a parasol, drawn in a rickshaw *ghari* by two pandies, with another couple marching as guard, and a *havildar* out in front brandishing a white flag. Wheeler ordered a stand-to when this strange little procession was seen approaching the east corner of the entrenchment, and went off himself with Moore to meet it, and a few minutes later word was passed for me and Vibart, who was up at my end of the parapet, to present ourselves.

Wheeler and the other senior men were grouped inside the parapet, while the old wife, fanning herself with a leaf and sipping at a *chatti*, was sitting just outside with her escort squatting round her. Wheeler was holding a paper, and glancing in bewilderment from it to the old woman; as we came up someone was saying: 'I wouldn't trust it a blasted inch! Why should they want to treat, at this time o'day? Tell

---

* Half-caste.

250

me that!', and Wheeler shook his head and passed the paper to Vibart.

'Read that,' says he. 'If what it says is true, the Nana wishes to make terms.'

It didn't sink in, at first; I studied the paper over Vibart's shoulder, while he read it out half-aloud. It was a brief, simple note, written in a good hand, in English, and addressed to Wheeler. As near as I recall, it said:

> To subjects of Her Most Gracious Majesty, Queen
> Victoria – all who are not connected with the acts of
> Lord Dalhousie and are willing to lay down their arms,
> shall receive a safe passage to Allahabad.

It was signed on behalf of Nana Sahib, with a name I couldn't make out, until Vibart muttered it out: 'Azeemoolah Khan'. He looked at Wheeler, then at the old woman, and Wheeler flapped a hand and says:

'This is Mrs Jacobs, of . . . ah, Cawnpore city. She has this note from Azeemoolah himself, in the presence of the Nana.'

'How-dee-do, gentlemen,' says Mrs Jacobs, bowing with a great creak of stays from her seat in the *ghari*. 'Such jolly weather we are having, yess?'

'I don't like it,' says Wheeler quietly, turning his back so that she shouldn't hear; the others grouped round us. 'As Whiting says, why should he offer terms when he must know we're at his mercy? All he needs do is wait.'

'Perhaps, sir,' says Vibart, 'he don't know how reduced we are.' He let out a deep breath. 'And we have our women and children to think of—'

At this the others broke in, in a fierce babble of low voices: 'It's a plot!' 'No, it ain't!' 'We've stood the bastards off this

251

long—' 'It's false – I can smell nigger treachery a mile away.' 'Why should it be treachery – my God, what have we to lose? We're done for as it is . . .', while I tried to keep my face straight and the delicious hope began to break over me – we were saved! For it seemed to me in that moment that whatever anyone said, whatever Wheeler felt, he was going to have to accept any terms the pandies offered – he couldn't refuse, and doom the women and children in that stinking barrack to certain death, however fearful of treachery he might be. We were being offered at least a chance of life against the certainty of death: he had to take it.

So I said nothing, while they wrangled in whispers there by the parapet, with every drawn face along the entrenchment on either side turned anxiously in our direction, and that painted old harridan sitting under the canopy of her *ghari*, nodding and bowing whenever anyone glanced at her. And sure enough, Wheeler finally says:

'What's your opinion, Colonel Flashman?'

The temptation to sing out: 'Take it, you bloody old fool – offer to crawl on your belly the whole way to Allahabad!' was strong, but I mastered it and looked pretty cool. 'Well, sir,' says I. 'It's an offer – no more. There's nothing to be decided until we've tested it.'

That shut them up. 'True enough,' says Wheeler, 'but—'

'Someone must talk to Nana Sahib,' says I. 'It may be that all isn't well with him, or that he thinks this siege ain't worth the candle. Maybe his precious pandies have had enough—'

'That's it, by God!' broke in Delafosse, but I went on, very steady:

'But we can't accept – or turn him down flat – till we've heard more than is written here,' and I tapped the paper in Vibart's hand. 'He hasn't approached us out of charity, we

252

may be sure – well, it may be treachery, or it may be weakness. Let's look him in the eye.'

It must have sounded well – bluff Flashy talking calm sense while others went pink in the face. They weren't to know I'd made up my trembling mind in the moment I'd read the note; the trick now was to make sure that Wheeler made up his, and in the right direction. For he was obviously full of suspicion about the Nana, and half-inclined to listen to the hotheads who were urging him to throw the offer back in the mutineers' teeth – you never heard such appalling nonsense in your life. Here we were, doomed for certain, being offered an eleventh-hour reprieve, and more than half the idiots in that impromptu council were for rejecting it out of hand. It made my innards heave to listen; thinks I, this is going to need delicate handling.

However, Wheeler saw the sense of what I'd said, and decided that Moore and I should go to see the Nana and hear precisely what he had to say. Thank God he chose me – I don't care, as a rule, to put my head into the lion's den, even under a flag of truce, but this was one negotiation I wanted to have a large hand in. I didn't want any hitches about the surrender – for surrender, if I had anything to do with it, was what it was going to be. All that mattered besides was that I should keep my credit intact.

So at noon Moore and I were escorted through the pandy lines, with Mrs Jacobs in her *ghari* jabbering about what a shame it was, oah yess, that the present unsettled state of affairs had prevented her getting up to the hills during the hot weather. Who she was, by the way, I never discovered; she looked like a typical half-caste bawd who'd been employed as a go-between because she was obviously neutral and inoffensive. But I may be misjudging the lady.

253

The notorious Nana Sahib was waiting for us in front of a great day-tent in a grove of trees, with a pack of servitors and minions attending him, and a score of Maharatta guardsmen, in breastplates and helmets, ranged either side of the great Afghan carpet before his chair. That carpet gave me an uneasy twinge – it reminded me of the one on which I'd seen McNaghten seized and chopped up outside Kabul, at just such a meeting as this; however, Moore and I put out our chests and looked down our noses, as true Britons ought to do in the presence of rebellious niggers who happen to have the drop on them.

Nana himself was a burly, fat-faced rascal with curly mustachioes and a shifty look – what they call a *tung admi*,* dressed in more silks and jewels than a French whore, sliding his eyes across Moore and me and whispering behind a plump hand to the woman beside him. She was worth a lewd thought or two, by the way; one of your tall, heavy-hipped beauties with a drooping lower lip – Sultana Adala, they called her, and I'm sorry I never got closer to her than twenty feet. We exchanged a glance or two during that interview, and let our mutual imaginations work; ten minutes alone together would have done the rest. On Nana's other side sat a nondescript and nasty-looking rascal, who I gather was his brother-in-crime, Tantia Tope.

However, the man who took things in hand was Azeemoolah Khan, a tall, handsome, light-skinned exquisite in a cloth-of-gold coat and with a jewelled aigret in his turban, who stepped smiling across the carpet with his hand out. Moore promptly put his hands behind his back, I contented myself by hooking my thumbs into my belt, and Azeemoolah smiled

* Literally, 'a tight man'.

254

even wider and withdrew his hand with a graceful flutter – Rudi Starnberg couldn't have done it better. I gave him our names, and he opened his eyes wide.

'Colonel Flashman! But this is an honour indeed! It has always been my regret that I missed you in the Crimea,' says he, flashing his teeth. 'And how is my dear old friend, Mr William Howard Russell?'

It was my turn to stare, at that; I didn't know then that this Azeemoolah was a travelled man, who spoke French and English as well as I did, had done diplomatic work in London – and gone through our sillier society women like a mad stallion at the same time. A charming, clever politician, whose urbanity masked a nature as appealing as a hooded cobra's;[30] for the occasion he was acting as interpreter for the Nana, who spoke no English.

I told him, fairly cool, that we were there to receive his master's proposals, at which he sighed and spread his hands.

'Well, gentlemen, it is a most distressing business, and no one is more deeply troubled by it than his highness, which is why he has sent his note to General Wheeler, in the hope that we can put an end to all this bloodshed and suffering—'

Moore interrupted at this to say that in that case it was a pity he hadn't sent his message earlier, or stayed loyal in the first place. Azeemoolah just smiled.

'But we are not talking politics, are we, Captain Moore? We are looking at military reality – which is that your gallant resistance is at an end, one way or another. His highness deplores the thought of useless slaughter; he is willing, if you will quit Cawnpore, to allow your garrison to depart with the honours of war; you shall have all necessary food and comforts for your women and children (for whom his highness is particularly concerned), and safe passage to Allahabad. It seems to me not an ungenerous offer.'

The Nana, who obviously knew the purport of what was being said, leaned forward at this, smiling greasily, and gabbled in Maharatta. Azeemoolah nodded, and went on:

'He says that baggage animals are already being collected to carry your wounded to the river, where boats will be waiting to take you all to Allahabad.'

I asked the question Wheeler wanted asked. 'What guarantees of safe-conduct does he offer?'

Azeemoolah lifted his brows. 'But are any necessary? If we intended you harm, we have only to attack, or wait. We know your situation, you see. Believe me, gentlemen, his highness is moved simply by humanity, the spirit of mercy—'

Whether it was deliberately timed or not, I don't know, but his words were interrupted by the most hideous scream of agony – a drawn-out, bubbling wail from behind the grove of trees. It rang out again, and then died into an awful whimper of pain, and I felt the hairs rise on my neck. Moore almost jumped out of his boots.

'What in God's name was that?' says he.

'Maharatta diplomacy, I imagine,' says I, with a straight face and my innards dissolving. 'Someone being flayed alive, probably, for our benefit – so that we could hear, and take note.'

'. . . but if his highness's word is not sufficient,' Azeemoolah went on blandly, 'he would raise no objection to your carrying away your personal arms and . . . shall we say, twenty rounds a man? With that, you will hardly be at a greater disadvantage in the open than behind that pathetic breastwork. But I repeat, gentlemen, his highness has nothing to gain by treachery – quite the reverse. It is repugnant to him, and would be politically damaging.'

I didn't trust the bastard an inch, but I was privately inclined to agree with him. Wiping out a British garrison entire was one thing, but he could do that anyway, without luring us into the open. On the other hand, getting a British garrison to haul down its flag would be a real feather in his cap – but Azeemoolah was a mile too shrewd to say so, for nothing would have been better calculated to stiffen Wheeler's resistance.

Nana started to chatter again in Maharatta, while I tried to efface the memory of that awful scream by exchanging a long look or two with Sultana Adala – it never does any harm. Azeemoolah heard him out, and then addressed us again.

'His highness asks you to reassure General Wheeler, and to add that while you are considering his most generous proposal, he is instructing our troops to observe an armistice. I myself will come tomorrow for General Wheeler's answer.'

And that was that. Moore and I trudged back through the pandy lines – and if anything was needed to convince me that surrender was imperative it was the sight of those glowering black faces at the gun emplacements and round the bivouacs. They might look less smart and orderly than they'd done as loyal Company troops, but by God there were plenty of them, and no signs of weakening or desertion.

It was touch and go, though, when we got back to the entrenchment and reported to Wheeler what Nana's proposals were. He called a council of all the officers, and we sat or stood crowded into the stifling corner of the barrack which was his office, with the moaning of the wounded beyond the partition, and the wailing of the children, while we heard rehearsed again all the arguments that had been whispered to and fro that morning. It frightened me, I may tell you, for Wheeler was still smelling treachery, and our younger sparks were in full cry against the notion of surrender.

'We've held out this long,' cries Delafosse, 'and now they're weakening. Tell him to go to blazes, I say, and ten to one he'll raise the siege.'

There were growls of approval at this, until Vibart says:

'And if he don't raise it? What then? We'll not have a child or woman alive in this hellish place three days hence. Are you prepared to accept that?'

'Are you prepared to accept a rebel's word?' retorts Delafosse. 'While we're in a defensive position here, at least we can make some show against him – and he may raise the siege, or Lawrence may march. But once we accept his terms and step into the open, we're at his mercy.'

'And we'll have hauled down our flag to a pack of rebels,' says Thomson bitterly. 'How do we go home to England and tell 'em that?'

At this some cried 'Bravo!' and urged Wheeler to answer Nana with defiance, but old Ewart, who was so sick that he had to attend the council lying on a stretcher, wondered what England would say if we condemned hundreds of women and children to die in the useless defence of a couple of ruined mud buildings. The older men nodded agreement, but the youngsters shouted him down, and Delafosse repeated the argument, red in the face, that Nana must be weakening or he'd never have made the offer.

Wheeler, who'd been sitting tugging his moustache while they bickered, looks at Moore and me.

'You saw his camp, gentlemen; what opinion did you form? Is he negotiating from weakness, because his troops have lost heart?'

I'd said nothing throughout; I was biding my time, and

258

let Moore answer. He said we'd seen no signs of flagging morale, which was true enough. Wheeler looked glum, and shook his head.

'I cannot think the Nana is to be trusted,' says he. 'And yet . . . it is a cruel choice. All my nature, every instinct, tells me to fight this command to the last; to die in my duty as a soldier should do, and let my country avenge me. But to do that at the cost of our loved ones' lives . . . already, so many . . .'

He broke off, and there was an uneasy silence; everyone knew that Wheeler's own son had died the day before. Finally he rubbed his face and looked round.

'If it were ourselves alone, there could be but one answer. As it is, I confess I should be tempted, for our women and children's sake, to accept this murderer's terms, were it not that my judgement tells me he will play us false. I . . .'

'Forgive me, sir,' says Moore, quietly, 'but if he does, we've lost nothing. For if we don't trust him, we're dead anyway – all of us. We know that, and—'

'At least we can die with honour!' cries some fool, and the younger chaps cheered like the idiots they were. At this Wheeler's head came up, and I saw his stubborn lip go out, and I thought, now, Flashy, now's your time, or the stupid old bastard will damn us all in the name of Duty and Honour. So I growled in my throat, and scraped my heel, and that caught his attention, just in time, and he looked at me.

'You've said nothing, Flashman,' says he. 'What is your thought?'

I felt all their eyes turn to me, and deliberately took my time, for I knew Wheeler was within an ace of deciding to fight it out to a finish, and I was going to have to humbug him, and the rest of them, into surrendering. But it was going to require my most artistic handling.

'Well, sir,' says I, 'like you, I wouldn't trust the Nana as far as the tuck-shop.' (Someone laughed; homely old Flashy, you see, with his schoolboy metaphors.) 'But as Moore here says – that don't matter. What does – or so it seems to me – is the fate of our ladies –' (here I looked red-faced and noble) '– and the . . . the youngsters. If we accept the Nana's offer, at least there's a chance they'll come off safe.'

'You'd surrender?' says Wheeler, in a strained voice.

'For myself?' growls I, and looked at the floor. 'Well, I never quite got the habit . . . goes against the grain, I reckon. Matter of honour – as someone said just now. And I suppose it can be said that honour demands we fight it out to the last –'

'*Shabash!*' cries Delafosse. 'Well done, Flashy!'

'– but, d'ye know, sir,' I went on, 'the day my honour has to be maintained by sacrificing Vibart's little boy – or Tunstall's mother – or Mrs Newnham's daughter, well . . .' I raised my head and stared at the circle of faces, a strong, simple man stirred to his depths; you could have heard a pin drop. 'I don't know – I may be wrong . . . but I don't think my honour's worth that much, d'ye know?'

The beauty of it was, while it was the most fearful gammon, coming from me – it was stark truth for the rest of them, gallant and honourable souls that they were. The irony was that for my own cowardly, selfish reasons, I was arguing the sane and sensible course, and having to dress it up in high-sounding bilge in order to break down their fatuous notions of Duty. Reason wouldn't have done it, but to suggest that the true honour demanded surrender, for the women and children's sake – that shamed 'em into sanity.

Old Ewart put the final touch to it. 'And that, gentlemen, you would do well to bear in mind –' he glared almost defiantly at Delafosse '– is the opinion of the man who held Piper's Fort, and led the Light Brigade.'

Wheeler put it to the formality of a vote, but it was foregone now. When Moore and Whiting voted to surrender, even the fieriest of the younger men gave way, and inside half an hour Wheeler's answer was on its way to Nana, agreeing to capitulate with the honours of war.[31] But he added the condition that we should not only keep our arms, but sixty rounds a man instead of the proposed twenty – 'then, if there is treachery, it will profit him little,' he told us, and echoed the thought Azeemoolah had expressed in the afternoon: 'We can fight as well in the open as in this death-trap.' That was all he knew.

He was still fearful of treachery, you see. I was not – you may think I was deluding myself, but the fact was I couldn't see that the Nana had anything to gain by playing us false. I state that honestly now, and I've explained the details of the Cawnpore surrender because it was a momentous thing, not only in the Mutiny, but in Indian history. I had spoken – and, as I've said, I believe mine was the decisive voice – for surrender, because I saw it as the only way to save my skin. But apart from that vital consideration, I still believe that surrender was right, by every canon of soldiering and common sense. Call me a fool if you like, and shake your heads in the light of history – nothing could have been worse than fighting on in that doomed entrenchment.

Whatever misgivings Wheeler may have had, hardly anyone else shared them when word got round of what had been decided, and Azeemoolah and Jwala Pershad had come to the entrenchment with the Nana's undertakings all signed

261

and witnessed: draught animals were to arrive at dawn for the mile-long journey to the river where boats would be waiting, and throughout the night there was bustle and eagerness and thanksgiving all through the garrison. It was as though a great shadow had been lifted; cooking fires blazed outside the barrack for the first time in weeks, the wounded were brought out of that stinking oven to lie in the open air, and even the children frolicked on the parapet where we'd been slashing at the sepoys two days before. Tired, worn faces were smiling, no one minded the dirt and stench any longer, or gave a thought to the rebels' massed guns and infantry a few hundred yards away; the firing had stopped, the fear of death had lifted, we were going out to safety, and throughout the night, over the din of packing and preparation, the sound of hymns rolled up to the night sky.

One of the few croakers was Ilderim. Wheeler had told those sepoys who had remained loyal and fought in the garrison to slip away over the southern rampart, for fear of reprisals from their mutinous fellows in the morning, but Ilderim wouldn't have it. He came to me in the dark at the north entrenchment, where I was smoking a cheroot and enjoying my peace of mind.

'Do I slip away like a cur when someone throws a stone at it?' says he. 'No – I march with Wheeler Sahib and the rest of you tomorrow. And so that no pi-dog of a mutineer will take me for anything but what I am, I have put this on, for a *killut*—'* and as he stepped closer in the gloom, I saw he was in the full fig of a native officer of cavalry, white coat, gauntlets, long-tailed *puggaree* and all. 'It is just a down-country regiment's coat, which I took from one of those we

---

* Dress of honour, usually on ceremonial occasions.

slew the other day, but it will serve to mark me as a soldier.'
He grinned, showing his teeth. 'And I shall take my sixty
rounds – do thou likewise, blood-brother.'

'We're not going to need 'em, though,' says I, and he
shrugged.

'Who knows? When the tiger has its paw on the goat's
neck, and then smiles in friendship . . . Wheeler Sahib does
not trust the Nana. Dost thou?'

'There's no choice, is there?' says I. 'But he's signed his
name to a promise, after all—'

'And if he breaks it, the dead can complain,' says he, and
spat. 'So I say – keep thy sixty rounds to hand, Flashman
sahib.'

I didn't heed him much, for Pathans are notoriously suspicious of everyone, reason or none, and when day broke there
was too much to do to waste time in thinking. The mutineers
came in the first mists of dawn, with bullocks and elephants
and carts to carry us to the river, and we had the herculean
task of getting everyone into the convoy. There were two
hundred wounded to be moved, and all the women and
children, some of them just babes-in-arms, and old people
who'd have been feeble enough even without three weeks on
starvation rations. Everyone was tired and filthy and oddly
dispirited now that the first flush of excitement had died
away. As the sun came up it shone on a strange, nightmare
sight that lives with me now only as a series of pictures as
the evacuation of Cawnpore began.

I can see the straggling mass of the procession, the bullock-
carts with their stretchers carrying the blood-stained figures
of the wounded, gaunt and wasted; bedraggled white women,
either sitting in the carts or standing patiently alongside, with
children who looked like Whitechapel waifs clinging to their

263

skirts; our own men, ragged and haggard, with their muskets cradled, taking up station along the convoy; the red coats and sullen faces of the mutineers who were to shepherd us across the maidan and down to the river ghat beyond the distant trees where the boats were waiting. The dawn air was heavy with mist and suspicion and hatred, as Wheeler, with Moore at his elbow as always, stood up on the rampart and reviewed the battered remnants of his command, strung out along the entrenchment, waiting listlessly for the word to move while all around was the confused babble of voices, orders being shouted, officers hurrying up and down, elephants squealing, the carts creaking, children crying, and the kites beginning to swoop down on the emptying barracks.

Incidents and figures remain very clear – two civilians hauling down the tattered flag from the barrack roof, rolling it up carefully and bringing it to Wheeler, who stood absent-mindedly with it trailing from one hand while he shouted: 'Sarn't Grady! Is the south entrenchment clear, Sarn't Grady?' A little boy with curly hair, laughing and shouting 'Plop-plop!' as one of the elephants dropped its dung; his mother, a harassed young woman in a torn ball-gown (it had rosebuds embroidered, I recall) with a sleeping infant in her arms, slapped and shook him with her free hand, and then straightened her hair. A group of mutineers walking round the barracks, belabouring one of our native cooks who was limping along under a great load of pans. A British private, his uniform unrecognisable, being railed at by an old mem-sahib as he helped her into a cart, until she was settled, when she said, 'Thank you, my good man, thank you very much,' and began searching her reticule for a tip. Four mutineers were hurrying up and down the untidy convoy, calling out and searching, until they spotted Vibart and his family – and then they ran hallooing and calling 'Colonel sahib! Mem-sahib!', and seized on the family's baggage, and one of them, beaming and chuckling, lifted Vibart's little lad on to his shoulders, piggy-back, while the others shouted and shoved and made room for Mrs Vibart in a wagon. Vibart was dumbfounded, and two of the mutineers were weeping as they took his hand and carried his gear – I saw another one at it, too, an old grizzled *havildar* of the 56th, standing on the entrenchment gazing down into the ruin of the barracks with tears running down his white beard; he was shaking his head in grief, and then he would look no more, but turned about and stared across the maidan, still crying.

Most of the mutineers weren't so sentimental, though. One tried to snatch a musket from Whiting, and Whiting flung him off snarling and shouting: 'You want it, do you? I'll give you its contents fast enough, you damned dog, if you don't take care!' The pandies fell back, growling and shaking their fists, and another gang of them stood and jeered while old Colonel Ewart was carried on a *palki* to his place in the line. 'Is it not a fine parade, colonel sahib?' they were jeering. 'Is it not well drawn up?' And they cackled and made mock of the drill, prancing up and down.

I didn't like the look of this a bit, or of the menacing-looking crowd of pandies which was growing across the maidan. Promises or no promises, it don't take much to touch off a crowd like that, and I was relieved when Moore, who had hurried to the head of the column, shouted and blew his whistle, and the procession began to move, creaking slowly, away from the entrenchment, and out on to the plain. I was near the rear of the line, where Vibart had charge of the supply-wagons; behind us the pandies were already scavenging in the deserted barracks – by God, they were welcome to anything they could find.

It was about a mile to the river, where the boats were, but we were so exhausted, and the convoy so haphazard and cumbersome, that it took us the best part of an hour to cross the maidan alone. It was a hellish trek, with the mutineers trying to drive us along, swearing and thrusting, and our fellows cursing 'em back, while wagons foundered, and one or two of the garrison collapsed and had to be loaded aboard, and the drivers thrashed at the beasts. Crowds of natives had come down from Cawnpore city to watch and jeer at us and get in the way; some of them, and the more hostile pandies, kept sneaking in close to shout taunts, or even to strike at us and try to steal our belongings. Something's going to crack in a moment, thinks I, and sure enough, just as we were trying to manhandle one of the store-wagons over a little white bridge at the far side of the maidan, where the trees began, there was a crackle of firing off to one side, and sudden shouting, and then more shots.

The driver of my store-wagon tried to whip up in alarm, a wheel caught on the bridge, and I and two civilians were struggling to keep it steady when Whiting comes up at the run, cocking his musket and demanding to know what the row was. In the same moment one of our corporals came flying out of the wood, rolled clean under the wagon in front of us, and jumps up yelling:

'Quick, sir – come quick! Them devils is murthering Colonel Ewart! They got 'im in the trees yonder, an'—'

Whiting sprang forward with an oath, but quick as light one of the mutineers who'd been watching us at the bridge jumps in his way and flung his arm round him. For a moment I thought, oh God, now they're going to ambush us, and the corporal must have thought the same, for he whipped out his bayonet, but the mutineer holding Whiting was just trying to keep him back and shouting:

'*Nahin*, sahib, *khabadan*!* If you go there, they will kill you! Let be, sahib! Go on – to the river!'

Whiting swore, and struggled with him, but the mutineer – a big, black-moustached *havildar* with a Chillian-wallah medal – threw him down and wrested his musket away. Whiting came up, furious, but the corporal understood, and grabbed his wrist.

''E's right, sir! Them swine'll just *sarf karo*† you, like they done the colonel! We got to git on to the river, like 'e says! Otherwise, maybe they'll do for everybody – the wimmen an' kids an' all, sir!'

He was right, of course – I'd been through the same sort of retreat as this, back in Afghanistan, and you've got to allow for a few stray slaughters and turn a blind eye, or the next thing you know you'll have a battle on your hands. Even Whiting realised it, I think, for he wheeled on the *havildar* and says:

'I must see. Will you come with me?'

The fellow says, '*Han*, sahib', and they strode into the trees. It seemed a sensible time to be getting on down to the river, so I told the corporal I must inform Wheeler of what was happening, ordered him to see the store-wagon safely over the bridge, and jumped up on to the coping, running past the carts ahead, with their passengers demanding to know what was happening. I hurried on through the trees, and found myself looking down the slope to the Suttee Choura Ghat, and beyond it the broad, placid expanse of the Ganges.

---

* Take care!

† To make clean – i.e., clean you up.

The slope was alive with people. The foremost wagons had reached the landing-stage, and our folk were already getting out and making their way to the water's edge, where a great line of thatched, clumsy-looking barges was anchored in the shallows. The wagons nearer me were splitting away from the convoy to get closer to the water, and everything was in confusion, with some people getting out and others sitting tight. Already the ground was littered with abandoned gear, the stretchers with the wounded were being unloaded just anywhere; groups of women and children were waiting, wondering which way to go, while their menfolk, red in the face and shouting, demanded to know what the orders for embarkation were. Someone was calling, 'All ladies with small children are to go in numbers twelve to sixteen!' but no one knew which barges were which, and you couldn't hear yourself think above the elephants squealing and the babble of voices.

On either side of the slope there were groups of pandies with their bayonets fixed, glowering but doing nothing to help, and off to one side I saw a little gaily-dressed group of natives by a temple on a knoll – Azeemoolah was there, talking to Wheeler, who was gesturing towards the barges, so I walked across towards them, through the silent groups of pandy riflemen, and as I came up Azeemoolah was saying:

'. . . but I assure you general, the flour is already in the boats – go and see for yourself. Ah, Colonel Flashman, good morning, sir; I trust I see you in good health. Perhaps, general, Colonel Flashman could be asked to examine the boats, and see that all is as I have told you?'

So I was despatched down to the water, and had to wade out through the shallows to the barges; they were great, musty-smelling craft, but clean enough, with half-naked nigger boatmen in charge, and sure enough there were grain sacks in most of them, as Azeemoolah had said. I reported accordingly, and then we set to with the embarkation, which simply meant telling people off at random to the various barges, carrying the women and children through the water, bearing the stretchers of the wounded head-high, stumbling and swearing in the stinking ooze of the shallows – I went under twice myself, but thank God I didn't swallow any; the Ganges is one river you don't want to take the waters of. It was desperate work, gasping in the steamy heat as the sun came up; the worst of it was getting the women and children and wounded properly stowed inboard – I remember thinking it was ironic that my experience of packing howling niggers into the slave-ship *Balliol College* some years before should come in so handy now. But there you are – any special knowledge comes in useful, sooner or later.

By God, though, the niggers had been easier to handle. I reckon I must have carried twenty females to the barges (and none of 'em worth even a quick fumble, just my luck), plucked one weeping child from the water's edge, where she was crying for her mama, put my fist into the face of a pandy who was pestering Mrs Newnham and trying to snatch her parasol, quieted an old crone who refused to be embarked until she was positive the barge she was going to was Number 12 ('Mr Turner said I *must* go to Number 12; I will go to *no other*' – it might have been the *Great Eastern* for all I knew, or cared), and stood neck-deep wrestling to replace a rotted rudder rope. Strange, when you're working all out with things like that, sweating and wrestling to make sense out of chaos, you forget about death and danger and possible treachery – all that matters is getting that piece of hemp knotted through the rudder stem, or finding the carpetbag that Mrs Burtenshaw's maid has left in the cart.

I was about done when I stumbled up through the litter of the bank for the last time, and looked about me. Nearly all the command was loaded, the barges were floating comfortably high on the oily surface, and beyond them the last dawn mists were receding across the broad expanse of the river to the far bank half a mile distant, with the eastern sun turning the water to a great crimson mirror.

There weren't above fifty of our folk, Vibart's rearguard mostly, left on the wreck-strewn, mud-churned slope; Wheeler and Moore and Vibart were all together, and as I came to them I heard Whiting's voice, shaking with anger:

'– and he was shot on his *palki*, I tell you – half a dozen times, at least! Those foresworn swine up yonder—' and he shook his fist towards the temple on the knoll, where Azeemoolah was sitting with Tantia Tope in a little group of the Nana's officers. There was no sign of Nana himself, though.

'There is nothing to be done, Captain Whiting!' Wheeler's voice was hoarse, and his gaunt face was crimson and sweating. He looked on the edge of collapse. 'I know, sir, I know – it is the basest treachery, but there is no remedy now! Let us thank God we have come this far – no, no, sir, we are in no case to protest, let alone punish – we must make haste down the river before worse befalls!'

Whiting stamped and cursed, but Vibart eased him away. The pandies who had lined the slope were moving down now, through the abandoned wagons, converging on the landing-place.

'Hollo, Flash,' says Moore, wearily. Like me, he was plastered with mud, and the sling was gone from his wounded arm. 'They settled Massie, too – did you know? He and

Ewart protested when the pandies dragged off four of our loyal sepoys – so they shot 'em all, out o' hand—'

'Like dogs, beside the road!' cries Whiting. 'By God, if I'd a gun!' He dashed the sweat from his eyes, glaring at the pandies on the slope. Then he saw me. 'Flashman – one of the sepoys was that Pathan orderly of yours – the big chap in the *havildar*'s coat – they shot him in the ditch!'

For a moment I didn't comprehend; I just stared at his flushed, raging face. 'Like a dog in the ditch!' cries he again, and then it hit me like a blow: he was telling me that Ilderim was dead. I can't describe what I felt – it wasn't grief, or horror, so much as disbelief. Ilderim couldn't die – he was indestructible, always had been, even as the boy I'd first met at Mogala years ago, one of those folk whose life is fairly bursting out of them; I had a vision of that grinning, bearded hawk-face of just a few hours ago – 'No pi-dog of a mutineer will take me for anything but what I am!' And he'd been right, and it had been the death of him – but not the kind of death the great brave idiot had always looked for, just a mean, covert murder at the roadside. Oh, you stupid Gilzai bastard, I thought – why didn't you go over the wall when you had the chance . . .

'Come on!' Moore was pushing at my shoulder. 'We'll be last aboard. We're in the – hollo, what's that?'

From the trees on the top of the slope a bugle sounded, the notes floating clearly down to us. I looked up the hill, and saw a strange thing happening – I suppose I was still shocked by the news of Ilderim's death, but what I saw seemed odd rather than menacing. The pandies on the slope, and there must have been a couple of hundred of them, were dropping to the kneeling firing position, their muskets were at their shoulders, and they were pointing at us.

'For Christ's—' a voice shouted, and then the hillside seemed to explode in a hail of musketry, the balls were howling past, I heard someone scream beside me, and then Moore's arm flailed me to the ground, and I was plunging through the ooze, into the water. I went under, and struck out for dear life, coming up with a shattering crash of my head against the middle barge. Overhead women were shrieking and muskets were cracking, and then there was the crash of distant cannon, and I saw the narrow strip of water between me and the shore ploughed up as the storm of grape hit it. I reached up, seizing the gunwale, and heaved myself up, and then the whole barge shook as though in a giant hand, and I was hurled back into the water again.

I came up gasping. The pandies were tearing down the slope now, sabres and muskets and bayonets at the ready, charging into the last of our shore-party, who were struggling in the shallows. Up on the slope others were firing at the boats, and in the shade beneath the trees there was the triple flash of cannon, sending grape and round-shot smashing down into the helpless lumbering boats. Men were struggling in the water only a few yards from me – I saw a British soldier sabred down, another floundering back as a sepoy shot him point-blank through the body, and a third, thrust through with a bayonet, sinking down slowly on the muddy shore. Wheeler, white-faced and roaring 'Treachery! Shove off – quickly! Treachery!', was stumbling out into the shallows, his sabre drawn; he slashed at a pursuing sepoy, missed his footing and went under, but a hand reached out from the gunwale near me and pulled him up, coughing and spewing water. Moore was in the water close by, and Vibart was trying to swim towards us with his wounded arm trailing. As Moore plunged towards him I sank beneath the surface, dived, and

272

struck out beneath the boat, and as I went I was thinking, clear enough, well, Flashy my lad, you were wrong again – Nana Sahib wasn't to be trusted after all.

I came up on the other side, and the first thing I saw was a body falling from the boat above me. Overhead its thatch was burning, and as a great chunk of the stuff fell hissing into the water I shoved away. I trod water, looking about me: in the next two barges the thatches were alight as well, and people were screaming and tumbling into the water – I saw one woman jumping with a baby in her arms: I believe it was the one who had cuffed the little boy for laughing at the elephant's dung. The shore was hidden from me by the loom of the barge, but the crash of firing was redoubling, and the chorus of screams and yells was deafening. People were firing back from the barges, too, and in the one down-river from me two chaps were beating at the burning thatch, and another was heaving at its tiller; very slowly it seemed to be veering from the bank. That's the boy for me, thinks I, and in the same moment the thatch of the barge immediately above me collapsed with a roar and a whoosh of sparks, with shrieks of the damned coming from beneath it.

It was obvious, even in that nightmare few moments, what had happened. Nana had been meaning to play false all along; he had just waited until we were in the boats before opening up with musketry, grape, and every piece of artillery he had. From where I was I could see one barge already sinking, with people struggling in the water round it; at least four others were on fire; two were drifting helplessly into midstream. The pandies were in the water round the last three boats, where most of the women and children were, but then a great gust of smoke blotted the scene from my view, and at the same time I heard the crackle of firing from the far bank

– the treacherous bastards had us trapped both sides. I put my head down and struck out for the next barge ahead, which at least had someone steering it, and as I came under its stern there was Moore in the water alongside, shoving for all he was worth to turn the rudder and help it from the shore. Beyond him I saw Wheeler and Vibart and a couple of others being dragged inboard, while our people blazed back at the pandies on the bank.

Moore shouted something incoherent at me, and as I seized on the rudder with him his face was within a foot of mine – and then it exploded in a shower of blood, and I literally had his brains blown all over me. I let go, shrieking, and when I had dashed the hideous mess from my eyes he was gone, the barge was surging out into the river as our people got the sweeps going, and I was just in time to grasp the gunwale and be dragged along, clinging like grim death, and bawling to be hauled aboard.

We must have gone several hundred yards before I managed to scramble up and on to the deck and get my bearings. The first thing I saw was Wheeler, dead or dying; he had a gaping wound in the neck, and the blood was pumping oozily on to his shirt. All around there were wounded men sprawled on the planks, the smouldering thatch filled the boat with acrid clouds of smoke, and at both gunwales men were firing at the banks. I clung to the gunwale, looking back – we were half a mile below Suttee Ghat by now, where most of the barges were still swinging at their moorings, under a pall of smoke; the river round them was full of people, floundering for the bank. The firing seemed to have slackened, but you could still see the sparkle of the muskets along the slope above the ghat, and the occasional blink of a heavy gun, booming dully across the water. Behind us, two of the barges seemed to have got clear, and were drifting helplessly across the river, but we were the only one under way, with half a dozen chaps each side tugging at the sweeps.

I took stock. We were clear; the shots weren't reaching us. Wheeler was dead, flopped out on the deck, and beyond him Vibart was lying against the gunwale, eyes closed, both arms soaked in blood; someone was babbling in agony, and I saw it was Turner, with one leg doubled at a hideous angle and the other lying in a bloody pool. Whiting was holding on to one of the awning supports, a gory spectre, fumbling one-handed at the lock of a carbine – there hardly seemed to be a sound man in the barge. I saw Delafosse was at one of the sweeps, Thomson at another, and Sergeant Grady, with a bandage round his brow, was in the act of loosing off a shot at the shore. And then, with a little shock of astonishment, I saw that one of the wounded men on the deck was East – and he was finished.

Why, I don't know, but I dropped down beside him and felt his pulse. He opened his eyes at that, and looked up at me, and someone at my elbow – I don't know who – says hoarsely:

'Pandy got him on the bank . . . bayonet in the back, poor devil.'

East recognised me, and tried to speak, but couldn't; you could see the life ebbing out of his eyes. His lips quivered, and very faintly I heard him say:

'Flashman . . . tell the doctor . . . I . . .'

That was all, except that he gripped my hand hard, and the man beside me said something about there not being any doctor on board.

'That ain't what he meant,' says I. 'It's another doctor he means – a schoolmaster, but he's dead.'

East gave a little ghost of a smile, and his hand tightened, and then went loose in mine – and I found I was blubbering and gasping, and thinking about Rugby, and hot murphies at Sally's shop, and a small fag limping along pathetically after the players at Big Side – because he couldn't play himself, you see, being lame. I'd hated the little bastard, too, man and boy, for his smug manly piety – but you don't see a child you've known all your life die every day. Maybe that was why I wept, maybe it was the shock and horror of what had been happening. I don't know. Whatever it was, I'm sure I felt it all the more sincerely for knowing that I was still alive myself, and no bones broken so far.[32]

Memory's the queerest thing. When you've been through a hellish experience – and the Cawnpore siege and surrender ranks high in that line, along with Balaclava and Kabul and Greasy Grass and Isandlhwana – the aftermath tends to be vague, until some fresh horror strikes. That barge is mercifully dim in my mind now – I know it was the only one that got away from Cawnpore, and that of the rest, all were shot to pieces or burned with their passengers, except those which had the women and children aboard. The pandies captured those, and took the women and kids back ashore – all the world knows what happened after that. But only a few things are clear about our trip down-river – Thomson has left a pretty full account of it, if you're interested. I remember Whiting dying – or rather I remember him being dead, looking very pale and small in the bows of the boat. I remember taking a turn at the rudder, and splashing and straining in the water when we grounded on a mudbank in the dark. I remember hearing drums beating on the bank, and Vibart biting on a leather strap as they set his broken arm, and the dull splashes as we put dead bodies over the side, and the musty taste of dry mealies which was all we had to eat – but the first time that memory becomes consecutive and coherent after East died was when a fire-arrow came winging out of the dark and thudded into the deck, and we were shooting away at dim figures on the nearest bank, and fire-arrows came down in a blazing rain as we hauled on the sweeps and forced the barge back into midstream out of range. We rowed like fury until the fiery pinpoints of light on the bank were far behind us, and the yelling and drumming of the niggers had died away, and then we flopped down exhausted and the current carried us and landed us high and dry on another mudbank just before dawn.

This time there was no shoving off; we were wedged tight in the mud, along a deserted jungly shore, with nothing to be heard but monkeys chattering and birds screeching in the dense undergrowth. The far bank was the same, a thick mass of green, with the brown oily river sliding slowly past. At least it looked peaceful, which was a pleasant change.

Vibart reckoned we must still be a hundred miles from Allahabad, and if the behaviour of the niggers who'd showered us with fire-arrows was anything to go by, we could count on hostile country most of the way. There were two dozen of us in the boat, perhaps half of whom were fit to stand; we were low on powder and ball, and desperately short of mealies, there were no medical supplies, and it was odds half the wounded would contract gangrene unless we reached safety quickly. Not a pleasant prospect, thinks I, as I looked round the squalid barge, with its dozen wounded groaning or listless on the planks, the stench of blood and death everywhere, and even the whole men looking emaciated and fit to croak. I was in better case than most – I hadn't been through the whole siege – and it was crossing my mind that I might do

277

worse than slip away on my own and trust to luck and judgement to get to Allahabad on foot; after all, I could always turn into a native again.

So when we held our little council, I prepared the way for decamping, in my own subtle style. The others, naturally, were all debating how we might get refloated again and press on to Allahabad; I shook them up by suddenly growling that I was in no hurry to get there.

'I agree we must get the barge refloated to take the wounded on,' says I. 'For the rest of us – well, for me, leastways, I'd sooner head back for Cawnpore.'

They gaped at me in disbelief. 'You're mad!' cries Delafosse.

'So I've been told,' says I. 'See here – while we had the women and children to think of, they were our first concern. That's the only reason we surrendered, isn't it? Well, now they're . . . either gone, or captives of those fiends – I don't much fancy running any longer.' I looked as belligerent as I knew how. 'There hasn't been much time to think things out these past hours – but now, well, I reckon I've a score to settle – and the only place I want to settle it is Cawnpore.'

'But . . . but . . .' says Thomson, 'we can't go back, man! It's certain death!'

'Maybe,' says I, very business-like. 'But I've seen my country's flag hauled down once – something I never thought to see – I've seen us betrayed, our . . . our loved ones ravished from us . . .' I managed a manly glisten about the eye. 'I don't like it above half! So – I'm going back, and I'm going to get a bullet into that black bastard's heart – I don't care how! And – that's that.'

'By God!' says Delafosse, taking fire, 'by God – I've half a mind to come with you!'

'You'll do no such thing!' This was Vibart; he was deathly

278

pale, with both arms useless, but he was still in command. 'Our duty is to reach Allahabad – Colonel Flashman, I forbid you! I will not have your life flung away in . . . in this rash folly! You will carry out General Wheeler's orders—'

'Look, old fellow,' says I. 'I was never one of General Wheeler's command, you recollect? I don't ask anyone to come with me – but I left a friend dead back there – a comrade from the old Afghan days – a salt man from the hills. Well, maybe I'm more of a salt man than a parade soldier myself – anyway, I know what I must do.' I gave him a quizzical little grin, and patted his foot. 'Anyway, Vibart, I'm senior to you, remember?'

At this they cried out together, telling me not to be a fool, and Vibart said I couldn't desert our wounded. He wanted to send a shore-party, to try to find friendly villagers who would tow us off; I was best fitted to lead it, he said, and my first duty was to carry out Wheeler's dying wishes, and get down-river. I seemed to hesitate, and finally said I would lead the shore-party – 'but you'll be going to Allahabad without me in the end,' says I. 'All I'll need is a rifle and a knife – and a handshake from each one of you.'

So we set off, a dozen of us, to try to find a friendly village. If we found one, and the prospects of getting off for Allahabad seemed good, I'd allow myself to be persuaded, and go along with them. If we didn't – I'd slip away, and they could imagine I'd gone back to Cawnpore on my mission of vengeance. (That's one thing about having a reckless reputation: they'll believe anything of you, and shake their heads in admiration over your dare-devilry.)

We hadn't gone five minutes into the jungle before I was wishing to God I'd been able to stay in the boat. It wasn't very thick stuff, once we got away from the river, but eerie and curiously quiet, with huge tall trees shadowing a forest-floor of creeper and swampy plants, like a great cathedral, and only the occasional tree-creature chirruping in the silence. We struck a little path, and followed it, and presently came on a tiny temple in a clearing, a lath-and-plaster thing that looked as though it hadn't been visited in years. Delafosse and Sergeant Grady scouted it, and reported it empty, and I was just ordering up the others when we heard it – very low and far-off in the forest: the slow boom-boom of drums.

I don't know any sound like it for shivering the soul. I've heard it in Dahomey, when the Amazons were after us, and in South American backwaters, and on a night on the Papar River in Borneo when the Iban head-hunters took the warpath – the muted rumble of doom that conjures up spectres with painted faces creeping towards you through the dark. They're usually damned real spectres, too – as they were here, for I'd barely given my order when there was a whistle and a thud, and Grady, on the edge of the clearing, was staggering with an arrow in his brow, and with a chorus of blood-chilling screams they were on us – black, half-naked figures swarming out of the trees, yelling bloody murder. I snapped off one shot – God knows where it went – and then I was haring for the temple. I made it a split second ahead of two arrows which quivered in the doorpost, and then we were tumbling inside, with Delafosse and Thomson crouched in the doorway, blazing away as hard as they could.

They came storming up to the doorway in a great rabble, and for the next five minutes it was as bloody and desperate a mêlée as ever I've been in. We were so packed in the tiny space inside the building – it wasn't more than eight feet square, and about that number of us had got inside – that only two of us could fire through the door at once. Whoever the attackers were – half-human jungle people, apparently, infected by the general Mutiny madness – they didn't appear to have firearms, and the foremost of them were shot down before they could get close enough to use their spears and long swords. But their arrows buzzed in like hornets, and two of our fellows went down before the attack slackened off. We were just getting our breath back, and I was helping Thomson push an arrow through and out of the fleshy part of Private Murphy's arm – and all the time we could hear our besiegers grunting and fumbling stealthily close under the temple wall – when Delafosse suddenly whoops out 'Fire, fire! They've set the place alight!'

Sure enough, a gust of smoke came billowing in the doorway, setting us coughing and stumbling; a fire-arrow came zipping in to bury itself in Private Ryan's side, and the yells of the niggers redoubled triumphantly. I staggered through the reek, and Thomson was clutching my arm, shouting:

'Must break out . . . two volleys straight in front . . . run for it . . .'

It was an affair of split seconds; there wasn't time to think or argue. He and Delafosse and two of the privates stumbled to the door, Thomson yells 'Fire!', they all let blast together, and then we put our heads down and went charging out of the temple, with the flames licking up behind us, and drove in a body across the clearing for the shelter of the jungle. The niggers shrieked at the sight of us, I saw the man before me tumble down with a spear in his back, I cannoned into a black figure and he fell away, and then we were haring through the trees, my musket was gone, and no thought but flight. Delafosse was in front of me; I followed him as he swerved on to the path, with the arrows whipping past us;

booted feet were thumping behind me, and Thomson was shouting, 'On, on – we can distance 'em! – come on, Murphy, Sullivan – to the boat!'

How we broke clear, God knows – the very suddenness with which we'd rushed from the temple must have surprised them – but we could hear their yells in the jungle behind, and they weren't giving up the hunt, either. My lungs were bursting as we ploughed through the thicker jungle near the river, tripping on snags, tearing ourselves, sobbing with exhaustion – and then we were on the bank, and Delafosse was sliding to a halt in the mud and yelling.

'It's gone! Vibart! My God, the boat's gone!'

The mudbank was empty – there was the great groove where the barge had been, but the brown stretch of water was unbroken to the wall of green on its far side; of the barge there wasn't a sign.

'It must have slid off—' Delafosse was crying, and I thought, good for you, my boy, let's stop to consider how it happened, eh, and the niggers can come up and join in. I didn't even check stride; I went into the water in the mightiest racing dive I ever performed, and I heard the cries and splashes as the others took to the river behind me. I was striking out blindly, feeling the current tugging me downstream – I didn't mind; anywhere would do so long as it was away from those black devils screeching in the forest behind. The far bank was too distant to reach, but downstream where the river curved there were islands and sandbanks, and we were being carried towards them far faster than our pursuers could hope to run. I swam hard with the current, until the yelping of the niggers had faded into the distance, and then glanced round to see how the others were getting along. There were four heads bobbing in the water – Delafosse, Thomson, Murphy, and Sullivan, all swimming in my wake, and I was just debating whether to make for the nearest sandbank or allow myself to be carried past, when Delafosse reared up in the water, yelling and gesturing ahead of me. I couldn't make him out, and then the single shrieked word 'Muggers!' reached me, and as I looked where he was pointing the steamy waters of the Ganges seemed to turn to ice.

On a mudbank a hundred yards ahead and to my right, shapes were moving – long, brown, hideously scaly dragons waddling down to the water at frightening speed, plashing into the shallows and then gliding out inexorably to head us off, their half-submerged snouts rippling the surface. For an instant I was paralysed – then I was thrashing at the water in a frenzy of terror, trying to get out into midstream, fighting the sluggish current. I knew it was hopeless; they must intercept us long before we could reach the islands, but I lashed out blindly, ploughing through the water, too terrified to look and expecting every moment to feel the agonising stab of crocodile teeth in my legs. I was almost done, with exhaustion and panic, and then Sullivan was alongside, tugging at me, pointing ahead – and I saw that the placid surface was breaking up into a long, swirling race where the water ran down between two little scrubby mudbanks. There was just a chance, if we could get into that broken water, that the faster current might carry us away – muggers hate rough water, anyway – and I went for it with the energy of despair.

One glance I spared to my right – my God, there was one of the brutes within ten yards, swirling towards me. I had a nightmare glimpse of that hideous snout breaking surface, of the great tapering jaws suddenly yawning in a cavern of

283

teeth – and I regret to say I did not notice whether the fourth tooth of the lower jaw was overlapping or not. A naturalist chap, to whom I described my experience a few years ago, tells me that if I'd taken note of this, I'd have known whether I was being attacked by a true crocodile or gavial, or by some other species, which would have added immense interest to the occasion.[33] As it was, I can only say that the bloody thing looked like an Iron Maiden rushing at me through the water, and I was just letting out a last wail of despair when Sullivan seized me by the hair, the current tore at our legs, and we were swept away into the rough water between the islands, striking out any old way, going under into the choking brown, coming up again and struggling to stay afloat – and then the water had changed to clinging black ooze, and Sullivan was crying:

'Up, up, sir, for Christ's sake!' and he was half-dragging me through the slime towards the safety of a tangled mass of creeper on top of a mudbank. Delafosse was staggering out beside us, Thomson was knee-deep in the water smashing with a piece of root at the head of a mugger which lunged and snapped before swirling away with a flourish of its enormous tail: Murphy, his arm trickling blood, was already up on the top of the bank, reaching down to help us. I heaved up beside him, shuddering, and I remember thinking: that must be the end, nothing more can happen now, and if it does, I don't care, I'll just have to die, because there's nothing I can do. Sullivan was kneeling over me, and I remember I said:

'God bless you, Sullivan. You are the noblest man alive,' or something equally brilliant – although I meant it, by God – and he replied: 'I daresay you're right, sir; you'll have to tell my missus, for damn me if she thinks so.' And then I must have swooned away, for all I can remember is Delafosse saying: 'I believe they are friends – see, Thomson, they are waving to us – they mean us no harm,' and myself thinking, if it's the muggers waving, don't you trust the bastards an inch, they're only pretending to be friendly . . .[34]

Luck, as I've often observed, is an agile sprite who jumps both ways in double quick time. You could say it had been evil chance that took me to Meerut and the birth of the Mutiny – but I'd escaped, only to land in the hell of Cawnpore, from which I was one of only five to get clear away after the ghat massacre. It had been the foulest luck to run into those wild men in the jungle, and the infernal muggers – but if they hadn't chased us, we mightn't have fetched up on a mudbank under the walls of one of those petty Indian rulers who stayed loyal to the Sirkar. For that was what had happened – the new niggers whom Delafosse saw waving and hallooing from the shore turned out to be the followers of one Diribijah Singh, a tough old maharaj who ruled from a fort in the jungle, and was a steadfast friend of the British. So you see, all that matters about luck is that it should run good on the last throw.

Not that the game was over, you understand; when I think back on the Mutiny, even on Cawnpore, I can say that the worst was still to come. And yet, I feel that the tide turned on that mudbank; at least, after a long nightmare, I can say that there followed a period of comparative calm, for me, in which I was able to recruit my tattered nerves, and take stock, and start planning how to get the devil out of this Indian pickle and back to England and safety.

For the moment, there was nothing to do but thank God and the loyal savages who picked us up from that shoal, with the muggers snuffling discontentedly in the wings. The natives took us ashore, to the maharaj's castle, and he was a brick – a fine old sport with white whiskers and a belly like a barrel, who swore damnation to all mutineers and promised to return us to our own folk as soon as we had recovered and it seemed safe to pass through the country round. But that wasn't for several weeks, and in the meantime the five of us could only lie and recuperate and contain our impatience as best we might – Delafosse and Thomson were itching to get back into the thick of things; Murphy and Sullivan, the two privates, kept their counsel and ate like horses; while I, making an even greater show of impatience than my brother-officers, was secretly well content to rest at ease, blinking in the sun and eating mangoes, to which I'm partial.

In the meantime, we later discovered, great things were happening in the world beyond. When news of Cawnpore's fall got out, it gave the Mutiny a tremendous fillip; revolt spread all along the Ganges valley and in Central India, the garrisons at Mhow and Agra and a dozen other places rebelled, and most notable of all, Henry Lawrence got beat fighting a dam' silly battle at Chinhat, and had to hole up in Lucknow, which went under siege. On the credit side, my old friend the First Gravedigger (General Havelock to you) finally got up off his Puritan rump and struck through Allahabad at Cawnpore; he fought his way in after a nine-day march, and recaptured the place a bare three weeks after we'd been driven out – and I suppose all the world knows what he found when he got there.

You remember that when we escaped the massacre at the Suttee Ghat, the barges with the women and children were caught by the pandies. Well, Nana took them ashore, all 200 of them, and locked them up in a place called the Bibigarh, in such filth and heat that thirty of them died within a week. He made our women grind corn; then, when word came that Havelock was fighting his way in, and slaughtering all opposition, Nana had all the women and children butchered. They say even the pandies wouldn't do it, so he sent in hooligans with cleavers from the Cawnpore bazaar; they chopped them all up, even the babies, and threw them, dead and still living, down a well. Havelock's people found the Bibigarh ankle-deep in blood, with children's toys and hats and bits of hair still floating in it; they had got there two days too late.

I don't suppose any event in my lifetime – not Balaclava nor Shiloh nor Rorke's Drift nor anywhere else I can think of – has had such a stunning effect on people's minds as that Cawnpore massacre of the innocents. I didn't see the full horror of it, of course, as Havelock's folk did, but I was there a few weeks after, and walked in the Bibigarh, and saw the bloody floor and walls, and near the well I found the skeleton bones of a baby's hand, like a little white crab in the dust. I'm a pretty cool hand, as you know, but it made me gag, and if you ask me what I think of the vengeance that old General Neill wreaked, making captured mutineers clean up the Bibigarh, flogging 'em and forcing 'em to lick up the blood with their tongues before they were hanged – well, I was all for it then, and I still am. Perhaps it's because I *knew* the corpses that went into that well – I'd seen them playing on the Cawnpore rampart, and being heard their lessons in that awful barrack, and laughing at the elephant dunging. Perhaps that baby hand I found belonged to the infant I'd seen in the arms of the woman in the torn gown. Anyway, I'd have snuffed out every life in India, and thought naught of it, in that moment when I looked at Bibigarh – and if you think that shocking, well, maybe I'm just more like Nana Sahib than you are.

Anyway, what I think don't signify. What mattered was the effect that Cawnpore had on our people. I know it turned our army crazy; they were ready to slaughter anything that even sniffed of mutiny, from that moment on. Not that they'd been dealing exactly kindly before; Havelock and Neill had been hanging right, left and centre from Allahabad north, and I daresay had disposed of quite a number of innocents – just as the pandies at Meerut and Delhi had done.[35]

What beats me is the way people take it to heart – what do they expect in war? It ain't conducted by missionaries, or chaps in Liberal clubs, snug and secure. But what amuses me most is the way fashionable views change – why, for years after Cawnpore, any vengeance wreaked on an Indian, mutineer or not, was regarded as just vengeance; nothing was too bad for 'em. Now it's t'other way round, with eminent writers crying shame, and saying nothing justified such terrible retribution as Neill took, and we were far guiltier than the niggers had been. Why? Because we were Christians, and supposed to know better? – and because England contains this great crowd of noisy know-alls that are forever defending our enemies' behaviour and crying out in pious horror against our own. Why our sins are always so much blacker, I can't fathom – as to Cawnpore, it don't seem to me one whit worse to slay in revenge, like

Neill, than out of sheer spite and cruelty, like Nana; at least it's more understandable.

The truth is, of course, that both sides were afraid – the pandy who'd mutinied, and feared punishment, decided he might as well be hanged for a sheep, and let his natural bloodlust go – they're cruel bastards at bottom. And our folk – they'd had an almighty scare, and Cawnpore brought *their* natural bloodlust to the top in turn; just give 'em a few well-chosen texts about vengeance and wrath of God and they could fall to with a will – as I've already observed about Rowbotham's Mosstroopers, there's nothing crueller than a justified Christian. Except maybe a nigger running loose.

So you can see it was a jolly summer in the Ganges valley, all right, as I and my four companions discovered, when Diribijah Singh finally convoyed us out from his fort and back to Cawnpore after Havelock had retaken it. I hadn't seen old Blood-and-Bones since he'd stood grumping beside my bed at Jallalabad fifteen years before, and time hadn't improved him; he still looked like Abe Lincoln dying of diarrhoea, with his mournful whiskers and bloodhound eyes. When I told him my recent history he just listened in silence, and then grabbed me by the wrist with his great bony hand, dragged me down on to my knees beside him, and began congratulating God on lugging Flashy out of the stew again, through His infinite mercy.

'The shield of His truth has been before thee, Flashman,' cries he. 'Has not the Hand which plucked thee from the paw of the bear at Kabul, and the jaws of the lion at Balaclava, delivered thee also from the Philistine at Cawnpore?'

'Absolutely, amen,' says I, but when I took him into my confidence – about Palmerston, and why I came to India in the first place, and suggested there was no good reason why

I shouldn't head for home at once – he shook his great coffin head.

'It cannot be,' says he. 'That mission is over, and we need every hand at the plough. The fate of this country is in the balance, and I can ill spare such a seasoned soldier as yourself. There is a work of cleansing and purging before us,' he went on, and you could see by the holy fire in his eyes that he was just sweating to get to grips with it. 'I shall take you on to my staff, Flashman – nay, sir, never thank me; it is I shall be the gainer, rather than you.'

I was ready to agree with him there, but I knew there was no point in arguing with the likes of Havelock – anyway, before I could think of anything to say he was scribbling orders for hanging a few more pandies, and dictating a crusty note to Neill, and roaring for his adjutant; he was a busy old Baptist in those days, right enough.

So there I was, and it might have been worse. I'd had no real hope of being sent home – no high command in their right mind would have dispensed with the famous Flash when there was a campaign on hand, and since I had to be here I'd rather be under Havelock's wing than anyone's. He was a good soldier, you see, and as canny as Campbell in his own way; there'd be no massacres or Last Stands round the Union Jack with the Gravedigger in charge.

So I settled in as Havelock's intelligence aide – a nice safe billet in the circumstances, but if you would learn the details of how I fared with him you must consult my official history, *Dawns and Departures of a Soldier's Life* (in three handsomely bound morocco volumes, price two gns. each or five gns. the set, though you may have difficulty laying hands on Volume III, since it had to be called in and burned by the bailiffs after that odious little Whitechapel sharper D'Israeli egged on one of his toadies to sue me for criminal information. Suez Canal shares, eh? I'll blacken the bastard's memory yet, though, just see if I don't. Truth will out).

However, the point is that my present tale isn't truly concerned with the main course of the Mutiny henceforth – although I bore my full reluctant part in that – but still with that mad mission on which Pam had sent me out in the first place, to Jhansi and the bewitching Lakshmibai. For I wasn't done with her, whatever Havelock might think, and however little I guessed it myself; the rest of the Mutiny was just the road that led me back to her, and to that final terrible adventure of the Jhansi flight and the guns of Gwalior when – but I'll come to that presently.

In the meantime I'll tell you as briskly as I can what happened in the few months after I joined Havelock at Cawnpore. At first it was damned bad news all round: the Mutiny kept spreading, Nana had sheered off after losing Cawnpore and was raising cain farther up-country, Delhi was still held by the pandies with our people banging away at it, and Havelock at Cawnpore didn't have the men or means to relieve Lucknow, only forty miles away, where Lawrence's garrison was hemmed in. He tried hard enough, but found that the pandy forces, while they didn't make best use of their overwhelming numbers, fought better defensive actions than anyone had expected, and Havelock got a couple of black eyes before he'd gone ten miles, and had to fall back. To make matters worse, Lloyd's advance guard got cut up at Arah, and no one down in Calcutta seemed to have any notion of overall strategy – that clown Canning was sitting like a fart in a trance, they tell me, and no proper order was taken.

I wasn't too upset, though. For one thing I was snug at

the Cawnpore headquarters, making a great *bandobast** over collecting information from our spies and passing the gist on to Havelock (intelligence work is nuts to me, so long as I can stay close to bed, bottle and breakfast and don't have to venture out). And for another, I could sense that things were turning our way; once the first flood of pandy successes had spent itself, there could only be one end, and old Campbell, who was the best general in the business, was coming out to take command-in-chief.

In September we moved on Lucknow in style, with fresh troops under Outram, a dirty-looking little chap on a waler horse, more like a Sheeny tailor than a general. They tell me it was a hell of a march; certainly it rained buckets all the way, and there was some stern fighting at Mangalwarh and at the Alum Bagh near Lucknow town – I know, because I got reports of it in my intelligence *ghari* at the rear of the column, where I was properly ensconced writing reports, examining prisoners, and getting news from friendly natives – at least, they were friendly by the time my Rajput orderlies had basted 'em a bit. From time to time I poked my head out into the rain, and called cheery encouragement to the reinforcements, or sent messages to Havelock – I remember one of them was that Delhi had fallen at last, and that old Johnny Nicholson had bought a bullet, poor devil. I drank a quiet brandy to him, listening to the downpour and the guns booming, and thought God help poor soldiers on a night like this.

However, having got Lucknow, Havelock and Outram didn't know what the devil to do with it, for the pandies were still thick around as fleas, and it soon became evident that

---

* Organisation, administration.

far from raising the siege, our forces were nothing but a reinforcement to the garrison. So we were *all* besieged, for another seven weeks, and the deuce of a business it must have been, with bad rations and the pandies forever trying to tunnel in under our defences, and our chaps fighting 'em in the mines which were like a warren underground. I say 'must have been', for I knew nothing about it; the night we entered Lucknow my bowels began to explode in all directions, and before morning I was flat on my back with cholera, for the second time in my life.

For once, it was a blessing, for it meant I was spared knowledge of a siege that was Cawnpore all over again, if not quite as bad. I gather I raved a good deal of the time, and I know I spent weeks lying on a cot in a beastly little cellar, as weak as a rat and not quite in my right mind. It was only in the last fortnight of the siege that I began to get about again, and by that time the garrison was cheery with the news that Campbell was on his way. I limped about gamely at first, looking gaunt and noble, and asking 'Is the flag flying still?' and 'Is there anything I can do, sir? – I'm much better than I look, I assure you.' I was, too, but I took care to lean on my stick a good deal, and sit down, breathing hard. In fact, there wasn't much to do, except wait, and listen to the pandies sniping away – they didn't hit much.

In the last week, when we knew for certain that Campbell was only a few days away, with his Highlanders and naval guns and all, I was careless enough to look like a whole man again – it seemed safe enough now, for you must know that at Lucknow, unlike Cawnpore, we were defending a large area, and if one kept away from the outer works, which unemployed convalescents like me were entitled to do, one could promenade about the Residency gardens without peril.

There were any number of large houses, half-ruined now, but still habitable, and we occupied them or camped out in the grounds – when I came out of my cellar I was sent to the bungalow, where Havelock was quartered with his staff people, but he packed me off to Outram's headquarters, in case I should be of some use there. Havelock himself was pretty done by this time, and not taking much part in the command; he spent most of his time in Gubbins's garden, reading some bilge by Macaulay – and was greatly intrigued to know that I'd met Lord Know-all and discussed his 'Lays' with the Queen; I had to tell Havelock all about that.

For the rest, I yarned a good deal with Vincent Eyre, who'd been in the Kabul retreat with me, and was now one of the many wounded in the garrison, or chaffed with the ladies in the old Residency garden, twitting them about their fashions – for after a six-month siege everyone was dressed any old how, with scraps and curtains and even towels run up into clothes. I was hailed everywhere, of course – jovial Flash, the hero on the mend – and quizzed about my adventures from Meerut to Cawnpore. I never mind telling a modest tale, if the audience is pretty enough, so I did, and entertained them by imitating Makarram Khan, too, which attracted much notice and laughter. It was an idiot thing to do, as you'll see – it earned another man the V.C., and nearly won me a cut throat.

What happened was this. One morning, it must have been about November 9th or 10th, there was a tremendous commotion over on the southern perimeter, where someone in Anderson's Post claimed he had heard Campbell's pipers in the distance; there was huge excitement, with fellows and ladies and niggers and even children hastening through the ruined buildings, laughing and cheering – and then everything went deadly still as we stood to listen, and sure enough, above the occasional crack of firing, far, far away there was the faintest whisper on the breeze of a pig in torment, and someone sings out, 'The Campbells are coming, hurrah, hurrah!' and people were embracing and shaking hands and leaping in the air, laughing and crying all together, and a few dropping to their knees to pray, for now the siege was as good as over. So there was continued jubilation throughout the garrison, and Outram sniffed and grunted and chewed his cheroot and called a staff conference.

He had been smuggling out messages by native spies all through the siege, and now that the relief force was so close he wanted to send explicit directions to Campbell on the best route to take in fighting his way through the streets and gardens of Lucknow to the Residency. It was a great maze of a place, and our folk had had the deuce of a struggle getting in two months earlier, being cut up badly in the alleys. Outram wanted to be sure Campbell didn't have the same trouble, for he had a bare 5,000 men against 60,000 pandies, and if they strayed or were ambushed it might be the end of them – and consequently of us.

I didn't have much part in their deliberations, beyond helping Outram draft his message in the secret Greek code he employed, and making a desperate hash of it. One of the Sappers had the best route all plotted out, and while they talked about that I went into the big verandah room adjoining to rest from the noon heat, convalescent-like. I sprawled on the cot, with my boots off, and must have dozed off, for when I came to it was late afternoon, the murmur of many voices from beyond the chick-screen had gone, and there were only two people talking. Outram was saying:

'. . . it is a hare-brained risk, surely – a white man proposing to make his way disguised as a native through a city packed with hostiles! And if he's caught – and the message falls into their hands? What then, Napier?'

'True enough,' says Napier, 'but to get a guide out to Campbell – a guide who can point his way for him – is better than a thousand messages of direction. And Kavanaugh knows the streets like a *bazaar-wallah*.'

'No doubt he does,' mutters Outram, 'but he'll no more pass for a native than my aunt's parrot. What – he's more than six feet tall, flaming red hair, blue eyes, and talks poor Hindi with a Donegal accent! Kananji may not be able to *guide* Campbell, but at least we can be sure he'll get a message to him.'

'Kananji swears he won't go if Kavanaugh does. He's ready to go alone, but he says Kavanaugh's bound to be spotted.'

'There you are, then!' I could hear Outram muttering and puffing on a fresh cheroot. 'Confound it, Napier – he's a brave man . . . and I'll own that *if* he could reach Campbell his knowledge of the byways of Lucknow would be beyond price – but he's harder to disguise than . . . damme, than any man in this garrison.'

I listened with some interest to this. I knew Kavanaugh, a great freckled Irish bumpkin of a civilian who'd spent the siege playing tig with pandy besiegers in the tunnels beneath our defences – mad as a hatter. And now madder still, by the sound of it, if he proposed to try to get through the enemy lines to Campbell. I saw Outram's problem – Kavanaugh was the one man who'd be a reliable guide to Campbell, if only he could get to him. But it was Tattersall's to a tin can that the pandies would spot him, torture his message out of him, and be ready and waiting for Campbell when he advanced. Well, thank God I wasn't called on to decide . . .

'. . . if he can disguise himself well enough to pass muster with me, he can go,' says Outram at last. 'But I wish to heaven Kananji would accompany him – I don't blame him for refusing, mind . . . but if only there were someone else who could go along – some cool hand who can pass as a native without question, to do the talking if they're challenged by the pandies – for if they are, and if Kavanaugh has to open that great Paddy mouth of his . . . stop, though! Of course, Napier – the very man! Why didn't it occur . . .'

I was off the cot and moving before Outram was half way through his speech; I knew before he did himself whose name was going to pop into his mind as the ideal candidate for this latest lunacy. I paused only to scoop up my boots and was tiptoeing at speed for the verandah rail; a quick vault into the garden, and then let them try to find me before sunset if they could . . . but blast it, I hadn't gone five steps when the door was flung open, and there was Outram, pointing his cheroot, looking like Sam Grant after the first couple of drinks, crying:

'Flashman! That's our man, Napier! Can you think of a better?'

Of course, Napier couldn't – who could, with the famous Flashy on hand, ripe to be plucked and hurled into the bloody soup? It's damnable, the way they pick on a fellow – and all because of my swollen reputation for derring-do and break-neck gallantry. As usual, there was nothing I could do, except stand blinking innocently in my stocking-soles while Outram repeated all that I'd heard already, and pointed out that I was the very man to go along on this hideous escapade to hold the great Fenian idiot's hand for him. I heard him in mounting terror, concealed behind a stern and thoughtful aspect, and replied that, of course, I was at his disposal, but really, gentlemen, was it wise? Not that I cared about the risk (Jesus, the things I've had to say), but I earnestly doubted whether Kavanaugh could pass . . . my convalescent condition, of course, was a trifling matter . . . even so, one wouldn't want to fail through lack of strength . . . not when a native could be certain of getting through . . .

'There isn't a loyal sepoy in this garrison who can come near you for skill and shrewdness,' says Outram briskly, 'or who'd stand half the chance of seeing Kavanaugh safe. Weren't you playing your old Pathan role the other day for the ladies? As to the toll of your illness – I've a notion your strength will always match your spirit, whatever happens. This thing's your meat and drink, Flashman, and you know it – and you've been fairly itching to get into harness again. Eh?'

'I'll hazard a guess,' says Napier, smiling, 'that he's more concerned for Kavanaugh than for himself – isn't that so, Flashman?'

'Well, sir, since you've said it—'

'I know,' says Outram, frowning at his damned cheroot. 'Kavanaugh has a wife and family – but he has volunteered, you see, and he's the man for Campbell, not a doubt of it. It only remains to get him there.' And the brute simply gave me a sturdy look and shook my hand as though that were the thing settled.

Which of course it was. What could I do, without ruining my reputation? – although such was my fame by this time that if I'd thrown myself on the floor weeping with fright, they'd probably not have taken me seriously, but thought it was just one of my jokes in doubtful taste. Give a dog a bad name – by God, it doesn't stick half as hard as a good one.

So I spent the evening dyeing myself with soot and *ghee*,

shuddering with apprehension and cursing my folly and ill luck. This, at the eleventh hour! I thought of having another shot at Napier, pleading my illness, but I didn't dare; he had a hard eye, and Outram's would be even worse if they suspected I was shirking. I near as a toucher cried off, though, when I saw Kavanaugh; he was got up like Sinbad the Sailor, with nigger minstrel eyes, harem slippers, and a great sword and shield. I stopped dead in the doorway, whispering to Napier:

'My God, man, he won't fool a child! We'll have the bloody pandies running after us shouting, "Penny for Guy Fawkes!"'

But he said reassuringly that it would be pretty dark, and Outram and the other officers agreed that Kavanaugh might just do. They were full of admiration for my get-up – which was my usual one of bazaar-ruffler – and Kavanaugh came up to me with absolute tears in his eyes and said I was the stoutest chap alive to stand by him in this. I nearly spat in his eye. The others were full of sallies about our appearance, and then Outram handed Kavanaugh the message for Campbell, biting on his cheroot and looking hard at us.

'I need not tell you,' says he, 'that it must never fall into enemy hands. That would be disaster for us all.'

Just to rub the point in, he asked if we were fully armed (so that we could blow our brains out if necessary), and then gave us our directions. We were to swim the river beyond the northern rampart, recross it by the bridge west of the Residency, and cut straight south through Lucknow city and hope to run into Campbell's advance pickets on the other side. Kavanaugh, who knew the streets, would choose our path, but I would lead and do the talking.

Then Outram looked us both in the eye, and blessed us, and everyone shook hands, looking noble, while I wondered if I'd time to go to the privy Kavanaugh, shaking with excitement, cleared his throat and says:

'We know what is to be done, sorr – an' we'll give our lives gladly in the attempt. We know the risks, ould fellow, do we not?' he added, turning to me.

'Oh, aye,' says I, 'that bazaar'll be full of fleas – we'll be lousy for weeks.' Since there was no escape, I might as well give 'em another Flashy *bon mot* to remember.

It moved them, as only jocular heroism can; Outram's aide, Hardinge, was absolutely piping his eye, and said England would never forget us, everyone patted us on the back with restrained emotion, and shoved us off in the direction of the rampart. I could hear Kavanaugh breathing heavily – the brute positively panted in Irish – and whispered to him again to remember to leave any talking to me. 'Oi will, Flashy, Oi will,' says he, lumbering along and stumbling over his ridiculous sword.

The thing was a farce from the start. By the time we had slipped over the rampart and made our way through the pitch dark down to the bank of the Goomtee, I had realised that I was in company with an irresponsible lunatic, who had no real notion of what he was doing. Even while we were stripping for our swim, he suddenly jerked his head up, at the sound of a faint plop out on the water.

'That's trout afther minnow,' says he, and then there was another louder plop. 'An' that's otter afther trout,' says he, with satisfaction. 'Are ye a fisherman, are ye?' Before I could hush his babbling, he had suddenly seized my hand – and him standing there bollock-naked with his togs piled on his head – and said fervently:

'D'ye know what – we're goin' to do wan o' the deeds that saved the Impoire, so we are! An' Oi don't moind tellin' ye somethin' else – for the first toime in me loife, Oi'm scared!'

'The first time!' squeaks I, but already he was plunging in with a splash like the launching of the *Great Eastern*, puffing and striking out in the dark, leaving me with the appalling realisation that for once I was in the company of someone as terrified as myself. It was desperate – I mean, on previous enterprises of this kind I'd been used to relying on some gallant idiot who could keep his head, but here I was with this buffoon who was not only mad Irish, but was plainly drunk with the idea of playing Dick Champion, the Saviour of the Side, and was trembling in his boots at the same time. Furthermore, he was given to daydreaming about trouts and otters at inappropriate moments, and had no more idea of moving silently than a bear with a ball and chain. But there was nothing for it now; I slid into the freezing water and swam the half-furlong to the far bank, where he was standing on one leg in the mud, hauling his clothes on, and making the deuce of a row about it.

'Are ye there, Flash?' says he, in a hoarse whisper you could have heard in Delhi. 'We'll have to be hellish quiet, ye know. Oi think there's pandies up the bank!'

Since we could see their pickets round the camp-fires not fifty yards away, it was a reasonable conclusion, and we hadn't stolen twenty yards along the riverside when someone hailed us. I shouted back, and our challenger remarked that it was cold, at which the oaf Kavanaugh petrified me by suddenly bawling out: '*Han, bhai, bahut tunder!*'* like some greenhorn reciting from a Hindi primer. I hustled him quickly away, took him by the neck, and hissed:

'Will you keep your damned gob shut, you great murphy?'

He apologised in a nervous whisper, and muttered

---

* 'Yes, brother, very cold!'

something about Queen and Country; his eye was glittering feverishly. 'Oi'll be more discreet, Flash,' says he, and so we went on, with me answering another couple of challenges before we reached the bridge, and crossed safely over into Lucknow town.

This was the testing part, for here there was lighting in the streets, and passers-by, and Kavanaugh might easily be recognised as counterfeit. The swim hadn't done his dyed skin any good, and apart from that his outlandish rig, the European walk, the whole cut of the man, was an invitation to disaster. Well, thinks I, if he's spotted, it's into the dark for Flashy, and old O'Hooligan can take care of himself.

The worst of it was, he seemed incapable of keeping quiet, but was forever halting to mutter: 'The mosque, ah, that's right, now – and then de little stone bridge – where the divil is it? D'ye see it, Flashy – it ought to be right by hereabouts?' I told him if he must chunter, to do it in Hindi, and he said absent-mindedly 'Oi will, Oi will, niver fear. Oi wish to God we had a compass.' He seemed to think he was in Phoenix Park.

It wasn't too bad at first, because we were moving through gardens, with few folk about, but then we came to the great Chauk Bazaar. Thank God it was ill-lit, but there were groups of pandies everywhere, folk at the stalls, idlers at every corner, and even a few *palkis* swaying through the narrow ways. I put on a bold front, keeping Kavanaugh between me and the wall, and just swaggered along, spitting. No one gave me a second glance, but by hellish luck we passed close by a group of pandies with some whores in tow, and one of the tarts plucked at Kavanaugh's sleeve and made an improper suggestion; her sepoy stared and growled resentfully, and my heart was in my mouth as I hustled Kavanaugh along, shouting over my shoulder that he'd just been married the previous day and was exhausted, at which they laughed and let us be. At least that kept him shut up for a spell, but no sooner were we clear of the bazaar than he was chattering with relief, and stopped to pick carrots in a vegetable patch, remarking at the top of his voice that they were 'the swaitest little things' he'd tasted in months.

Then he lost our way. 'That looks devilish like the Kaiser Bagh,' says he, and fell into a monsoon ditch. I hauled him out, and he went striding off into the dark, and to my horror stopped a little old fellow and asked where we were. The man said 'Jangli Ganj', and hurried off, glancing suspiciously at us. Kavanaugh stood and scratched himself and said it wasn't possible. 'If this is Jangli Ganj,' says he, 'then where the hell is Mirza Kera, will ye tell me that? Ye know what, Flashman, that ould clown doesn't know where he's at, at all, at all.' After that we blundered about in the dark, two daring and desperate men on our vital secret mission, and then Kavanaugh gave a great laugh and said it was all right, he knew where we were, after all, and that must be Moulvie Jenab's garden, so we should go left.

We did, and finished up striking matches along Haidar's Canal – at least, that's what Kavanaugh said it was, and he should have known, for he was in it twice, thrashing about in the water and cursing. When he had climbed out he was in a thundering rage, swearing the Engineers had got the map of Lucknow all wrong, but we must cross the canal anyway, and bear left until we hit the Cawnpore road. 'The bloody thing's over dere somewhere!' cries he, and since he seemed sure of that, at least, I stifled my growing alarm and off we went, with Kavanaugh tripping over things and stopping every now and then to peer into the gloom wondering: 'D'ye

304

think that garden could have been the Char Bagh, now? No, no, niver – and yet agin, it moight be – what d'ye think, Flashy?'

What I thought you may guess; we must have been wandering for hours, and for all we knew we might be heading back towards the Residency. Kavanaugh's slippers had given out, and when he lost one of them we had to grope about in a melon patch until he found it; his feet were in a deplorable condition, and he'd lost his shield, but he was still convinced our plight was all the fault of the ancient he had asked the way from. He thought we might try a cast to our right, so we did, and found ourselves wandering in Dilkoosha Park, which was full of pandy artillery; even I knew we were quite out the way, and Kavanaugh said, yes, he had made a mistake, but such mishaps were of frequent occurrence. We must bear away south, so we tried that, and I asked a peasant sitting out with his crops if he would guide us to the Alam Bagh. He said he was too old and lame, and Kavanaugh lost his temper and roared at him, at which the fellow ran off shrieking, and the dogs began to bark and we had to run for it and Kavanaugh went headlong into a thorn bush. (And this, as he'd remarked, was one of the Deeds that Saved the Empire; it's in all the books.)

There was no end to the fellow's capacity for disaster, apparently. Given a choice of paths, he headed along one which brought us full tilt into a pandy patrol, and I had to talk our way out of it by saying we were poor men going to Umroula to tell a friend the British had shot his brother. Arriving in a village, he wandered into a hut when I wasn't looking, and blundered about in the dark, seized a woman by the thigh – fortunately she was too terrified to cry out, and we got away. After that he took to crying out 'That's

Jafirabad, Oi'm certain sure. And that's Salehnagar, over there, yes.' Pause. 'Oi think.' The upshot of that was that we landed in a swamp, and spent over an hour ploshing about in the mud, and Kavanaugh's language was shocking to hear. We went under half a dozen times before we managed to find dry land, and I spotted a house not far off, with a light in an upper window, and insisted that Kavanaugh must rest while I found out where we were. He agreed, blaspheming because the last of his dye had rubbed off with repeated immersions.

I went to the house, and who should be at the window but the charmingest little brown girl, who said we were not far from Alam Bagh, but the British had arrived there, and people were running away. I thanked her, inwardly rejoicing, and she peeped at me over the sill and says:

'You are very wet, big man. Why not come in and rest, while you dry your clothes? Only five rupees.'

By George, thinks I, why not? I was tired, and sick, and it had been the deuce of a long time, what with sieges and cholera and daft Irishmen falling in bogs; this was just the tonic I needed, so I scrambled up, and there she was, all chubby and brown and shiny, giggling on her charpoy and shaking her bouncers at me. I seized hold, nearly crying at this unexpected windfall, and in a twinkling was marching her round the room, horse artillery fashion, while she squeaked and protested that for five rupees I shouldn't be so impatient. I was, though, and it was just as well, for I'd no sooner finished the business than Kavanaugh was under the window, airing his Urdu plaintively in search of me, and wanting to know what was the delay?

I leaned out and cadged five rupees off him, explaining it was a bribe for an old sick man who knew the way; he passed it up, I struggled into my wet fugs, kissed my giggling Delilah good night, and scrambled down, feeling fit for anything.

It took us another two hours, though, for Kavanaugh was about done, and we had to keep dodging behind trees to avoid parties of peasants who were making for Lucknow. I was getting a mite alarmed, because the moon was up, and I knew that dawn couldn't be far off; if we were caught by daylight, with Kavanaugh looking as pale as Marley's ghost, we were done for. I cursed myself for a fool, whoring and wasting time when we should have been pushing on – what had I been thinking of? D'you know, I suddenly realised that in my exasperation with Kavanaugh, and all that aimless wandering in wrong directions, and watching him fall in tanks and canals, I'd forgotten the seriousness of the whole thing – perhaps I was still a trifle light-headed from my illness, but I'd even forgotten my fears. They came back now, though, in full force, as we staggered along; I was about as tuckered as he was, my head was swimming, and I must have covered the last mile in a walking dream, because the next thing I remember is bearded faces barring our way, and blue-tunicked troopers with white *puggarees*, and thinking, 'These are 9th Lancers.'

Then there was an officer holding me by the shoulders, and to my astonishment it was Gough, to whom I'd served brandy and smokes on the verandah at Meerut. He didn't know me, but he poured spirits into us, and had us borne down into the camp, where the bugles were blowing, and the cavalry pickets were falling in, and the flag was going up, and it all looked so brisk and orderly and *safe* you would have wept for relief – but the cheeriest sight of all, to me, was that crumpled, bony figure outside the headquarter tent, and the dour, wrinkled old face under the battered helmet. I hadn't seen Campbell close to, not since Balaclava; he was an ugly old devil, with a damned caustic tongue and a grave-yard sense of humour, but I never saw a man yet who made me feel more secure.

He must have been a rare disappointment to Kavanaugh, though, for at the sight of him my blundering Paddy threw off his tiredness, and made a tremendous parade of announcing who he was, fishing out the message, and presenting it like the last gallant survivor stumbling in with the News; you never saw suffering nobility like it as he explained how we'd come out of Lucknow, but Campbell, listening and tugging at his dreary moustache, just said 'Aye', and sniffed, and added after a moment: 'That's surprising.' Kavanaugh, who had probably expected stricken admiration, looked quite deflated, and when Campbell told him to 'Away you and lie down', he obeyed pretty huffily.

I knew Campbell, of course, so I wasn't a bit astonished at the way he greeted me, when he realised who I was.

'It's no' you again?' says he, like a Free Kirk elder to the town drunk. 'Dearie me – ye're not looking a whit better than when I saw ye last. I doot ye've nae discretion, Flashman.' He sighed and shook his head, but just as he was turning away to his tent he looked back and says: 'I'm glad tae see ye, mind.'

I suppose there are those who'd say that there's no higher honour than that, coming from Old Slowcoach; if that's so, I must make the most of it, for it's all the thanks I ever got for convoying Kavanaugh out of Lucknow. Not that I'm complaining, mind, for God knows I've had my share of undeserved credit, but it's a fact that Kavanaugh stole all the limelight when the story came out; I'm certain it was sheer lust for glory that had made him undertake the job in the

308

first place, for when I joined him in the rest-tent after we'd left Campbell, he broke off the kneeling-and-praying which he was engaged in, looked up at me with his great freckled yokel face, and says anxiously:

'D'yez think they'll give us the Victoria Cross?'

Well, in the end they did give him the V.C. for that night's work, while all I got was a shocking case of dysentery. He was a civilian, of course, so they were bound to make a fuss of him, and there was so much V.C.-hunting going on just then that I suppose they thought recognised heroes like me could be passed over – ironic, ain't it? Anyway, I wasn't recommended at the time for any decoration at all, and he was, which seemed fairly raw, although I don't deny he was brave, you understand. Anyone who's as big a bloody fool as that, and goes gallivanting about seeking sorrow, must be called courageous. Still . . . if it hadn't been for me, finding his blasted slipper for him, and fishing him out of canals – and most important of all, getting the right direction from that little brown banger – friend Kavanaugh might still have been traipsing along Haidar's Canal asking the way. But thinking back, perhaps I got the better of the bargain – she was a lissome little wriggler, and it was Kavanaugh's five rupees, after all.[36]

If Campbell was sparing with his compliments, he was equally careful of his soldiers' lives, especially his precious 93rd Highlanders. He took a week to relieve Lucknow, feeling his way in along the route our message had suggested, battering the pandies with his artillery, and only turning his kilties and Sikhs on them when he had to. They butchered everything in sight, of course, between them, but it was a slow business, and he was much abused for it afterwards. In my opinion, he was dead right – as he and Mansfield, his staff chief, were when they wouldn't risk lives simply to pursue and punish fleeing mutineers. A general's job is to win campaigns with as little loss as may be, but of course that don't suit the critics in clubs and newspaper offices – they're at a safe distance, and they want blood, rot them, so they sneer at Old Slowcoach, and call him a stick-in-the-mud soldier.[37]

In fact, his relief of Lucknow, in the face of odds that were sometimes fifteen to one, was a model of sound sense. He got in, he took the garrison out, and he retired in good order, scratching his ear and looking glum, while ignorant asses like

Kavanaugh danced with impatience. D'ye know, that Irish lunatic absolutely ran the gauntlet of pandy fire to get back *into* Lucknow, and bring out Outram and Havelock in person (with the poor old Gravedigger hardly able to hobble along) just so that they could greet Sir Colin as he covered the last few furlongs? Bloody nonsense, but it looked very gallant, and has since been commemorated in oils, with camels and niggers looking on admiringly, and the Chiefs all shaking hands. (I'm there, too, like John the Baptist on horseback, with one aimless hand up in the air, which is rot, because at the time I was squatting in the latrine working the dysentery bugs out of my system and wishing I was dead.)[38]

Poor old Gravedigger – he didn't last more than a few days after. The dysentery bugs did for him in earnest, and we buried him under a palm tree by the Alam Bagh at the start of the retreat. I guess that suited him, and I remember the text running through my head, 'And Nicanor lay dead in his harness' – it was what he'd said to me fifteen years earlier, when he'd told me of Sergeant Hudson dying at Piper's Fort. Aye, well, none of us lives forever.

Anyway, Lucknow had to be left in rebel hands, and Campbell took our army back to Cawnpore, where Tantia Tope was raging around the garrison; Campbell whipped him in quick time, and then started clearing up rebel resistance along the Ganges, while at the same time assembling a new force which would march back to Lucknow after Christmas, clear the pandies out properly, and subdue the whole of Oudh kingdom. It was fairly obvious that although mutineers were still thick as mosquitoes everywhere, and had several armies in the field, Campbell's methodical operations would have the whole business settled in a few months, if only Calcutta let him alone. I lent my gallant assistance by supervising intelligence work at Unao, just across the river from Cawnpore, where our new army was assembling; easy work, and nothing more dangerous than occasional brawls and turn-ups between the Pathan Horse and the Devil's Own,* which suited me. The only thing that ruffled my surface at all that winter was a rebuke from Higher Authority when I squired an upper-class half-caste whore to a band parade at Cawnpore,[39] which shows you better than anything how things were beginning to quieten down: when generals have nothing better to do than worry about the morals of staff colonels, you may be sure there's no great work on hand.

And indeed, we were beginning to make things so hot for the pandies along the Grand Trunk that winter that it seemed the bulk of their power was being forced farther and farther south, into the Gwalior country, where Tantia Tope had taken his army, and the rebel princelings had still to be dealt with. That was where Jhansi was: I used to see its name daily in the intelligence reports, with increasing references to Lakshmibai – 'the rebel Rani' and 'the traitor queen' was what they were calling her now, for in the past few months she'd thrown off the pretence of loyalty which she had maintained after the Jhansi massacre, and cast in her lot with Nana and Tantia and the other mutinous princes. That had shocked me when I first heard it, and yet it wasn't so surprising really – not when I recalled her feelings towards us, and her grievances, and that lovely dark face so grimly set – 'Mera Jhansi denge nay! I won't give up my Jhansi!'

She'd have to give it up fast enough, though, presently, with our southern armies under General Rose already advancing north to Gwalior and Bandelkand. She would be

---

* The Connaught Rangers (88th Foot).

crushed along with the other monarchs and their sepoy-cum-bandit armies, and I didn't care to think about that, much. When my thoughts turned towards her – and for some reason they did increasingly in the leisure of that winter – I couldn't think of her as belonging in this world of turmoil and blood and burning and massacre: when I read about 'the Jhansi Jezebel' plotting with Nana and whipping up revolt, I couldn't reconcile it with my memory of that bewitching figure swinging gently to and fro on her silken swing in that mirrored fairy palace. I found myself wondering if she was still swinging there, or playing with the monkeys and parrots in her sunny garden, or riding in the woods by the river – who with? How many new lovers had she taken since that night in the pavilion? That was enough to set the flutters going low down in my innards – and farther up, in my midriff, for it wasn't only lust. When I thought of those slanting eyes, and the grave little smile, and the smooth dusky arm along the rope of her swing, I was conscious of a strange, empty longing just for the sight of her, and the sound of her voice. It was downright irritating, for when I reflect on an old love it's usually in terms of tits and buttocks pure and simple – after all, I wasn't a green kid, and I didn't care to find myself thinking like one. What I needed to cure me, I decided, was two weeks' steady rogering at her to get these moon-calf yearnings out of my mind for good, but of course there was no chance of that now.

Or so I thought, in my complacent ignorance, as the winter wore through, and our campaign in the north approached its climax. I knew it was as good as over when Billy Russell of *The Times* showed up to join Campbell's final march on Lucknow – it's a sure sign of victory when the correspondents gather like vultures. We marched with 30,000 men and strong artillery, myself piling up great heaps of useless paper in Mansfield's intelligence section and keeping out of harm's way. It was an inexorable, pounding business, as our gunners blew the pandy defences systematically to bits, the Highlanders and Irish slaughtered the sepoy infantry whenever it stood, the engineers demolished shrines and temples to show who was master, and everyone laid hands on as much loot as he could carry.

It was a great bloody carnival, with everyone making the most of the war: I recall one incident, in a Lucknow courtyard (I believe it may have been in the Begum's palace) in which I saw Highlanders, their gory bayonets laid aside, smashing open chests that were simply stuffed with jewels, and grinning idiot little Goorkhas breaking mirrors for sheer sport and wiping their knives on silks and fabrics worth a fortune – they didn't know any better. There were Sikh infantry dancing with gold chains and necklaces round their necks, an infantry subaltern staggering under a great enamelled pot overflowing with coins, a naval gunner bleeding to death with a huge shimmering bolt of cloth-of-gold clasped in his arms – there were dead and dying men everywhere, our own fellows as well as pandies, and desperate hand-to-hand fighting going on just over the courtyard wall; muskets banging, men shrieking, two Irishmen coming to blows over a white marble statuette smeared with blood, and Billy Russell stamping and damning his luck because he had no rupees on him to buy the treasures which private soldiers were willing to trade away for the price of a bottle of rum.

'Gi'es a hunnerd rupees, now!' one of the Micks was shouting, as he flourished a gold chain set with rubies – they were as big as gull's eggs. 'Jist a hunnerd, yer honour, an' dey're yours!'

314

'But . . . but they're worth fifty times that!' cries Russell, torn between greed and honesty.

'Ah, the divil wid that!' cries Paddy. 'Oi'm sayin' a hunnerd, an' welcome!'

All right, says Russell, but the man must come to his tent for the money that night. But at this Paddy cries out:

'Oh, God, Oi can't, sorr! How do Oi know you or me won't be dead by then? Ready money, yer honour – say jist fifty chips, an' yer spirit flask! Come, now?'

But Billy hadn't even fifty rupees, so the Mick shook his head sorrowfully and swore he couldn't trade, except for cash down. Finally he burst out:

'But Oi can't see a gintleman in yer honour's position goin' empty-handed! Here, take dis for nuthin', an' say a prayer for O'Halloran, Private Michael,' and he thrust a diamond brooch into Russell's hand and ran off, whooping, to join his mates.

You may wonder what I was doing there, so close to the fighting: the answer is I was keeping an eye on my two Rajput orderlies, who were picking up gold and jewellery for me at bargain prices, using intelligence section funds. I paid it all back, mind, out of profits, no irregularities, and finished with the handsome surplus which built Gandamack Lodge, Leicestershire, for my declining years. (My Rajputs bought O'Halloran's ruby chain, by the way, for ten rupees and two ounces of baccy – say for £2 all told. I sold it to a Calcutta jeweller for £7,500, which was about half its true value, but not a bad stroke of business, I think.)[40]

I asked Billy later what value he would have put on all the loot that we saw piled up and scrambled for in that one yard, and he said curtly: 'Millions of pounds, blast it!' I'd believe it, too: there were solid gold and silver vessels and ornaments,

315

crusted with gems, miles of jewel-sewn brocade, gorgeous pictures and statues that the troops just hacked and smashed, beautiful enamel and porcelain trampled underfoot, weapons and standards set with rubies and emeralds which were gouged and hammered from their settings – all this among the powder smoke and blood, with native soldiers who'd never seen above ten rupees in their lives, and slum-ruffians from Glasgow and Liverpool, all staggering about drunk on plunder and killing and destruction. One thing I'm sure of: there was twice as much treasure destroyed as carried away, and we officers were too busy bagging our share to do anything about it. I daresay a philosopher would have made heavy speculation about that scene, if he'd had time to spare from filling his pockets.

I was well satisfied with my winnings, and pondered that night on how I'd employ them when I went home, which couldn't be long now: I remember thinking 'This is the end of the war, Flash, old buck, or near as dammit, and well out of it you are.' I was very much at ease, sitting round the mess-fire in the dusk of a Lucknow garden, smoking and swigging port and listening to the distant thump of the night guns, while I yarned idly with Russell and 'Rake' Hodson (who'd fagged me at Rugby) and Macdonald the Peeler and Sam Browne and little Fred Roberts, who wasn't much more than a griff,[41] but knew enough to hang around us older hands, warming himself in the glow of our fame. Thinking of them, it strikes me how many famous men I've run across in the dawn of their careers – not that Hodson had long to go, since he was shot while looting next day, with his glory all behind him. But Roberts has gone to the very top of the tree (pity I wasn't more civil to him when he was green; I might have been higher up the ladder myself now), and I suppose Sam Browne's name is known today in every army on earth. Just because he lost an arm and invented a belt, too – get them to call some useful article of clothing after you, and your fame's assured, as witness Sam and Raglan and Cardigan. If I had my time over again I'd patent the Flashman fly-button, and go down in history.[42]

I don't remember much of what we discussed, except that Billy was full of indignation over how he'd seen some Sikhs burning a captured pandy alive, with white soldiers looking on and laughing: he and Roberts said such cruelty oughtn't to be allowed, but Hodson, who was as near a wild beast as I ever met, even among British irregular cavalry, said the viler deaths the rebels died, the better; they'd be less ready to mutiny again. I can see him yet, sitting forward glaring into the fire, pushing back his fair hair with that nervous gesture he had, and steady Sam Browne squinting at him quizzically, drawing on his cigar, saying nothing. I know we talked too of light cavalry, and Russell was teasing Hodson with the prowess of the Black Sea Cossacks, winking at me, when Destiny in the unlikely shape of General Mansfield tapped me on the shoulder and said: 'Sir Colin wants you, directly.'

I didn't think twice about it, but pitched my cheroot into the fire and sauntered through the lines to the Chief's tent, computing my loot in my mind and drinking in the warm night air with sleepy content. Even when Campbell's greeting to me was: 'How well d'ye know the Rani of Jhansi?' I wasn't uncomfortably surprised – there'd been a despatch in about the Jhansi campaign that very day, and Campbell already knew about my mission for Palmerston; it all seemed a long way away now.

I said I had known her very well; we had talked a great deal together.

317

'And her city – her fortress?' says Campbell.

'Passably, sir. I was never in her fort proper – our meetings were at the palace, and I'm not over-familiar with the city itself—'

'More familiar than Sir Hugh Rose, though, I'll be bound,' says he, tapping a paper in front of him. 'And that's his own opeenion – he mentions ye by name in his latest despatch.' I didn't care for that; it don't do to have generals talking about you. I didn't care for the way Campbell was looking at me, either, tapping a nail against those beautifully kept teeth that shone so odd in his ancient face.

'This Rani,' says he at length. 'What's she like?'

I began to say that she was a capable ruler and nobody's fool, but he interrupted with one of his barbarous Scotch noises.

'Taghaway-wi-ye! Is she pretty, man? Eh? How pretty?'

I admitted that she was strikingly beautiful, and he grinned and shook his grizzly head.

'Aye, aye,' says he, and squinted at me. 'Ye're a strange man, Flashman. I'll confess to ye, I've even-on had my doots aboot ye – don't ask me what, for I don't know. I'm frank wi' ye, d'ye see?' I'll say that for him, he always was. 'This much I'm certain of,' he went on, 'ye always win. God kens how – and I'm glad I don't ken mysel', for I wish to think well of ye. But there – Sir Hugh needs ye at Jhansi, and I'm sending ye south.'

I didn't know what to think of this – or of his curious opinion of me. I just stood and waited anxiously.

'This mutiny mischief is just aboot done – it's a question of scattering the last armies – here, in Oudh and Rohilkand, and there, in Bandelkand – and hanging Nana and Tantia and Azeemoolah higher than Haman. Jhansi is one of the last nuts tae be cracked – and it'll be a hard one, like enough. This bizzum of a Rani has ten thousand men and stout city walls. Sir Hugh will have her under siege by the time ye get there, and nae doot he'll have to take the place by storm. But that's not enough – which is why you, wi' your particular deeplomatic knowledge of the Rani and her state, are essential to Sir Hugh. Ye see, Flashman, Lord Canning and Sir Hugh and mysel' are agreed on one thing – and your experience of this wumman may be the key to it.' He looked me carefully in the eye. 'Whatever else befalls, we must contrive tae capture the Rani of Jhansi alive.'

If she'd been ugly as sin, or twenty years older and scrawny, it would never have happened. Jhansi would have been taken, and if a plain, elderly Rani had been bayoneted or shot in the process, no one would have given a damn. But Canning, our enlightened Governor-General, was a sentimental fool, intent on suppressing the Mutiny with the least possible bloodshed, and already alarmed at the toll of vengeance that people like Neill and Havelock had taken. He guessed that sooner or later the righteous wrath of Britons at home would die down, and that if we slaughtered too many pandies a revulsion would set in – which, of course, if did. My guess is that he also feared the death of a young and beautiful rebel princess (for her fame and likeness had spread across India by now) might just tip the balance of public conscience – he didn't want the liberal press depicting her as some Indian Joan of Arc. So, however many other niggers died, male and female, she was to be taken alive.

Mind you, I could see Canning's point, and personally I was all for it. There wasn't a life anywhere – except Elspeth's and little Havvy's – that was as precious to me then as Lakshmibai's, and I don't mind admitting it. But fair's fair; I wanted her saved without any dangerous intervention on my part, and the farther I could have kept away from Jhansi the better I'd have liked it. It wasn't a lucky place for me.

So I took as long as I decently could getting there, in the hope that it might be all over by the time I arrived. I had the excuse that the two hundred miles between Lucknow and Jhansi was damned dangerous country, with pandies and the armies of rebel chiefs all over the place; I had a strong escort of Pathan Horse, but even so we went warily, and didn't sight that fort of ill-omen on its frowning rock until the last week in March. Rose was just getting himself settled in by then, battering away at the city defences with his guns, his army circling the walls in a gigantic ring, with observation posts and cavalry pickets all prettily sited to bottle it up.

He was a good soldier, Rose, careful as Campbell but twice as quick, and one glance at the rebel defences told you that he needed to be. Jhansi lay massive and impregnable under the brazen sun, with its walls and outworks and the red rebel banner floating lazily above the fort. Outside the walls the dusty plain had been swept clear of every scrap of cover, and the rebel batteries thundered out in reply to our gunners, as though warning the besiegers what would happen if they ventured too close. And inside there were ten thousand rebels ready to fight to the finish. A tough nut, as Campbell had said.

'We'll have them out in a week, though, no fears about that,' was Rose's verdict. He was another Scotsman (India was crawling with them, of course, as always), brisk and bright-eyed and spry; I knew him well from the Crimea, where he'd been liaison at the Frog headquarters, and less objectionable than most diplomat-soldiers. He was new to India, but you'd never have guessed it from his easy confidence and dandy air – to tell the truth, I have difficulty in memory separating his appearance from George Custer's, for they both had the same gimlet assurance, as well as the carefully wind-blown blond hair and artless moustaches. There the resemblance ended – if we'd had Rose at Little Big Horn, Crazy Horse and Gall could have whistled for their dinners.

'Yes, a week at most,' says he, and pointed out how he had sited his left and right attacks opposite the strongest points in the rebel defences, which our gunners were pounding with red-hot shot, keeping the pandy fire-parties busy quelling the flames which you could see here and there behind the walls, flickering crazily through the heat-haze. 'Frontal night assault as soon as the breaches are big enough, and then . . .' He snapped his telescope shut. 'Bloody work, since the pandies are sure to fight to the last – but we'll do the business. The question is: in all that carnage, how do we preserve her ladyship? You must be our oracle on that subject, what? Would she personally surrender, d'you suppose?'

I looked about me from the knoll on which we stood, with his staff officers. Just before us were the lines of siege-guns in their earthworks, shaking the ground with their explosions, the smoke wraithing back towards us as the gunners, crawling like ants round their pieces, reloaded and fired again. Either side the pickets of the flying cavalry camps were strung out as far as the eye could see – the red jackets of the Light Dragoons, and the grey khakee of the Hyderabad troopers' coats, dusty with the new curry-powder dye. Two miles behind us, near the ruins of the old cantonment, were the endless tent-lines of the infantry brigades, waiting patiently till the guns had done their work on the massive walls of Jhansi city, behind which the jumble of distant houses stretched in the smoky haze up to the mighty crag of the fortress. She'd be up there, somewhere, perhaps in that cool durbar room, or on the terrace, playing with her pet monkeys; perhaps she was with her chiefs and soldiers, looking out at the great army that was going to swallow her up and reduce her city and fairy palace to rubble. *Mera Jhansi denge nay*, thinks I.

'Surrender?' says I. 'No, I doubt if she will.'

'Well, you know her.' He gave me that odd, leery look that I'd got used to even in the few hours I'd been at his headquarters, whenever her name was mentioned. The popular view was that she was some gorgeous human tigress who prowled half-naked through sumptuous apartments, supervising the torture of discarded legions of lovers – oh, my pious generation had splendid imaginations, I may tell you.[43]

'We've tried proclamation, of course,' says Rose, 'but since we can't guarantee immunity to her followers, we might as well save our breath. On the other hand, she may not be eager to see her civilians exposed to continuous bombardment followed by the horrors of assault, what? I mean, being a woman . . . what *is* she like, by the way?'

'She's a lady,' says I, 'extremely lovely, uses French scent, is kind to animals, fences like a Hungarian hussar, prays for several hours each day, recreates herself on a white silk swing in a room full of mirrors, gives afternoon tea-parties for society ladies, and hangs criminals up in the sun by their thumbs. Useful horse-woman, too.'

'Good God!' says Rose, staring, and behind him his staff were gaping at me round-eyed, licking their lips. 'Are you serious?'

'What about lovers, hey?' says one of the staff, sweating

and horny-eyed. 'They say she keeps a harem of muscular young bucks, primed with love-potions—'

'She didn't tell me,' says I, 'and I didn't ask her. Even you wouldn't, I fancy.'

'Well,' says Rose, glancing at me and then away. 'We must certainly consider what's to be done about her.'

That was how I employed myself for the next three days, while the guns and eight-inch mortars smashed away in fine style, opening a sizeable breach in the south wall, and burning up the rebels' repair barricades with red-hot shot. We blew most of their heavy gun posts into rubble, and by the 29th Rose was drawing up final orders for his infantry stormers – and still we had reached no firm plan for capturing Lakshmibai unharmed. For the more I thought about it, the more certain I became that she'd fight it out, in person, when our infantry fought their way hand-to-hand into her palace – it was easy, after Lucknow, to imagine bloody corpses on that quilted Chinese carpet, and the mirrors shattered by shot, and yelling looters smashing and tearing in those price-less apartments, sabring and bayoneting everything that stood in their way. God knows it was nothing new to me, and I'd lent a hand in my time, when it had been safe to do so – but these would be *her* rooms, *her* possessions, and I was senti-mental enough to be sorry for that, because I'd liked them and been happy there. By George, I'd got her into my blood-stream though, hadn't I just, when I started worrying about her damned furniture.

And what would happen to her, in that madhouse of blood and steel? Try as I might, I could see nothing for it but to tell off a picked platoon with orders to make straight for the palace and secure her unharmed at any price – provided she didn't get in the way of a stray shot, there was no reason why they shouldn't bring her out safe. By God, though, that was one detail I'd have to avoid – no, my job would be her reception and safe-keeping when the slaughter was safely over: Flashy the stern and sorrowful jailer, firm but kindly, shielding her from prying eyes and lecherous staff-wallopers with dirty minds, that was the ticket. She'd have to be escorted away, perhaps even to Calcutta, where they'd decide what to do with her. A nice long journey, that, and she'd be grateful for a friendly face among her enemies – especially one for which she'd shown such a partiality in the past. I thought of that pavilion, and that gleaming bronze body undulating towards me, quivering voluptuously to the music – we'll have dancing every night, thinks I, in our private hackery, and if I'm not down to twelve stone by the time we reach Calcutta, it won't be for want of nocturnal exercise.

I explained my thoughts to Rose – the first part, about the special platoon, not the rest – at dinner in his tent, and he frowned and shook his head.

'Too uncertain,' says he. 'We need something concerted and executed before the battle has even reached her palace; we must have her snug and secure by then.'

'Well, I don't for the life of me see how you're going to do that,' says I. 'We can't send anyone in ahead of the troops, to kidnap her or any such thing. They wouldn't get a hundred yards through the streets of Jhansi – and if they did, she has a Pathan guard hundreds strong covering every inch of the palace.'

'No,' says he, thoughtfully, picking at his cheroot. 'Force wouldn't serve, I agree – but diplomacy, now? What d'ye think, Lyster?'

This was young Harry Lyster, Rose's galloper, and the only other person present at our talk. I'd known him any time the past ten years; he'd been a special constable with me at the Chartist farce of '48 when I took up old Morrison's truncheon and did his duty for him – me and Gladstone and Louis Napoleon holding the plebeian mob at bay, I don't think. Lyster was a smart 'un, though; given a silver spoon he'd have been a field marshal by now.

'Bribery, perhaps – if we could smuggle a proposal to some of her officers?' says he.

'Too complicated,' says Rose, 'and you'd probably just lose your money.'

'They've eaten her salt,' says I. 'You couldn't buy 'em.' I was far from sure of that, by the way, but I wanted to squash all this talk of intrigue and secret messages – I'd heard it too often before, and I know who finishes up sneaking through the dark with his bowels gurgling and his hair standing on end in the enemy's lair. 'I'm afraid it comes down to the special platoon after all, sir. A good native officer, with intelligent *jawans*—'

'Counsel of despair, Flashman.' Rose shook his head decisively. 'No – we'll have to trick her out. Here's a possibility – storm the city, as we intend, but leave her a bolthole. If we draw off our cavalry pickets from the Orcha Gate, they'll spot the weakness, and when our rebel lady sees that her city's doomed, I'll be much surprised if she don't try to make a run for it. How well do Indian women ride?'

'This one? Like a Polish lancer. It might work,' says I, 'if she don't suspicion what we're up to. But if she smells a rat—'

'She'll be smelling too much powder smoke by then to notice anything else,' says Rose confidently. 'She'll break for the open, to try to join Tantia, or some other rebel leader – and we'll be waiting for her on the Orcha road. What d'you say, gentlemen?' says he, smiling.

Well, it suited me, although I thought he underrated her subtlety. But Lyster was nodding agreement[44] and Rose went on:

'Yes, I think we'll try that – but only as a long stop. It's still not enough. Lord Canning attaches the utmost importance to capturing the Rani unscathed; that being so, we must play every card in our hand. And we have a trump which it would be folly not to use for everything it's worth.' He turned and snapped a pointing finger at me. 'You, Flashman.'

I choked on my glass, and covered my dismay with a shuddering cough. 'I, sir?' I tried to get my breath back. 'How, sir? I mean, what—?'

'We can't afford to neglect the opportunity which your knowledge of this woman – your familiarity with her – gives us. I don't suppose there's a white man living who has been on closer terms with her – isn't that so?'

'Well, now, sir, I don't know—'

'I still think we can talk her out. Public offers of surrender are useless, we agree – but a private offer, now, secretly conveyed, with my word of honour, and Lord Canning's, attached to it . . . that might be a different matter. Especially if it were persuasively argued, by a British officer she could trust. You follow me?'

All too well I followed him; I could see the abyss of ruin and despair opening before my feet once again, as the bright-eyed lunatic went eagerly on:

'The offer would assure her that her life would be spared, if she gave herself up. She doesn't have to surrender Jhansi, even – just her own person. How can she refuse? She could even keep her credit intact with her own people – that's it!' cries he, smacking the table. 'If she accepts, all she has to do is take advantage of the bolthole we're going to leave her, through the Orcha Gate! She can pretend to her own folk that she's trying to escape, and we'll snap her up as she emerges. No one would ever know it was a put-up business – except her, and ourselves!' He beamed at us in triumph.

Lyster was frowning. 'Will she accept – and leave her city and people to their fate?' He glanced at me.

'Oh, come, come!' cries Rose. 'She ain't European royalty, you know! These black rulers don't care a snuff for their subjects – ain't that so. Flashman?'

I seized on this like a drowning man. 'This one does, sir,' says I emphatically. 'She wouldn't betray 'em – never.' The irony of it was, I believed it to be true.

He stared at me in disappointment. 'I can't credit that,' says he. 'I can't. I'm positive you're mistaken, Flashman.' He shook his head. 'But we have nothing to lose by trying, at any rate.'

'But if I went in, under a flag of truce, demanding private audience with her—'

'Pshaw! Who said anything about a flag of truce? Of course, that would blow the gaff at once – her people would know there was something up.' He tapped the table, grinning at me, bursting with his own cleverness. 'Didn't I say you were the trump card? You not only know her well, you're one of the few men who can get inside Jhansi, and into her presence, with no one the wiser – as a native!' He sat back, laughing. 'Haven't you done it a score of times—? Why, all the world knows about how you brought Kavanaugh out of Lucknow! What d'ye think they're calling you down in Bombay these days – the Pall Mall Pathan!'

There are times when you know it absolutely ain't worth struggling any longer. First Palmerston, then Outram, and now Rose – and they were only the most recent in a long line of enthusiastic madmen who at one time or another had declared that I was just the chap they were looking for to undertake some ghastly adventure. I made one attempt at a feeble excuse by pointing out that I didn't have a beard any longer; Rose brushed it aside as of no importance, poured me another brandy, and began to elaborate his idiot plan.

In essence it was what I've already described – I was to convince Lakshmibai of the wisdom of giving herself up (which I reckoned she'd never agree to do), and if she accepted, I was to explain how she must make an attempt to escape through the unguarded Orcha Gate at the very height of our attack on Jhansi city – the timing, said Rose, was of the utmost importance, and the further advanced our attack was before she made her bolt, the less suspicion her people might feel. (I couldn't see that this mattered much, but Rose was one of these meticulous swine who'll leave nothing to chance.)

'And if she rejects the offer – as I know she will?' I asked him.

'Then on no account must you say anything about the Orcha Gate,' says he. 'Only when she has accepted the offer must you explain how her "capture" is to be contrived. But if she *does* refuse – well, she may still be tempted to use a bolthole in the last resort, if we leave her one. So we shall nab her anyway,' he concluded smugly.

'And I – if she refuses?'

'My guess,' says he airily, puffing at his cheroot, 'is that she'll try to keep you as a hostage. I hardly think she'd do more than that, what? Anyway,' says he, clapping me on the arm, 'I know you've never counted risk yet – I saw you at Balaclava, by George! Did you know about that, Lyster?' he went on, 'charging with the Heavies wasn't enough for this beauty – he had to go in with the Lights as well!' And, do you know, he actually sat laughing at me in admiration? It would turn your stomach.

So there it was – again. Hell in front and no way out. I tried to balance the odds in my mind, while I kept a straight face and punished the brandy. Would Lakshmibai listen to me? Probably not; she might try to escape when all was lost, but she'd never give herself up and leave her city to die. What would she do with me, then? I conjured up a picture of that dark face, smiling up at me with parted lips when I pinned her and kissed her against the mirrored wall; I remembered the pavilion – no, she wouldn't do me harm, if she could help it. Unless . . . *had* she set those Thugs after me? No, that had been Ignatieff. And yet – there was the Jhansi massacre – how deep had she been in that? Who knew what went on in an Indian mind, if it came to that? Was she as cruel and treacherous as all the rest of them? I couldn't say – but I was going to find out, by God, whether I liked it or not. I'd know, when I came face to face with her – and just for an instant I felt a leap of eagerness in my chest at the thought of seeing her once more. It was only for an instant, and then I was sweating again.

I'll say this for Hugh Rose – along with his fiendish ingenuity for dreaming up dangers for me, he had an equally formidable talent of organisation. It took him a good thirty seconds to think of a fool-proof way of getting me safe inside Jhansi – I would have the next day to prepare my disguise, with skin-dye and the rest, and the following night he would loose a squadron of Hyderabad Cavalry in a sudden raid on the breach in the city wall. They would break through the flimsy barrier which the defenders had thrown up, sabre a few sentries, create a hell of a row, and then withdraw in good order – leaving behind among the rubble one native *badmash* of unsavoury appearance, to wit, Colonel Flashman, late of the 17th Lancers and General Staff. I'd have no difficulty, said Rose breezily, in lying low for half an hour, and then emerging as one of the defenders. After that, all I had to do was tool up through the streets to the palace and knock on the door, like Barnacle Bill.

Speaking from a safe distance, I can say it was a sound scheme. Hearing it propounded at the time I thought it was fit to loosen the bowels of a bronze statue – but the hellish thing is, whatever a general suggests, you can do nothing but grin and agree. And, I have to admit, it worked.

I don't remember the agonising day I must have spent waiting, and attiring myself in a filthy sepoy uniform, so that I could pass in my old role of 3rd Cavalry mutineer. But I'll never forget the last moment of suspense beside the siege guns, with the Hyderabadi troopers round me in the gloom, and Rose clasping my hand, and then the whispered order, and the slow, muffled advance through the cold dark, with only the snorting of the horses and the creak of leather to mark our passing towards that looming distant wall, with the dull crimson glow of the city behind it, and the broad gap of the breach where the watch-fires twinkled, and we could even see figures silhouetted as they moved to and fro.

Away to our left flank the night-batteries were firing, distant tiny jets of flame in the dark, pounding away at the flank of the city which faced the old cantonment. That was for diversion; I could smell the bazaar stink from Jhansi, and still we hadn't been spotted. Even through my genuine funk, I could feel that strange tremor of excitement that every horse-soldier knows as the squadrons move forward silently in the gloom towards an unsuspecting enemy, slowly and ponderously, bump-bump-bump at the walk, knee to knee, one hand on the bridle, t'other on the hilt of the lamp-blacked sabre, ears straining for the first cry of alarm. How often I'd known it, and been terrified by it – in Afghanistan, at Cawnpore with Rowbotham, in the Punjab, under the walls of Fort Raim when I rode against the Russians with old Izzat Kutebar and the Horde of the Blue Wolves, and that lovely witch, Ko Dali's daughter, touching my hand in the dark . . .

The crack of a rifle, a distant yell, and the thunderous roar of the *rissaldar*: 'Aye-hee! Squah-drahn – charge!' The dark mass either side seemed to leap forward, and then I was thundering along, flat down against my pony's flanks like an Oglala, as we tore across the last furlong towards the breach. The Hyderabadis screamed like fury as they spread out, except for the four who remained bunched ahead and either side of me, as a protective screen. Beyond them I could see the smoky glare of the fires in the breach, a rubble-strewn gap a hundred yards wide, with a crazy barricade thrown across it; pinpoints of flame were twinkling in the gloom, and shots whistled overhead, and then the first riders were at the barrier, jumping it or bursting through, sabres swinging. My front-gallopers swerved in among the jumble of fallen masonry and scorched timbers, howling like dervishes; I saw one of them sabring down a pandy who thrust up at him with musket and bayonet, while another rode slap into a big, white-dhotied fellow who was springing at him with a spear. His horse stumbled and went down, and I scrambled my own beast over a pile of stones and plaster, from which a dark figure emerged, shrieking, and vanished into the gloom.

There was a fire straight ahead, and men running towards me, so I jerked my beast's head round and made for the shadows to my right. Two Hyderabadis surged up at my elbow, charging into the advancing group, and under their cover I managed to reach the lee of a ruined house, while the clash of steel, the crack of musketry, and the yells of the fighters sounded behind me. Close by the house there was a tangle of bushes – one quick glance round showed no immediate enemy making for me, and I rolled neatly out of the saddle into what seemed to be a midden, crawled frantic- ally under the bushes, and lay there panting.

I'd dropped my sabre, but I had a stout knife in my boot and a revolver in my waist under my shirt; I snuggled back as far into cover as I could and kept mum. Feet went pounding by towards the tumult at the barricade, and for two or three minutes the pandemonium of shooting and yelling continued. Then it died down, to be replaced by a babble of insults from the defenders – presumably directed at our retreating cavalry – a few shots went after them, and then comparative peace descended on that small corner of Jhansi. So far, so good – but, as some clever lad once said, we hadn't gone very far.

I waited perhaps quarter of an hour, and then burrowed through the bushes and found myself in a narrow lane. There was no one about, but round the corner was a watch-fire, with a few pandies and bazaar-wallahs round it; I ambled past them, exchanging a greeting, and they didn't do more than give me an idle glance. Two minutes later I was in the bazaar, buying a chapatti and chilli, and agreeing with the booth- wallah that if the *sahib-log* couldn't do better than the feeble skirmish there had just been down at the breach, then they'd never take Jhansi.

Although it was three in the morning, the narrow streets were as busy as if it had been noon. There were troops on the move everywhere – rebels of the 12th N.I., regulars of the Rani's Maharatta army, Bhil soldiers-of-fortune, and every sort of armed tribesman from the surrounding country, with spiked helmets, long swords, round shields, and all kinds of firearm from Minies to matchlocks. It looked to me as though Jhansi knew our main attack was soon coming, and they were moving reserves down to the walls.

There were ten civilian townsfolk about for every soldier, and the booths were doing a roaring trade. Here and there were ruined shops and houses where some of our stray shots had fallen, but there was no sign of unease, as you'd have expected – rather a sense of excitement and bustle, with everyone wideawake and chattering. A party of coolies went by, dragging a cart piled with six-pounder cartridges, and I took the opportunity to remark to the booth-wallah:

'There go a thousand English lives, eh, brother?'

'Like enough,' says he, scowling. 'And every cannon-shot means another anna in market-tax. Lives can be bought too dear – even English ones.'

'Nay, the Rani will pay it from her treasury,' says I, giving him my shrill sepoy giggle.

'Ho-ho-ho, hear him!' says he, scornfully. 'You should set up a stall, soldier, and see how fat you get. When did the Rani ever pay – or any other prince? What are we for but to pay, while the great ones make war?'

Just what they'd be saying in the Reform Club or the Star and Garter, thinks I. Aloud I said:

'They say she holds a great council in the fort tonight. Is it true?'

'She did not invite me,' says he, sarcastically. 'Nor, strangely enough, did she offer me the use of the palace when she left it. That will be three pice, soldier.'

I paid him, having learned what I wanted to know, and took the streets that led up to the fort, with my knees getting shakier at every step. By God, this was a chancy business; I had to nerve myself with the thought that, whatever her feelings towards my country and army, she'd never shown anything but friendliness to me – and she'd hardly show violence to an envoy from the British general. Even so, when I found myself gazing across the little square towards that squat, frowning gateway, with the torches blazing over it, and the red-jacketed Pathan sentries of her personal guard standing either side, I had to fight down the temptation to scuttle back into the lanes and try to hide until it was all over. Only the certainty that those lanes would shortly be a bloody battleground sent me reluctantly on. I wound my *puggaree* tightly round head and chin, hiding half my face, slipped from my pocket the note which Rose and I had carefully prepared, walked firmly across to the sentry, and demanded to see the guard commander.

He came out, yawning and expectorating, and who should it be but my old acquaintance who spat on shadows. I gave him the note and said: 'This is for the Rani's hand, and no other. Take it to her, and quickly.'

He glowered from me to it and back. 'What is this, and who may you be?'

'If she wishes you to know, belike she'll tell you,' I growled, and squatted down in the archway. 'But be sure, if you delay, she'll have that empty head off your shoulders.'

He stood glaring, turning the note in his hands. Evidently it impressed him – with a red seal carrying young Lyster's family crest, it should have done – for after an obscene inquiry about my parentage, which I ignored, he scratched himself and then loafed off, bidding the sentries keep an eye on me.

I waited, with my heart hammering, for this was the moment when things might go badly astray. Rose and I had cudgelled our brains for wording that would mean nothing to anyone but her, in case the note fell into the wrong hands. As an added precaution, we'd written it in schoolboy French, which I knew she understood. It said, simply:

One who brought perfume and a picture is here. See him alone. Trust him.

Rose had been delighted with this – he was plainly one who enjoyed intrigue for its own sake, and I've no doubt would have liked to sign it with a skull and crossbones. Squatting in the doorway, I couldn't take such a light-hearted view. Assuming that Pathan blockhead took it straight to her, she'd guess who it was from fast enough – but suppose she didn't want to see me? Suppose she thought the best way of answering the message would be to send me back in bits to Rose's headquarters? Suppose she showed it to someone else, or it miscarried, or . . .

The sound of marching feet came from the gloom beyond the archway, and I got to my feet, quivering. The *havildar* came out of the dark, with two troopers behind him. He stopped, gave me a long, glowering look, and then jerked his head. I went forward, and he motioned me on into the courtyard beyond, falling in beside me with the two troopers behind. I wanted to ask him if he'd given the note to the Rani personally, but my tongue seemed to have shrivelled up; I'd know soon enough. As my eyes became accustomed to the gloom after the glare of the torches by the gate, I saw that we were heading across the yard, with high black walls on either side, and another torch at the far end over a doorway, guarded by two more Pathans.

'In,' growls the *havildar*, and I found myself in a small vaulted guard room; I blinked in the sudden glare of oil lamps, and then my heart lurched down into my boots, for the figure peering intently towards me from the centre of the room was the little fat chamberlain whom I knew so well from Lakshmibai's durbar.

The stupid bitch had told him who I was! There was no hope of a secret offer now – Rose's fat-headed scheme had sprung a leak, and –

'You are the officer who brought gifts from the British Queen?' he squeaked. 'The Sirkar's envoy – Colonel Flashman?' He was squinting at me in consternation, as well he might, for I didn't look much like the dandy staff officer he'd known. Sick and fearful, I peeled off my *puggaree* and pushed my hair back.

'Yes,' said I. 'I'm Colonel Flashman. You must take me to the Rani, at once!'

He goggled at me, his little eyes wide in that fat face, twisting his hands nervously. And then something fluttered in the air between us – for an instant I thought it was a moth – and fell to the floor with a tiny puff of sparks. It was a cigarette, smoking on the flags; a long yellow tube with a mouthpiece.

'All in good time,' said Ignatieff's voice, and I believe I actually cried out with shock, as I spun round to stare in horrified disbelief at the doorway. He was standing there, his hand still frozen in the act of flicking away the cigarette – Ignatieff, whom I'd supposed a thousand miles away by now, looking at me with his dreadful cold smile, and then inclining his tawny head.

337

'All in good time,' he repeated in English, as he came forward. He ground his heel on the fallen cigarette. 'After we have resumed the . . . discussion? . . . which was so unfortunately interrupted at Balmoral.'

How I've survived four-score years without heart seizure I do not know. Perhaps I'm inured to the kind of shock I experienced then, with my innards surging up into my throat; I couldn't move, but stood there with my skin crawling as he came to stand in front of me – a new Ignatieff, this, in flowered shirt and *pyjamy* trousers and Persian boots, and with a little gingery beard adorning his chin. But the rat-trap mouth was still the same, and that unwinking half-blue half-brown eye boring into me.

'I have been anticipating this meeting,' says he, 'ever since I learned of your mission to India – did you know, I heard about it before you did yourself?' He gave a chilly little smile – he could never resist bragging, this one. 'The secret deliberations of the astute Lord Palmerston are not as secret as he supposes. And it has been a fool's errand, has it not? But never so foolish as now. You should have been thankful to escape me . . . twice? . . . but you come blundering back a third time. Very well.' The gotch-eye seemed to harden with a brilliant light. 'You will not have long to regret it.'

With an effort I got my voice back, damned shaky though it was.

'I've nothing to say to you!' cries I, as truculently as I could, and turned on the little chamberlain. 'My business is with the Rani Lakshmibai – not with this . . . this renegade! I demand to see her at once! Tell her—'

Ignatieff's hand smashed across my mouth, sending me staggering, but his voice didn't rise by a fraction. 'That will not be necessary,' says he, and the little chamberlain dithered submissively. 'Her highness is not to be troubled for a mere spy. I shall deal with this jackal myself.'

'In a pig's eye you will!' I blustered. 'I'm an envoy from Sir Hugh Rose, to the Rani – not to any hole-and-corner Russian bully! You'll hinder me at your peril! Damn you, let me loose!' I roared as the two troopers suddenly grabbed my elbows. 'I'm a staff officer! You can't touch me – I'm—'

'Staff officer! Envoy!' Ignatieff's words came out in that raging icy whisper that took me back to the nightmare of that verminous dungeon beneath Fort Arabat. 'You crawl here in your filthy disguise, like the spy you are, and claim to be treated as an emissary? If that is what you are, why did you not come in uniform, under a flag, in open day?' His face was frozen in fury, and then the brute hit me again. 'I shall tell you – because you are a dishonoured liar, whose word no one would trust! Treachery and deceit are your trade – or is it assassination this time?' His hand shot out and whipped the revolver from my waist.

'It's a lie!' I shouted. 'Send to Sir Hugh Rose – he'll tell you!' I was appealing to the chamberlain. 'You know me, man – tell the Rani! I demand it!'

But he just stood gaping, waiting for Ignatieff, whose sudden anger had died as quickly as it came.

'Since Sir Hugh Rose has not honoured us with a parley, there is no reason why we should address him,' says he softly. 'We have to deal only with a night prowler.' He gestured to the troopers. 'Take him down.'

'You've no authority!' I roared. 'I'm not answerable to you, you Russian swine! Let me go!' They were dragging me forward by main strength, while I bawled to the chamberlain, pleading with him to tell the Rani. They ran me through a doorway, and down a flight of stone steps, with Ignatieff following, the chamberlain twittering in front of him. I struggled in panic, for it was plain that the brute was going to prevent the Rani hearing of my arrival until after he'd done . . . I nearly threw up in terror, for the troopers were hauling me across the floor to an enormous wheel like a cable drum, set perpendicular above ground level. There were manacles dangling from it, and fetters attached to the stone floor beneath it – Jesus! They had racked Murray to death in this very fort, Ilderim had said, and now they flung me against the hellish contraption, one grinning trooper pinning me bodily while the other snapped the floor-chains round my ankles. I yelled and swore, the chamberlain sank down fearfully on the bottom step, and Ignatieff lit another cigarette.

'So much would not be necessary if I only sought information,' says he, in that dreadful metallic whisper. 'With such a coward as you, the threat is sufficient. But you are going to tell me why you are here, what treachery you intended, and for what purpose you wished to see her highness. And when I am satisfied that you have told me everything –' he stepped close up to me, that awful eye staring into mine, and concluded in Russian, for my benefit alone '– the racking will continue until you are dead.' He signed to the troopers, and stepped back.

'For Christ's sake, Ignatieff!' I screamed. 'You can't do this! I'm a British officer, a white man – let me go, you bastard! Please – in God's name, I'll tell you!' I felt the drum turn behind me as the troopers put their weight on the lever, drawing my arms taut above my head. 'No, no! Let me go, you foul swine! I'm a gentleman, damn you – for pity's sake! We've had tea with the Queen! No, please—'

There was a clank from the huge wheel, and the chains

wrenched at my wrists and ankles, sending shoots of pain through my arm and thigh muscles. I howled at the top of my voice as the wheel turned, stretching me to what seemed the limit of endurance, and Ignatieff stepped closer again.

'Why did you come?' says he.

'Let me go! You vile bloody dog, you!' Behind him I saw that the chamberlain was on his feet, white with horror. 'Run!' I yelled. 'Run, you stupid fat sod! Get your mistress – quickly!' But he seemed rooted to the spot, and then the drum clanked again, and an excruciating agony flamed through my biceps and shoulders, as though they were being hauled out of my body (which, of course, they were). I tried to scream again, but nothing came out, and then his devil's face was next to mine again, and I was babbling:

'Don't – don't, for Jesus' sake! I'll tell you – I'll tell you!' And even through the red mist of pain I knew that once I did, I was a dead man. But I couldn't bear it – I had to talk – and then inspiration came through the agony, and I let my head loll sideways, with a groan that died away. If only I could buy a moment's time – if only the chamberlain would run for help – if only Ignatieff would believe I'd fainted, and I could keep up the pretence with my whole body shrieking in pain. His palm slapped across my face, and I couldn't restrain a cry. His hand went up to the troopers, and I gasped:

'No – I'll tell you! Don't let them turn it again! I swear it's the truth – only don't let them do it again – oh, God, please, not again!'

'Well?' says he, and I knew I couldn't delay any longer. I couldn't bear another turn.

'General Rose—' My voice seemed to be a whisper from miles away. 'I'm on his staff – he sent me – to see the Rani

– please, it's the God's truth! Oh, make them let me down!'

'Go on,' says that dreadful voice. 'What was your message?'

'I was to ask her . . .' I was staring into his horrible eye, seeing it through a blur of tears, and then somewhere in the obscured distance behind him there was a movement, at the top of the steps, and as I blinked my vision was suddenly clear, and my voice broke into a shuddering sigh of relief, and I let my head fall back. For the door at the top of the steps was open, with my red-coated guard sergeant, that wonderful, bearded genius of a Pathan who spat on shadows, holding it back, and a white figure was stepping through, stopping abruptly, staring down at us. I had always thought she was beautiful, but at that moment Lakshmibai looked like an angel pavilioned in splendour.

I was in such anguish that it was even an effort to keep my eyes open, so I didn't, but I heard her cry of astonishment, and then the chamberlain babbling, and Ignatieff swinging round. And then, believe it or not, what she said, in a voice shrill with anger, was:

'Stop that at once! Stop it, do you hear?' for all the world like a young school-mistress coming into class and catching little Johnny piddling in the ink-well. I'll swear she stamped as she said it, and even at the time, half-fainting with pain that I was, I thought it sounded ridiculous; and then suddenly with an agonising jerk that made me cry out, the fearful traction on my limbs was relaxed, and I was sagging against the wheel, trying to stop my tortured legs from buckling under me. But I'm proud to say I still had my wits about me.

'You won't get anything out of me!' I groaned. 'You Russian hound – I'll die first!' I fluttered an eye open to see how this was received, but she was too busy choking back her fury as she confronted Ignatieff.

'This is by your order?' Lord, it was a lovely voice. 'Do you know who this is?'

I'll say this for him, he faced her without so much as a blink – indeed, he even tossed his blasted cigarette aside in deference before giving his little bow to her.

'It is a spy, highness, who stole into your city in disguise – as you can see.'

'It is a British officer!' She was blazing, trembling from her white head-veil all down her shapely sari-wrapped body to her little pearled sandals. 'An envoy of the Sirkar, who brings a message for me. For me!' And she stamped again. 'Where is it?'

Ignatieff pulled the note from his girdle, and handed it to her without a word. She read it, and then folded it deliberately, and looked him in the face.

'Sher Khan tells me he had orders to deliver it into my hands alone.' She was holding in her anger still, with an effort. 'But seeing him with it, you asked what it might be, and the fool gave it you. And having read it, you dared to question this man without my leave—'

'It was a suspicious message, highness,' says Ignatieff, dead level. 'And this man was obviously a spy—'

'You bloody liar!' croaks I. 'You knew damned well what I was! Don't listen to him, Lakshmi – highness – the swine's got it in for me! He was trying to murder me, out of spite!'

She gave me one look, and then fronted Ignatieff again. 'Spy or not, it is I who rule here. Sometimes I think you forget it, Count Ignatieff.' She faced him eye to eye for a long moment, and then turned away from him. She looked at me, and then away, and we all waited, in dead silence. Finally she said quietly:

'I shall see to this man, and decide what is to be done with him.' She turned to Ignatieff. 'You may go, Count.'

He bowed, and said: 'I regret if I have offended your highness. If I have done so, it was out of zeal for the cause we both serve – your highness's government –' he paused '– and my imperial master's. I would be failing in my duty to both if I did not remind you that this man is a most dangerous and notorious British agent, and that—'

'I know very well who and what he is,' says she quietly, and at that the gotch-eyed son-of-a-bitch said no more, but bowed again and took himself off, with the two troopers sidling hastily after him, salaaming nervously as they passed her. They clattered up the steps behind Ignatieff, and Sher Khan closed the door after them, and that left the four of us, all cosy as ninepence – Lakshmibai standing like a glimmering white statue, the little chamberlain twitching in anxious silence, Sher Khan on the door, and H. Flashman, Esq., doing his celebrated imitation of a Protestant martyr. Damned uncomfortable, too, but something told me grateful babblement wouldn't be in order, so I said as steadily as I could:

'Thank you, your highness. Forgive me if I don't make my bow, but in the circumstances . . .'

Very gallant, you see, but the truth was that fiery pains were still shooting through my arms and legs, and it was all I could do to keep from gasping and groaning. She was standing looking at me, quite expressionless, so I added hopefully:

'If your *havildar* would release me . . .'

But she didn't move a muscle, and I felt a sudden thrill of unease under the steady gaze of those dark eyes, the whites so clear against her dusky skin. What the hell was she up to,

344

keeping me strung up on this bloody machine, and not so much as a glimmer of a smile, or recognition even? I palpitated while she stood, watching me and thinking, and then she came up within a yard of me, and spoke, in a flat hard voice.

'What did he want to know from you?'

The tone took my breath away, but I held my head up. 'He wanted to know my business with your highness.'

Her glance went to the chains on my wrists, then back to my face.

'And did you tell him?'

'Of course not.' I thought a brave smile mightn't be out of place, so I tried one. 'I like people to ask me questions – politely.'

She turned her head towards the little chamberlain.

'Is this true?'

He puffed and flapped his arms, all eagerness. 'Indeed, exalted highness! Not a word did the colonel sahib say – not even under the cruel torture! He did not even cry out – much . . . oh, he is an officer sahib, of course, and—'

Poor little bastard was hoping to butter his bread on the right side, of course, but I wasn't sure he was backing a winner here; she was still looking at me as if I was some carcase on a butcher's slab. The chilling thought struck me that it probably wasn't the first time she'd contemplated some poor devil in my situation . . . God, perhaps even Murray . . . and then she turned her head and called to Sher Khan, and he came tumbling down the steps double quick, while the sweat broke out on me. Surely she wasn't going to order him to –

'Release him,' says she, and I near fainted with relief. She watched impassively while he unclamped me, and I took a few staggering and damned painful steps, catching at that hellish wheel for support. Then:

'Bring him,' says she curtly. 'I shall question him myself,' and without another word she turned and walked up the steps, out of the dungeon, and with the little chamberlain bobbing nervously behind her, and Sher Khan spitting and grunting as he assisted me to follow.

'Speak well of me to her highness, *husoor*,' he muttered as he gave me a shoulder. 'If I blundered in giving thy *kitab* to the Ruski sahib, did I not make amends? I went for her, when I saw he meant to ill-use thee . . . I had not recognised thee, God knows—'

I reassured him – he could have had a knighthood and the town hall clock for my part – as he conducted me up through the guard room to a little spiral stair, and then along a great stone passage of the fort, which gave way to a carpeted corridor where sentries of her guard stood in their steel caps and backs-and-breasts. I limped along, relieved to find that apart from a few painfully pulled muscles and badly skinned wrists and ankles, I wasn't much the worse . . . yet, and then Sher Khan was ushering me through a door, and I found myself in a smaller version of the durbar room at the palace – a long, low richly furnished apartment, all in white, with a quilted carpet, and silk hangings on the walls, divans and cushions and glowing Persian pictures, and even a great silver cage in which tiny birds cheeped and fluttered. The air was heavy with perfume, but I still hadn't got the stink of fear out of my nostrils, and the sight of Lakshmibai waiting did nothing to cheer me up.

She was sitting on a low backless couch, listening to the little chamberlain, who was whispering fifteen to the dozen, but at sight of me she stopped him. There were two of her ladies with her, and the whole group just looked at me, the women curiously, and Lakshmibai with the same damned disinheriting stare she'd used in the dungeon.

'Set him there,' says she to Sher Khan, pointing to the middle of the floor, 'and tie his hands behind him.' He jumped to it, wrenching the knots with no thought for my flayed wrists. 'He will be safe enough so,' she added to the little chamberlain. 'Go, all of you – and Sher Khan will remain beyond the door within call.'

Dear God, was she going to set about me herself, I wondered, as the ladies swiftly rustled out, and the chamberlain hurried by, eyeing me apprehensively. I heard Sher Khan withdraw, and the door close, leaving me standing and her sitting erect, staring at me – and then to my amazement she sprang from the seat and was flying across the room towards me, with her arms out and her face trembling, throwing herself against me, clinging to me, and sobbing:

'Oh, my darling one, my darling, my darling! You have come back – oh, I thought I should never see you again!' And her arms were round my neck, and that lovely dark face, all wet with tears, was upturned to mine, and she was kissing me any old how, on the cheeks and chin and eyes and mouth, sobbing out endearments and shuddering against me.

I'm an easy-going chap, as you know, and can take things pretty well as they come, but I'll admit that I wondered if I was mad or dreaming. Not much above two hours ago I'd been in Rose's tent in the safety of British lines, gulping down a last brandy and trying to read the advertisements in an old copy of *The Times* to take my mind off the ordeal ahead, with young Lyster humming a popular song – and since then I'd taken part in a cavalry skirmish, and skulked through a hostile nigger city in disguise, and been scared out of my senses by

347

that fiend Ignatieff's appearance, and stretched on a rack in fearful physical and even worse mental agony, and been rescued at the last minute and dragged and bound in the presence of a female despot – and here she was clinging and weeping and slobbering over me as though I were Little Willie the Collier's Dying Child. It was all a shade more than enough for my poor bemused brain, and body, and I just sank to my knees under the weight of it all, and she sank with me, crying and kissing.

'Oh, my sweet, have they hurt you? I thought I should swoon when I saw – ah, your poor flesh!' Before I knew it she was down at my legs, soothing my scraped ankles with one hand while she kept the other behind my head, and kissed me long and lingeringly on the mouth. My amazement was giving way to the most wonderful mixture of relief and joy, and pure ecstatic pleasure in that scented dark skin pressed against my face, her open mouth trembling on mine. I could feel her breasts hard against me – and, dammit, my hands were tied, and I could only strain against her until she freed her lips and looked at me, holding my face between her hands.

'Oh, Lucky – Lucky Lakshmi!' I was babbling out of sheer delight. 'Oh, you wonderful, beautiful creature!'

'I thought you were dead,' says she, cradling my head down against her bosom – by George, that was the place to be, and I struggled my hands desperately to try to free them. 'All these months I have mourned you – ever since that dreadful day when they found the dead dacoit near the pavilion, and I thought . . .' She gave a little sob and pulled up my face to kiss me again. 'And you are safe, and back again with me . . . my darling.' The great eyes were brimming with tears again. 'Ah, I so love you!'

Well, I'd heard it before, of course, expressed with varying degrees of passion by countless females, and it's always gratifying, but I couldn't recall a moment when it had been more welcome than now. If ever I needed a woman to be deeply affected with my manly charms, this was the moment, and being half in love with her myself it required no effort at all to play up and make the most of it. So I put my mouth on hers again, and used my weight to bear her down on the cushions – damned difficult with my hands bound, but she was all for it, and lay there drinking me in, teasing with her tongue and stroking my face gently with her fingertips until I thought I'd burst.

'Lakshmi, *chabeli* – untie my hands!' I croaked, and she disengaged herself, glancing towards the door and then smiling at me longingly.

'I cannot . . . not now. You see, no one must know . . . yet. To them, you are a prisoner – a spy sent by the British soldiers . . .'

'I can explain all that! I had to come secretly, in disguise, to bring you a message from General Rose. Lakshmi, dearest, you've got to accept it – it's an offer of life! Please, untie me and let me tell you!'

'Wait,' says she. 'Come, sit here.' And she helped me up, pausing on the way to fondle me again and kiss me before seating me on the edge of a divan. 'It is best for the moment that we leave you bound – oh, beloved, it will not be for long, I promise . . . but in case someone comes suddenly. See, I shall get you a drink – you must be parched – ah, and your poor wrists, so cruelly torn!' The tears welled up again, and then such a look of blazing hatred passed across her face that I shrank where I sat. 'That beast of Russia!' says she, clenching her tiny fist. 'He will pay for it – I will have him

349

drawn apart, and make him eat that hideous eye of his! And the Tsar his master may go straight to hell, and look for him!'

Excellent sentiments, I thought, and while she filled a goblet with sherbet I thought I'd improve the shining hour.

'It was Ignatieff who set the Thugs on me that night – he's been dogging me ever since I came to India, spying and trying to stir up rebellion . . .'

I suddenly stopped there; she, after all, was now one of the leaders of that rebellion, and obviously Ignatieff was her ally, whatever her personal feelings towards him. She put the cup to my lips, and I drank greedily – being put on the rack's the way to raise a thirst, you know – and when I'd finished she stood up, with the cup between her hands, looking down at me.

'If I had only listened to you,' says she. 'If there had only been more time! I did not know . . . if only I could make you understand – all the years of waiting, and trying to right injustice to . . . to me, and my son, and my Jhansi . . .'

'How is the young fella, by the way? Well, eh, and thriving – fine lad, that . . .'

'. . . and waiting turns to despair and despair to hatred, and I thought you were another cold and unfeeling creature of the Sirkar – and yet . . .' she suddenly knelt down in front of me, and caught my hands, and there was a look in her great almond eyes that made even my experienced old heart skip a beat '. . . and yet, I knew that you were not like the others. You were gentle, and kind, and you seemed to understand. And then . . . that day when we fenced, in the durbar room . . . I felt something inside me that – that I had not known before. And later . . .'

'In the pavilion,' says I, hoarsely. 'Oh, Lakshmi, that was

350

the most wonderful moment of my life! Really capital, don't ye know . . . beat everything . . . darling, couldn't you untie my hands a second . . .?'

Just for an instant there was a strange, distant look in her eyes, and then she turned her head away, and her hands tightened on mine.

'. . . and when you disappeared, and I thought you dead, there was such an emptiness.' She was trying not to cry. 'And nothing else seemed to matter – not I, or Jhansi, even. And then came news of the red wind, sweeping through the British garrisons in the north – and even here, in my own state, they killed them all, and I was helpless.' She was biting her lip, staring pleadingly at me, and if she'd been before the House of Lords the old goats would have been roaring 'Not guilty, on my honour!' with three times three. 'And what could I do? It seemed that the Raj – and I hated the Raj! – was falling, and my own cousin, Nana, was raising the standard of revolt, and to stand idle was to lose Jhansi, to the jackals of Orcha or Gwalior, or even to the sepoys themselves . . . oh, but you are British, and you cannot understand!'

'Dearest,' says I, 'you don't have to excuse yourself to me, of all people. What else could you do?' It wasn't an idle question, either; the only treason is to pick the wrong side, which, in the long run, she had done. 'But it doesn't matter, you see – that's why I'm here! It can all come right again – at least, you can be saved, and that's what counts.'

She looked at me and said simply: 'I do not care, now that you have come back.' And she leaned forward and kissed me again, gently, on the lips.

'You must care,' says I. 'See here – I've come from General Rose, and what he says comes straight from Lord Canning in Calcutta. They want to save you, my dear, if you'll let them.'

351

'They want me to surrender,' says she, and stood up. She walked away to set the cup down on a table, and the sight of the tight-wrapped sari stirring over those splendid hips set my fingers working feverishly at the knots behind my back. She turned, with her bosom going up like balloons, and her face was set and sad. 'They want me to give up my Jhansi.'

'Darling – it's lost anyway. Any day now they'll storm the walls, and that's the end. You know it – and so must your advisers. Even Ignatieff – what the devil's he doing here, anyhow?'

'He has been here – and at Meerut and Delhi – everywhere, since the beginning. Promising Russian help – making rebellion, as you say, on his master's behalf.' She made a little helpless gesture. 'I do not know . . . there has been talk of a Russian army over the Khyber – some would welcome it; myself . . . I fear it – but it does not matter, now. He remains, I suppose, as long as he may do your government some harm . . . if Jhansi falls, he will go to Tantia or Nana.' And she added, with a shrugged afterthought that somehow prickled my spine. 'Unless I have him killed, for what he has done to you.'

All in good time, thinks I, happily, and got back to the matter in hand.

'But it isn't Jhansi they want – it's you.' She opened her eyes at that, and I hurried on. 'They can't make terms with rebels – why, half your garrison must be pandies, with nothing to hope for; there's no pardon for them, you see. So they'll storm the city, whatever you do. But they want to save you alive – if you will give yourself up, alone, then . . . then they won't –' I couldn't meet her eye, though '– punish you.'

'Why should they spare me?' For a minute the fire was

back in her eye. 'Who else have they spared? Why should they want to keep me alive – when they blow men away from guns, and hang them without trial, and burn whole cities? Will they spare Nana or Tantia or Azeemoolah – then why the Rani of Jhansi?'

It wasn't an easy one to answer – not truthfully, anyway. She wouldn't take it too kindly if I said it was just politics, to keep the public happy.

'Does it matter?' says I. 'Whatever their reasons . . .'

'Is it because I am a woman?' She said it softly, and came to stand in front of me. 'And the British do not make war on women.' She looked steadily at me for several seconds. 'Is it because I am beautiful? And do they wish to take me to London, as the Romans did with their captives, and show me as a spectacle to the people—'

'That ain't our style,' says I, pretty sharp. 'Of course, we don't make war on women . . . and, well, you see, you're – well, you're different—'

'To them? To Lord Canning? To General Rose? They do not know me. Why should they care? Why should any of you . . .' And then she stopped, and dropped to her knees again, and her lip was trembling. 'You? Have you spoken – for me? You came from Lord Palmerston – have you asked them to save me?'

By George, here was an unexpected ball at my foot, with a vengeance. It hadn't crossed my mind that she'd think I was behind Rose's remarkable offer. But when the chance arises, I hope I know how to grasp it as well as the next man – carefully. So I looked at her, steady and pretty grim, and made myself go red in the face, and then looked down at the carpet, all dumb and noble and unspoken emotion. She put out a hand and lifted my chin, and she was absolutely frowning at me.

'Did you – and have you risked so much, to come here – for me? Tell me.'

'You know what I think about you,' says I, trying to look romantically stuffed. 'I've loved you since the moment I clapped eyes on you – on that swing. More than anything else in the world.'

At that moment, mind you, it wasn't all gammon. I did love her – pretty well, anyway, just then. Not as much as Elspeth, I daresay – although, mind you, put 'em together, side by side, both stripped down, and you'd think hard before putting England in to bat. Anyway, I'd no difficulty in looking sincere – not with that flimsy bodice heaving almost under my nose.

She looked at me in silence, with strange, grave eyes, and then said, almost in a whisper:

'Tonight – I did not think . . . I only knew that you were here with me again – when I had thought you lost. It did not matter to me, whether you loved me truly or not – only that you were with me again. But now . . .' she was looking at me in the strangest way, sorrowfully almost, and with a kind of perplexity '. . . now that you tell me that it was . . . for love of me, that you have done this . . .' I wondered if she was going to fling herself on me again in tears, but after a moment she just kissed me, quite gently, and then said:

'What do they wish me to do?'

'To surrender, yourself. No more than that.'

'But how? If the city is to be taken, and there is no pardon for the mutineers, how can I—'

'Don't fret about that,' says I. 'It can all be arranged. If I tell you how – will you do it?'

'If you will stay with me – afterwards.' Her eyes were fixed on mine, soft but steady. 'I will do whatever they ask.'

354

Persuasively urged, Rose had said, but I'll bet he'd never envisaged the likes of this – by George, his randy staff men wouldn't have been able to believe their eyes.

'When the city is stormed,' says I, 'our fellows will fight their way in to the fortress. You must be ready to make an escape – through the Orcha Gate. We'll have drawn off our cavalry picket just there, so it can be done in safety. You must ride out on the Orcha road – and then, you will be captured. It will look as though . . . well, it will look all right.'

'I see.' She nodded gravely. 'And the city?'

'Well, it'll be taken, of course – but there'll be no looting –' Rose had promised that, for what it was worth '– and of course, the people will be all right, provided they lie low and don't resist. The mutineers . . . well, it'll all be the same for them, anyway.'

'And what will they do . . . with me? Will they . . . imprison me?'

I wasn't sure about this, and had to go careful. They'd exile her for certain, at least to a distant part of India where she could do no harm, but there was no point in telling her that. 'No,' says I. 'They'll treat you very well, you'll see. And then – it'll all blow over, don't you know? Why, I can think of a score of nig— native chieftains and kings, who've been daggers drawn with us, but their wars have got by, and then we've been the best of friends, and so forth. No hard feelings, you see – we ain't vindictive, even the Liberals . . .'

I was smiling to reassure her, and after a while she began smiling back, and gave a great sigh, and settled against me, seemingly content, and I suggested again that it might be a capital notion to unslip my hands, just for a moment – I was most monstrously horny with her nestling up against me – but at this she shook her head, and said we had delayed already, and must not excite suspicion. She kissed me a lingering goodbye, and told me to be patient a little longer; we must bide our time according to Rose's plan, and since her people must have no inkling of it I would have to be treated as a prisoner, but she would send for me when the time was ripe.

'And then we shall go together . . . with only a trusted few?' She held my face in her hands, looking down at me. 'And you will . . . protect me, and love me . . . when we come to the Sirkar?'

Till you're blue in the face, you darling houri, thinks I – but for answer all I did was kiss her hands. Then she straightened her veil, and fussed anxiously with her mirror before seating herself on her divan, and it was the charmingest thing to see her give me a last radiant smile and then compose her face in that icy mask, while I waited suitably hangdog, standing in the middle of the floor at a respectful distance. She struck her little gong, which brought Sher Khan in like the village fire brigade, with chamberlain and ladies behind him.

'Confine this prisoner in the north tower,' says she, as if I were so much dross. 'He is not to be harshly used, but keep him close – your head on it, Sher Khan.'

I was bustled away forthwith – but it's my guess that Sher Khan, with that leery Pathan nose of his, guessed that all was not quite what it seemed, for he was a most solicitous jailer in the days that followed. He kept me well provisioned, bringing all my food and drink himself, seeing to it that I was comfortable as my little cell permitted, and showing me every sign of respect – mind you, in view of my Afghan reputation, that might have been natural enough.

It took me a few hours to settle down after what I had

been through, but when I came to cast up the score it looked none so bad. Bar my aching joints and skinned limbs, I was well enough, and damned thankful for it. As to the future – well, I'd thought Rose's plan was just moonshine, but then I'd never dreamed that Lakshmibai was infatuated with me. Attracted, well enough – it's an odd woman that ain't, but the force of her passion had been bewildering. And yet, why not? I'd known it happen before, after all, and often as not with the same kind of women – the high-born, pampered kind who go through their young lives surrounded by men who are forever deferring and toadying, so that when a real plunger like myself comes along, and treats 'em easy, like women and not as queens, they're taken all aback. It's something new to them to have a big likely chap who ain't abashed by their grandeur, but looks 'em over with a warm eye, perfectly respectful but daring them just the same. They resent it, and like it, too, and if you can just tempt them into bed and show them what they've been missing – why, the next thing you know they're head over heels in love with you.

That's how it had been with Duchess Irma, and that wild black bitch Ranavalona in Madagascar (though she was so stark crazy it was difficult to be sure), so why not the Rani of Jhansi? After all, her only husband had been as fishy as Dick's hatband, by all accounts, and however many young stalwarts she'd whistled up since then, they wouldn't have my style. Well, it was a damned handy stroke of luck – as well as being most flattering.

As to the surrender – well, she wasn't a fool. Here was a way out for her, with more credit and safety than she could have expected, under the wing of the adored Flashy, who she imagined would protect and cherish her happy ever after. I

357

was all for that – for a few months, anyway, which was more than most females could expect from me. Mark you, I was famously taken with her (I still am, somehow) but I guessed I'd cool after a spell. Couldn't take her home, anyway – she'd just have to reconcile herself to waving me goodbye when the time came, like all the others.

In the meantime, I could only wait, in some excitement, for Rose to mount his assault. When a tremendous cannonading in the city broke out on the following day, with native pipes and drums squealing and thundering, I thought the attack had begun, but it was a false alarm, as Sher Khan informed me later. It seemed that Tantia Tope had suddenly hove in sight with a rebel army twenty thousand strong, to try to relieve Jhansi; Rose, cool as a trout as usual, had left his heavy artillery and cavalry to continue the siege, and had turned with the rest of his force and thrashed Tantia handsomely on the Betwa River, a few miles away. At the same time he'd ordered a diversionary attack on Jhansi to keep the defenders from sallying out to help Tantia; that had been the noise I'd heard.[45]

'So much for our stout-hearted mutineers in Jhansi,' sneers Sher Khan. 'If they had sallied out, your army might have been caught like a nut between two stones, but they contented themselves with howling and burning powder.' He spat. 'Let the Sirkar eat them, and welcome.'

I reminded him he was on the rebel side, and that it would be short shrift for mutineers when Jhansi fell.

'I am no mutineer,' says he, 'but a paid soldier of the Rani. I have eaten her salt and fight for her like the Yusufzai I am – even as I fought for the Sirkar in the Guides. The sahibs know the difference between a rebel and a soldier who keeps faith; they will treat me with honour – if I live,' he added carelessly. He was another Ilderim, in his way – shorter and uglier, with a smashed nose and pocked face, but a slap-up Pathan Khyberie, every inch.

'With any luck they will have hanged thy Ruski friend by now,' he went on, grinning. 'He rode out to join Tantia in the night, and has not returned. Is that good news, Iflass-man *husoor*?'

Wasn't it just, though? Of course, Ignatieff would have been daft to stay in Jhansi – we'd have hanged him high enough for the foreign spy he was. He'd be off to assist the leading rebels in the field; I felt all the better for knowing he was out of distance, but I doubted if he'd allow himself to be killed or taken – he was too downy a bird for that.

With Tantia whipped, it seemed to me Rose would lose no further time assaulting Jhansi, but another day and night passed in which I waited and fretted, and still there was nothing but the distant thump of cannon-fire to disturb my cell. It wasn't till the third night that the deuce of a bombardment broke out, in the small hours, and lasted until almost dawn, and then I heard what I'd been waiting for – the crash of volley-firing that signified British infantry, and the sound of explosions within the town itself, and even distant bugle calls.

'They are in the city,' says Sher Khan, when he brought my breakfast. 'The mutineers are fighting better than I thought, and it is hot work in the streets, they say.' He grinned cheerfully and tapped the hilt of his Khyber knife. 'Will her highness order me to cut thy throat when the last attack goes home, think ye? Eat well, *husoor*,' and the brute swaggered out, chuckling.

Plainly she hadn't confided her intentions to him. I guessed she'd wait for nightfall and then make her run; by that time

359

our fellows would be thumping at the gates of the fort itself. So I contained myself, listened to the crackle of firing and explosion, drawing always nearer, until by nightfall it seemed to be only a few hundred yards off – I was chewing my nails by then, I may tell you. But the dark came, and still the sound of battle went on, and I could even hear what I thought were English voices shouting in the distance, among the yells and shrieks. Through the one high window of my cell the night-sky was glaring red – Jhansi was dying hard, by the look of it.

I don't know what time it was when I heard the sudden rattle of the bolt in my cell-door, and Sher Khan and two of his guardsmen came in, carrying torches. They didn't stand on ceremony, but hustled me out, and down narrow stone stairs and passages to a little courtyard. The moon wasn't up yet, but it was light enough, with the red glare above the walls, and the air was heavy with powder smoke and the drift of burning; the crashing of musketry was close outside the fort now.

The yard seemed to be full of red-coated troopers of the Rani's guard, and over by a narrow gateway I saw a slim figure mounted on a white horse which I recognised at once as Lakshmibai. There were mounted guardsmen with her, and a couple of her ladies, also mounted, and heavily veiled; one of the mounted men had a child perched on his saddlebow: Damodar, her stepson. I was about to call out, but to my astonishment Sher Kahn suddenly stooped beside me, there was a metallic snap, and he had a fetter clasped round my left leg. Before I could even protest, he was thrusting me towards a horse, snarling: 'Up, *husoor*!' and I was no sooner in the saddle than he had passed a short chain from my fetter under the beast's belly, and secured my other ankle, so that I was effectively shackled to the pony.

'What the hell's this?' I cried, and he chuckled as he swung aboard a horse beside me.

'Heavy spurs, *husoor*!' says he. 'Peace! – it is by her order, and doubtless for your own safety. Follow!' And he shook my bridle, urging me across the square; the little party by the gate were already passing out of sight, and a moment later we were riding single file down a steep alleyway, with towering walls either side, Sher Khan just ahead of me and another Pathan immediately behind.

I couldn't think what to make of this, until it dawned on me that she wouldn't have let her entourage into the whole secret – they would know she was escaping, but not that she intended to give herself up to the British. So for form's sake I must appear to be a prisoner still. I wished she'd given me the chance of a secret word beforehand, though, and let me ride with her; I didn't want us blundering into the besieging cavalry in the dark, and perhaps being mistaken.

However, there was nothing for it now but to carry on. Our little cavalcade clattered down the alleyways, twisting and turning, and then into a broader street, where a house was burning, but there wasn't a soul to be seen, and the sound of firing was receding behind us. Once we'd passed the fire it was damned dark among the rickety buildings, until there were torches and a high gateway, and more of her guardsmen in the entry-way; I saw her white horse stop as she leaned from the saddle to consult with the guard-commander, and waited with my heart in my mouth until he stepped back, saluting, and barked an order. Two of his men threw open a wicket in the main gate, and a moment later we were filing through, and I knew we were coming out on to the Orcha road.

It was blacker than hell in November under the lee of the great gateway, but half a mile ahead there was the twinkling line of our picket-fires, and flashes of gunfire as the artillery pieces joined in the bombardment of the city. Sher Khan had my bridle in his fist as we moved forward at a walk, and then at a slow trot; it was easy going on the broad road surface at first, but then the dim figures of the riders ahead seemed to be veering away to the right, and as we followed my horse stumbled on rough ground – we were leaving the road for the flat maidan, and I felt the first prickle of doubt in my mind. Why were we turning aside? The path to safety lay straight along the road, where Rose's pickets would be waiting – she knew that, even if her riders didn't. Didn't she realise we were going astray – that on this tack we would probably blunder into pickets that weren't expecting us? The time for pretence was past, anyhow – it was high time I was up with her, taking a hand, or God knew where we would land. But even as I stiffened in my saddle to shove my heels in and forge ahead, Sher Khan's hand leaped from my wrist to my bridle, there was a zeep of steel, and the Khyber knife was pricking my ribs with his voice hissing out of the dark:

'One word, Bloody Lance – one word, and you'll say the next one to Shaitan!'

The shock of it knocked my wits endways – but only for a moment. There's nothing like eighteen inches of razor-edged steel for turning a growing doubt into a stone-ginger certainty, and before we'd gone another five paces I had sprung to the most terrifying conclusion – she was escaping, right enough, but not the way Rose and I had planned it – she was using the information I'd given her, but in her own way! It rushed in on me in a mad whirl of thoughts – all her protestations, her slobbering over me, those tear-filled eyes, the lips on mine, the passionate endearments – all false? They couldn't be, in God's name! Why, she'd been all over me, like a crazy schoolgirl . . . but now we were pacing still faster in the wrong direction, the knife was scoring my side, and suddenly there was a shouted challenge ahead, and a cry, the riders were spurring forward, a musket cracked, and Sher Khan roared in my ear:

'Ride, *feringhee* – and ride straight, or I'll split your backbone!'

He slashed his reins at my pony, it bounded forward, and in a second I was flying along in the dark, willy-nilly, with him at my elbow and the thundering shadows surging ahead. There was a fusillade of shots, off to the left, and a ball whined overhead; as I loosed the reins, trusting to my pony's feet, I saw the picket-fires only a few hundred yards off. We were racing towards a gap between one fire and the next, perhaps two furlongs across; all I could do was career ahead, with Sher Khan and a Pathan either side of me – I couldn't roll from the saddle, even if I'd dared, with that infernal chain beneath my horse's belly; I daren't swerve, or his knife would be in my back; I could only gallop, cursing in sick bewilderment, praying to God I wouldn't stop a blade or a bullet. Where the hell were we going – was it some ghastly error after all? No, it was treachery, and I knew it – and now the picket-fires were on our flanks, there were more shots, a horse screamed ahead of us, and my pony swerved past the dim struggling mass on the ground, with Sher Khan still knee to knee with me as we sped on. A trumpet was sounding behind, and faint voices yelling; ahead was the drumming of hooves and the dim shapes of the Rani's riders, scattered now as they galloped for their lives. We were clear through, and every stride was taking us farther from Jhansi and Rose's army, and safety.

How long we kept up that breakneck pace I don't know, or what direction we took – I'd been through too much, my mind was just a welter of fear and bewilderment and rage and stark disbelief. I didn't know what to think – she couldn't have sold me so cruelly, surely – not after what she'd said, and the way she'd held my face and looked at me? But I knew she had – my disbelief was just sheer hurt vanity. God, did I think I was the only sincere liar in the world? And here I was, humbugged to hell and beyond, being kidnapped in the train of this deceitful rebel bitch – or was I wrong, was there some explanation after all? That's what I still wanted to believe, of course – there's nothing like infatuation for stoking false hope.

However, there's no point in recounting all the idiot arguments I had with myself on that wild ride through the night, with the miles flying by unseen, until the gloom began to lighten, the scrub-dotted plain came into misty view, and Sher Khan still clung like a bearded ghost at my elbow, his teeth bared as he crouched over his pony's mane. The riders ahead were still driving their tired beasts on at full stretch; about a hundred yards in front I could see Lakshmibai's slim figure on her white mare, with the Pathans flanking her. It was like a drunken nightmare – on and on, exhausting, over that endless plain.

There was a yell from the flank, and one of the Pathans up in his stirrups, pointing. A shot cracked, I saw a sudden flash of scarlet to our left, and there was a little cloud of horsemen bursting out of a nullah – only half our numbers, but Company cavalry, by God! They were careering in to take our leaders in the flank, pukka light cavalry style, and I tried to yell, but Sher Khan had my bridle again, wrenching me away to the right, while the Pathan guardsmen drew their sabres and wheeled to face the attackers head on. I watched them meet with a chorus of yells and a clash of steel; the dust swirled up round them as Sher Khan and his mate herded me away, but half-slewed round in my saddle I saw the sabres swinging and the beasts serving and plunging as the Company men tried to ride through. A Pathan broke from the press, shepherding away a second rider, and I saw it was one of the Rani's ladies – and then more figures were wheeling out of the dust, and one of them was Lakshmibai, with a mounted man bearing down on her, his sabre swung aloft. I heard Sher Kahn's anguished yell as her white mare seemed to stumble, but she reined it up somehow, whirling in her tracks, there was the glitter of steel in her hand, and as the Company man swept down on her she lunged over her beast's head – the sabres clashed and rang, and he was past her, wheeling away, clutching at his arm as he half-slipped from his saddle.[46]

That was all I saw before Sher Khan and the other herded me down a little nullah, where we halted and waited while the noise of the skirmish gradually died away. I knew what was happening as well as if I was seeing it – the Company riders, out-sabred, would be drawing off, and sure enough presently the Pathans came down the nullah in good order, clustered round Damodar and the Rani's women; among the last to come was Lakshmibai.

It was the first clear look at her that I'd had in all that fearful escape. She was wearing a mail jacket under her long cloak, with a mail cap over her turban, and her sabre was still in her hand, blood on its blade. She stopped a moment by the rider who carried Damodar, and spoke to the child; then she laughed and said something to one of the Pathans and handed him her sabre, while she wiped her face with a handkerchief. Then she looked towards me, and the others looked with her, in silence.

As you know, I'm a fairly useful hand on social occasions, ready with the polite phrase or gesture, but I'll confess that in that moment I couldn't think of anything appropriate to say. When you've just been betrayed by an Indian queen who has previously professed undying love for you, and she confronts you – having just sabred one of your countrymen, possibly to death – and you are in the grip of her minions, with your feet chained under your horse . . . well, the etiquette probably takes some thinking about. I suppose I'd have come out with something in a minute or two – an oath, or a squeal for mercy, or a polite inquiry, perhaps, but before I had the chance she was addressing Sher Khan.

'You will take him to Gwalior.' Her voice was quiet and perfectly composed. 'Hold him there until I send for you. At the last, he will be my bargain.'

You may say it served me right, and I can't disagree. If I weren't such a susceptible, trusting chap where pretty women are concerned, I daresay I'd have smelled a rat on the night when Lakshmibai rescued me from Ignatieff's rack and then flung herself all over me in her perfumed lair. A less warm-blooded fellow might have thought the lady was protesting rather too much, and been on his guard when she slobbered fondly over him, vowing undying love and accepting his proposal for her escape. He might – or again, he mightn't.

For myself, I can only say I had no earthly reason to suppose her false. After all, our last previous meeting had been that monumental roll in her pavilion, which had left me with the impression that she wasn't entirely indifferent to me. Secondly, her acceptance of Rose's proposal seemed natural and sensible. Thirdly, I'll admit to being enthralled by her, and fourthly, having just finished a spell on the rack I was perhaps thinking less clearly than usual. Finally, m'lud, if you'd been confronted by Lakshmibai, with that beautiful dusky face looking pleadingly up at you, and those tits quivering under your nose, I submit that you might have been taken in yourself, and glad of it.

In any event, it didn't make a ha'porth of difference. Even if I'd suspected her then, I was in her power, and she could have wrung all the details of Rose's scheme out of me and made her escape anyway. I'd have been dragged along at her tail, and finished up in the Gwalior dungeons just the same. And mind you, I'm still not certain how far she *was* humbugging me; all I know is that if she was play-acting, she seemed to be enjoying her work.

More than I enjoyed Gwalior, at any rate. That's a fearful place, a huge, rocky fortress of a city, bigger than Jhansi, and said to be the most powerful hold in India. I can speak with authority only about its dungeons, which were a shade worse than a Mexican jail, if you can imagine that. I spent the better part of two months in them, cooped in a bottle-shaped cell with my own filth and only rats, fleas and cockroaches for company, except when Sher Khan came to have a look at me, about once a week, to make sure I hadn't up and died on him.

He and his fellow-Pathan took me there on Lakshmibai's orders, and it was one of the most punishing rides I've ever endured. I was almost unconscious in the saddle by the time we reached it, for the brutes never took my chain off once in the hundred miles we covered: I think, too, that my spirit had endured more than I could stand, for after all I'd gone through there were moments now when I no longer cared whether I lived or died – and I have to be pretty far down before that happens. When they brought me to Gwalior by night, and half-carried me into the fortress, and dropped me into that stinking, ill-lit cell, I just lay and sobbed like an infant, babbling aloud about Meerut and Cawnpore and

Lucknow and Thugs and crocodiles and evil bitches – and now this. Would you believe it, the worst was yet to come?

I don't care to dwell on it, so I'll hurry along. While I was in that dungeon at Gwalior, waiting for I didn't know what, and half-believing that I'd rot there forever, or go mad first, the final innings of the Mutiny was being played out. Campbell was settling things north of the Jumnah, and Rose, having captured Jhansi, was pushing north after Tantia Tope and my ministering angel, Lakshmibai, who'd taken the field with him. He beat them at Calpee and Kanch, driving them towards Gwalior where I was enjoying the local hospitality. The odd thing was, that at the time I was incarcerated there, Gwalior's ruler, Maharaja Scindia, had remained neutral in the rebellion, and had no business to be allowing his prison to be used for the accommodation of captured British officers. In fact, of course, he (or his chief advisers) were sympathetic to the rebels all along, as was proved in the end. For after their defeat at Calpee, Tantia and Lakshmibai turned to Gwalior, and the Maharaja's army went over to them, almost without firing a shot. So there they were, the last great rebel force in India, in possession of India's greatest stronghold – and with Rose closing inexorably in on them.

I knew nothing of all this, of course; mouldering in my cell, with my beard sprouting and my hair matting, and my pandy uniform foul and stinking (for I'd never had it off since I put it on in Rose's camp), I might as well have been at the North Pole. Day followed day, and week followed week without a cheep from the outside world, for Sher Khan hardly said a word to me, although I raved and pleaded with him whenever he poked his face through the trap into my cell. That's the worst of that kind of imprisonment – not knowing, and losing count of the days, and wondering

369

whether you've been there a month or a year, and whether there is really a world outside at all, and doubting if you ever did more than dream that you were once a boy playing in the fields at Rugby, or a man who'd walked in the Park, or ridden by Albert Gate, saluting the ladies, or played billiards, or followed hounds, or gone up the Mississippi in a side-wheeler, or watched the moon rise over Kuching River, or – you can wonder if *any* of it ever existed, or if these greasy black walls are perhaps the only world that ever was, or will be . . . that's when you start to go mad, unless you can find something to think about that you *know* is real.

I've heard of chaps who kept themselves sane in solitary confinement by singing all the hymns they knew, or proving the propositions of Euclid, or reciting poetry. Each to his taste: I'm no hand at religion, or geometry, and the only repeatable poem I can remember is an Ode of Horace which Arnold made me learn as a punishment for farting at prayers. So instead I compiled a mental list of all the women I'd had in my life, from that sweaty kitchen-maid in Leicestershire when I was fifteen, up to the half-caste piece I'd been repri-manded for at Cawnpore, and to my astonishment there were four hundred and seventy-eight of them, which seemed rather a lot, especially since I wasn't counting return engagements. It's astonishing, really, when you think how much time it must have taken up.

Perhaps because I'd been listing them I had a frightful dream one night in which I had to dance with all of them at a ball on the slave-deck of the *Balliol College*, with the demoniac Captain Spring conducting the music in a cocked hat and white gloves. They were all there – Lola Montez and Josette and Judy (my guvnor's mistress, she was), and the Silk One and Susie from New Orleans and fat Baroness

370

Pechmann and Narreeman the nautch, and all the others, and each one left her slave-fetters with me so that I must dance on loaded and clanking, crying out with exhaustion, but when I pleaded for rest Spring just rolled his eyes and made the music go faster, with the big drum booming. Elspeth and Palmerston waltzed by, and Pam gave me his false teeth and cried: 'You'll need 'em for eating chapattis with your next partner, you know' – and it was Lakshmibai, naked and glitter-eyed over her veil, and she seized me and whirled me round the floor, almost dead with fatigue and the cruel weight of the chains, while the drum went boom-boom-boom faster and faster – and I was awake, gasping and clutching at my filthy straw with the sound of distant gunfire in my ears.

It went on all that day, and the next, but of course I couldn't tell what it meant or who was firing, and I was too done to care. All through the morning of the third day it continued, and then suddenly my trap was thrown open, and I was being dragged out by Sher Khan and another fellow, and I hardly knew where I was. When you're hauled out of a dead captivity like that, everything seems frighteningly loud and fast – I know there was a courtyard, full of nigger soldiers running about and shouting, and their pipes blaring, and the gunfire crashing louder than ever – but the shock of release was too much for me to make sense of it. I was half-blinded just by the light of the sky, although it was heavy with red and black monsoon clouds, and I remember thinking, it'll be capital growing weather soon.

It wasn't till they thrust me on a pony that I came to myself – instinct, I suppose, but when I felt the saddle under me, and the beast stirring, and the smell of horse in my nostrils and my feet in stirrups, I was awake again. I knew this was Gwalior fortress, with the massive gate towering in

371

front of me, and a great gun being dragged through it by a squealing elephant, with a troop of red-coated nigger-prince's cavalry waiting to ride out, and a bedlam of men shouting orders: the din was still deafening, but as Sher Khan mounted his pony beside me I yelled:

'What's happening? Where are we going?'

'She wants you!' cries he, and grinned as he tapped his hilt. 'So she shall have you. Come!'

He thrust a way for us through the crowd milling in the gateway, and I followed, still trying to drink in the sights and sounds of this madhouse that I had all but forgotten – men and carts and bullocks and dust and the clatter of arms: a *bhisti* running with his water-skin, a file of pandy infantry squatting by the roadside with their muskets between their knees, a child scrambling under a bullock's belly, a great-chested fellow in a spiked cap with a green banner on a pole over his shoulder, a spindly-legged old nigger shuffling along regardless of them all, the smell of cooking *ghee*, and through it all that muffled crash of cannon in the distance.

I stared ahead as we emerged from the gate, trying to understand what was happening. Gunfire – that meant that British troops were somewhere near, and the sight that met my eyes confirmed it. Before me there was miles of open plain, stretching to distant hills, and the plain was alive with men and animals and all the tackle of war. Perhaps a mile ahead, in the haze, there were tents, and the unmistakable ranks of infantry, and gun emplacements, and squadrons of horse on the move – a whole army stretched across a front of perhaps two miles. I steadied myself as Sher Khan urged me forward, trying to take it in – it was a rebel army, no error, for there were pandy formations moving back towards us, and native state infantry and riders in uniforms I didn't know, men in crimson robes with little shields and curved *tulwars*, and gun-teams with artillery pieces fantastically carved in the native fashion.

That was the first fact: the second was that they were retreating, and on the edge of rout. For the formations were moving towards us, and the road itself was choked with men and beasts and vehicles heading for Gwalior. A horse-artillery team was careering in, the gunners clinging to the limbers and their officer lashing at the beasts, a platoon of pandies was coming at the double-quick, their ranks ragged, their faces streaked with dust and sweat, and all along the road men were running or hobbling back, singly and in little groups: I'd seen the signs often enough, the gaping mouths, the wide eyes, the bloody bandages, the high-pitched voices, the half-ordered haste slipping into utter confusion, the abandoned muskets at the roadside, the exhausted men sitting or lying or crying out to those who passed by – this was the first rush of a defeat, by gum! and Sher Khan was dragging me into it.

'What the blazes is happening?' I asked him again, but all I got was a snarl as he whipped my pony to a gallop, and we clattered down the roadside, he keeping just to rear of me, past the mob of men and beasts streaming back to Gwalior. The formations were closer now, and not all of them were retreating: we passed artillery teams who were unlimbering and siting their guns, and regiments of infantry waiting in the humid heat, their faces turned towards the distant hills, their ranks stretched out in good order across the plain. Not far in front artillery was thundering away, with smoke wreathing up in the still air, and bodies of cavalry, pandy and irregular, were waiting – I remember a squadron of lancers, in green coats, with lobster-tail helmets and long ribbons trailing from their lance-heads, and a band of native musicians, squealing and droning fit to drown the gunfire. But less than half a mile ahead, where the dust-clouds were churning up, and the flashes of cannon shone dully through the haze, I knew what was happening – the army's vanguard was slowly breaking, falling back on the main body, with the weaker vessels absolutely flying down the road.

We crossed a deep nullah, and Sher Khan wheeled me off along its far lip, towards a grove of palm and thorn, where tents were pitched. A line of guns to my left was crashing away towards the unseen enemy on the hills – enemy, by God, that was my army! – and round the oasis of tents and trees there was a screen of horsemen. With a shock I recognised the long red coats of the Jhansi royal guard, but for the rest they were only the ragged ghosts of the burly Pathans I remembered, their uniforms torn and filthy, their mounts lean and ungroomed. We passed through them, in among the tents, to where a carpet was spread before the biggest pavilion of all; there were guardsmen there, and a motley mob of niggers, military and civilian, and then Sher Khan was pulling me from the saddle, thrusting me forward, and crying out:

'He is here, highness – as you ordered.'

She was in the doorway of the tent, alone – or perhaps I just don't remember any others. She was sipping a glass of sherbet as she turned to look at me, and believe it or not I was suddenly conscious of the dreadful, scarecrow figure I cut, in my rags and unkempt hair. She was in her white jodhpurs, with a mail jacket over her blouse, and a white cloak; her head was covered by a cap of polished steel like a Roman soldier's, with a white scarf wound round it and under her chin. She looked damned elegant, I know, and even when you noticed the shadows on that perfect coffee-coloured face, beneath the great eyes, she was still a vision to take your breath away. She frowned at sight of me, and snapped at Sher Khan:

'What have you done to him?'

He mumbled something, but she shook her head impatiently and said it didn't matter. Then she looked at me again, thoughtfully, while I waited, wondering what the devil was coming, dimly aware that the volume of gunfire was increasing. Finally she said, simply:

'Your friends are over yonder,' and indicated the hills. 'You may go to them if you wish.'

That was all, and for the life of me I couldn't think of anything to say. I suppose I was still bemused and in a shocked condition – otherwise I might have pointed out that there was a battle apparently raging between me and those friends of mine. But it all seemed unreal, and the word which I finally managed to croak out was: 'Why?'

She frowned again at that, and then put her chin up and snapped her cloak with one hand and said quickly:

'Because it is finished, and it is the last thing I can do for you – colonel.' I couldn't think when she'd last called me that. 'Is that not enough? Your army will be in Gwalior by tomorrow. That is all.'

It was at this moment that I heard shouting behind us, but I paid it no heed, not even when some fellow came running and calling to her, and she called something to him. I was wrestling with my memory, and it will give you some notion of how foundered I was when I tell you that I absolutely burst out:

'But you said I would be your bargain – didn't you?'

She looked puzzled, and then she smiled and said to Sher

Khan: 'Give the colonel sahib a horse,' and was turning away, when I found my tongue.

'But . . . but you! Lakshmibai! I don't understand . . . what are you going to do?' She didn't answer, and I heard my own voice hoarse and harsh: 'There's still time! I mean – if you . . . if you think it's finished – well, dammit, they ain't going to hang you, you know! I mean Lord Canning has promised . . . and – and General Rose!' Sher Khan was growling at my elbow, but I shook him off. 'Look here, if I'm with you, it's sure to be all right. I'll tell 'em—'

God knows what else I said – I think I was out of my wits just then. Well, when the shot's flying I don't as a rule think of much but my own hide, and here I was absolutely arguing with the woman. Maybe the dungeon had turned my brain a trifle, for I babbled on about surrender and honourable terms while she just stood looking at me, and then she broke in:

'No – you do not understand. You did not understand when you came back to me at Jhansi. But it was for me you came – for my sake. And so I pay my debt at the end.'

'Debt?' I shouted. 'You're havering, woman! You said you loved me – oh, I know now you were tricking me, too, but . . . but don't it count for anything, then?'

Before she could answer there was a flurry of hooves, and some damned interfering scoundrel in an embroidered coat flung himself off his horse and started shouting at her; behind me there was a crackle of musketry, and shrieks and orders, and a faint trumpet note whispering beyond the cannon. She cried an order, and a groom hurried forward, pulling her little mare. I was roaring above the noise, at her, swearing I loved her and that she could still save herself, and she shot me a quick look as she took the mare's bridle – it was just for an instant, but it's stayed with me fifty years, and you may think me an old fool and fanciful, but I'll swear there were tears in her eyes – and then she was in the saddle, shouting, and the little mare reared and shot away, and I was left standing on the carpet.

Sher Khan had disappeared. I was staring and yelling after her, as her riders closed round her, for beyond them the gunners were racing towards us, with pandy riflemen in amongst them, turning and firing and running again. There were horsemen at the guns, and sabres flashing, and above the hellish din the trumpet was blaring clear in the 'Charge!' and over the limbers came blue tunics and white helmets, and I couldn't believe my eyes, for they were riders of the Light Brigade, Irish Hussars, with an officer up in his stir-rups, yelling, and the troopers swarming behind him. They came over the battery like a wave, and the scarlet-clad Pathan horsemen were breaking before them. And I'll tell you what I saw next, as plain as I can.

Lakshmibai was in among the Pathans, and she had a sabre in her hand. She seemed to be shouting to them, and then she took a cut at a Hussar and missed him as he swept by, and for a moment I lost her in the mêlée. There were sabres and pistols going like be-damned, and suddenly the white mare was there, rearing up, and she was in the saddle, but I saw her flinch and lose the reins; for a moment I thought she was gone, but she kept her seat as the mare turned and raced out of the fight – and my heart stopped as I saw that she was clutching her hands to her stomach, and her head was down. A trooper drove his horse straight into the mare, and as it staggered he sabred at Lakshmibai back-handed – I shrieked aloud and shut my eyes, and when I looked again she was in the dust, and even at that distance I could see the crimson stain on her jodhpurs.

I ran towards her and there must have been riders charging past me as I ran, but I don't remember them – and then I stumbled and fell. As I scrambled up I saw she was writhing in the dust; her scarf and helmet were gone, she was kicking and clawing at her body, and her face was twisted and working in agony, with her hair half across it. It was hideous, and I could only crouch there, gazing horrified. Oh, if it were a novel I could tell you that I ran to her, and cradled her head against me and kissed her, while she looked up at me with a serene smile and murmured something before she closed her eyes, as lovely in death as she'd been in life – but that ain't how people die, not even the Rani of Jhansi. She arched up once, still tearing at herself, and then she flopped over, face down, and I knew she was a goner.[47]

It was only then, I believe, that I began to think straight again.

There was one hell of a skirmish in progress barely twenty yards away, and I was unarmed and helpless, on all fours in the dirt. Above all other considerations, I'm glad to say, one seemed paramount – to get to hell out of this before I got hurt. I was on my feet and running before the thought had consciously formed – running in no particular direction, but keeping a weather eye open for a quiet spot or a riderless horse. I dived into the nullah, barged into someone, stumbled up and raced along it, past a group of pandies in pill-box hats who were scrambling into position at the nullah's edge to open fire, leaped over a wrecked cart – and then, wondrous sight, there *was* a horse, with a wounded nigger on his knees holding the bridle. One kick and he was sprawling, I was aboard and away; I put my head down and fairly flew – a fountain of dirt rose up just ahead of me as a cannon-shot from somewhere ploughed into the nullah bank, and the last thing I remember is the horse rearing up, and something smashing into my left arm with a blinding pain; a great weight seemed to be pressing down on my head and a red smoke was drifting above me, and then I lost consciousness.

I told you the worst was still to come, didn't I? Well, you've read my chronicle of the Great Mutiny, and if you've any humanity you're bound to admit that I'd had my share of sorrow already, and more – even Campbell later said that I'd seen hard service, so there. But Rose himself declared that if he hadn't been told the circumstance of my awakening at Gwalior by an eyewitness, he wouldn't have believed it – it was the most terrible thing, he said, that he had ever heard of in all his experience of war, or anybody else's, either. He wondered that I hadn't lost my reason. I agreed then, and I still do. This is what happened.

I came back to life, as is often the case, with my last waking moment clear in my mind. I had been on horseback, riding hard, seeing a shot strike home in a sandy nullah – so why, I wondered irritably, was I now standing up, leaning against something hard, with what seemed to be a polished table top in front of me? There was a shocking pain in my head, and a blinding glare of light burning my eyes, so I shut them quickly. I tried to move, but couldn't, because something was holding me; my ears were ringing, and there was a jumble of voices close by, but I couldn't make them out. Why the hell didn't they shut up, I wondered, and I tried to tell them to be quiet, but my voice wouldn't work – I wanted to move, to get away from the thing that was pressing against my chest, so I tugged, and an unspeakable pain shot through my left arm and into my chest, a stabbing, searing pain so exquisite that I screamed aloud, and again, and again, at which a voice cried in English, apparently right in my ear.

''Ere's another as can't 'old 'is bleedin' row! Stick a gag in this bastard an' all, Andy!'

Someone grabbed my hair and pulled my head back, and I shrieked again, opening my eyes wide with the pain, to see a blinding light sky, and a red, sweating face within a few inches of mine. Before I could make another sound, a foul wet rag was stuffed brutally into my mouth, choking me, and a cloth was whipped across it and knotted tight behind my head. I couldn't utter a sound, and when I tried to reach up to haul the filthy thing away, I realised why I hadn't been able to move. My hands were lashed to the object that was pressing into my body. Stupefied, blinking against the glare, in agony with my arm and head and the gag that was suffocating me, I tried to focus my eyes; for a few seconds there was just a whirl of colours and shapes – and then I saw.

I was tied across the muzzle of a cannon, the iron rim biting into my body, with my arms securely lashed on either side of the polished brown barrel. I was staring along the top of that barrel, between the high wheels, to where two British soldiers were standing by the breech, poking at the touch-hole, and one was saying to the other:

'No, by cripes, none o' yer Woolwich models. No lanyards, Jim my boy – we'll 'ave to stick a fuse in, an' stand well clear.'

'She's liable to blow 'er flamin' wheels off, though, ain't she?' says the other. 'There's a four-pahnd cartridge in there, wiv a stone shot. S'pose it'll splinter, eh?'

'Ask 'im – arterwards!' says the first, gesturing at me, and they both laughed uproariously. 'You'll tell us, won't yer, Sambo?'

For a moment I couldn't make it out – what the devil were

380

they talking about? And how dared the insolent dogs address a colonel as 'Sambo' – and one of 'em with a pipe stuck between his grinning teeth? Fury surged up in me, as I stared into those red yokel faces, leering at me, and I shouted 'Damn your eyes, you mutinous bastards! How dare you – d'ye know who I am, you swine? I'll flog the ribs out of you . . .' but it didn't come out as a shout, only as a soundless gasp deep in my throat behind that stifling gag. Then, ever so slowly, it dawned on me where I was, and what was happening, and my brain seemed to explode with the unutterable horror of it. As Rose said afterwards, I ought to have gone mad; for an instant I believe I did.

I don't have to elaborate my sensations – anyway, I couldn't. I can only say that I was sane enough after that first spasm of dreadful realisation, because behind the fog of panic I saw in a second what had happened – saw it with blinding certainty. I had been knocked on the head, presumably by a splinter of flying debris, and picked up senseless by our gallant troops. Of course they'd taken me for a pandy – with my matted hair and beard and filthy and ragged sepoy uniform; they'd seen I wasn't dead, and decided to execute me in style, along with other prisoners. For as I flung my head round in an ecstasy of such fear as even I had never known before, I saw that mine was only one in a line of guns, six or seven of them, and across the muzzle of each was strapped a human figure. Some were ragged pandies, like me, others were just niggers; one or two were gagged, as I was, the rest were not; some had been tied face to the gun, but most had the muzzles in their backs. And shortly these brutes who loafed about the guns at their ease, spitting and smoking and chaffing to each other, would touch off the charges, and a mass of splintering stone would tear through my vitals – and there was nothing

I could do to stop them! If I hadn't screamed when I regained consciousness, I wouldn't have been gagged, and three words would have been enough to show them their ghastly error – but now I couldn't utter a sound, but only watch with bulging eyes as one of the troopers, in leisurely fashion, pushed a length of fuse into the touch-hole, winked at me, and then sauntered back to rejoin his mates, who were standing or squatting in the sunlight, obviously waiting for the word to start the carnage.

'Come on, come on, where the 'ell's the captain?' says one. 'Still at mess, I'll lay. Christ, it's 'ot! I want ter get on my charpoy, I do, an' bang me bleedin' ear-'ole. 'E couldn't blow the bloody pandies away arter supper, could 'e? Oh, no, not 'im.'

'Wot we blowin' 'em up for?' says one pale young trooper. 'Couldn't they 'ang the pore sods – or shoot 'em? It 'ud be cheaper.'

'Pore sods my arse,' says the first. 'You know what they done, these black scum? You shoulda bin at Delhi, see the bloody way they ripped up wimmen an' kids – fair sicken yer, wot wi' tripes an' innards all over the plice. Blowin' away's too — good for 'em.'

'Not as cruel as 'angin', neither,' says a third. 'They don't feel nothin'.' He strolled past my gun, and to my horror he patted me on the head. 'So cheer up, Sambo, you'll soon be dead. 'Ere, wot's the matter wiv 'im, Bert, d'ye reckon?'

I was writhing frenziedly in my bonds, almost fainting with the agony of my wounded arm, which was gashed and bleeding, flinging my head from side to side as I tried to spit out that horrible gag, almost bursting internally in my effort to make some sound, any sound, that would make him understand the ghastly mistake they'd made. He stood, grinning

382

stupidly, and Bert sauntered up, knocking his pipe out on the gun.

'Matter? Wot the 'ell d'yer think's the matter, you duffer? 'E don't want 'is guts blew all the way to Calcutta – that's wot's the matter! Gawd, 'e'll kill 'isself wiv apple-plexy by the look of 'im.'

'Funny, though, ain't it?' says the first. 'An' look at the rest of 'em – jes' waitin' there, an' not even a squeak from 'em, as if they didn't care. Pathetic, ain't it?'

'That's their religion,' pronounced Bert. 'They fink they're goin' to 'eaven – they fink they're goin' to get 'arf-a-dozen rum bints apiece, an' bull 'em till Judgement Day. Fact.'

'Go on! They don't look all that bleedin' pleased, then, do they?'

They turned away, and I flopped over the gun, near to suffocation and with my heart ready to burst for misery and fear. Only one word – that was all I needed – Christ, if I could only get a hand free, a finger even! Blood from my wounded arm had run on to the gun, drying almost at once on the burning metal – if I could even scrawl a message on it – or just a letter – they might see it, and understand. I must be able to do something – think, think, think, I screamed inside my head, fighting back the madness, straining with all my power to tear my right wrist free, almost dislocating my neck in a futile effort to work the gag-binding loose. My mouth was full of its filthy taste, it seemed to be slipping farther into my gullet, choking me – God, if they thought I was choking, would they pull it out, even for a second? . . . that was all I needed, oh God, please, please, let them – I couldn't die like this, like a stinking nigger pandy, after all I'd suffered – not by such cruel, ghastly, ill-luck . . .

'Aht pipes, straighten up – orficer comin',' cries one of

the troopers, and they scrambled up hastily, adjusting their kepis, doing up their shirt-buttons, as two officers came strolling across from the tents a couple of hundred yards away. I gazed towards them like a man demented, as though by staring I could attract their attention; my right wrist was raw and bleeding with my dragging at it, but the rope was like a band of steel round it, and I couldn't do more than scrabble with my fingers at the hot metal. I was crying, uncontrollably; my head was swimming – but no, no, I mustn't faint! Anything but that – think, think, don't faint, don't go mad! They've never got you yet – you've always slid out somehow . . .

'All ready, sergeant?' The leading officer was glancing along the line of guns, and my eyes nearly started from my head as I saw it was Clem Hennidge[48] – Dandy Clem of the 8th Hussars, whom I'd ridden with at Balaclava. He was within five yards of me, nodding to the sergeant, glancing briefly round, while beside him a fair young lieutenant was staring with pop-eyes at us trussed victims, going pale and looking ready to puke. By heaven, he wasn't the only one!

He shuddered, and I heard him mutter to Hennidge: 'Christ! I shan't be writing to mother about this, though!'

'Beastly business,' says Hennidge, slapping his crop on his palm. 'Orders, though, what? Very good, sergeant – we'll touch 'em off all together, if you please. All properly shotted and primed? Very good, then.'

'Yessir! Beg pardon, sir, usual orders is to touch 'em off one arter the other, sir. Leastways, that's 'ow we done it at Calpee, sir!'

'Good God!' says Hennidge, and contained himself. 'I'll be obliged if you'll fire all together, sergeant, on this occasion!' He muttered something to the lieutenant, shaking his head as in despair.

Two men ran forward to my gun, one of them pulling matches from his pocket. He glanced nervously back and called.

'Sarn't – sir! This 'un ain't got no lock, nor lanyard, please! See, sir, it's one o' them nigger guns – can't fire it 'cept with a fuse, sir!'

'What's that?' cries Hennidge, coming forward, 'Oh – I see. Very well, then, light the fuse at the signal, then, and – Good God, is this fellow having a fit?'

I had made one last desperate effort to pull free, hauling like a mad thing, flinging myself as far as my lashing would allow, tossing my head, jerking to and fro, my head swimming with the pain of my arm. Hennidge and the boy were staring at me – the boy's face was green.

''E's been carryin' on like that since we triced 'im up, sir,' says one of the gunners. 'Screamin', 'e was – we 'ad ter gag him, sir.'

Hennidge swallowed, and then nodded curtly, and turned away, but the lieutenant seemed to be rooted with horrified fascination, as though he couldn't tear his eyes away from me.

'Ready!' bawls the sergeant, and 'Light the fuse now, Bert,' says the man at my gun. Through a red haze I saw the match splutter, and go out. Bert cursed, struck a second, and touched it to the fuse. A moment, and it fizzed, and the gunners retreated.

'Best stand back, sir!' cries Bert. 'Gawd knows what'll happen when she goes off – might blow wide open!'

The lieutenant shuddered, and seemed to collect himself, and then the strangest thing happened. For I absolutely heard a voice, and it seemed to be very close in my ear, and the oddest thing was, it was Rudi Starnberg, my old enemy from Jotunberg, and as clear as a bell across the years I heard him laughing: 'The comedy's not finished yet! Come on, play-actor!'

No doubt it was the product of a disordered mind, as I stared at Death in the spluttering fuse, but just for a second I realised that if there was the ghost of a chance left, it depended on keeping ice-cold – as Rudi would have done, of course. The lieutenant's eyes were just on mine for an instant before he turned away, and in that instant I raised my brows and lowered them, twice, quickly. It stopped him, and very carefully, as he stared, I closed one eye in an enormous wink. It must have been a grotesque sight; his mouth dropped open, and then I opened my eye, turned my head deliberately, and stared fixedly at my right hand. He must look, he must! My wrist was as fast as ever, but I could just turn my hand, palm upwards, fold the thumb and last three fingers slowly into my palm, and beckon with my fore-finger, once, twice, thrice – and still beckoning, I stared at him again.

For a moment he just gaped, and closed his eyes, and gaped again, and I thought, oh Christ, the young idiot's going to stand there until the bloody fuse has burned down! He stared at me, licking his lips, obviously flabbergasted, turned to glance at Hennidge, looked back at me – and then, as I tried to bore into his brain, and crooked my finger again and again, he suddenly yelled 'Wait! Sergeant, don't fire!' and striding forward, he yanked the burning fuse from the touchhole. Clever boys they had in the Light Brigade in those days.

'What the devil? John – what on earth are you doing?' cries Hennidge. 'Sergeant, hold on there!' He came striding up, demanding to know what was up, and the lieutenant, pale and sweating, stood by the breech pointing at me.

'I don't know! That chap – he beckoned, I tell you! And he winked! Look, my God, he's doing it again! He's . . . he's trying to say something!'

'Hey? What?' Hennidge was peering across at me, and I wobbled my eyebrows as ludicrously as I could, and tried to munch my lips at the same time. 'What the deuce – I believe you're right . . . you, there, get that gag out of his mouth – sharp, now!'

'Arise, Sir Harry' was one of the sweetest sounds I ever heard; so was Abe Lincoln's voice in that house at Portsmouth, Ohio, asking 'What do you want with me?' when the slave-catchers were on my tail. I can think of many others, but so help me God, none of them rang such peals of hope and joy in my ears as those words of Hennidge's beside the guns at Gwalior. Even as the cloth was wrenched loose, though, and the gag was torn out of my mouth, and I was gasping in air, I was thinking frantically what I must say to prevent the appalling chance of their disbelieving me – something to convince them instantly, beyond any doubt, and what I croaked out when my breath came was:

'I'm Flashman – Flashman, d'ye hear! You're Clem Hennidge! The curfew tolls the knell of parting day, God save the Queen. I'm English – English – I'm in disguise! Ask General Rose! I'm Flashman, Harry Flashman! Cut me loose, you bastards! I'm Flashman!'

You never saw such consternation in your life; for a moment they just made pop-eyed noises, and then Hennidge cries out:

'Flashman? Harry Flashman? But . . . but it's impossible – you can't be!'

387

Somehow I didn't start to rave, or swear, or blubber. Instead I just leered up at him and croaked:

'You give me the lie, Hennidge, and I'll call you out, d'you know? I called a man out in '39, remember? He was a cavalry captain, too. So – would you mind just cutting these damned ropes – and mind my arm, 'cos I think it's broken . . .'

'My God, you are Flashman!' cries he, as if he was looking at a ghost. Then he just stuttered and gaped, and signed to the gunners to cut me loose, which they did, lowering me gently to the ground, horror and dismay all over their faces, I was glad to see. But I'll never forget what Hennidge said next, as the lieutenant called for a water-bottle and pressed it to my lips; Hennidge stood staring down at me appalled, and then he said ever so apologetically:

'I say, Flashman – I'm most frightfully sorry!'

Mark you, what else was there to say? Oh, aye, there was something – I hadn't reasoned it, as you can imagine, but it leaped into my mind as I sat there, almost swooning with relief, not minding the pains in my head and arms, and happened to glance along the guns. I was suddenly shuddering horribly, and bowing my head in my sound hand, trying to hold back the sobs, and then I says, as best I could:

'Those niggers tied to the guns. I want them cut loose – all of 'em, directly!'

'What's that?' says he. 'But they've been condem—'

'Cut 'em loose, damn you!' My voice was shaking and faint. 'Every mother's son-of-a-bitch, d'you hear?' I glared up at him, as I sat there in the dust in my rags, with my back to the gun-wheel – I must have been a rare sight. 'Cut 'em loose, and tell 'em to run away – away, as far as they know how – away from us, and never to get caught again! Blast you, don't stand there gawping – do as I say!'

'You're not well,' says he. 'You're distraught, and—'

'I'm also a bloody colonel!' I hollered. 'And you're a bloody captain! I'm in my right mind, too, and I'll break you, by God, if you don't attend to me this minute. So . . . set – them – loose! Be a good chap, Clem – very well?'

So he gave the orders, and they turned them free, and the young lieutenant knelt beside me with the water-bottle, very respectful and moist-eyed.

'That was merciful,' says he.

'Merciful be damned,' says I. 'The way things are hereabouts, one of 'em's probably Lord Canning.'

There isn't much more to tell. The Great Mutiny ended there, under the walls of Gwalior, where Rose broke the last rebel army, and Tantia Tope fled away. They caught him and hanged him in the end, but they never found Nana Sahib, and for the rest, a few bands of pandies roamed about like bandits for a month or two, but were gradually dispersed.

I was back in the pavilion then, with my pads off, recovering from a broken arm and a battered head, to say nothing of a badly disarranged nervous system. I was exhausted in body and mind, but it's surprising how you pick up when you realise that it's all over, and there's nothing to do but lie back and put on weight, and you can sleep sound at nights. In the weeks of my convalescence at Gwalior I wrote my reports for Rose and Campbell, and composed another, at great length, for Palmerston, in which I detailed all my doings at Jhansi and elsewhere so far as they concerned the mission he'd given me. I told him what had happened with the Rani (the respectable bits, you understand, no romantic nonsense) and how I had been there at the end; I also warned him that

Ignatieff had not been heard of again, and might still be abroad, doing mischief, though I doubted it.

(I've met the gotch-eyed bastard on two occasions since, by the way, both of 'em diplomatic bunfights, I'm happy to say. We used each other with perfect civility, and I kept my back carefully to the wall and left early.)

It was autumn before I was up and about again at Gwalior, and had received word from Campbell that I was released from my duties and might go home. I was ready for it, too, but before I left I found myself riding out on the road to Kota-ki-serai, to have a look at the spot where her people had made a little shrine to Lakshmibai, near the nullah – they thought no end of her, you know, and still do.

Well, I could understand that; I hadn't been indifferent myself, although it all seemed far past now, somehow. They had cremated her, in the Hindoo fashion, but there was this little painted model temple, which I took to be her memorial, and withered flowers and wreaths and little pots round it, and I mooched about, scuffing the dust with my boots, while a few old niggers squatted under the thorns, watching me curiously, and the bullock-carts went by. There wasn't much sign of the skirmish where she'd died – a few trifles of broken gear, a rusty stirrup, that sort of thing. I wondered why she'd done it all, and in spite of what she said to me at the last, I believe I did understand. As I'd said in my report to Pam, she didn't give up her Jhansi. That was what had mattered to her, more than life. As to what she may have thought or felt about me, truly – and for that matter, what I'd really felt about her – I couldn't make up my mind.[49] It didn't matter now, anyway, but I could always make the best of it, and remember those eyes above the veil, and the soft lips brushing my cheek. Aye, well. Damned good-looking girl.

I went up the Agra trunk on my way home, and down to Cawnpore, where there were letters waiting for me, including one from Billy Russell, congratulating me on my escape and recovery, which he said had been the talk of Simla, where he had been taking things easy with a game leg. He was down at Allahabad now, following the seat of government on its peregrinations, as he put it, and I must stop off and celebrate with him. I didn't mind that a bit; I was ready to start enjoying life again, after all the nonsense I'd been through, and to put me in the best fettle there were several letters from Elspeth, in her usual rattle-pated style; full of loving slush about her dear, darling champion whom she was yearning to clasp again to her Loving Bosom (hear! hear! thinks I) when he returned with his Laurels fresh upon his Brow. She absolutely did write like this; came from reading novels, I suspect:

> . . . the Town is full of talk of you and your Gallant Comrades, especially Sir Hugh Rose and dear Sir Colin – or Lord Clyde as we must now call him – I own I felt a Flush of Pride when I thought that my Distinguished Countryman had chosen for his title the name of the Beauteous Stream beside which I – humble little Me – was born, and where I spent such Blissful Hours with my Own True Love – yourself, dear, dear, Harry!! Do you remember?

I did – and the thought of that first splendid gallop we'd had together in the bushes brought sentimental tears to my eyes and set me bursting to be at her again, back in green England, away from this bloody beastly country and its stench of death and war and dust. Elspeth, with her golden hair and blue eyes and adoring idiot smile and resplendent – oh, that was certainty, and happiness and jollity and be-damned!

. . . and even Lord Cardigan is civil – altho' he thinks Sir Colin was tardy, and can have made but poor use of his Light Cavalry, I think it was, in punishing the Rascally Sepoys – and Lord Cardigan was very full in his attentions to me when we met in the Row, but I gave him the Right About, for I was certain you would wish it, and he went off not too pleased, I thought, but perhaps he is disposed to Toady, for he sent me a new book as a gift for you, saying he was sure it must interest you most particularly, but I have glanced at it and don't care for it much, since it seems to be about rustics, and quite without that Tender Passion which I admire in writing, and which Fills my Thoughts whenever they turn to my Dearest of Husbands and Lovers, as they do every minute, and my legs go quite weak. Still, I send it to you, with his Lordship's compliments. Now then, there is the finest scandal about Daisy Marchmont's footman . . .

I didn't care to hear about Cardigan – the mention of the name was enough to set my jealous bile working, for it reminded me that my darling Elspeth wasn't always the dutiful and loving wife she pretended to be, and heaven knew how many randified admirers had been beating our door-knocker in my absence. She'd have no time or opportunity for dalliance when Flashy roared back into residence, though . . . I chuckled at the thought, threw Cardigan's present into my valise without looking at it, and caught the train to Allahabad, where Billy Russell was at the station with a *ghari* to meet me.

He was all beams and whiskers as usual, full of fun, and demanding my news of the Jhansi and Gwalior affairs – which he knew already, of course, in their essentials, 'but it's the spice and colour I'm after, old fellow, and devil a bit of those d'ye get in despatches. This business of your stealing into the Jezebel of Jhansi's fortress in disguise, now, and being carried away prisoner in the night, eh . . .?'

I parried his questions, grinning, as we bowled away towards the Fort, and then he says:

'I've got your winnings from Lucknow safe, by the by, and your prize-money. It's about all you've had out o' this campaign, ain't it – bar a few wounds an' grey hairs?'

I knew what he meant, blast him. While orders and ribbons and medals and titles had been flying about like hail among the Indian heroes, devil a nod had come my way – nor would it. You see, the irony was that while I'd seen more than my share of hell and horror in the Mutiny, I knew that in official eyes, my service must have been a pretty fair frost. I'd failed entirely in the original mission Pam had given me, and Rose had been damned stuffy that the plan to save Lakshmibai had come adrift; Lord Canning, he'd said, would be profoundly disappointed – as though it was my fault, the ungrateful bastard. But these are the things that matter, when they come to passing out the spoils, and I knew that while the likes of Rose and Campbell were having honours showered on them, and the prowess of Outram and Sam Browne and the snirp Roberts were being trumpeted round the world, poor old Flash would be lucky to get an address of welcome and a knife-and-fork supper at Ashby Town Hall.

'There's others have been well rewarded,' says Billy. 'Slow-coach is a lord – but ye know that. There must be about fifty Crosses flying about, and God knows how many titles . . .

394

they might ha' done something for you. I wonder,' says he, as we got out at the Fort and went along the verandah, 'if a leaderette in the old Thunderer might stir 'em up, what? We can't have Horse Guards neglectin' our best men.'

I liked the sound of that, rather, but as he conducted me across the hall, where Sikh sentries stood and the *punkahs**hissed, I thought it best to say I didn't mind, really – and then I found he was grinning all over his whiskers as he ushered me through a doorway, and I stopped dead in amazement.

It was a big, airy room, half office and half drawing-room, with a score of people standing at the far end, beyond the fine Afghan carpet, all looking in my direction, and it was sight of them that had checked me – for there was Campbell, with his grizzled head and wrinkled Scotch face, and Mansfield smiling, very erect, toying with his dark whiskers, and Macdonald grinning openly, and Hope Grant, stern and straight. In the middle was a slim, elegant civilian in a white morning coat with a handsome woman smiling beside him; it took me a moment to realise that they were Lord and Lady Canning.

Then Russell was pushing me forward, and Canning was smiling and shaking hands, and I was bowing to Lady Canning, wondering what the devil this was all about, and then there was silence, and Canning was clearing his throat and addressing me. I wish I could remember all of it, but I was quite taken aback to find myself thrust into this company, so unexpected . . . what was this? – 'distinguished conduct on many numerous occasions, familiar to all . . . Afghanistan, Crimea, Balaclava, Central Asia . . . lately, and most

---

* Fans.

exemplary, service in the insurrection of the Bengal Army . . . most gallant conduct in the defence and evacuation of Cawnpore . . . and most signally, at the direction of Sir Hugh Rose, in undertaking service of the most dangerous and difficult nature in the Gwalior campaign . . . warmest approval of Her Majesty and of her Ministers and principal advisers . . . recognition of conduct far beyond the call of duty . . .'

I listened to all this in a daze, and then Canning was passing something to Campbell, and he was coming up to me, glowering under his brows, and harrumphing.

'It is at my perr-sonal request,' growls he, 'that I have been purr-meeted tae bestow a disteenction that should rightly have come from Her Majesty's ain – own – gracious hands.'

He reached up, and I felt a sudden keen pain in my left tit as he stuck a pin in it – I gasped and looked down, and there it was, on its ribbon, the shabby-looking little bronze cross against my jacket; at first I didn't even recognise it, and then Lady Canning was leading the clapping, and Campbell was pumping my right hand and staring at me with his brows down.

'The Order o' the Victoria Cross,' says he, and then he added, 'Flashman . . .', but there he stopped and shook his head. 'Aye,' says he, and grinned at me – and God knows he didn't often grin, that one, and went on shaking his head and my hand, and the clapping and laughter rang in my ears.

I couldn't speak; I was red in the face, I knew, and almost in tears, as they clustered round me, Mansfield and Macdonald and the rest of them, and Billy slapping me on the back (and then scribbling quickly in his book and sticking it in his pocket) and I was trembling and wanted ever so much to sit down – but what I was thinking was, by God, you don't deserve it, you know, you shifty old bastard of a Flashy – not if it's courage they're after . . . but if they hand out medals for luck, and survival through sheer funk, and suffering ignobly borne . . . well, grab 'em with both hands, my boy – and then, in the august presence of the Governor-General and the Commander-in-Chief, someone started to sing, 'For he's a jolly good fellow', and there were happy faces all round me, singing, until Canning led me out on to the verandah, and in the garden there seemed to be crowds of soldiers, and civilians – bearded Sikhs and ugly little Goorkhas, Devil's Own and Highlanders, artillerymen and sappers, chaps in white coats and sun-helmets, ladies in garden-party dresses, and as Canning waved to them someone shouted 'Hip-hip-hip!' and the crashing 'Hurrah!' sounded three times and a tiger – and I looked out at them through a mist of tears, and beyond them to the Gwalior guns and the Cawnpore barricade and the burning lines of Meerut and the battery reek of Balaclava and the bloody snow of Gandamack, and I thought, by God, how little you know, or you wouldn't be cheering me. You'd be howling for my blood, you honest, sturdy asses – and then again, maybe you wouldn't, for if you knew the truth about me, you wouldn't believe it.

'What a gratifying experience to relate to your children, colonel,' says Canning, and on the other side Lady Canning smiled at me and says: 'And to Lady Flashman.'

I mumbled yes, indeed, so it would be; then I noticed that she was looking at me a trifle arch, and cudgelled my wits to think why – she couldn't be wanting to get off with me, not with Canning there – and then her last words sank in, my legs went weak, and I believe I absolutely said, 'Hey?'

They both laughed politely at my bewilderment, Canning

looking fond reproval at her. 'That must be under the rose, my dear, you know,' says he. 'But of course we should have informed you, colonel, privately.' He beamed at me. 'In addition to the highest decoration for valour, which has been justly bestowed on many gallant officers in the late campaigns, Her Majesty wished to distinguish your service by some additional mark of favour. She has therefore been graciously pleased to create you a Knight of the Bath.'

I suppose I was already numb with shock, for I didn't faint, or cry 'Whoops!' or even stand gaping at the man in disbelief. In fact, I blew my nose, and what I was thinking as I mopped away my emotion was: by God, she's got no taste, that woman. I mean, who but little Vicky would have thought to pile a knighthood on top of the V.C., all at one go? It didn't seem scarcely decent – but, by God, wasn't it bloody famous! For over everything the words were revolving in my mind in a golden haze – 'Sir Harry Flashman, V.C.' It wasn't believable . . . Sir Harry . . . Sir Harry and Lady Flashman . . . Flashman, V.C. . . . my stars, it had come to this, and when least expected – oh, that astonishing little woman . . . I remembered how she'd blushed and looked bashful when she'd hung the Queen's Medal on me years before, and I'd thought, aye, cavalry whiskers catch 'em every time . . . and still did, apparently. Who'd have thought it?

'Well . . . God save the Queen,' says I, reverently.

There was no taking it in properly at the time, of course, or indeed in the hours that followed; they remain just a walking dream, with 'Sir Harry Flashman, V.C.' blazing in front of my eyes, through all the grinning faces and back-slapping and cheering and adulation – all for the V.C., of course, for t'other thing was to remain a secret, Canning said, until I got home. There was a great dinner that evening, at the Fort, with booze galore and speeches and cheering, and chaps rolling under the table, and they poured me on to the Calcutta train that night in a shocking condition. I didn't wake up till noon the following day, with a fearful head; it took me another night to get right again, but on the next morning I had recovered, and ate a hearty breakfast, and felt in capital shape. Sir Harry Flashman, V.C. – I could still hardly credit it. They'd be all over me at home, and Elspeth would go into the wildest ecstasies at being 'My lady', and be insufferable to her friends and tradesmen, and adoringly grateful to me – she might even stay faithful permanently, you never knew . . . I fairly basked in my thoughts, grinning happily out at the disgusting Indian countryside in the sunrise, reflecting that with luck I'd never see or hear or smell it again, after this, and then to beguile the time I fished in my valise for something to read, and came on the book Cardigan had sent to Elspeth – what could have possessed Jim the Bear, who detested me, to send me a present?

I opened it at random, idly turning the pages . . . and then my eye lit on a paragraph, and it was as though a bucket of icy water had been dashed over me as I read the words:

'But that blackguard Flashman, who never speaks to one without a kick or an oath—' 'The cowardly brute,' broke in East, 'how I hate him! And he knows it, too; he knows that you and I think him a coward.'

I stared at the page dumbfounded. Flashman? East? What the blind blue blazes was this? I turned the book over to look at the title: 'Tom Brown's School Days', it said, 'by an Old Boy'. Who the hell was Tom Brown? I whipped quickly through the pages – rubbish about some yokels at a village fair, as Elspeth had said . . . Farmer Ives, Benjy . . . what the deuce? Tom trying his skill at drop-kicks . . . 'Rugby and Football' . . . hollo, here we were again, though, and the hairs rose on my neck as I read:

> 'Gone to ground, eh?' roared Flashman. 'Push them out then, boys; look under the beds . . . Who-o-o-p!' he roared, pulling away at the leg of a small boy . . . 'Young howling brute. Hold your tongue, sir, or I'll kill you!'

By God, it was me! I mean, it wasn't only my style, to a 't', I even remembered doing it – years ago, at Rugby, when we flushed the fags out and tossed them in blankets for a lark . . . Yes, here it was – 'Once, twice, thrice, and away' . . . 'What a cursed bully you are, Flashy!' I sped through the passage, in which the horrible ogre Flashman, swearing foully, suggested they be tossed two at a time, so that they'd struggle and fall out and get hurt – it's true enough, that's the way to get the mealy little bastards pitched out on to the floor.

But who on earth could have written this? Who had dared – I tore the pages over, scanning each one for the dread name, and by God wasn't it there, though, in plenty? My eyes goggled as I read:

> 'Flashman, with an oath and a kick, released his prey . . .' '. . . the tyranny of Flashman . . .' '. . . Flashman was on the look-out, and sent an empty pickle-jar whizzing after them, which narrowly missed Tom's head. "He wouldn't mind killing one, if he wasn't caught," said East . . .' '. . . "Was Flashman here then?" – "Yes, and a dirty little snivelling sneaking fellow he was, too . . .

used to toady the bullies by offering to fag for them, and peaching against the rest of us . . .'"

I was red and roaring with rage by this time, barely able to see the pages. By God, here was infamy! Page after foul page, traducing me in the most odious terms – for there wasn't a doubt I was the villain referred to; the whole thing stank of Rugby in my time, and there was the Doctor, and East, and Brooke, and Crab Jones – and me, absolutely by name, for all the world to read about and detest! There was even a description of me as big and strong for my age – and I 'played well at all games where pluck wasn't much wanted' if you please, and had 'a bluff, offhand manner, which passed for heartiness, and considerable powers of being pleasant'. Well, that settled it – and my reputation, too, for not a page went by but I was twisting arms, or thrashing weaklings, or swearing, or funking, or getting pissy drunk, or roasting small boys over fires – oh, aye, *that* brought back Master Brown to memory sharp enough. He was the mealy, freckled little villain who tried to steal my sweepstake ticket, damn him – a pious, crawling little toad-eater who prayed like clockwork and was forever sucking up to Arnold and Brooke – 'yes, sir, please, sir, I'm a bloody Christian, sir,' along with his pal East . . . and now East was dead, in the boat by Cawnpore.

Someone was alive, though – alive and libelling me most damnably. Not that it wasn't true, every vile word of it – oh, it was all too true, that was the trouble, but the devil with that, it was a foul, malicious blot on my good name . . . dear Christ, here was more!

'. . . Flashman's brutality had disgusted most even of his intimate friends . . .' No, by God, there was *one*

401

downright, shameful lie – the kind of friends I had at Rugby you *couldn't* have disgusted, not Speedicut and Rattle and that lot . . . What next? 'Coward as he was, Flashman couldn't swallow such an insult . . .' and then followed a description of a fight, in which I ('in poor condition from his monstrous habit of stuffing') was soundly thrashed by a couple of fags and skulked off whining: 'You shall pay for this . . .'

I believe I foamed at the mouth at this point, and yet again at the description of my drunken expulsion from Rugby, but what was even worse was the scene in which the unctuous little swabs, Brown and East, were described as praying for 'poor Flashman'. I hurled the book across the carriage, and set about thrashing my bearer, and only when I'd driven him howling on to the carriage-roof did I settle down and realise the full bitterness of what this vindictive biographer had done.

He'd ruined me – half England must have read the beastly thing by now. Oh, it was plain enough why Cardigan had sent it to me, the spiteful swine. How could I ever hold up my head again, after this poisonous attack? – my God, just in my moment of supreme glory, too! What would my Cross and my Knighthood be worth now, with this venom spewed on me by 'an Old Boy'?, whoever the brute was . . . probably some greasy little sneak whom I'd disciplined for his own good, or knocked about in boyish fun . . . well, by heaven he'd pay for it! I'd sue the wicked, scribbling son-of-a-bitch through every court in England, I'd have every lousy penny he owned, and the shirt off his back, and see him starve in the gutter, or rot in jail for criminal slander –

'No!' I roared, shaking my first, 'I'll kill the bastard, that's what I'll do – after I've sued him! I'll call him out, if he's a

civilian, and blow his mangy head off on Calais sands – I'll
horsewhip him publicly . . .'

[At this point, with a torn page and several explosive blots,
the fifth packet of the Flashman Papers comes to an end.]

[N.B. – Flashman apparently never took action against
Thomas Hughes, the author of *Tom Brown's Schooldays*, which
first appeared in 1857 and had achieved immense success
before Flashman saw it in India. Probably he came to realise,
after his first understandable indignation had subsided, that
any harm it did to his reputation was trifling, and that the
publicity of litigation could only make things worse. But it
is possible that he made the threat of legal action, and
demanded some retraction; it is at least interesting that when
the sequel, *Tom Brown at Oxford*, appeared in 1861, Hughes
devoted a preface to denying any identification of himself
with Tom Brown: '. . . neither is the hero a portrait of myself
[he wrote] *nor is there any other portrait in either of the books*,
except in the case of Dr Arnold, where the true name is
given.' The italics are the editor's; the satisfaction was presumably Flashman's.]

APPENDIX I:

The Indian Mutiny

As far as it goes, and leaving aside those more personal experiences and observations which there is no confirming or denying, Flashman's account of his service in the Mutiny seems both generally accurate and fair. His descriptions of Meerut, before and during the outbreak, of Cawnpore and Lucknow and Jhansi and Gwalior, are consistent with other eye-witness accounts; at worst, he differs no more from them than they do from each other. As to causes and attitudes, he seems to give a sound reflection of what was being said and thought in India at the time.

It is still difficult to discuss certain aspects of the Mutiny without emotion creeping in; it was an atrociously bloody business, and it is not easy to appreciate entirely the immense intensity of feeling on both sides. How to explain the conduct of Nana Sahib at Cawnpore, on the one hand, or on the other, the attitude of the Christian and personally kindly John Nicholson, who wanted legislation passed for the flaying, impaling, and burning of mutineers? Flashman's observations are not without interest, but it is really superfluous to comment on them; there should not be, for intelligent people, any question of trying to cast up the atrocious accounts, or attempting to discover a greater weight of 'blame' on one side or the other. Fashions in these things change, as Flashman remarks, and one should beware of fashionable judgements. Sufficient to say that fear, shock, ignorance, and racial and religious intolerance, on both sides, combined to produce a hatred akin to madness in some individuals and groups – British, Hindoo and Muslim – but by no means among all.

At the same time, it is worth remembering that the struggle which produced so much cruelty and shame was also marked by countless examples of self-sacrifice and human kindness almost beyond understanding, and by devotion and heroism which will last as long as British and Indian memory: the spirit which inspired the last stand of a handful of unnamed mutineers in Gwalior fortress was the same as that which held the wall of Wheeler's entrenchment at Cawnpore.

APPENDIX II:

The Rani of Jhansi

Lakshmibai, Maharani of Jhansi, was one of the outstanding leaders of the Mutiny, and a heroine of Indian history. She has been compared, not unjustly, to Joan of Arc; on the other hand, while the evil reputation which propaganda gave her in her lifetime has now been largely discounted, there remain some shadows over her memory.

The general facts about her career, as Flashman learned them from Palmerston and Skene, and as he himself describes them, are accurate – her upbringing, marriage, political attitudes, part in the Mutiny, escape, campaigning, and death. What is less clear is when and why she became actively involved in the Mutiny, for even after the Jhansi massacre (see Notes) she professed friendship for the Sirkar; it may even be that, despite her bitterness towards the British, she would have stayed clear of rebellion if she could. What is certain is that, once committed, she led her troops with great resolution and personal bravery – she was, in fact, a fine swordswoman and rider, and a good shot, as a result of her upbringing among boys (Nana Sahib among them) at the Peshawa's court.

On a more everyday level, Flashman's impressions of Lakshmibai and her court are borne out by contemporary accounts. He seems to have given a fair picture of her conduct of affairs and public behaviour, as well as of such details as her daily routine, her apartments, private zoo, recreations and tea-parties, and even clothing and jewellery. Other Britons who met her shared at least some of his enthusiasm for her looks ('remarkably fine figure . . . beautiful eyes . . . voluptuous . . . beautiful shape', are among the descriptions, although one added that he thought her 'not pretty'). The most apparently authentic surviving portrait shows her much as Flashman first describes her. Her personality seems to have been pleasant enough, if forceful (her two most quoted remarks are 'I will not give up my Jhansi', and the taunt thrown at Nana Sahib when they were children: 'When I grow up I'll have ten elephants to your one!').

But her true character remains a mystery. Whether she is regarded as a pure-hearted patriot, or as a devious and cruel opportunist is a matter of choice – she may have been something of each. Her epitaph was given by her most persistent enemy, Sir Hugh Rose, speaking of the rebel leaders; he called Lakshmibai 'the best and bravest'.

(For biographies see *The Rebellious Rani*, by Sir John Smyth, V.C., and *The Ranee of Jhansi*, by D. V. Tahmankar. Also in Sylvester, Forrest, Kaye/Malleson.)

NOTES

1. Lord Cardigan, who led the Charge of the Light Brigade, was a popular hero after Balaclava, but a reaction set in against him in 1856, with rumours that he had shirked his duty, and even that he had not reached the Russian guns at all. The law-suit did not take place until 1863, when Cardigan sued Colonel Calthorpe for libel on the subject; it was established that he had been at the guns, and also that he had left his brigade during the action which, although it did not reflect on his personal courage, left a large question-mark over his fitness for command.

2. *Punch* also noted that at this dinner champagne was served at the rate of only one bottle per three guests.

3. For once Flashman is exact with a date – it was on the 21st that Florence Nightingale had a two-hour meeting with the Queen at Balmoral. In fact, his recollections of Balmoral are so exact, even down to topics of conversation and the state of the weather on particular days, that one suspects he is indebted to the detailed diary which his wife Elspeth kept during their married life, and which forms part of The Flashman Papers. (For corroboration,

see *Queen Victoria's Letters*, 1827–61, ed. Benson and Esher; *The Queen at Balmoral* by F. P. Humphrey (1893); *Life of the Prince Consort*, 5 vols., by Sir T. Martin (1875–80); *Twenty Years at Court*, by Eleanor Stanley (1916); and *A Diary of Royal Movements . . . in the life of Queen Victoria* (1883).

4. No record can be found of a visit by Lord Palmerston to Balmoral in late September, 1856; obviously it must have been kept secret, along with the disturbing news that chapattis had appeared in an Indian regiment: most histories of the Mutiny do not mention chapattis as appearing until early in 1857.

    For the rest, Flashman gives a fair picture of 'Pam' as his contemporaries saw him – a popular, warm-hearted, impulsive, and (to some eyes) deplorable figure whom Disraeli described as a 'painted old pantaloon'. Lord Ellenborough was a former Governor-General of India, and Sir Charles Wood, although at the Admiralty when Flashman met him, had been President of the Board of Control for India from 1853–55, and was to return to the India Office from 1859–66.

5. The missionaries were greatly displeased at a government decision in 1856–7 that education in Indian schools should be secular. The fear of Christianisation was certainly present among Indians at this time, and is considered to have been a main cause of the Mutiny. Preaching army officers were regarded as especially dangerous: Governor-General Canning, who was was unjustly suspected of being an ardent proselytiser, actually said of one religiously minded colonel that he was unfit to be trusted with his native regiment, and Lord Ellenborough delivered a strong warning in the House of Lords on June 9, 1857, against 'colonels connected with missionary operations . . . You will see the most bloody revolution which has at any time occurred in India. The English will be expelled.' This

409

contrasts with the statement of Mr Mangles, chairman of the East India Company: 'Providence has entrusted the empire of Hindoostan to England in order that the banner of Christ should wave triumphant from one end of India to the other.'

6. John Nicholson (1821–57) was one of the legendary figures of British India, and an outstanding example of the type of soldier-administrator who became known as 'the desert English', possibly because many of them were Scots or Irish. Their gift, and it was rare, was of winning absolute trust and devotion from the people among whom they worked in the East; Nicholson had it to an unusual degree, and when he was only twenty-seven the religious sect of 'Nikkulseynites' was formed, worshipping him with a fervour which caused him much annoyance. As a soldier and administrator he was brilliant; as a Victorian case-study, fascinating. Since he served in the First Afghan War he would certainly have known Flashman, but it is interesting that they met as described here, since in late 1856 Nicholson should have been far away on the frontier. However, as he was about to enter on new duties at Peshawar about this time, it is conceivable that he came south first, and that they met on the Agra Trunk Road.

7. The Guides was perhaps the most famous fighting unit in the history of British India. Raised by Henry Lawrence in 1846, and commanded by Harry Lumsden, it became legendary along the frontier as an intelligence and combat force of both infantry and cavalry (Kipling, it will be remembered, used the Guides' *mystique* in his 'Ballad of East and West'). It is interesting that Flashman recognised Sher Khan as an ex-Guide by his coat, since the regiment normally wore nondescript khaki rather than a military colour.

410

8. Flashman's assumption that the Rani would be much older was not unnatural. He had heard Palmerston describe her as 'old when she married', which, by Indian standards, she was, being well into her teens.

9. The General Service Enlistment Act (1856) required recruits to serve overseas if necessary. This was one of the most important grievances of the sepoys, who held that crossing the sea would break their caste.

10. Irregular cavalry units of the British Indian armies occasionally dressed in a highly informal style, so the Afghan *rissaldar* might conceivably have been wearing an old uniform coat of Skinner's Horse ('The Yellow Boys'). But it is unlikely that he had ever served in that unit – the Guides would have been more his mark.

11. The society of Thugs (lit. deceivers) were worshippers of the goddess Kali, and practised murder as a religious devotion which would ensure them a place in paradise. They preyed especially on travellers, whom they would join on the road with every profession of friendship before suddenly falling on them at a prearranged signal; the favourite method of killing was strangulation with a scarf. The cult numbered thousands before Sir William Sleeman stamped them out in the 1830s, but since many continued at large, and the Jhansi region was traditionally a hotbed of *thugee*, it is perfectly possible that ex-Thugs were active as Flashman says. In some cases it was possible to identify a former Thug by a tattoo on his eyelid or a brand on his back.

12. 'Pass him some of his own tobacco' – a grim joke by Ilderim's companion. 'Pass the tobacco' was the traditional verbal signal of the Thugs to start killing.

13. There was indeed a Makarram Khan, who served in the Peshawar Police, and later became a notable frontier raider at the head of a band of mounted tribesmen, fighting against the Guides cavalry. (See *History of the Guides, 1846–1922*.)

14. The offering and touching of a sword hilt, in token of mutual respect, was traditional in the Indian Cavalry. (See *From Sepoy to Subedar*, the memoirs of Sita Ram Pande, who served in the Bengal Army for almost fifty years. They were first published a century ago, and recently edited by Major-General James Lunt.)

15. It is curious that Flashman makes no reference to dyeing his skin (as Ilderim had suggested) and indeed seems to imply that he found it unnecessary. But dark as he was, and light-skinned as many frontiersmen are, he must surely have stained his body, or he could hardly have passed for long in a sepoy barrack-room.

16. Of the sepoys whom Flashman mentions by name, only two can be definitely identified as serving in the 3rd N.C. skirmishers at this time – Pir Ali and Kudrat Ali, who were both corporals, although Flashman refers to Pir Ali as though he were an ordinary sepoy.

17. 'Addiscombe tripe' refers to the officers, not the *jemadars* and n.c.o.s. Addiscombe was the military seminary which trained East India Company cadets from 1809 to 1861. Flashman's prejudice may be explained by the fact that Lord Roberts, among other famous soldiers, went there.

18. The fears and grievances which Flashman recounts probably give a fair reflection of the state of mind of many sepoys in early 1857. Rumours of polluted flour and greased cartridges, and stories like that of the Dum-Dum sweeper,

reinforced the suspicion that the British were intent on interfering with their religion, breaking their caste, altering terms of enlistment, and generally changing the established order. To these were added the Oude sepoys' discontent at the recent annexation of their state, which cost them certain privileges, and resentment at the changed attitude towards them (by no means imaginary, according to some contemporary writers) of a new generation of British officers and troops, who seemed more ignorant and contemptuous than their predecessors; this unfortunately coincided with the arrival in the Bengal Army of a better class of sepoys, possibly quicker to take offence – or, according to some writers, more spoiled.

All these things combined to undermine confidence and cause unrest, and there was no lack of agitators ready to play on the sepoys' fears. The belief that the British intended to Christianise India (see Note 5) was widespread, and reinforced by such reforms as the suppression of *thugee* and *suttee* (widow-burning). The resentment which reform had created among Indian princes has been referred to: in addition, educational innovations created disquiet (see Lawrence's evidence to the Select Committee on India, July 12, 1859, E.I. Parliamentary Papers, vol. 18); so even did the development of the railway and telegraph. With all these underlying factors, it will be seen that the greased cartridge was eventually only the spark to the tinder. (See also Sita Ram, Lord Robert's *Forty-one Years in India*, Kaye and Malleson's *History of the Sepoy War* and *History of the Indian Mutiny* (1864–80), G. W. Forrest's *History of the Indian Mutiny* (1904–12), and the same author's *Selections from the Letters, Despatches and C.S.P. . . . Government of India*, 1857–8.)

19. Mrs Captain MacDowall's advice on the running of an Indian household might serve as a model for its time. (See the

Complete Indian Housekeeper, by G. G. and F. A. S. published in 1883.)

20. The 19th N.I., who had rioted in February, were disbanded at the end of March, having refused the new cartridge. The paper which Mangal showed to Flashman was undoubtedly the March 28 issue of *Ashruf-al-Akbar*, of Lucknow, which predicted a great holy war throughout India and the Middle East; however, it gave a warning against relying on Russian assistance, describing them as 'enemies of the faith'.

21. Sepoy Mangal Pandy (? –1857), of the 34th Native Infantry, ran amok on the parade ground at Barrackpore on March 29, apparently drugged with *bhang*, trying to rouse a religious revolt and claiming that British troops were coming against the sepoys. He attacked one of his officers, and then tried to kill himself. Pandy was subsequently hanged, along with a native officer whose offence apparently was that he did not try to stop the attack. However, this first of the Indian sepoy rebels gained an appropriate immortality: the British word for any native mutineer thereafter was 'pandy'.

22. For the loading drill, see Forest's *Selections*, and J. A. B. Palmer's *The Mutiny Outbreak in Meerut in 1857* referring to the Platoon Exercise Manual. While there is general agreement among historians on what happened at the firing-parade, some differ over precise technical details; Flashman's account is sound on the whole. He states that the cartridges were not greased, but waxed, and since he does not refer to them as ball cartridges, this would seem to confirm that they were ungreased blanks. However, this would not allay the fears of the sepoys, who were apparently suspicious of any cartridge with a shiny appearance. Nor do they seem to have been impressed by the

repeated assurances that it was unnecessary to bite the cartridge (which, if it were greased, would be highly polluting); as early as January, 1857, when it was announced that the sepoys could grease their own loads with non-polluting substances, it was also stated that they could tear the cartridges with their fingers (see Hansard, 3rd series 145, May 22, 1857); the response of some sepoys to this was that they might forget, and bite.

23. The British were, in fact, more considerate and humane towards their native troops than they were to their white ones. Flogging continued in the British Army long after it had been abolished for Indian troops, whose discipline appears to have been much more lax, possibly in consequence – a point significantly noted by Subedar Sita Ram when he discusses in his memoirs the causes of the Mutiny.

24. Lieutenant (later Lieutenant-General Sir Hugh) Gough was warned by one of the native officers of his troop on May 9 that the sepoys would rise to rescue their comrades from the jail. Carmichael-Smith and Archdale Wilson both rejected the warning.

25. One of the first casualties of the Meerut mutiny was, in fact, a British soldier murdered in a bazaar lemonade shop.

26. Hewitt and Archdale Wilson were extraordinarily slow in getting the British regiments on the move after the outbreak; they did not reach the sepoy lines until after the mutineers had set off for Delhi.

27. Altogether thirty-one Europeans are known to have been murdered in the Meerut massacre, including the Dawson family, and Mrs Courtney and her three children (all mentioned by Flashman). The full list is given in the *Records of the Intelligence Department of the N.W. Provinces, 1857*, vol.

ii, appendix. The circumstances of their deaths are horrifying enough – Surgeon Dawson was shot on his verandah, while Mrs Dawson was burned by thrown torches, and at least one pregnant woman, Mrs Captain Chambers, was murdered – but even so, greatly overstated reports of Meerut atrocities were circulated, including tales of sexual violation. It is worth quoting the statement of Sir William Muir, then head of the N.W. Intelligence Department, in a letter to Lord Canning (Agra, December 30, 1857), that several British witnesses at Meerut were confident that no rapes took place, and they believed that the atrocities, appalling as they were, had been exaggerated. It was alleged, for example, that Riding-Master Langdale's (not Langley's, as Flashman says) little daughter was tortured to death; she had, in fact, been killed by a *tulwar* blow while sleeping on her charpoy (see the Rev. T. C. Smith's letter, dated Meerut, December 16, 1857). This tendency of many British observers to be strictly fair and impartial, even in the highly emotional atmosphere of the Mutiny and its immediate aftermath, should not be seen as playing down the atrocities; they were merely concerned to correct the wilder stories, and give an honest account.

28. The mutiny and massacre at Jhansi took place exactly as Ilderim Khan described it. The mass murder of the 66 Britons (30 men, 16 women, and 20 children) was carried out in the Jokan Bagh on June 8, 1857; the only details which Ilderim's narrative adds to historical record are the quoted remarks of the victims and their killers. It was the second largest massacre in the entire Mutiny, and in some ways the most cruel, although it has been over-shadowed in popular infamy by Cawnpore. What is by no means certain is how far Rani Lakshmibai was responsible, if at all: she protested her innocence afterwards and there

is considerable doubt what her attitude was to Skene's three envoys before the Town Fort surrendered. (No record exists of the death of 'Murray sahib' as described by Ilderim Khan, and the quotation that the Rani 'had no concern with English swine', which is to be found in at least one other contemporary source, appears to rest on the evidence of a suspect Indian witness.) It is possible that Lakshmibai was powerless to prevent either the mutiny or the massacre; on the other hand, there is no evidence that she tried to, and there is no doubt that soon afterwards she was most effectively in control of Jhansi, and capable of dealing with any threat to her sovereignty.

29. The quotation given by Flashman is the substance of the last letter which Wheeler sent out of Cawnpore after one of the most heroic defences in the history of war. Later events were to overshadow it, but it remains an epic of the Mutiny, for the conditions within the entrenchment, the figures of casualties, and even small details of the siege, were as Flashman describes them: for example, Bella Blair did die, John McKillop of the Civil Service did draw water under constant fire for a week before he was killed, and the reference to shooting horses for food, rather than riders, is authentic.

30. Azeemoolah Khan had been sent to London in 1854 by Nana Sahib, the adopted son of the Maharatta Peshawa, to petition against the disallowance of Nana's pension and title after his father's death. The petition failed, but Azeemoolah, by his own account, had immense success in his pursuit of London society women – a boast which did not endear him to W. H. Russell of *The Times* when the two met at Missirie's Hotel, Constantinople, in 1856, and subsequently in the Crimea. Apart from being a nobleman, Azeemoolah is also believed to have worked as a teacher and as a waiter. Nana Sahib, who

had joined the rebellion on the outbreak at Cawnpore, was to become the most famous of the Mutiny leaders, but Tantia Tope, whom Flashman barely noticed, was to be a far greater menace in the field.

31. While Flashman's account of the council of war is new, it supports the known facts: Wheeler wanted to fight on, and his younger officers supported him; the older men wished to surrender for the sake of the women and children, and Wheeler finally agreed, although he was deeply suspicious of the rebels' good faith. Nana Sahib's offer of terms, in the words which Flashman gives, was brought to the entrenchment by Mrs Jacobs, described by one contemporary as an 'aged lady'.

32. Details of the massacre at Suttee Ghat are necessarily confused, but the broad facts are as narrated, and again many of Flashman's incidental memories are confirmed by other accounts. For example, Ewart was killed on the way to the ghat in a palankeen; Vibart's kit was carried and his wife escorted by rebels of his regiment; five loyal sepoys were murdered; Moore ('the real defender of Cawnpore') was killed in the water, shoving off. Some versions say that the thatch in the barges was fired before the shooting began, and one of Wheeler's servants, a nurse, said the general was killed on the shore, his head being cut off as he leaned from his stretcher; however, the probability is that he died in one of the boats. What appears to be in no doubt is the premeditated treachery of the attack; only one boat (Vibart's) escaped.

33. The reptiles which attacked the swimmers can hardly have been gavials, which feed exclusively on fish. True crocodiles have an overlapping fourth tooth.

34. The account of the escape down-river is true. This is independently confirmed by the narrative of Lieutenant Thomson,

which describes the fire-arrows, the boat's grounding, the temple siege, escape to the shore, the boat's disappearance, crocodiles, etc. Apart from Flashman, there were four survivors – Thomson, Delafosse, Sullivan, and Murphy – who were eventually rescued by Diribijah Singh.

35. The massacre of women and children at Cawnpore was the most notorious atrocity of the Mutiny, and provoked the most notorious reprisal by General Neill. It has been suggested that Nana was not himself responsible, and that the massacre may have been in retaliation for the indiscriminate punishment which Neill's troops had visited earlier on Allahabad and on villages during their march to Cawnpore. Without in any way condoning Neill's behaviour, which has been justly condemned by historians, it is only fair to point out that there had been no element of retaliation in previous massacres by Indians, at Meerut, Jhansi, and Delhi. What is not in dispute is the effect which Cawnpore had on British opinion, or the fury it caused in the army – a curious echo of this even lingered on into the Second World War, when tattooists in Hogg Market, Calcutta, were still offering to imprint the arms of British recruits with the legend 'Cawnpore Well'.

36. Flashman does T. Henry Kavanaugh considerably less than justice. The big Irishman was undeniably eccentric – one Mutiny historian, Rice Holmes, has called him vain and self-important to the point of insanity – but his night journey to Campbell, in his ludicrous disguise, was an act of the most calculated courage. Possibly Flashman was nettled by the fact that other accounts of the exploit describe Kavanaugh's companion as an Indian; he may also have been unfavourably impressed by the somewhat immodest title of the book in which Kavanaugh described his adventure: *How I Won the V.C.* It tallies fairly closely, in general

facts if not in spirit and interpretation, with Flashman's version. An excellent map of the scene of the journey is in Forrest, vol. ii.

37. Campbell has been much criticised by some military theoreticians for his caution, and for his (and Mansfield's) reluctance to shed lives – British and mutineer; Fortescue thinks this policy may even have helped to lengthen the Mutiny. It is not a view which Flashman could be expected to share. (See Fortescue, vol. xiii.)

38. The painting to which Flashman refers, of Havelock and Outram greeting Campbell at Lucknow, is by a celebrated Victorian painter of military scenes, T. J. Barker. The mounted figure shown raising a hand in acclamation may indeed be intended to be Flashman; it bears some resemblance to the only other identifiable picture of him as a comparatively young man – in a group of Union staff officers with President Lincoln during the U.S. Civil War.

39. Flashman's old friend, William Howard Russell, *The Times* correspondent, makes an obvious reference to this incident in *My Diary in India* (p. 188, vol. 1).

40. Flashman's description of the looting is borne out by Russell, who described his attempt to buy the jewelled chain from an Irish soldier in his *Diary*; their accounts are almost word for word, and Russell even confirms that the chain subsequently fetched £7,500, as Flashman says.

41. Griff, or griffin – a greenhorn, a young officer. Hardly a fair description of Roberts who, although still young, was to win his Victoria Cross only a few weeks later. But Flashman plainly had little liking for the legendary 'Bobs', who was to become Field-Marshal Lord Roberts of Kandahar; no doubt he was jealous of him.

42. Roberts apart, it seems to have been a distinguished gathering round the fire that night. William Stephen Raikes Hodson (1821–58) was already renowned as an irregular cavalry leader and the founder of Hodson's Horse. He was a year older than Flashman and since they were at Rugby together it seems quite feasible that Flashman had been his fag. Hodson has left a mixed reputation; a brilliant soldier, he was capable of cold-blooded cruelty, as when he murdered the Delhi princes while they were his prisoners. He was shot at Lucknow on March 11th, 1858, and there was a rumour (repeated by Flashman) that he was in the act of looting at the time. Roberts firmly denied this, with convincing evidence (see note, page 404, *Forty-one Years in India*, vol. 1). Sam Browne, inventor of the belt which bears his name, was another celebrated cavalry leader, who became a general and won the V.C. He lost his left arm in a skirmish some months after Lucknow. 'Macdonald the Peeler' was probably Macdonald who had been provost-marshal in the Crimea.

43. As one of the Jhansi besiegers later put it: 'The Ranee, young, unwedded, jealous of power, sat watching the puny figures below . . . we watched and wondered what she said and did to those best-favoured among a band of chieftains, and imagination ran wild in the fervid heat.' (See J. H. Sylvester, *Cavalry Surgeon*, ed. A. McKenzie Annand, 1971.)

44. Until the discovery of The Flashman Papers, Lyster (later General Sir Harry Hamon Lyster, V.C.) was the only authority for the plan to capture the Rani of Jhansi alive. No other contemporary writer on the Mutiny mentions the scheme, and it was not until 1913, when the Rev. H. H. Lyster Denny published a little-known work, *Memorials of an Ancient House*, containing some of General Lyster's recollections, that the story came out. According to Lyster, Rose

confided the plan to him in strict confidence, and Lyster himself did not reveal it until many years after Rose's death. The plan was substantially as Flashman recounts it, and involved luring the Rani into attempting an escape by withdrawing a British picket from its position covering one of the Jhansi gates.

45. The battle on the Betwa (April 1, 1858) is one of the forgotten actions, but it is a striking illustration of Rose's coolness and tactical brilliance. Caught at an apparent disadvantage, he turned from Jhansi and attacked the new rebel force, which outnumbered him ten to one; Rose led the cavalry charge in person, and Tantia's army was routed with the loss of 1,500 dead and 28 guns captured. (See Fortescue, *History of the British Army*, vol. xiii.)

46. This incident took place about twenty miles from Jhansi, following the Rani's escape, when a party of British cavalry under Lieutenant Dowker caught up with her. According to popular tradition (now confirmed by Flashman's account) the rebel horseman who wounded Dowker was the Rani herself. Incidentally, Flashman is probably in error when he says the Rani left Jhansi through the Orcha Gate; other authorities specify the Bandhari Gate, and say that the Rani herself had the child Damodar on her saddle.

47. There are differing accounts of Lakshmibai's death, but Flashman's accords with the generally accepted version. This is that she was killed in the action of Kota-ki-serai, before Gwalior, when the 8th Hussars charged the rebel camp at Phool Bagh. She was seen in the mêlée, with her horse's reins in her mouth, and was struck in the body, probably by a carbine bullet: she swayed in the saddle, crossed swords with a trooper, and was cut down. According to tradition, she was wearing the priceless necklace of Scindia, which she gave away

to an attendant as she lay dying. Her tent on the battlefield was later found to contain a full-length mirror, books, pictures, and her swing.

48. Captain Clement Heneage took part in the Charge of the Light Brigade at Balaclava, and also charged with the 8th Hussars in the action of June 17, 1858, in which the Rani of Jhansi was killed. Flashman's misspelling may have arisen through his never having seen the name written.

49. Deplorable though Flashman's attitude to women was, there were obviously some for whom he felt a genuine attachment, and even respect – Lola Montez and the Rani of Jhansi among them. Lakshmibai obviously captivated him, but how far she returned his affection is debatable. He would turn in his grave at the suggestion, but it seems highly questionable that she spent the night with him in the Jhansi pavilion (see pages 114–116). It may be significant that he never saw her face clearly on that occasion, and his description of the encounter might seem to suggest that the lady who entertained him was a professional nautch-dancer or courtesan, rather than the Rani. It is unfortunately true that in the climate created by the Mutiny, Lakshmibai was credited with every vice ('ardent' and 'licentious' were two of the adjectives employed) but there is no evidence that her private life and behaviour were not entirely respectable.

That is not to say that she would not use her feminine power (or any other weapon) for political ends; in this may be found a logical explanation of the pavilion incident. It is possible, on the basis of Flashman's account, that at that time the Rani was already deep in mutinous conspiracy, perhaps with agitators like Ignatieff, and either at their prompting or on her own initiative, decided to destroy Flashman, a potentially dangerous British agent. To lead him on, to lure him to the pavilion, and to arrange for an attack on him by professional assassins, was simple; that something of the sort actually happened is indicated by the confession which Ilderim Khan extracted from the captured Thug.

As to the Rani's display of affection for Flashman on his last visit to Jhansi, it may well have been entirely (and not partially, as he complacently assumed) prompted by her need to extract every scrap of information from him. Or – perhaps she was not entirely indifferent to him, after all; he seemed to think so, and he was not inexperienced.

The FLASHMAN Papers
(In chronological order)

The FLASHMAN Papers
(In order of publication)

Also by George MacDonald Fraser

Mr American
The Pyrates
The Candlemass Road
Black Ajax
The Reavers

Short Stories
The General Danced at Dawn
McAuslan in the Rough
The Sheikh and the Dustbin

History
The Steel Bonnets:
The Story of the Anglo-Scottish Border Reivers

Autobiography
Quartered Safe Out Here
The Light's on at Signpost

*

The Hollywood History of the World